The Road Not Travelled

The Road Not Travelled

Alternative Tales of the Wars of the Roses

Various Authors

Joanne R Larner (Editor)

ISBN-13: 9798502367400

Cover illustrationss by: Riikka Nikko

Dedication

***

This book is dedicated to Richard Tearle, the author of '**By the Grace of God**', one of the stories. He wrote his story when already ill and, sadly, did not live to see it published. I hope he is looking down from above and feeling very proud.

Table of Contents

✮✮✮

Foreword

by Matthew Lewis
Chairman of the Richard III Society

✫✫✫

The story of Richard III is shrouded in mystery and uncertainty at many moments. Historians struggle to penetrate the veil without taking subjective leaps influenced by a personal outlook on the events of the second half of the fifteenth century. Authors of fiction have the freedom to fill in the gaps with a smattering of artistic license. The exploration of alternative histories is a fascinating avenue that allows some of the greatest 'what ifs' of the period to be investigated. What if Richard, Duke of York had become king? What if Edward IV had confronted the suggestion that he had married bigamously during his lifetime? How different might England have been if Richard III had won the Battle of Bosworth?

The Road Not Travelled is a unique and intriguing dive into what might have been. Richard, Duke of York is a man who has fascinated me for a long time. I believe he would have made a good king, and now you can join me in indulging that possibility, and many more. Some moments in history, as in our own lives, feel like big turning points that define what follows, but smaller, seemingly innocuous decisions can radically alter the course of history, and life, too. *The Road Not Travelled* offers a broad platter of thought-provoking investigations of what might have been.

King Richard III has been a focal point of interest for hundreds of years, and has had a Society dedicated to studying him and his times for almost a century now. Richard's reputation has fluctuated over time. Within a few years of the end of the Tudor dynasty, there was an emerging fascination with him and a conviction that Richard couldn't possibly have been as bad as his reputation had become. During the nineteenth century the reign of Richard III, and the whole period of the Wars of the Roses, was viewed with some dismay and consternation as self-destructive and failing to contribute to the development of the empire then held in such high esteem.

The 1950s saw a turning point again, as Isolde Wigram breathed new life into the Order of the White Boar, the precursor to the Richard III Society, which took that name in 1959. In the same decade, Josephine Tey's ***The Daughter of Time*** piqued interest as a (then) modern criminal investigation into Richard III. Since the discovery of his remains in 2012 by the Looking For Richard Project, Richard III has been historical hot property. Yet the popular image of Richard as a monstrous child killing tyrant clings defiantly to the popular consciousness, often in direct opposition to demonstrable fact. Shakespeare has a lot to answer for, but Ricardians should be wary of punishing The Bard for the acceptance of his dramatic fiction as fact. How to dissect that popular image from the collective mind is an old problem, here tackled in a brand new way.

Ricardians will often find themselves asked why they expend time and energy on a man who ruled England for two years half a millennium ago. It's a good question that remains difficult to answer. I think it appeals to the part of us that wants to discover a truth that has been obscured, painted over with layers of myth and legend. Once we find a peel in the paint and start picking, we can't stop until the layers have been stripped away and the job is complete. There is also a facet of the human condition that ensures we are acutely aware of an unfair set of odds stacked against someone, and that causes us to root for the underdog.

Richard III had his history written by those hostile to him. A little light is enough to begin chasing away the shadowy parts of his story. This collection of talented writers have gathered together their lights to illuminate a part of history often overlooked, but relevant to each of us in our own lives. The What Ifs? Perhaps things might have worked out differently based on one solitary choice made, or maybe the result would have been the same however it was arrived at. We can never know, but here we can indulge our curiosity by considering how history might have been different. The stories within are informed by an impressive depth of research into a complex and fascinating period and cast of characters. They are also freed from the shackles of what we know did transpire to allow the creation of a historical multiverse in which anything is possible and the possibilities are endless. Enjoy them.

Matt Lewis
June 2021

Introduction

by
Joanne R Larner

★★★

I had the idea for this book when I read a similar one, dealing with the momentous year of 1066. It was called *1066 Turned Upside Down* and had tales of different scenarios which, had they actually happened, would have changed history forever and thus affected thousands, if not millions, of lives.

I immediately thought of doing the same thing for the period of history I am most familiar with, the Wars of the Roses. There are many pivotal moments in that period: the death of Richard, Duke of York (Richard III's father); the rebellion and downfall of Warwick, the Kingmaker; the marriage of Edward to Elizabeth Woodville; the revelation of Edward's previous marriage to Eleanor Talbot/Butler and Richard's decision to reveal it; Buckingham's rebellion and execution; and many more.

I enlisted the help of about twenty other, very talented authors, some established and successful novelists, some new. They all had their own take on what might have happened to change history if a different choice had been made...

We decided to call the book *The Road Not Travelled* because it encapsulates what happens whenever we reach a fork in the road of our life's journey: we choose one path and the other one, unchosen, remains a mystery. In this book these mysteries are revealed and the reader can discover how our history might have been very different if only some of the major characters in those times had made a different choice.

There is an introduction to each story to explain the historical background for readers who are unfamiliar with it and an author bio of each of the contributors with links to their other works, websites, blogs, etc.

There are some stories that deal with the same event or time but they all have their own take on what could have happened and show how different things could be if one little thing had changed.

I have placed the stories in a rough chronological order, according to when the events would have happened should that particular road have been travelled. I hope you enjoy exploring those roads.

Joanne R Larner

The Unwritten Story (Part 1)
by
Maria Grazia Leotta

Introduction

This story was written by accident. I was just writing in my diary about a strange dream I had had a couple of nights before, and I was suddenly inspired to turn it into a story. It was tweaked a little to fit in with the Alternative History theme.

✮✮✮

It had been an extraordinarily busy day at White Rose Publishing. Brian, the Editor in Chief, had come up with a most original idea and, even though it would take a whole working day, he strongly wanted the workshop to happen. It was a huge challenge; even for a skilled author, writing a short story in just five hours was incredibly difficult – and the topic too! Only three hundred minutes to write a unique alternative history story about King Richard III and the Wars of the Roses! Brian had made it absolutely clear: 'No more than five thousand words, no more than five hours, original content, no copying and pasting from other stories. At the end, we will sit in a circle and read all our stories.'

'Oh, my word, Brian! How can we write and read so many stories and all of them about Richard III and his times?' Sandra jumped up from her chair with her perennial cup of tea in her left hand, narrowly avoiding spilling it. 'That will take ages!' She sank down again on her chair with a gesture of despair.

'So what?' replied Brian. 'It will be interesting though! Can't wait!'

Brian was a tall, fat, middle-aged man, always dressed in light colours, his belly protruding over his trousers, the buttons too tight, and reading glasses attached to a gold chain around his neck. He was a good boss, always willing to give advice, help everyone. He enjoyed eating a fig roll with his black coffee. He was exceptionally creative and organised fascinating projects, but sometimes they were really odd!

He was a staunch Ricardian, born and bred in York and he paid a fortune to rent a flat with a view of Monk Bar and the Minster. Brian was also a cheerful man with a great sense of humour and, when he started to laugh, nobody could stop him. His laughter was contagious and resounded through the whole floor. He had wonderful green eyes and light brown hair, which he only cut when it touched his shoulders; not because that was his style but just because he hated wasting time at the barber's.

He announced the workshop by saying: 'Tomorrow, you will all become writers!' He was sure that the workshop would be a worthwhile exercise and also a unique working day. Besides, he had read every possible book available about Richard III and he thought it would be a great opportunity to read something new and avoid the rather depressing repetition of Richard's gruesome death at Bosworth.

'Can I write about Henry VII?' goaded Joanne, laughing loudly.

'There is plenty of space left at the Tower, just for you!' replied Brian. 'I will have your head, don't you worry!' And he started laughing so loudly that Maria heard him from the floor above.

He had invited some other writer friends to join the workshop so, apart from him, Joanne, Maria, Alex and Clare, about fifteen other people attended. Brian asked them not to mention their names so that the stories would be anonymous and nobody would be able to guess who was the author of each one. Only at the end could they reveal their identities and the titles of their tales.

The meeting room was the medium one and the larger one would be used for refreshment. Brian would never relinquish a tea break at around 11am. A long table had been prepared, covered with a clean, white cloth, with kettles for tea and coffee plus an unbelievable quantity of biscuits, Jaffa Cakes, brownies, apple pies, iced rings and his favourite, his fantastic fig rolls. He was not interested in a low-calorie diet.

People arrived at nine to start at about nine thirty, after the first coffee. They sat in a circle, over twenty in all and, an incredible coincidence, everyone was dressed in light colours such as white, beige, cream, mustard and light green. Brian had a light blue shirt, a blue tie scattered with little white roses, the symbol of Yorkshire, and white trousers. He sat down facing an empty chair; one participant was late, although he soon appeared, apologising for the delay.

The newcomer immediately caught everyone's attention. He was a most strange man. Awfully thin, not overly tall, long fingers, a prominent nose, a wide jaw line, piercing blue eyes and a clear, alluring voice. He couldn't have been described as beautiful but he was fascinating and his glance seemed to draw people into those eyes. Everyone noticed his appearance; he was totally dressed in black, except for a white collar, visible under his black velvet Korean jacket. He sat down facing Brian and then remained almost unnaturally still.

Maria glanced at him from the corner of her eye, behind her glasses. She was a tall woman, who always wore skirts and high heels. Her short, grizzled hair gave her a stern air. Her character was serious and committed and she had worked there for almost fifteen years. She tried to take her eyes off the man but she couldn't. She noticed he had a massive ruby on his right little finger and he had beautiful hands. She always looked at men's hands and she realised that he must surely come from a classy background. He appeared very young, she thought he could have been in his early thirties. Mysterious and silent, he glanced at her while Brian was giving instructions: 'Behind you are your desks with wooden panels around so nobody can see what their neighbours are writing. It is not just for privacy but above all to allow you to concentrate. You will find paper, pen and an envelope there for you. When you finish writing your story, put it inside the envelope, seal it and bring to me. Is that clear? Ready? Good luck!'

All participants sat at their desks. Brian was himself taking part. There were no prizes, just a certificate of attendance.

The five hours, with a comfort break halfway through, were finally up and everyone handed Brian their envelope. 'Let's have a late lunch break before reading the first stories,' he said.

'What a great idea this was, Brian!' said Alex. 'I really enjoyed it.'

'You will enjoy it even more when we read the stories.'

'You know what, Brian? I've never tried to write anything like this before but it was not as difficult as I thought. Words flowed easily and the plot came to me like it was dictated!'

'I told you, Alex. I was sure it would be an exciting experience. Richard and his times are so fascinating!'

'I would give anything to discover whether he killed his nephews!' Alex exclaimed.

'For heaven's sake, Alex!' shouted Brian. 'I am sick and tired of this story! He had no reason to kill those boys; he was already king and the boys declared bastards!'

'OK, OK! Blimey, Brian, I am not against him, but every book I have read…'

'Is rubbish! Bin them! They're not even good enough for recycling!'

Brian couldn't stand people who still believed in Thomas More and Shakespeare's fairy tales. He hated those two for all their slander and lies about the last Plantagenet king.

'He died in battle, he was a man of honour, loyal to his brother, never killed a woman or a priest, never tortured prisoners, he was just and pious and treated everyone fairly without distinction between nobles and commoners!' thundered Brian.

16

'That was his weakness, Brian. That is the point! He was a threat to the nobles and he preferred Northerners to Southerners.'

'He loved the North, he established his house in Middleham and above all, he adored York, the city I am proud to have been born in!'

Brian pointed to his tie and the boar badge he had on his shirt pocket. He gritted his teeth and clenched his fists so hard his knuckles were white. He always did that when he was upset.

Slightly subdued by Brian's emotional outburst, they slowly drifted back to their seats in the circle again. Maria did everything in her power to sit near the man in black. He was silent, as before. He smelled of rosemary and rose but it was not an aftershave like the others wore, nor a perfume; it seemed to be some kind of essential oil. Perhaps, it was a shaving foam, since he had such a smooth face that it was almost like that of a young boy.

'Well done all of you. I'm sure you have written interesting and unique stories.'

'You will like them if they are favourable to King Richard,' twittered Clare, laughing at Brian.

'That's not true! Why are you always so scornful?' Brian replied.

'Oh, come on, I was just joking…'

'No, you were making fun of me and won't stand for it!'

'Brian, it's fine! You know I am just teasing…'

'Clare, I can laugh at anything but not about Richard's reputation. Why are you so sceptical?'

'I am not, the problem is that we have no proof he is innocent.'

'Have you any he was guilty?' Brian's face had started to redden, which occurred when he was fuming and trying to hide his fury.

'No, I haven't, but he possibly did it… I wouldn't blame him, his times were horrible, he had to protect himself and his family, he…'

'No! He wouldn't have done that. A valiant man like him! Can you see him asking someone to kill two children?'

Clare became silent then she drew closer to him.

'Brian, I am sorry, I didn't mean to… '

She looked at him coyly. She had a secret passion for him although Brian was about the only one who didn't know. He had a difficult situation at home. His wife was a frivolous woman and resented Brian reading and writing articles about medieval history, finding his passion for Richard III a total waste of time. Clare sipped her hot tea and tried to meet Brian's eyes. He was silent, deep in his thoughts and staring straight at the man in black. Maybe he also felt intimidated by his mysterious attitude. The man was alone, sitting in his chair with a fig roll in his hand. He observed everyone as if he wanted to read their inner secrets. His blue eyes seemed like razors when he stared at people.

Maria, seated close to him, tried to start a discussion with him, but was getting nowhere. She was normally a good conversationalist and knew how to attract the interest of men, but this one was different. He started to fidget again with his ring. She looked at it and noticed that the gold surrounding the ruby was finely decorated. The ring seemed a very old one, the shape reminded her of something…someone… Suddenly, she realised! That ring was exactly the same as the one Richard III had on his left hand in the portrait that was displayed in Brian's room.

'*Maybe he is a re-enactor,*' she thought. '*Or an antiquarian… When we read all the stories, I will try to approach him.*'

She couldn't stop looking at the man's hands. He had fantastic, long, slender fingers. He continued to fidget with his ring.

'*He must be very nervous or he is bored,*' she thought. '*I wonder what his job is… Maybe he is a writer or a banker, or possibly a lawyer…*'

He looked at her from the corner of his eye. She felt his gaze on her and lowered her eyes, feeling as if he knew what she had just been thinking. He stood up and started to pace up and down, thus avoiding any possible contact.

'I find Richard III very fascinating. I read a book about him and, from then on, I couldn't stop reading about him.' An old lady was explaining her passion for the king to Brian, who was listening to her, obviously delighted.

The man in black was close to them. He was having a Jaffa cake with his tea, his back to the two of them. But he was listening. He seemed interested in the conversation, although he didn't join in.

'I am obsessed with his nephews. I wonder if he really killed them or if the boys were sent abroad, as some new theories suggest.' This was a man aged about forty, who was talking to Janet, another attendee of the workshop.

'I don't think he did it.' Janet replied. 'I have read so many books about the Princes in the Tower, but I can't see any reason why he would have killed them. They were declared bastards, so what was the point? Buckingham maybe, Margaret Beaufort or Henry Tudor but not Richard, not him.'

The mysterious man smiled while sipping his tea. He seemed happy to hear that and chewed his lip thoughtfully while turning his head towards Janet, who didn't fail to notice and reciprocated with a smile.

Maria came back and tried to sit in a chair near where the man with wonderful hands had been seated before, hoping he would come back. There was a small space between him and the couple still speaking about the Princes and she had to pass between them. She accidentally touched his left shoulder with her arm and he turned his head towards her. That physical contact made her shiver.

'Sorry,' she murmured. He made a gesture with his hand as if saying 'No problem' but he didn't speak. She was totally fascinated by the man. She had to admit that looking at him from close up he appeared even more interesting.

Brian was still chatting with Clare. 'Let's have another coffee and cake. We have five minutes left,' he said, and he rushed to the buffet table, but he was not paying attention, so he stumbled against Maria. She would have fallen down, but her wrist was caught by a powerful hand and when she raised her eyes it was the man in black. He had grabbed her, preventing her fall.

'Sorry, love,' apologized Brian. 'I'm always so clumsy. Are you all right?'

'Yes, I am fine, no worries,' replied Maria in confusion. 'Thank you, you saved me,' she said to the mysterious man, who replied with a quick bow.

Maria rubbed her wrist. He had an incredible grip and such quick reflexes! His hand was like a steel cuff, so powerful! But it was cold, like marble, and as pale as his face. She wouldn't have imagined he had such strength; he didn't look that strong, as he was not very tall or stocky but appearances could be deceptive sometimes.

The man disappeared for a couple of minutes and Brian decided to start reading the first stories. All the participants were back in their seats.

'I will read the stories in the order I received them, so I will start with number one,' announced Brian, opening the envelope with satisfaction. 'Here we go....'

York Ascendant
by
Jennifer Bradley

✯✯✯

Introduction

Richard III's father, Richard, Duke of York, was killed at the Battle of Wakefield in December 1460 and his son, Edward continued to fight the Lancastrians, becoming King Edward IV in 1461, but this story explores a different scenario...

✯✯✯

Ludlow Castle, October 1459

Behind her rose the market cross of Ludlow. Cecily Neville, Duchess of York, was surrounded by growing numbers of soldiers, mounted and on foot. Lancastrian soldiers, overexcited with the adrenalin of victory. She sensed her youngest son Richard, just past his seventh birthday, cling closer to her leg. She knew he could feel its trembling, a weakness that no one else would see; she was not worried that the boy would know. He had always been sensitive to emotions around him. When he had first clung close to her, he was two years old and she wondered if he was looking for comfort or protection, something her other sons had never needed. They were proud and confident, sure of their place in the world in one of England's foremost families, educated and trained to take whatever actions were necessary. She soon learned that Richard stood so close for information, rather than comfort; he knew that the face she presented in public was not necessarily the true one.

Now she felt fear – the future of Ludlow could be in her hands – but most of all she felt anger. She was so angry it almost consumed her, threatening to burst out in rage.

It was vital she hide her feelings. She was a Duchess, a Neville and she knew what she had to do. It could make the difference between survival and destruction, not just for her family but for all the people of Ludlow, who had never been anything more than English citizens, loyal to the Crown. They did not deserve being treated like the villages in France she'd seen laid waste.

In this war, women and children had usually been treated well and she planned to ensure this would continue. Her upright body, her haughty expression, were to assure her enemies that she was not afraid. She expected the Lancastrian nobles to behave as well. She watched as two of the younger Beaufort men walked towards her. Of the families who supported the King and Margaret, she hated the Beauforts most. Descended from the illegitimate half-brothers of Henry IV, who had deposed Richard II, setting in train this ongoing feud, they were determined to make Lancaster the permanent dynasty on the English throne. Her hatred and fury kept her left leg trembling, her face a mask of calm.

For many years, the unreasoning malice of that bitch queen, Margaret, had made her families' lives complete misery. At any moment, everything Cecily cared about could be ripped out from under her. Margaret had certainly tried to eliminate the man she saw as her greatest threat several times before this.

From the day of her marriage to Henry VI in 1445, Margaret of Anjou had seen herself as the champion of her husband's Crown, protecting him from everything she imagined might threaten him. He was a gentle man, totally unsuited for kingship. He loved prayers and priests, he saw sin and evil everywhere he looked. And he trusted his advisors blindly, allowing them to transgress justice, to fleece the Crown's riches of land and treasure, leaving the King in severe debt.

Cardinal Beaufort's party, which had been supreme since 1440, used the King's favour to get whatever they chose. And Henry, unaware of the increasingly wretched state of his realm, loved and trusted those who were causing the wretchedness. His new bride saw as her few friends the men who had arranged her marriage and wanted peace with France. Her enemies were therefore those who opposed his advisers, Humphrey of Gloucester and his party.

Close behind the elderly Duke Humphrey was Richard, Duke of York, Cecily's husband, perceived as even more dangerous a threat than the old Duke because he was young and his claim to the throne surpassed that of her own husband.

In 1447, Duke Humphrey was arrested as he arrived at Bury St Edmunds for a meeting of Parliament. He died five days later, of a 'stroke', it was explained.

And the Duke of York was exiled to Ireland, appointed as its Lieutenant.

He was never meant to reach his destination. Royal commands were sent to ensure York never arrived in Ireland.

He evaded them and made his exile a triumph. He made friends of the Irish, he settled quarrels amongst the English, he produced order and even justice. And while York was demonstrating that he could rule, in England, the 'favourites' were losing France. Suffolk and Somerset surrendered Maine in 1448, in 1449 Normandy fell to the French armies and by 1451 only Calais remained English. Uprisings against the greedy barons who 'advised' the King were growing.

In 1450 Richard returned to England. Queen Margaret tried to have him killed on his way home, but he again evaded those assassins arriving safely but increasingly angry.

He protested his loyalty to the King himself and was welcomed as a true subject and cousin, a view that only lasted for a few months. For the last ten years York and his family had been seen as the major threat, THE enemy.

Margaret's enmity had turned him into what she had always assumed. Her enemy and therefore that of King Henry. Richard knew that while ever Margaret was Queen, he and his family would never be safe.

At this moment, York's safety had never been more in peril. Little Richard's hand in Cecily's skirt clutched the fabric in terror, but he held himself upright and looked steadily at the lords and soldiers in front of them. George stood a few inches away, certain that nobody could touch him; George's total self-absorption had always both entertained and exasperated his brothers and sisters.

The Duchess had been left alone at Ludlow, with her two youngest sons, while her husband, her brother Salisbury and her nephew Warwick and her two eldest sons Edward and Edmund, had fled from the might of the King's army. It had been the only sensible thing to do after Anthony Trollope and his Calais troops deserted them, taking their numbers and knowledge of all the Yorkist plans to the King and the King's pardon; The Lancastrian army was too numerous and close to fight. Surviving to raise their own army meant escaping immediately.

If Cecily hoped to save the people of Ludlow, her effort was in vain. She and her boys were hustled off to the royal camp, with minimal courtesy, while Ludlow was pillaged, looted and its people raped and killed. The castle was robbed to the bare walls.

She knew her boys had heard the screams of the Ludlow men and women and the shouts of increasingly drunken soldiers. She hoped they had seen little of what was happening. She had caught glimpses of blood and dead bodies as the soldiers took them to the camp. She pulled her boys closer, hoping to protect them.

They were then taken to Coventry, where a Lancastrian Parliament promptly attainted the Dukes of York and Salisbury, and the Earl of Warwick and their chief followers. Their estates were forfeited to the Crown.

Cecily and her children were placed in the custody of her sister, the Duchess of Buckingham, but given one thousand marks per year for maintenance. Just before Christmas 1459 they took up residence as prisoners of the Crown, while her menfolk became fugitives.

The Duke of York and his son Edmund, Earl of Rutland, found a ship and sailed for Ireland, where they were welcomed. The Irish Parliament recognised York as the virtual ruler of Ireland and declared that only those writs of the English King that were approved by the Parliament would have any force.

The Earls of Warwick, Salisbury and March bought a ship and escaped to Calais. Edward, Earl of March found time to write to his kinsman the Archbishop of Canterbury, asking him to befriend his two young brothers, George and Richard. The two boys moved into his household and were put to serious study.

The Yorkist lords prepared to invade England, and collected supporters and troops.

The scene was set for the next moves in the war.

☆☆☆

Sandal Castle, December 1460

'For pity's sake, Edmund, sit down and stop prowling!' Richard, Duke of York glared at his son. Sandal Castle was not the most comfortable place to be holed up in winter. It was both cold and draughty, despite fires and large smoke faded tapestries. They hadn't visited for some time and it felt neglected, dust motes visible in the air.

Perhaps Edmund was trying to keep warm, but it was still annoying and disrupted his father's thought processes. The seventeen-year-old Earl of Rutland was like an overgrown pup, with limbs and feet that were still growing. And a mind, his father thought with a smile, a mind that was growing from boyhood to manhood and sometimes ran in all directions at once. Even annoyed, Richard looked forward to seeing the man he would become.

He was often in the shadow of his elder brother Edward, the golden son, taller and brighter than his siblings and with an outgoing, confident manner that appealed to both nobility and servants. Not that he was popular with Lancastrian supporters, who rightly thought he might prove dangerous to them. He was a seasoned fighter, who had won battles for York, supported by Edmund.

Richard wondered where Edward was. When they had split up, he had been heading to Wales, intending to quell difficulties there, then collect troops to boost his father's army, and shore up support for York.

His mind wandered over the Act of Accord, which made him the heir to Henry VI, instead of Edward, Prince of Wales, son of Margaret of Anjou and Henry. It should have settled the warring factions but given the deeply held beliefs of those who supported the King, this was unlikely.

When he looked up again, Edmund had disappeared. For a few minutes he enjoyed the quiet, but then realised that it was too quiet. He called to Warren, a close servant, to enquire.

'I think he heard there had been a scuffle at the gate and thought he ought to check.'

The Duke, thinking he would be grateful when Edmund had outgrown his impetuosity, shrugged and went back to planning the coming battle.

He knew he had 9000 men but had no intelligence about the size of his foes' army. The Duke of Somerset, Earl of Northumberland, Barons Clifford, Neville and Ros could summon thousands between them, and might easily outnumber his own troops.

If only Edward were close. The Duke had sent a messenger when he'd first arrived at Sandal on 21 December, but the messenger had yet to return.

Richard was startled by shouts, and clashing metal from outside the castle. He hurried to see what was happening.

He had half dressed in his battle clothing, but stopped to add his hauberk, and grab his sword and helmet before rushing down the stairs. The northern gate was a mess of men, Yorkists and Lancastrians, swords clashing, grunts and yells. As he paused, more men arrived, and for a few moments, he could not see whose troops they were.

Surrounded by his men, he rushed towards the melee, sure they were about to be overrun. He recognised Salisbury, struggling to contain men who surged towards him, but he could not see well enough to identify anyone else.

Then he heard a furious and familiar shout, one full of pain and anger.

Edward! He still could not see him, but his voice was unmistakable.

'Edmund!!!'

Richard's heart dropped, but it only strengthened his desire to reach the men. His sword at the ready, he barged straight into the mass, slicing almost at random. A path seemed to clear for him, and he joined Edward, whose fury had reached berserker levels. They stood, protected by their men, fighting off the attack from the Lancastrians.

Richard saw what had happened. A small group with Andrew Trollope at its head, had approached the gate, seeking parlay with the Duke. It seemed entry was denied, at least initially, and some of the group had become annoyed, taunting and pricking the guards. Edmund had seen his guards in trouble and rushed to join them, as the troops of Somerset and Clifford began to swarm down to the base of the motte.

What had been intended as a push, before an invasion, turned into a small scuffle, and the armies led by Edward had rushed to join in. If Lancaster thought they outnumbered the York troops, now Edward had arrived with his tired men, York was far more numerous and furious.

What had enraged Edward was seeing his beloved Edmund on the ground, blood seeping from his neck and a sword thrust under his hauberk. There was no doubt he was dead. His father and brother looked in horror at his body. Their lovable Edmund, dead before his life had virtually begun.

How would they tell his mother?

But they had no time to think about that, or to mourn. They were all in danger and needed to fight for their lives if they were to survive.

The Duke stopped long enough to detail two of the guards to take up Edmund's body and place it in the castle, then grabbed his sword with determination. He and Edward glanced at each other and nodded.

For the next two hours they slashed and sliced, killed and moved on. Slipped in blood and kicked aside bodies and swords, fury and grief lending their battle skills an edge. Some men fell beside them, but more of their opponents dropped, as they moved outwards from the castle, pushing further with each minute.

With one part of his mind, Richard registered the falls of Clifford and Neville, the wounding of Somerset and many of their men. He was fleetingly sorry to see Somerset still living, the man who had replaced him as Lieutenant of France and then failed to defend Normandy. On his own side he saw Salisbury fall and other good and loyal men, but had no time to dwell on any of it.

He and Edward fought on, as their enemies fell back. The extra Lancastrian troops, under Ros and Wiltshire, had been hidden in woods, ready to fall upon the York army. They awaited the word to join the battle, but it never came. They could not clearly see the battle and assumed that Lancaster was the winning side, certain they outnumbered the Yorkists.

When the battle outside Sandal castle was dying down, Edward sent troops towards the woods. The army in the woods had grown bored, assuming they would not be needed. Complacent, they lounged and were an easy target when Edward's well-trained men burst through the trees. Those that were not killed, fled when they realised that it was York triumphant.

By late afternoon, it was all over. The land around Sandal was a scene of carnage – with bodies and weapons, horses and bits of armour spread out. It was winter, so dark quickly, and they could do little to retrieve bodies for burial that night.

Except for Edmund. He was laid out in the castle chapel. His body was lovingly tended by his brother Edward, whose tears of grief dripped onto the cleaned limbs and face. Richard, Duke of York, his own scratches ignored, knelt beside the bier and vowed that his death would be avenged.

28

And that he, Richard would not wait for the king to die, but would seize the throne now.

Margaret of Anjou and her snivelling brat would be exiled, where her enmity could fester to no effect.

Long live King Richard III!

★★★

Baynard's Castle, London, January 1471

Queen Cecily propped herself higher on the pillows as she watched her husband get ready for bed.

'Richard,' she began. 'I've been thinking about Henry II.'

He looked at her in amazement. 'Who? Why?'

'You know who – he ruled from 1154 until he died in 1189.'

'Yes, and why him now?'

'It was more how he ended his reign, warring with his sons.'

King Richard III pushed his cold feet into the bed as he joined her. He fluffed his own pillows so he could sit and watch his wife.

'Do you think that's going to happen to me?'

'Not exactly, but I was concerned by the boys at dinner.'

Richard thought about her words. 'Mmmm. They were scrapping more than usual.'

Or rather, he thought, as usual, George managed to rile both his brothers. Mostly, both Edward and Dickon managed to deal well with him, damping down his sniping and bad temper, but this day, they had both bit back, loudly and with complaint. Almost vicious complaint.

'George always feels hard done by. What do you suggest, then?'

Cecily thought for a moment before replying.

'I think they all need more to do. Idle hands as they say.'

29

'All three of them, not just George?'

'George always wants more. He's sure his brothers are loved, appreciated and rewarded more than he is.'

'Ha! We've rewarded his bad behaviour more than I've ever wanted to. If anything, his brothers have reason to feel they've been treated less well because of him.'

'Dickon in particular.'

'He is the youngest – and he's still only eighteen. What does he expect?'

'Nothing. He's always more concerned for Edward than for himself. I think his jumping down George's throat today was more about Edward than himself.'

'Edward's my heir. And you're right. Edward needs more responsibility. When he hasn't enough to do, he gets into bother.'

Cecily winced. 'Yes, like getting married without your permission. And to a woman whom I have difficulty liking.'

She giggled. 'She patronises me. I'm Queen and she looks down her elegant little nose at me! She's got minimal breeding and considers me not good enough.'

'Or maybe she's looking forward to being Queen herself.' Richard looked sideways at his wife.

'I'm sure she is. And there's part of the problem. Edward wants to please her.'

'You don't seriously think she'd persuade him to try to take the throne?'

'No, I don't, but he might get impatient if you live too long!'

Richard leaned over and kissed her goodnight. 'I'll think about it,' he assured her as he rolled over, dragging the bedcovers over his legs.

'Huh'. Cecily dragged some of the covers back and settled down for sleep.

King Richard raised his goblet to all those gathered in the hall. It was a merry crowd, who had been feasting and drinking for some hours, and were soothed and entertained by some of the best musicians in the country.

'Thank you all for coming to help us celebrate Twelfth Night. It has been a good year and we have all benefitted. I want to drink to the next year being even better.'

He looked around the hall. At his side Cecily, his Queen, and beside her his sons, Edward, George and Dickon.

His family, his legacy. York sons to inherit the throne of England.

In front of him, representatives of the nobility, from the Duke of Salisbury, now very elderly and still not recovered fully from his wounds at Sandal, his son the Earl of Warwick, somewhat impatient to take his father's place. The Dukes of Suffolk and Norfolk, Oxford and even some of the Beauforts had come. If he was being sceptical, the King knew that they all owed him – their status and indeed their wealth owed much to the pleasure of the Crown.

Richard did not take their support for granted. In his lifetime he had seen disaffected aristocrats move their allegiance from one king to a claimant of the throne, sometimes for good reason, but often for pure self-interest.

He never underestimated the strength of human selfishness, and it was this knowledge that had allowed him to rule England's warring factions and keep peace. He was always aware peace was a fragile thing, which could fall at the drop of an over ambitious desire on the part of any noble who decided he deserved to be king. And there were still disgruntled Lancastrian supporters who believed that they would be better off with a Lancastrian king who owed them his throne.

He could not take his kingship for granted.

And he never took the uncritical support of his sons for granted either. They all needed something more challenging to do than being king's sons in a country at peace.

Something he planned to change that night.

The King, Queen and their sons rose and bowed to their guests. They would retire to the solar upstairs and have a family discussion. He hoped his sons would welcome his orders.

'Anyone want another drink?'

Only George raised his goblet for a refill. The others shook their heads. King Richard was aware of his Queen watching him carefully. She knew what he was planning and, like him, was worried about George, the son who had inherited the worst Neville traits, she often thought. Both Edward and young Richard had the ability to see beyond their immediate desires and consider what might happen if they behaved in a certain way.

Not George though. The world began and ended with what was best for George. What George thought he deserved. And what George wanted NOW.

Soon they would find out what that was.

King Richard swallowed the wine.

'We need to talk about what happens next for all of us. I've been on the throne now for ten years and turn sixty this year. I have three adult sons, so the succession should be secure.

'This last year has been peaceful. We've managed to get some good legislation through parliament and most of the nobles went along with us. No uprisings, few skirmishes either in England or elsewhere. But we cannot guarantee this will continue and we need to be prepared. We all grow fat and lazy and an organised army could easily overrun us.

'Retaining power is not just about battles. We need to practise the skills of ruling in peacetime and that requires managing people and their expectations.

'First, you, Edward, my Prince of Wales and heir. You have a wife and young family, and you don't really have enough to do, apart from carousing. You helped with our legislative program, both its content and persuading parliament that it was in their interests. But you're hardly stretched and are apt to get up to mischief if you're bored.'

Edward had secretly married the young widow Elizabeth Woodville, Lady Grey, several years before. She proved to be a fertile choice, if not one the King considered suitable. What he did not say was that his wife's family, the Woodvilles were numerous and seeking to marry within the English nobility. When Edward came to the throne, they would be everywhere, and Richard could not decide if that would be a good or bad thing. Being related to the king was not a guarantee of support for that king as the history of the Plantagenets showed.

'I think it's time for you to leave England to be in charge at Calais. It's an important posting and it's more than time for you to be fully in charge.'

And it would keep him far from those of his cronies who encouraged and joined in his drinking.

Edward looked thoughtful, then nodded slowly. His father was right. He needed a challenge that would help prepare him for kingship. He was becoming too fat and lazy.

'And George,' the king looked at his second living son. 'I think it's time for you to take on more responsibility. I would like you to be my representative in Ireland.'

He stopped there, watching the young Duke's face. George was looking his usual discontented self, and would no doubt tell everyone what he thought.

'Ireland!!' George spluttered. 'I don't want Ireland'.

'Then what do you want?' his father asked.

'I want more power in England. Isobel didn't bring me many titles, and I want to take on more of the south, and there are several wards I should get.'

'That, George, is not going to happen. Ireland needs a strong and careful hand. I put considerable effort into gaining Irish support for York and reaching a peace. But I've been away now for some years and I hear it's becoming more unsettled by the day. It will build your skills to ensure an ongoing peace there.'

George frowned and began to argue for what he wanted. He yelled, stomped around and threatened. He re-iterated his desires and why the King should agree. King Richard listened and responded but did not give an inch. George was going to Ireland and might even learn something useful. Richard had strong doubts, but George was still young and not having to compete with his brother – either of them, although he tended to discount Dickon.

George looked at Edward and his frown turned into a smirk. His mother felt cold. George had always been jealous of Edward – and Edmund when he was alive – and that look did not imply brotherly love. Given an opportunity, he would harm his brother and smile.

'And you, young Dickon,' said the King, 'I'd like to send you north. It's still a nest of Lancastrian support, as well as being subject to forays from the Scots.'

And, thought the King, become your own person rather than an acolyte of Edward, who relies on you and takes you for granted.

Dickon beamed. 'Thank you, my Lord. I'd like that.'

Cecily looked around her sons. This would help for a while at least, as the boys became independent men.

But in a few years, as the King aged towards his three score years and ten, things might be different. Edward's impatience might grow, especially if he was egged on by his ambitious wife, who had not yet produced any sons, only a brood of daughters and the two sons from her first marriage. But being in charge of Calais would be good for both him and England.

She wondered what George was thinking.

As for Dickon, like his father, he had the makings of a good administrator and should manage the north well, despite being so young. It was also nearly time Dickon was married. Being the youngest, neither she nor Richard had pushed his betrothal to a useful ally. Partly that was because there was no suitable heiress or princess in the wings, but also because he had not wanted anyone they'd mentioned. She knew he would do what was required, but she had thought he had an inclination for young Anne Neville, the younger sister of George's wife Isabel. There was money there and she suspected that George wanted it all. If Anne were married to his brother, he'd have to share. Sharing was not something George did well, if at all.

Her mind spiralled back to Henry II's quarrelsome and acquisitive sons and what happened when they decided Henry had been on the throne long enough. Surely that could not happen again?

About Jennifer Bradley

From Canberra, Australia, Jennifer Bradley is a long-term public servant and writer, with one book, ***Girls with Wings***, in print (historical fiction of 1930s aviation in rural NSW). She developed a passion for medieval history in high school after finding Shakespeare's ***Richard III*** unbelievable, and has been reading about the period, in both fiction and non-fiction, ever since.

If Only…

by

Alex Marchant

✩✩✩

'If Only…' was previously published in the Richard III-inspired charity anthology **Right Trusty and Well Beloved…**

Introduction

In the early summer of 1483, evidence was placed before the Royal Council that the recently deceased king, Edward IV, had been secretly married to Lady Eleanor Butler (née Talbot) at the time of his – also secret – wedding to Dame Elizabeth Grey (née Woodville). Elizabeth became his queen in 1464, once their marriage was finally made public. Lady Eleanor died in 1468, but her death did not make the marriage between Edward and Elizabeth legal – it was still bigamy and the children born to them deemed illegitimate, and therefore unable to inherit the throne. The revelation of the prior marriage led to Edward's son, briefly King Edward V, being put aside by Parliament and the throne being offered to the next heir, his uncle, Richard. He reigned for a little over two years as King Richard III, until a certain battle on an August morning in 1485. But what if Edward had acted to put this right…?

✩✩✩

L ady Eleanor Butler?'

I search my memory, trying to recall the lady of whom he speaks. But, though the name tugs at the edges of my mind, I have to admit defeat.

'Who is – was she, brother?'

His face bears a look I rarely see upon it – discomfort, embarrassment even. But at what?

'She was a lady I – I met. Once or twice.'

'Once or twice? Why then is her death so important?'

'Important?' His laugh is strained, an attempt at light-heartedness. 'Maybe it is not – not really. And it was so long ago.'

'Long ago?' Now my perplexity is heightened. 'Hers is not a recent death? There are no legal matters that require urgent attention?'

'No, indeed – it is some years ago now – I do not quite recall how many. No, perhaps – perhaps it is no matter at all.'

'No matter? It is surely a great matter if you should summon me the length of England to attend you at such short notice.'

Has impatience crept into my voice? I abandoned important work at home in the north to respond to his summons. Yet though he is my brother, he is also King of England. I must be careful in my words, my tone. I must not offend. I must not try his patience – like George.

But, if he hears aught in my speech, he does not heed it. He throws his arm about my shoulders. His great bear-like arm. It is all I can do to stop myself recoiling from the stab of pain it causes. I must not remind him of it, the curve in my back that continues to grow, lest he fears I can no longer serve him so well. But he does not notice, as he draws me to the deep-recessed window. He stands silent for a time, staring out at the teeming traffic on the Thames, while I steal a glance askance at him. His eyes, usually so clear, so merry, are brooding, cloudy like the sky reflected in the busy waterway.

He speaks again, gazing still, but perhaps not seeing.

'There is none I trust so well as you, little brother.'

I smile at his words. That he should still call me that, even now I am no longer a boy, but a full-grown man. Though, to be sure, I will never now reach his stature. He stands a full head and more above me, as he clasps me so close to him I almost feel, rather than hear, his next words.

'You have ever proved true – throughout all my many trials. And now, now I must have a witness – witnesses – whom I trust completely. No one else must ever know.'

'Witnesses? To what?'

Silence. For a second. As his grip tightens, as his lips tighten. Then...

'Elizabeth is not happy. She says there is no need. That we should continue as before. That nothing need change. That no one need know. But I ...'

This sudden mention of his wife. The queen. Why...?

'But I – I fear for my son. What may happen if ... His right to the throne must be secure if I should die while he is yet young.'

First, talk of his wife. Now of his son. Young Edward. My bafflement is no less. Why does he speak like this? Of such a thing as his death? He is young still himself – in his prime, at least. And why worry about the succession? I do not speak, but he blunders on, his eyes fixed still on the distant river. A feverishness tinges their depths.

'How could I ride to battle again in the knowledge that ... Before now – at Barnet, Tewkesbury – I knew you or George could – would succeed me should I fall on the battlefield. That a Plantagenet king would continue to rule in my stead, though he were my brother, not my son. But now ... now my son is born, is my heir – now it would be his right to rule. But – but he must be legitimate...'

Understanding strikes me like a blow from a halberd. This puzzle he has skirted round. The lady he spoke of, this Eleanor Butler ...

She – she he had wed before ... before he wed Elizabeth...

Elizabeth. The queen. Yet ... not ... not his queen. For the Lady Eleanor still lived until – when? Some years at least after my brother's marriage to the mother of his children. That marriage that had itself been secret – and against the wishes of Parliament, of our cousin Warwick. When a foreign alliance had been needed, a foreign princess prepared – a princess then spurned when news of this marriage to Elizabeth emerged.

And now? Now he seeks a second marriage ceremony – as secret as that first – with witnesses he can trust not to tell...

Or rather – a third ceremony as secret as both those 'marriages'... secret in the world, but known before God...

My mind whirls, my world in turmoil. All the certainties of my life dropping away one by one. Darkness spins my thoughts around, clouds befog my sight. I close my eyelids, a defence against the hammering reality.

'Your Grace? It's time to wake.'

The words, the voice, though quiet, slice through my reverie. But they do not wake me into the grey glimmer of the dawn.

For I was not asleep.

But I raise my head from the silk pillow as though it were heavy with slumber, as though brushing away the gentle touch of dreams.

My attendants and gentlemen must not know I had been awake. They must not think I have slept ill. In truth, indeed, my sleep was like a babe's this night – till I was stirred by the first cock crow in the village nearest to the royal camp. And then I lay a while, raking across the events of my life so far. Events that brought me to this dawn, this day of reckoning. When I must face he who would take my crown – once my brother's crown – that should have been our father's – and perhaps... perhaps also my brother's son's.

And I thought of how that life might have been so different if – if only...

If only my brother had summoned me the length of England one day, some years ago...

39

About Alex Marchant

Alex Marchant was born and raised in the rolling Surrey downs, but, following stints as an archaeologist and in publishing in London and Gloucester, now lives surrounded by moors in King Richard III's northern heartland, not far from his beloved York and Middleham.

A Ricardian and writer since a teenager, Alex's first novel, *Time Out of Time* (due out June 2021), won the 2012 Chapter One Children's Book Award, but was put on the backburner in 2013 at the announcement of the rediscovery of King Richard's grave in a car park in Leicester.

Discovering there were no books for children telling the story of the real Richard III, Alex was inspired to write them, and so *The Order of the White Boar* and its sequel *The King's Man* were born. Together they tell King Richard's story through the eyes of a young page in his service and have been called 'a wonderful work of historical fiction for both children and adults' by the Bulletin of the Richard III Society. The third book in the White Boar sequence, *King in Waiting*, will be published in 2021.

Alex has also edited two anthologies of short stories by authors inspired by King Richard III: *Grant Me the Carving of My Name* and *Right Trusty and Well Beloved...*, both sold to raise money for Scoliosis Association UK (SAUK), which supports people with the same condition as the king.

Website: alexmarchantblog.wordpress.com

Amazon: https://tinyurl.com/2dcnpfu4

Facebook: www.facebook.com/AlexMarchantAuthor/

Twitter: twitter.com/AlexMarchant84

GoodReads: https://tinyurl.com/etbyw4w7

Instagram: www.instagram.com/alexmarchantauthor/

The Desmond Papers

by
CJ Lock

★★★

Introduction

'A great deed was done in Drogheda this year; to wit, the Earl of Desmond, namely, Thomas son of James, son of Earl Gerald, was beheaded. And the learned relate that there was not ever in Ireland a foreign youth that was better than he. And he was killed in treachery by a Saxon Earl...'

So do the Annals of Ulster record the death of Thomas Fitzgerald, Seventh Earl of Desmond, on 15th February 1468 in Drogheda. A man who fought, and won, the only battle of the Wars of the Roses fought in Ireland. A man who served Edward IV as Lord Deputy of Ireland until he was replaced in 1467 by John Tiptoft, Earl of Worcester. Desmond's descendants argued over many a year that the accusations of treason against him were false. Desmond, charismatic and charming, had a love of Irish culture, something that was frowned on by many an Anglo-Irish lord. He had many friends, but also enemies.

More importantly, he was at court during the fateful summer of 1464 when Edward secretly married Elizabeth Woodville. Desmond left England in September, around the time that Edward revealed the identity of his bride to a stunned court at Reading Abbey. Four years later, he was dead.

In 1484 Richard III wrote to Desmond's son, the Eighth Earl, offering him kind words and gifts to lure the family back into the *adoption of English ways, something the family eschewed after the unjust murder of their father. Richard promised justice, to pursue whomever was responsible for his father's death. In 1484, there was only one person alive to whom he could have been referring: Elizabeth Woodville. For Desmond's death was rumoured to be the searing revenge of a woman scorned. A woman who took offence at the honest words of an Irish Lord, his only sin being to speak a frank opinion to his king, when asked what he made of the new English queen.*

Yet, was there something else? Something other than a bawdy jest which was more dangerous, should the words ever be uttered. What if, then, the swing of the executioner's axe was stalled? If, on the 15th February 1468, his lips were not sealed for eternity. What would Desmond's words have told us, if he had lived on to bear witness to the truth...?

23rd day of February, Aboard 'La Katerine'

I should be dead.

My head and body encased in cold, damp soil. Lifelong companions separated by the executioner's blade. Yet, I live. Breathe. Eyes fortunate enough to stare across a massive heaving ocean instead of a sightless void. When the keys turned in the lock on my prison door, the cold hard rattle of an old man's final breath, I was ready. Soul purged. Final goodbyes whispered.

Yet it was not my gaolers who greeted me. Two men, yes, but these bore the faces of friends not foes. Richard Neville, Earl of Warwick and George Plantagenet, Duke of Clarence. Lord Lieutenant of Ireland. I was saved from an undeserved fate. For a while at least. Long enough for me to travel to England, for the king to hear my own account of the charges railed against me. As he had promised he would, some years ago. A promise I thought he had forgotten. Or ignored. Leaving me to perish at the hands of a vengeful servant, the man who had replaced me as Lord Deputy of Ireland, John Tiptoft, Earl of

Worcester. An envious man. A cold man. An Englishman. I was bundled away far too swiftly to gain a satisfactory slightest glimpse of his astonished face. That was a frustration. At least until Warwick told me the reason for his absence. My sons, James and Maurice, had raised arms in anger at my arrest. At the charges of treason they knew to be false. My sons, two siblings who constantly quarrelled when under the same roof were now united in a common cause. I had to smile.

I still do, despite the rolling motion of the ship. The lurching of the table where I sit writing these words. The planks around me creaking in protest. The smell of candlewax, damp wool, salt and sweat. A single flame guiding my pen. My companions are asleep, but I have slept too much these past days, for what else is a condemned man to do? Sleep stopped my restless thoughts, tossing and tumbling like the waves around us. The charges against me were a farce. Did Edward truly believe I sought to make myself King of Ireland? That I had conspired against him with Irish rebels? I will admit that I did use, and defend, my use of an old Gaelic custom to pay for the billeting of my men. Coyne and livery, outlawed in laws drawn up by English lords who knew little of the ways of our land. A land they had never fully conquered, and never would. Not until they understood.

A proud race, the Irish. Proud and ancient. Brave and fearless hearts that were a match for any armour plate. No one man should underestimate them for the lack of steel. Warwick knew it. So did Richard, Duke of York, the Lord bless his soul. A man who tried his best for my land. Whilst a feeble king poured English taxes into the defence of his territories in France, Richard paid us out of his own coffers, more than once. I know of no one alive who is his equal. Certainly not his eldest son. Not too many years ago, I held a secret for a king. For Richard's son. He married in secret all whilst the land believed he was seeking the hand of a foreign princess. Leaving his cousin and mentor to seek out a bride whose slender hand brought with it a French treaty. Alliances. The meat and mead of kings. Yet, not Edward. Rashly, and in secret, he chose his own bride and married her before anyone could whisper the folly of his actions. In one foolish afternoon, he plunged the court into a swirling river of dissent.

Yet, all storms cease. Winds calm. Boats glide into smoother waters, in time. Just, not forever. I am alive thanks to his intervention, but two of my sons suffered at the same axe blade that was sharpened for me. My own fate had been postponed, but Edward still allowed my boys to die. Innocent boys, guilty only of my sin. My sin? They were Irish boys whom I took under my roof after their own father was killed in battle by one of my men. In a battle fought for Edward in an Irish town that I doubt many Englishmen have heard of. A battle that expunged the Lancastrian threat from Ireland for good. But even that did not save my sons. It did not, alone, save me.

Edward was no longer my friend. He allowed my sons, my fostered sons, to die. Boys who sat at the board and shared chambers with my very own blood. Rather I had died instead of two young boys with their lives still to live. I had not been given that choice. Edward had taken it away from me, and now, I could pay back the compliment. Not too many years ago I held a secret for a king. Now I held another. A secret passed to me by an enemy of the crown. A man bloated with the pleasure his knowledge gave him. At least he was, until my fostered son ran a sword through his gut, leaving his knowledge to seep into the ground with his blood. They are both dead now. But I know. I know that secret and I am alive. My son lost his life despite protecting his king against that dreadful secret. I cannot forgive Edward. Soon he will wish I too had been kissed by the executioner's axe.

Feast of the Annunciation, Minster Lovell, England

The deed is done. Not that I feel any better for it. I thought I would. I thought the sharing of it would assuage the anger inside me. Give me the courage I needed to be able to face Ellice. To look my dear wife in the face and tell her that I did what I could to avenge their deaths. Ellice was closer to them than I, having spent many an hour in their company whilst I governed the land for our king. I was proud to serve Richard's son. I do not feel proud now. It is a beautiful place, this house. Warwick holds it as part of a wealthy wardship. A noble young lad who lost both father and mother now relies on the earl for his keep. A fortunate arrangement for Warwick. For many an English lord who takes such unfortunates under their wing. How is that different to what I did? What did it matter that those two boys belonged to a native Irishman, not the offspring of nobility? Boys murdered for the misfortune of their birth, yet the MacCarthy Reagh of southern Ireland are an ancient line. I do not know if Ellice even knows as yet. I am sure she must. Word travels faster than the wind in our land. A bird sings throatily outside the window as a rainbow dusk falls. The constant babble of a river a welcome companion. My chamber is a better prison than the Tholsel in Drogheda, but a prison just the same.

The king is in a high state and it is my fault. Warwick and George know not what to say. To me. To anyone. Not since Edward stormed out of the large, sunlit room they call a solar. Tall windows line one end, bathing it in golden light, washing away the darkness of the secret. It could have been summer, apart from the chill. Warwick negotiated the meeting here. Neutral territory he called it. He is a good friend and it is some surprise to me that Edward agreed. That I was not dragged before him in the great hall at Westminster to answer for my treasons. Would I have dared to speak up then? Instead, there was just Edward, George and Warwick. Edward's younger brother Richard, a solemn young boy the image of his father. My heart ached, such did his face touch my heart. He is the same age as my own daughter, Katherine. A girl with true Irish spirit, with the clear sparking air of our land in her eyes and skin. She smiles a lot. I can hear her laughter even now as I write of it. Then, two sombrely robed members of the clergy. George Neville, Warwick's brother and Archbishop of York, and Bourchier, Archbishop of Canterbury. And William Hastings. The king's Chamberlain.

No one is allowed to see Edward without his express permission. I imagine they sorely wish they had not been invited to today's events now, for all our tomorrows are now changed. Was I right to speak out, to allow my smouldering anger to flare and spit? Had I held my tongue, could I now be planning to return home to Youghal? To my family? To a life of peace? Ellice's face appears before me. Cheeks tearstained, eyes dulled with grief. No. I had been right. How could I return without defending them? No matter the dictats of English law.

I can still see his face, Edward. First deathly pale, before it flushed slowly, from the chin up, like wine filling a flagon. His bright eyes watered. He was enraged, but there was one comfort for me in my final betrayal. I saw. I knew his face well. It was true. He could yell and bluster and thump massive, curled fists on the oaken table hard enough to make the candles leap from their sconces and the clergy soil their holy robes, but it was true. What Edmund Butler told me. What he had learned during his time in England, before he returned to Ireland to fight with the Irish and hopefully reclaim his ancestral rights. Before he left the grand estates of the Talbot earls. Old Shrewsbury, who died at Castillion back in Henry's time, once he was governor of Ireland, as I had been.

There had been a bitter feud between the Talbots and Butlers. There were many such between the lords over the years. The Irish nobility fought between themselves just as fiercely as the Irish clans themselves, despite their airs and graces and grand velvet robes. We are all just men underneath. Old Talbot and James Butler of Ormond never did see eye to eye. We all paid, in those days, for the rule of an ineffectual king. Warwick tells me he is a prisoner in the Tower. I am surprised Edward hasn't had him done away with. They say the man is harmless and so he may be, but a puppet will dance again if someone picks up its strings. Then it dances like a demon!

Butler gave his daughter in marriage to Shrewsbury's heir. A good match, or it was until my own father heard of it. For the girl was already promised in marriage to me. A marriage which fractured the bond between my family and the Butler's to this very day. A marriage. Another marriage. A marriage took a Butler over to England and a Butler came back to Ireland with news of a marriage. The irony. So, I told him. I told Edward, in the presence of his brothers, the clergy and his closest friends. I told him. I told him what Butler had told me. That not long after Edward won his crown, a widow petitioned him for return of her lands. He met her, in person, only to be captivated by her cool, demure beauty. But the woman was pious. Godfearing. She did not respond to his amorous advances. She intended to remain a maid and only submit to a man who had been joined to her in the eyes of God. So, Edward did what any young, foolish man with lust pounding through his limbs and the whole world at his feet would do. He had conquered the world. He believed he could do whatever he wished.

So, he married her. In secret. In a small chapel with one witness. A secret. The same sort of secret I held for him that fair summer, four years ago. Only this time, the bride was the daughter of nobility. The daughter of Old Shrewsbury. And her name was Eleanor Butler.

✫✫✫

Feast of St Ruadan, Le Herber, London

I have written to Ellice today. Written of all that has happened. Assured her I am safe and well, for surprisingly, I am. Before we left Minster Lovell, young Richard of Gloucester came to see me. Before the beauty of Minster Lovell became a memory, unmarked by any repercussions of my revenge. There were bound to be some, it was true. I had understood that the moment I left Ireland. Edward could surely not allow me to live with the knowledge I held. The knowledge that invalidated his marriage and made bastards of his children. But fortune hears our words, listens to our hopes and fears yet still spins her wheel, smiling as she does so, for even she knows not who will rise and who will fall. Knows not, cares not. Cruel mistress to some, blessed angel to others. Am I caught on the spindle for I feel neither blessed nor cursed? I long for Ireland. England could never be my home.

He asked me if it was true, young Richard. Looking at me with his father's stormy eyes, pale face framed by auburn tinged hair, only his youth and an air of sobriety was different. He asked me if it was true. What I had said in the solar. I told him I found it hard to doubt, given Edward's reaction. Would I not be angered too, he asked of me, had a man I thought of as my true friend accused me thus? Would a true friend murder two innocent boys, I replied? He looked shocked, his face greyer than a winter dawn, for surely, he could never contemplate such a thing. Why would he? All Edward had to do was banish the boys down to Munster, back to Ellice's care. Or even back to their clan.

I knew Dermod MacCarthy well. He had known their father, a foolish drunk. Half in his cups even in battle. No wonder he met his end at Piltown. There were other fates the boys could have suffered. They did not have to die. They had committed no crime. All of this he heard, my shoulders heavy under the burden of his stare. He loved his brother. I knew that. I understood. To believe what I was saying was a grave disloyalty. The boy was being torn apart before me. He didn't need to tell me, I knew. I could see. He had sworn to serve his king above all and he loved his brother deeply, but as for what he had done? A king could not ride roughshod over the law. Especially God's law.

Richard paced the floor before me, distracted. He wore a jewelled ring on his thumb which he twisted round and round, a form of comfort it seemed. It was only when he came to a halt that I knew he would speak. Would I swear, he asked me. That was an easy answer. I would swear to what I was told. Only God, Edward and the woman herself knew if it was true. I had lost two sons but would willing swear on the lives of my children who still lived. His mood lightened, relief flashed behind his eyes, like lightning silvering the clouds. It was easy for him with his love for Edward, to reach out for that hope. To believe that what I had been told was a lie. His belief gave me hope and sadness in equal measure. I had long wished that my boys, James and Maurice, would love each other as he loved Edward, yet they were as cocks baited for a fight. Only too willing to believe the worst of each other. Such unflinching trust brought tears to my eyes. A moment short lived. The door to the chamber flew open, and the flower of hope was blasted by the hard frost of truth. Warwick. A man had come forward. A man of the law. It was unbelievable, even for me, who had known this secret for so long. This man had known it much, much longer. A man by the name of William Catesby.

48

✩✩✩

18th day of April, Coldharbour, London

God forgive me! What have I done? What devil did I release with my words? I should have known. Should have understood the resentment and hatred that boiled and simmered over four long years. I had known. I had known when I left these shores, fearful for the outcome of Edward's rash actions. Terrified of the anger of a nobility shunned and snubbed. Even abused. Commoners married to noble children. Old dowagers. And one proud man bearing the brunt of it all. Swallowing the bitter truth down every single day and still managing to smile. A painted smile, hiding the desperate desire to change all before him. I have delivered it to him, in my anger. In my despair. Edward is dead. I still cannot believe it, but I was witness myself. Saw his bloodied hand clutching the jewelled handle of the dagger, his eyes wide with disbelief. George's dagger.

I too had been duped. I had believed my friend's words when he told me he would persuade Edward to put Elizabeth to one side. That the church would annul his union. The pope himself would agree. Why would he not? All was agreed, or so I, in my blind trust, believed.

Until Lady Fortune stepped in again, with one careless wave of a deadly hand the wheel spun, spokes blurring before my eyes. Three days ago, it was, we all met together here. Edward strangely calm. George excitable. Agitated. A usual state for him. The boy burned with an inner energy that reminded me of my own Maurice. Envy was a murderous emotion. I do not even recall how the argument started. There was wine, but then where there was Edward, there was always wine. There was no secret now, even though just the few of us knew it, for the moment at least. The whole sorry tale. How this William Catesby came to know, to be able to bear witness to events some years ago. How his father, Sir William, was a man of law in the service of the Talbot family. How he came to find out about the marriage, to draw up the agreement which later saw Eleanor Butler agree to enter a nunnery, not long after that fateful council meeting at Reading where Edward revealed his Woodville bride. Eleanor, tucked away neatly so there would be no one to rail against the king's recent marriage. Tossed aside like a discarded robe, she entered a nunnery and there she perished. The king's wife. The queen.

She died there mere weeks ago, the news only recently reaching us as confirmation of the sorry tale was sought. Saw Edward gloatingly announce that there was no need for him to put Elizabeth aside now, causing George to leap up from his chair. Was he truly angry? Or was it rehearsed? Arranged? Screaming words which were hard to hear. How did Edward dare to pick his own bride, even now, when George had been denied his choice? Edward stood too, chair toppling over in his haste. George called his brother a Flemish bastard. That all knew he was the product of his mother's infidelity. Of a night of passion snatched whilst his father was away on campaign in France.

All before me became a blur of noise and light. Of Richard's stunned expression. Of Warwick's smouldering glare. We were in George's house. Warwick's men, and George's, lined the halls outside. Edward had come lightly accompanied, believing the matter was only a formality. All settled. Mere ripples in a pond which was once again calm. At least until the sun glinted on the rubies in the dagger hilt as George sunk it into his brother's gut, lips peeled back in seething anger. My throat aches as I write the words. The king is dead. Long live...? I cannot write...

My head throbs. How has this happened? One jealous act has plunged the country into danger. All of this, because I was saved the executioner's axe? I have no notion of what will happen now. Warwick is mustering his men, hundreds of them coming down from the north. From all his lands and territories. He has arrested George for regicide. He lingers in the tower as I linger here, in his home. I have nowhere else to go. Other than home, but that is a dream, as yet. I must see out what I started, wracked by guilt and grief as I am. For my anger was misplaced. It was not Edward's doing. Why did I not see that? Know that? Deep in my gut. Warwick knew. Yet only this day had he told me.

It was Elizabeth. Elizabeth and Worcester working in tandem. Elizabeth, scarred by my words. Frightened of what I might know. I had told Edward she was not a suitable bride and she had not been. For, if nothing else, stealing the seal, ordering my death and the death of my boys, in Edward's name, was proof itself. It was not Edward who was hard and cruel. I had known that, so why had I been so determined to shame him? All I have done is shame myself.

Eve of St John's Day, Baynard's Castle, London

This will be my last day in London. One of my last few in England, at least for now. The duchess, shocked, if not surprised by recent events, insists I return for the coronation. It seems wrong, somewhere deep down, but Cecily reminded me, sitting calmly by the river, running rosary beads through her fingers. Grief etched deep in her face, darkening her eyes. The death of no one man will hinder the progress of time. She knows that more than anyone. We remembered time past spent at Trim Castle. Pleasant memories. We pray for more to come. God willing, we will see them. Time indeed stops for no-one. George faces a trial for the sin of regicide. Cecily hopes for mercy but understands there may well be none. The dowager queen, Elizabeth, has been sent north with her children. To one of Warwick's many strongholds. He demurs when asked which one, or what will become of them. He was always a majestic man, yet his shoulders lift higher these days. I understand. I truly do, but still regret my part in it. I told the duchess as much, but she sighed and told me not to waste my energy on events I could not change. That what had happened must have been God's will. Maybe she is right.

Warwick stood true by Richard of York and by his eldest son. Fought brave and hard to avenge York's death and fulfil his son's ambition. Without the mighty Warwick, his power and influence, would Edward ever have sat upon the throne? These questions are as nothing now. The city is calm. The country too. The court, when given a choice between a loyal Yorkist cousin and a pack of Woodvilles, knew where they were best served. The halls of Westminster now hum with excitement. The joy and celebration that a new king can bring. This one as yet untested in battle or in character, but I have no worries on that score. For the boy is his father, and will be every bit the man, and the king, that he would have been. Sometimes, God has a way of enacting his plans in ways none of us expect. I should stay, but I too have an important duty to perform. To fulfil one of Richard's first duties as king. I am now Lord Lieutenant of Ireland and must go to my land and escort Worcester back for his trial. Guilty of misprision of treason at best, treason at worst. I care not which.

In lighter moments, I allow myself some semblance of mercy. That Edward and his queen brought their fates upon themselves. A true king should care for his country before all. My gut tells me that Richard will be such a king. For myself I long to be reunited with my family in Dublin. There will be sadness, I am sure. Our sons, those two innocent boys, will not be forgotten. Wheresoever Worcester saw fit to rest them, I will ensure they receive reburial in a place of sanctity and repose. Is it not what all men desire, when we imagine our ending? Dignity. Respect. I will swear before God to rule Ireland with renewed vigour, in service of Richard. In service to the house of York, now free of secrets and stain.

Warwick made me smile last evening as we sat before the fire. Once again, the conversation was of marriage. Of how he had planned for his daughters to wed George and Richard. Only now could he see those wishes had been a reaction to Edward's obstinacy. The more he resisted, the more important it became. Still, Richard would need a bride. The country a queen. You have a daughter, he said to me. Is she not the same age as Richard? Katherine. Fair Katherine. Born the same year as Richard. Ellice and Cecily were both with child at the same time. That was what made me smile. Often, in Ireland, our lilting manner of speech could mangle many a name. We named her Katherine. More than once I had heard her called Caitlin. I know not if he was jesting, all I could answer was that a king of England deserved a foreign princess. One who could bring powerful alliances. Trade and goodwill. He shrugged, for his mind was already on other matters for he will be the boy's right hand, his Lord Protector. Charged in a duty to continue nurturing and advising Richard as he has for the past few years. He will guide him wisely and with a country united I know he is already casting his predatory gaze across the sea. Eager to secure the future of his progeny. To rip up the final roots of future rebellion and strangle their ambitions before they can flower and seed. Lancastrian weeds. Margaret of Anjou, old Henry's queen, and a young boy he calls the Whelp of Lancaster, Henry Tudor. Having fought so hard, he is not about to allow any lingering ghosts to haunt his new vision for England.

Tomorrow I leave for the coast. For my passage on a ship back to Ireland leaving England in Warwick's capable hands. These have been tumultuous days in which I have played my part. It will be hard not to dwell on the disaster which could have overcome this realm had Edward continue to hold his secret from the world. As it is, this time I can leave England with peace in my heart, looking forward with hope to a long and prosperous reign for our most glorious sovereign, King Richard III.

Thomas Fitzgerald

Seventh Earl of Desmond, Lord Lieutenant of Ireland. The year of our Lord Fourteen hundred and sixty-eight.

★★★

About C J Lock

C J Lock writes historical fiction but hates writing about herself. Much happier wandering the medieval highways and byways, she penned the **Desmond's Daughter** series of books based on a fictional mistress of King Richard III. This was followed by the **Semper Fidelis** stories giving the same timeline from the perspective of Francis Lovell. Current work includes **Tales Cordis** – which will follow the same story in first person from the viewpoint of Richard Plantagenet himself.

When back in the real world, she is a former Communications Manager of the Richard III Society and had the privilege to be one of a small group of people who gained 'behind the scenes' access to the Leicester Cathedral Team during the run up to the reinterment of the king in Leicester in 2015.

Amazon: https://tinyurl.com/3ttm58b9

The Rose of Ireland
by
Toni Mount

✭✭✭

Introduction

Years ago, I read a throw-away line at the end of a book about the battle of Bosworth, to the effect that one reason among others for Richard III's loss of support was his lack of a wife and a legitimate heir. I didn't give it much credence at the time – after all, Henry Tudor didn't have a wife or an heir either when he came to the throne. However, I never forgot the statement and it set me thinking about what if Richard hadn't married the Earl of Warwick's daughter, Anne Neville? Anne gave him just one son who died in 1484 and she followed their child to the grave in spring 1485. But we know Richard had two illegitimate children, Katherine and John. Supposing he had wed their mother, instead? Might Bosworth have had a different outcome? And who could have been this mysterious unidentified woman?

Well, I think I've found her: her name is Katherine – like her daughter. She was born in 1452, so is the same age as Richard. She's an earl's daughter and the couple definitely have many things in common. Serendipitously, everything seems to fit, even as far as foreshadowing future events, such as the revelation of King Edward's bigamous marriage and the disappearance of two young princes. Katherine FitzGerald was real enough but here's my version of the couple's possible alternative history.

By the way (spoiler alert), in the fifteenth century, a marriage contracted between two people in private, without a priest or even witnesses, was recognised as a legal union by the Church if both had made their vows willingly in the present tense and sealed the deal by consummating it.

I'm grateful for the opportunity to put my ideas into words in support of a worthy cause.

May 1469

The gardens were alive with birdsong, the scent of thyme rising from the neat turf path at my every step. A beautiful morning and seeming full of hope. Mayhap, this day, the king would consent to grant me audience though, thus far, I had hoped in vain.

A young man sat upon a bench beside the fragrant rose arbour. Much of an age with me; I had not seen him before but then I was but lately arrived at the great royal Palace of Westminster from Ireland. I knew few people among the courtiers.

I approached him, my tread silent upon the soft path.

'God give you good day, sir.' I spoke boldly, startling him. 'It is a fine morn, is it not?'

He glanced up. I was shocked now, seeing a great black bruise, like an ink stain upon his cheek. Otherwise, he might have been accounted handsome, if he did not frown so deeply that twin furrows formed betwixt his dark brows.

'Is it? I had not paid it any mind.' His voice sounded harsh but then he attempted a smile which became a wince. His cheek must hurt him. He stood and gestured to the bench. 'Will you sit, my lady? I crave pardon for my lack of courtesy. I am out of humour and not good company, I fear.'

'Thank you, sir.' Though I had intended to walk on, I sat, doing my best to appear graceful and elegant. He sat also and I arranged my skirts so the cloth should not touch his dove-grey hose. He had a well-shaped thigh; I could not help but take note.

'I have not seen you at court before.' His hand strayed to his injured cheek, as though attempting to hide the ugly bruise. 'I am certain I should have recalled one so fair as you, lady.'

I sighed, disappointed. He was just another court flatterer, spilling honey-sweet words that meant naught at all.

'And I you, sir.'

He nodded and gave a wry – careful – smile. Somewhat lopsided, even so, it transformed his face, lighting his eyes.

'Aye, you could not fail to note this face,' he said. 'I am Richard, at your service, my lady.'

'And I am Katherine, also at yours, good sir.' I fussed with the folds of my gown, wondering what to say next. The honey-tongued courtier seemed to have run out of words also. Perhaps he was not so well practised as I thought. 'Why were you sitting alone on –'

'You are not from these parts –'

We both spoke at once, laughed at our fault and fell silent again. After a lengthy pause, I began anew.

'You appeared to be quite forlorn, sir, when first I saw you. Why so alone?'

'That is no man's concern but mine.' He spoke right sharply and I knew I had ventured too far. 'Forgive me,' he said softly. 'Did I not warn you I was out of humour? This place... I like it not these days, since...'

'Since when?'

'I am summoned upon a whim, to leave my friends behind in the North Country. Here, I am mocked as a bumpkin: my clothes criticised as being of last year's fashion, my speech not of the fancy courtier's tongue and my preference for plain meats at board to be unsophisticated as a labourer's. And I will not pretend to be otherwise than I am. No mincing, prinked up jackanapes I. I am a soldier and when I refuse to play that foolish part – you see my reward.' He pointed to his bruise which, I swear, had grown worse with the telling of its cause. He cast his gaze downwards, watching his shoe nudging at a daisy flower. 'I apologise, Katherine. You did not need to hear that rant but my blood rises whenever I think of it.' He breathed deeply and let his braced shoulders ease.

'But you also have been summoned to court?' he asked, sounding more calm. 'All the way from Ireland, I would judge from the lilt of your words.'

'You have a good ear, sir. I am from County Cork, in the south. To answer your enquiry: no. I was not summoned but came, uninvited, to make request of King Edward, to beg his sympathy for an orphaned daughter in need.'

'May I offer you my most sincere condolences? I know full well the aching loss of a father. And not the loss alone but the sudden change of situation for those loved ones left behind. Did he die in battle?'

'If only he had, I could understand his death but he was slain in cold blood, named for a traitor...' Tears came, unbidden. I had not meant to weep, not before a man I hardly knew, yet I accepted the small kerchief pressed into my hand. '...they murdered my younger brothers too, so young, so innocent... dragged from their school books...' I dried my eyes and composed myself. 'My father was no traitor. He stood ever loyal to the House of York since Duke Richard's time as the King's Lieutenant of Ireland.'

I realised his arm held me steady, comforting. His skin was warm and firm.

'I believe I know the deed of wickedness of which you speak. Your father was Thomas FitzGerald, Earl of Desmond, if I recall correctly?'

I nodded and returned the damp kerchief which he tucked into his sleeve.

He sighed and turned aside a little. Changing the purpose of his speech, he asked:

'My lady, pray tell me which of the blossoms here you most favour?' His arm swept to encompass the tapestry of flowers spread before us. 'The white rose of York, maybe, symbol of purity and loyalty?'

'Why, sir, if you would know, then, I prefer red blooms, the colour of passion and vibrancy.' I thought to tease him. 'Red roses speak of joy and love of life.'

A shadow flitted across his features but then was gone. He leapt to his feet and ran among the rose bushes and flower beds. Laughing, he returned with a haphazard posy of crimson roses, dark clove-red gillyflowers and vermillion poppies. He knelt and offered them to me.

'In recompense for my previous discourtesies, my lady, I make amends to you.'

As I received his gift, a thorn pricked my thumb.

'Oh, dearest lady...' Again, he took out his kerchief and offered to bind my injury. 'I fear the red rose is always untrustworthy. Forgive me. In my haste, I forgot to remove the thorns.' He enclosed my hand in his. Only the layer of finest Holland cloth kept our flesh from touching.

Our eyes met. I cannot say what he saw in mine but his were grey and fathomless as the Irish Sea. But his hand felt strong enough to rescue me from an ocean of loneliness; his arms a safe harbour.

The moment passed. The voices of other courtiers coming into our paradise garden, raucous as crows, complaining as magpies, drowned out the soft music of birdsong.

'Come, let us find a cup of wine to strengthen you, Katherine. Fear not, you will have your audience with the king and my full support for your request. I shall ensure he gives you a favourable hearing, if my counsel counts for anything these days, in a court overrun with Woodvilles like a midden heap with rats.' He raised me up with gentle hands and we walked together, back into the labyrinth that was the Palace of Westminster. I wondered at his certainty that he could persuade the king to grant audience to anyone, this country bumpkin in his outmoded dress.

This Richard.

✩ ✩ ✩

King Edward had been in jovial spirits until his little brother sent a request to speak with him and he knew the subject of their speech before ever Richard said a word. Money. It was certain to concern the lad's lack of funds; it always was. Edward was extremely fond of his youngest sibling – more trustworthy and loyal than any of his sycophantic, arse-licking courtiers – but the trouble was that his dukedom of Gloucester, though well deserved, came with little in the way of estates to support so illustrious a rank. And the money that did come in passed straight to Edward as Richard's guardian, since the lad was yet a minor at sixteen years of age. Richard was due a quarterly allowance from that income but, somehow, it always disappeared into the ever-hungry royal coffers and proved nigh impossible to prise from its jaws.

Richard made his due reverence before Edward – always kingship came before brotherhood to the younger man's mind.

'Get up, Dickon. Do not grovel like a lackey. Besides, you wear holes in those hose, you will be demanding I pay for a new pair. Have some wine.'

'Thank you, your Grace.' Richard went to the table to pour wine from the pitcher. Not that he had much liking for this dark red stuff, his unaccustomed taste-buds preferring the pale Rhenish wines, if there was no ale offered.

'Matthew!' the king bellowed to a servant standing in the shadows. 'Pour his bloody wine for him, you idle knave. Dickon, put the pitcher down; you are not our cousin of Warwick's esquire here. Behave like a royal duke, can you not?'

'My apologies, sire, I...'

'Just sit, drink your wine and state your purpose. It is about your allowance, no doubt? I am well aware your money is in arrears but you know how it is. You were paid at Christmas, were you not?' The king accepted a cup from the servant and gulped his much-needed wine to brace himself for talk of finances – ever a sore issue.

'Aye, somewhat but not the full amount and now my Easter payment is overdue... but it is not that I would discuss. My concern is for another's problem, if you allow?'

'Whose?'

'A lady's.'

Edward's face evolved into a huge grin. He was always willing to speak of ladies.

'Is she comely? Do you have a fancy for her? Have I made her acquaintance?'

'What? No. I mean, aye, but...' Richard's face turned crimson beneath his bruises. 'It is not like that.'

'Oh. A pity, indeed. I thought you had found yourself a pretty piece to warm your bed at last. At your age, I had long since found a dozen places to cast my spear. So, who is she and what is her problem? And for the saints' sake do not tell me it is bloody money. I have none to spare.'

'The lady's name is Katherine FitzGerald, the Earl of Desmond's daughter. A year ago, her father, Thomas FitzGerald – always loyal to York – was arrested, accused of treason and murdered...'

'I do not need to hear it. I recall those... er... unfortunate events.' Edward raised his hands to halt Richard's speech.

The brothers exchanged a glance in which much was said in silence. Both were aware that the queen had overstepped her authority by a mile and more, ordering Desmond's arrest and summary execution without trial because he had referred to her, in jest, as 'the king's old Grey mare' – an insult Elizabeth Woodville-Grey, Queen of England, could not tolerate. The punishment had somehow been extended to encompass the disappearance of two of Desmond's young sons who had been neither seen nor heard of since. What Richard did not know was that the queen had 'borrowed' Edward's personal seal to authenticate the death warrant – a fact the king found hard to forgive even whilst infatuated with the perpetrator of so infamous a deed.

'Once declared traitor and attainted, all Desmond's estates and property were ceded to the Crown. Katherine has come to plead her family's case,' Richard explained.

'Why not her elder brothers? It is more their affair than hers.'

'Aye, I suppose it is.' Richard squirmed on the cushioned seat, his face flushing anew. 'They... it was thought a, er, pretty lass might gain a fairer hearing from your Grace.'

Edward laughed loudly, spilling droplets of wine from his cup.

'And they may be right at that.'

'She hopes also that you will see fit to grant her something from her father's estates for a dowry, that she may take a husband.'

'A bold lass then but not pretty enough to attract a man without some pecuniary enticement.'

'On the contrary. Katherine is... is quite lovely to look upon,' the young duke ended lamely, wishing he could prevent the blood from rushing to his cheeks, knowing his obvious embarrassment caused his brother – and others – great mirth.

'I shall see what I can do, though I promise naught to her or you, Dickon. Oh, and I have had words in certain ears, concerning your bruises. If the Grey boys do not keep their fists to themselves, I grant you permission to return the favour in kind. They have been warned.'

'You know? I never said.'

'I am the king. I know everything.'

Perhaps that was true, Richard thought but, upon reflection, it seemed unlikely as future events would reveal.

★★★

King Edward's Whitsuntide court, to which he had been summoned for a display of York family unity, was no longer the lonely, heartless affair Richard had been dreading. He now had a dear friend, a partner in the dance and an exquisite ornament to present to envious eyes. The bumpkin in his outmoded doublet had won the supreme accolade of a beautiful woman. Better yet, she treated the queen's sons – Richard's bitterest rivals and the main source of his misery at court – with impeccable courtesy but utter disdain. No wonder when their mother had caused the FitzGeralds' downfall.

Richard could not hope for better. Katherine was perfect.

☆☆☆

At the Whitsuntide feast, to my great delight, I found a place had been set for me at the high table, next to my Richard. Thus honoured, I could click my fingers at the queen's obvious ire, though Richard warned me not to offend her further, as if I did not know from my family's own experience that Elizabeth Woodville was a dangerous woman and a mortal enemy. But for those few hours, I did not care.

Richard and I danced the evening away, until my thin-soled slippers wore into holes. He was a fine dancer, nimble, graceful and light upon his feet. I was grateful for the first time that my mother had seen to it I was well schooled in such arts when, at that age, I would rather have been grooming the horses or, more likely, at my father's kennels with his much-prized wolf-hounds. At last I had a reason to act the lady and I put my heart into playing the part. I did not want to let Richard down.

It was twilight when he led me out into the garden, away from the smoky torchlit gaiety and the press of hot, sweaty bodies. We made for the bench where we had sat on that first day. Richard stretched out his long legs, spread his arms wide to embrace the joy of living and blew out his breath.

'Kate, Kate, my own sweet Rose of Ireland, what pleasure you have given me this eve. I thank you from the bottom of my very soul. How may I ever repay your kindness and friendship towards this lonely, undeserving fellow? This night would have been a very torture without you at my side.'

'It was not all generosity on my part, so do not make out it was. I enjoyed myself, too. You know full well I did.' I leant against his velvet-clad arm, weary from so much dancing. He put his arm around me. He smelled of spices and smoke and sunlight – at least he seemed so to me.

'Are you chilled, sweeting? I would not have you catch a cold. You are too precious.'

'No, not cold. I like to have you hold me close. I feel safe in your arms.'

'Naught will harm you, Kate. I shall defend you with my life.'

I thought to laugh at this mighty declaration but somehow I knew they were not empty words. He truly meant what he said and to make light of it would give deep offence to my gracious knight.

'I have something to tell you, Kate. I know it will please you.'

'Oh, what is it?' I asked eagerly.

'You have an audience with the king tomorrow. At last. I am certain he will see you get the generous dowry you deserve. Is that not good tidings?'

'Aye, I suppose...' I could not conceal my disappointment.

'But is that not why you came to Westminster? Is that not what you wanted all along?' He sounded confused and no wonder. 'I prevailed upon Edward because I thought you wanted me to do so.'

'I thought so, too, but now...'

'What is amiss? What has changed?'

'You, Richard. You have changed everything. If the king grants my dowry, I shall have no reason to remain in England any longer. I shall return home with my wretched dowry and have my brother find me some worthy but unwanted husband.'

'The line of eager suitors will be of great length, no doubt.' His jest fell flat; there was no hint of merriment in his voice.

'But none of them will be you.'

'What do you mean, Katherine?'

'You know full well what I mean. I do not want some other eager suitor. I want you. I love you, Richard.'

64

He pushed me away a little, turning my face in his hands so he could look into my eyes in the fast-fading light of dusk. 'You truly mean it?'

'Of course I do.'

'I felt that way on the first morning I saw you,' he admitted in a whisper. 'But how could I believe any woman would return the sentiment? A lovely woman like you could have any man...'

'I want you; no one else,' I told him. My heart was afire, leaping within my ribs as if it would escape and fly to him.

'I love you, Kate, and here is my seal upon it.' He kissed me beneath the star-studded heavens.

My Richard.

☆☆☆

May 1471 [Two years later]

King Edward was jubilant: back at Westminster, his enemies defeated and – most joyous of all – during his absence in exile, the queen had borne him a son and heir at last. Now he would set his regained kingdom to rights and reward those who had proved steadfast in their loyalty. At the head of that short but worthy list stood his youngest brother, Richard of Gloucester. What a revelation the lad had been, so capable, constant and quite the hero on the battlefield.

'Well, Dickon,' Edward clapped his slender sibling on the back with such enthusiasm as to unbalance him. 'You have proved your manhood in two pitched battles; time you had your reward. I have determined you shall be my Lieutenant in the North, replacing that treacherous cousin of ours. Now Warwick is gone, I shall need a trustworthy replacement to keep the Nevilles and the Percies from each others' throats and the Scots in their rightful place on their own side of the border. Are you the man for that task, Dickon?'

'Aye. You know I will serve you as well as I may. I shall not fail you, Ned, I swear upon our father's soul; may God assoil...'

'To which end,' Edward continued, unable to keep from grinning, 'I have a bride in mind for you.'

'A bride?'

'Aye. Come, sit. We can discuss the matter. You cannot expect to remain a foot-loose bachelor forever. Here, have some wine. You are of an age now to take on the responsibilities of a wife, beget yourself an heir but my choice of a lady for you will likely come as a surprise. You will wed Warwick's daughter, Anne.'

'But...'

'I know I forbade the union before but that was because Warwick was too self-important, thinking he could enhance his power by marrying his girls to you and George. When George wed Isobel despite me... at least you obeyed. But the situation is very different now. I want you to wed Anne so you can divide the Neville inheritance betwixt you and George in right of your wives as Warwick's heiresses. It will also aid you, having a Neville wife, to gain the loyalty of her kin and affinity in the north. You will have all Warwick's castles and estates north of the River Trent. George can have everything to the south to keep him content.'

'My lord, sire...' Richard's face wore an expression Edward had not seen before. He had set down his wine, untouched, and was knotting his fingers in his lap. Unable to be still, he sprang from his seat. 'Ned, I cannot marry Anne.'

'Of course, you can. The necessary dispensation to marry your cousin is in hand. I have told you...'

'I am already wed to another! I cannot commit bigamy.' Richard braced himself for an explosion of rage. Edward possessed that legendary Plantagenet temper as had many of their forbears but it did not happen. Instead, the king turned corpse-white, groping for his wine.

'How? When? Who is she?' Edward spoke so quietly.

'Katherine FitzGerald, daughter to the late Earl of Desmond. We wed at the end of summer last. We knew Warwick was raising rebellion and it must surely come to war or exile or, as it proved, both. Katherine was fearful of what might happen to me... to her. She was with child – my child – and would not have it bastard born.

'If I was slain, I wanted to leave behind an heir to bear my name. It was the eve before we marched forth that she told me of the babe. There was no time for ceremony, priests and witnesses. We stood in the garden here, beneath the stars where God might see us clearly. We plighted our troths, each to the other, and begged God's blessing upon our union. I gave her a ring from my finger, to serve until...'

'Why did you not tell me until now? By the bloody saints. All this time, Dickon, and you never said a word.'

'Forgive me. I would have confided my tidings to you but it was never the right moment, what with councils of war, exile, riding all around Burgundy, the Low Countries, Germany even, persuading dukes, princes and Hanse merchants to support our cause with men, money, ships, weapons, horses... The opportune occasion did not come amidst so many distractions. I am sorry. I admit such excuses are feeble. I should have told you...' Richard hung his head.

Edward sighed heavily. He could hardly berate his brother for doing exactly as he had done: marrying in secret and lacking the courage to own it until the truth became unavoidable.

'You have destroyed my plans for you as my Lieutenant in the North.'

'How so? You are the king. If you would have me hold such office then appoint me.'

'You need Anne at your side...'

'Why? Because she has Neville blood? Upon our mother's side, we have as much Neville blood in our veins as she. Would that not count as well? As for Warwick's northern estates, he died a traitor, his properties ceded to the Crown. Most surely, you may grant them as you will, to whoever you wish. Besides, Anne is too much her father's daughter to ever make a kindly wife. Traits such as pride, aggression and determination are admirable in a man but, in a woman, they become haughtiness, spite and obstinacy. You would do no bridegroom any favours by shackling him to Lady Anne for life. And she would not want me. She not only blames me, in person, for her father's downfall, she has known the highest position in the land as Princess of Wales to Edward Lancaster and prospective Queen of England. A mere duke will not be grand enough for her now.'

'Better than being a humble sister in a convent which will now be her fate.' Edward had regained his good humour. 'And you are right, Dickon. You can still command the North in my stead because I say you will.'

Richard smiled.

'And in right of my wife, sire, I also have influence in southern Ireland since you were generous in giving her some valuable estates there as her dowry. The Irish have always supported our House of York.'

'I shall bear it in mind, little brother. Now when do I get to meet my sister-by-marriage?'

'Katherine returned to Ireland for safety's sake during our troubled times. Our child was born in March last. I received the letter just yesterday. Both mother and daughter are well and thriving. As soon as possible, Katherine will come to England for I am eager to meet my child. They named her Kate also.'

August 1485

The town of Leicester was celebrating the king's triumph at Redemore. Not that it had been much of a battle – a waste of His Grace's famed military prowess; little more than a skirmish. Bloody Tudor though, had to have his day, putting everyone to much inconvenience. But he was done with now.

King Richard was in high spirits, dispensing largesse to all as though his royal coffers were a bottomless well. In truth, they were kept filled by the king's excellent management of his vast estates, comprising those of the Crown, the dukedoms of Lancaster, York,

Gloucester and Buckingham, the earldoms of Cambridge, Richmond – regardless of Tudor's spurious claim – and Cork in Ireland. Justice was all in Richard's England. Every man had his rights and his responsibilities and the king was the golden example of what could be achieved. Beloved by his people; feared by his enemies.

Richard claimed it was all down to strength and unity within the royal family. Queen Katherine was his staff, his counsel and his soul mate. Without her he was naught, so he said. She had given him four beautiful, intelligent daughters to make fine marriage alliances, though parting with them caused much anguish. Kate – or rather Katherine, Princess of Scots, to give her due respect – had wed Prince James, heir to the king of those turbulent people two years since. Eleanor was betrothed to the heir of King Christian of Denmark and Sweden, improving trade across the Northern Seas. Cecily would be sailing to Spain all too soon to seal an alliance with the joint monarchs of Castile and Aragon. As for little Ellice, named for the queen's mother, her destiny was undecided, as yet, although her doting Papa had his eye on little Philip, Duke of Burgundy, as a possible suitable spouse.

But what had made the Tudor's effort to unseat the House of York so absurd were the three fine sons the king had. John, Prince of Wales, was a paragon of virtue, the perfect king-in-waiting, and none dare disagree with his father's opinion on the matter. Edmund was Duke of York and Earl of Cork and, nominally at present, Viceroy in Ireland, ruling on his father's behalf from his mother's estates there. Young Richard, Duke of Gloucester, his father's namesake and, though it was never made overly plain, his parent's favourite, would become Lieutenant in the North when he was of an age for such office. Mind, the title was not the onerous burden it once had been, in his father's younger days. The North was peaceful now; the Scots kept quiet by Katherine's marriage alliance and the squabbling Nevilles and Percies subdued to peace by a strong monarchy.

Tudor's promise of worthy kingship and a new dynasty was laughed at. Who could better King Richard on either score? No wonder few had turned up to support so risible a claim. With the upstart Welshman slain by the king's own hand in the field, the resounding cry now echoed through the streets of Leicester as the sun sank low in a blaze of crimson and gold on 22nd August 1485:

Long live King Richard III!

✩✩✩

About Toni Mount

Toni Mount is the author of many factual history books, published by Amberley and Pen & Sword, as well as the Sebastian Foxley *The Colour of...* series of whodunit novels, set in fifteenth-century London, published by MadeGlobal. She is a member of the Research Committee of the Richard III Society and of the Crime Writers' Association, running history classes online for mature students and a creative writing group. She writes regular articles for history magazines and has a series of educational courses online.

Although born in London and living in Kent with her husband and best friend, Glenn, at heart she's a Yorkshire lass and a loyal supporter of the House of York – no red roses in her garden.

Website: www.tonimount.com

Seb Foxley's Website: www.SebastianFoxley.com

Facebook.com/toni.mount.10

Facebook.com/medievalengland

Twitter.com/tonihistorian

Online educational courses at www.medievalcourses.com

How George Clarence Became King

by
Brian Wainwright

✰✰✰

Introduction

George, Duke of Clarence, younger brother of Edward IV, came under the influence of his cousin, Richard, Earl of Warwick, as both of them became increasingly discontented with the King's rule and the influence of his favourites. Notably the Woodville relatives of Edward's Queen, Elizabeth, a Lancastrian widow of no importance whom Edward had married for love – or lust.

George wished to marry Warwick's elder daughter (and potential heiress) Isabelle, but Edward forbade the match. Defying him, George and Isabelle were married in Calais, Warwick having procured the necessary dispensation from Rome. Warwick and Clarence then returned to England, overthrew Edward and made him their prisoner. (This meant that two English kings were prisoners at the same time, as the deposed Lancastrian Henry VI was still in the Tower.) They also executed the Queen's father and one of her brothers.

Finding it difficult to rule and faced with increasing chaos, Warwick and Clarence were forced to release Edward but this did not resolve the political situation. They were soon plotting against the King again, but with the defeat of their allies at Losecote Field they had to flee to France.

There Warwick was induced by the French King, Louis XI, to enter into a pact with the exiled Lancastrian Queen Margaret of Anjou. Margaret's son was to marry Warwick's younger daughter, Anne. Although Clarence was included in the arrangement, he was not content and was soon involved in secret negotiations for a reconciliation with his brother. However, when Warwick and Clarence landed in England again, this time as 'Lancastrians', Edward was forced to flee to Burgundy and Henry VI was restored.

Some months later Edward landed in Yorkshire with a small invasion force. George Clarence, who had raised men nominally to fight for Henry VI, now went over to his brother. Warwick and a Lancastrian army were defeated at Barnet and Warwick killed. Margaret of Anjou and her son landed at Weymouth, and Edward (and Clarence) marched to meet them at Tewkesbury. So far, this is history. But what if the Battle of Tewkesbury had had a slightly different ending? Let George tell the tale...

I was terrified at Barnet, and the battle, fought in dense fog, could have gone either way. I counted myself lucky to survive. But Tewkesbury was different. We had caught the Lancastrians with their backs to a river, we had the numbers, and I never doubted we would win. They were led by Somerset, but we had Edward, and there was no question which of them was the better general.

Edward kept me close to him, as he had at Barnet, instead of giving me a division to command. In a way, this was an insult, especially given that our left was led by my younger brother, Richard, and our right by Hastings, who had been but a squire ten years earlier – though he was some sort of distant cousin. However, I could not really blame the King. When you have changed sides twice in two years it does provoke suspicion.

It did not surprise me much when the Lancastrian centre began to buckle and break, and after that it was only a matter of time before the rout. I sent the best-mounted of my men into the pursuit, with orders to take Margaret's son, the so-called 'Prince of Wales' if they could, or better still to make an end of him.

Almost at once Edward sent me after them, because, he said, he did not want a massacre, at least not of the ordinary fellows. But by the time I caught up with them, they were already dealing with the 'Prince of Wales', poking their knives into his face as he screamed for mercy. I was too late to prevent them but even if I had it would have been no great mercy. Such an enemy could never have been allowed to live, and it's better to die in battle than on a scaffold. The boy was only seventeen, but then so was my brother Edmund of Rutland when the Lancastrians butchered him at Wakefield. I felt no great regret. There were hundreds of good men lying around dead and wounded because of this brat and his wretched mother, and no one wept for them.

There was another Edward, though, that we did weep for. My brother, the King, killed by what must have been the last arrow loosed that day, a random arrow shot in despair as some fellow ran away in panic.

It took him in the eye, killed him in an instant, and all we could do was stand around, and look at one another, and wonder what to do next. I could not believe it, though the freezing thought struck me that if it had happened ten minutes earlier the battle might have gone the other way, and I might have been dead too.

'George, you must take command now. Say what is to be done.' It was my friend, John Mowbray, the Duke of Norfolk, who spoke – very decisively for him given that he was usually a man of few words. He was one of the few friends I had around me. Lord Hastings glared at me, in floods of tears, as if I had killed Edward. Even my brother Richard was giving me a strange look, as if he expected me to be pleased.

I was *not* pleased, for what it's worth. I was horrified. I would have to take charge knowing that most of those who had fought on our side were about as fond of George Clarence as they were of Edward of Lancaster. I had no idea what to say.

'Somerset has fled the field,' Richard said, 'and should be pursued.'

'Yes,' I said, gratefully, gulping for air. 'Of course. Richard, take some men and see to it, will you? I don't think you need to take prisoners, not now.'

He was off in an instant, Hastings with him, burning for revenge. I gazed around at those who were left, my brain slowly beginning to function again. Nothing seemed quite real. I shook myself.

'Margaret of Anjou must be somewhere nearby,' I said. 'I want her secured as well. Sir William, will you deal with that?'

I addressed Sir William Stanley, a man with a face like a rusty hatchet. He was Lord Stanley's brother, but at least he had always fought for us – for York I mean – unlike his elder sibling who could never be trusted to turn up for either side. He grunted something and hurried off, gathering his men about him. They would search far and wide until that woman and her entourage were captured.

'Now,' I said to those that remained, 'let us advance into the town. My dear brother the King must lie this night before the high altar of the abbey, with all due ceremony. This victory is his and his alone, and dearly bought. We must see that he is honoured as his greatness deserves.'

So we went forward in slow, sad procession, Edward's body laid in a cart. It seemed to take an hour to reach the abbey, though in truth it cannot have been more than a quarter of that. As we drew closer I saw Richard's banner, and Hastings's above a great press of men gathered about the precincts. I guessed at once what had happened. Somerset and the other fugitives had gone inside for sanctuary.

So they had, and some of them had been bloodied in the process. Those of our men who had arrived first were not restrained by their surroundings and sought them out among the tombs and holy statues, slashing and stabbing. The abbot had come forward with the sacred Host and threatened them with excommunication and other dire penalties, and Richard, arriving at this point, had somehow regained control and withdrawn our people from the building. All this he reported to me, in breathless tones. It now fell to me to resolve the situation.

I entered the great church, Richard at my side, Norfolk and Hastings not so far behind. The abbot was standing in our way, still clutching a monstrance in his hands, another monk behind him with a crucifix on a pole and a few more wandering aimlessly about in the background. Beyond them I caught sight of Somerset, hiding behind a tomb, and various other fellows of his party. I suppose there might have been twenty of them in all.

'Abbot,' I said, 'I am the Duke of Clarence, and I have brought my royal brother, King Edward, to lie this night before your altar. I expect you and your monks to receive his body and do it due honour. I myself will be spending the night here in vigil, as will most of the King's nobles here present. As to this rabble of rebels, they may stay within your precincts this one night, to be confessed and reconciled to God. In the morning though, they must come forth. They will be given a trial, and some may be shown mercy. If they do not surrender, then they will be dragged out like so many rats and torn to pieces. I cannot prevent it. Those men out there, by and large, are not my men, they are not answerable to me, and they are very, very angry. Do you understand me?'

Abbot Strensham looked extremely uncomfortable. It was of course, understandable. His precincts had been invaded by hundreds of armed men, many of us still splattered with blood and gore from the battle. He had seen fighting in his church, which no priest can be expected to enjoy, and now he was threatened with even more violence. (Although it was not really a threat, more a simple prediction. I was by no means certain that I could control the men of Edward's army.) Moreover, he was required to sing dirige over the body of a King of England, not something he had anticipated when he ate his breakfast. Such an agenda was enough to dismay the Archbishop of Canterbury, or even the Holy Father himself, let alone a simple country abbot.

'The abbey has been polluted by this bloodshed,' he spluttered, waving his arms about, 'it will need to be reconsecrated.'

'Then do what has to be done, man. That is not my business. But be aware that if those traitors do not yield at dawn tomorrow, there will be more bloodshed. It's beyond my control.'

'Tomorrow,' he gasped, 'is Sunday.'

'I'm well aware of it,' I snapped. 'Very well, I take your point. They can have until dawn on Monday. But they must give up their arms and be prepared to yield.'

I stepped outside and explained the arrangements to the assembled troops, who responded with much angry growling and loud protests. I told them to show some respect; that the King was to be laid before the altar, and prayers said for him, and that all who wished might be in attendance. They were, however, to leave their weapons outside. (I allowed my brother Richard and a select group of chosen men to retain their swords. Richard was High Constable, so it was his business to maintain order, and there was a risk that the Lancastrians in the church might start something if they saw that all our people were disarmed.)

For my own part I retired into the town of Tewkesbury, where some of my men had secured suitable lodgings for me, hung the Black Bull of Clarence above the door by way of guidance. Here I was stripped of my armour, cleaned up as best as I could be in the absence of a bath, and allowed to climb into bed for a few hours. I was utterly exhausted, and I had the night's vigil before me.

I was not allowed to sleep long. There were too many men gathered in the next room, most of them wanting to ask me damn fool questions, to demand direction on matters which they ought to have handled on their own initiative. They had no authority, you see. Nor did I, if it came to that, but as Edward's elder surviving brother it seemed to fall upon me without any formal process.

✯✯✯

I performed the night's vigil for Edward, kneeling on the hard stones of the abbey floor, half asleep after the exertions of the day. In the morning, I had the heralds proclaim my baby nephew, King Edward V, and gathered everyone who was anyone to swear allegiance to him.

A few hours later, William Stanley returned, bringing with him Margaret of Anjou, my sister-in-law Anne of Warwick (widow of the so-called prince) with their ladies and various other non-combatants.

Margaret was a broken woman. She did not even bother to spit at me, as I thought she might. I said they might all rest for the day, then in the morning go on to London, Margaret to the Tower to be with her husband, old Harry VI. Anne to the Erber to lodge with her sister, my Isabelle. Among the others was one unctuous priest by the name of Morton. He swore that he was now ready to change his allegiance, and that he would serve me well if I gave him a chance. I liked not the cut of his jib, so I sent him to the Tower as well. He's probably there to this day – one forgets to enquire.

I told Richard that he and Norfolk must constitute a court for Monday, to deal with Somerset and his friends. 'No need for mercy,' I said.

They were all executed, there by the cross at Tewkesbury. They say Somerset died well. I can't vouch for it, as I didn't bother to witness the event. I was in the abbey, praying over Edward, wondering how I was going to manage. I had sixteen years – at least – before his son was deemed to be of age, and during that time the whole rule of England would fall on me. I was surrounded by men who did not trust me a yard, and it made me sweat just to think of it.

That evening, Richard and I relaxed together over a glass of wine. We were quite alone, which was, of course, unusual. He had made a point of sending our attendants out, telling them to take their ease, for we had all worked hard of late, and deserved our rest.

'George,' he said, so quietly that I had to bend forward to hear him properly, 'we have had our differences, but you are still my brother, and you will have my loyalty. Not everyone thinks you should be Protector. Hastings says the Council should govern, and there are even those who would give power to the Queen. It's ridiculous, isn't it? But there you are. Some can't forget that until very recently you were with Warwick on the other side.'

I felt my anger rising. 'Without my four thousand men, Edward would have been trampled into the mud at Barnet. I saved his cause. Who are these dogs to judge me?'

He shrugged. 'You had your reasons, no doubt. You thought Edward was unfair to you, now I ask you to be fair to me. I have my title, George, I am Duke of Gloucester, but I have very little else.'

I sighed. If he wanted to bargain for his support, it was reasonable enough. 'What do you want?'

'The hand of Anne of Warwick, now she is widowed, and her share of the Warwick inheritance. A just partition. I thought that she and I might live in Yorkshire. At Barnard Castle, perhaps, or Middleham. You will need someone to manage the North for you. If it isn't me, it will have to be Percy or Stanley. Consider it.'

It didn't take long. Percy, Earl of Northumberland, was only lately pardoned by Edward and restored to his estates. He was an unknown quantity, and Thomas Stanley was a snake. I had hoped to keep most of the Warwick inheritance myself, but now the Lancastrians were out of the way, I could at least retain all the estates Edward had given me, and half the Warwick lands would be a fair addition.

'Very well,' I said, suppressing a sigh.

'Of course, I shall continue as Constable and Admiral of England.'

'Naturally.'

He took a long sip of his wine. 'You see, I am not unreasonable, dear brother, and nor, as it proves, are you. As long as we two stick together, no one can touch us. You should keep an eye on Hastings, though. This talk of the Council ruling – it's a nonsense. He means himself. One man must rule, you cannot manage everything by Committee.'

✩✩✩

I will pass lightly over what followed: the various sparks of rebellion that had to be stamped out; the long obsequies for Edward at

Windsor, where I, of course, had to be Chief Mourner; the endless press of business.

When all this was done, the Council gathered at Westminster, and with no fuss at all appointed me Protector and Defensor – to give the full title – subject only to the confirmation of Parliament, which all agreed must now be summoned. However, the Queen's brother, Anthony Woodville, Earl Rivers, supported by Hastings, said that – following the precedent of Harry VI, who had come to the throne as a babe – there should be another person appointed to have custody of the King's person.

'Well,' I said, leaning back in my chair at the head of the table, 'it would never do to flout precedent. I agree, and I hereby nominate my well-beloved brother, Richard, Duke of Gloucester, to that office.'

Richard looked gratified. Rivers and Hastings looked as if their favourite dogs had just died. But others slapped their hands on the table in table in thunderous approval, led by Norfolk, his cousin, Lord Howard, and my brother-in-law, Suffolk, and I smiled knowing that I had judged well.

'Of course,' I added, 'I do not propose that the King should leave his mother's care at this time. While he is of such tender age, he is better left to women. My brother shall have care for his interests and later, when the time is right, take him into his household.'

Rivers looked sulky, and it was clear to me that he had envisaged the office for himself. He was a strange fellow – fancied himself a poet, and had a taste for jousting, but I could never make sense of him or understand quite what he was about. As for Hastings, I was disappointed in him. He had been Edward's friend, but that was no real reason for him to be hostile to me. I had left him in his offices of Lord Chamberlain and Master of the Mint. Indeed, at this point I had made no changes at all in the principal appointments, though I was now minded that Rivers should not remain Lieutenant of Calais for too long, in case it gave him ideas.

As the meeting ended, the Lord Chancellor, Robert Stillington, Bishop of Bath and Wells, asked to speak to me in private. I sighed, and assented. I was in no mood for more tedious business, and hoped it would not take too long. I thought him a dull stick, overly serious and obsessed with state business, and suspected I was about to be burdened with a thousand tedious decisions. I had no idea of the storm that was about to break over my head.

☆☆☆

That night I scarcely slept at all. I turned on one side, then another, then lay on my back, sighing and staring up at the canopy. Stillington had managed to give me more of a shaking than the two battles of Barnet and Tewkesbury put together.

At last, my Isabelle stirred. 'What is it?' she asked. 'Go to sleep, for the love of God.'

'You are the Queen of England,' I said.

'Oh, George, what are you babbling about?'

'Bishop Stillington says that Edward and Elizabeth were never lawfully married. That he was already married to someone else. That their children are bastards. That I am King. I, George Clarence, King!'

'Is it true?' she asked, suddenly awake.

'How do I know? But he isn't just a bishop. He's Lord Chancellor of England. Edward's Chancellor. Why should he lie?'

There was silence for a good two minutes. I could almost hear my wife thinking. You must remember, she was Warwick's daughter. She knew about plots and intrigue and ambition.

'This is dangerous,' she said at last. 'Who will stand with you?'

She meant, if it came to a fight. It was a very good question.

'Norfolk,' I said. 'His wife's sister was the other woman. She's dead now, but they knew of it. Richard perhaps. Those who hate the Woodvilles even more than they hate me. You're right, Isabelle. It is dangerous. Bloody dangerous. What am I to do?'

'Take what is yours,' she said. Warwick's daughter. It was never in doubt.

✫✫✫

Next morning, I asked Richard to come to me. He did not keep me waiting long.

'I need you to arrest Rivers and Hastings,' I said. 'They must go to the Tower for a while.'

He gaped at me for a moment, and then I explained the reasons. It was for the sake of peace. I knew that those two would resist me in arms if they were left at liberty, and the one thing I wanted to do was to avoid bloodshed. Especially mine.

'You believe this tale?' he asked, tilting his head to one side like a bewildered dog.

'Well, no, of course not. I'm sure the Lord Chancellor of England has invented the whole thing to make life more interesting, and that Norfolk – and the other witnesses he has promised – are just playing along with it for a joke. After all, that's much more likely, isn't it?'

'People are bound to question it, and I'm not sure Hastings and Rivers are the only ones you need to worry about.'

I shook my head. 'Richard, I am not simply going to take the crown tomorrow! Do you think me stupid? Look, this is not a matter for me to decide. Nor even the Council. It must go before Parliament and they must judge. I intend that they will hear the evidence, and the learned fathers in God who sit on the bishops' benches must have their full say. If they decide our nephew is the lawful King, I will accept that without question. But you must see that this is not something that can be left to hang. It must be resolved, one way or the other.'

He considered that for a moment. 'Very well,' he said. 'Rivers should be straightforward enough. Hastings, though, will have Edward's household men at his back, or at least some of them. That might mean a fight.'

'You are Lord High Constable,' I said, 'and you can have as many of my men as you need as well as your own. Charge them with conspiracy against the Lord Protector, something like that. It needs to happen before they get a smell of this news – it's only a matter of time

81

before it's common knowledge. I've sworn Stillington and Norfolk to secrecy – but you know as well as I that this cannot be kept close for long.'

So it was done, and no one was hurt in the process, though Richard found it necessary to lock up half a dozen of our brother's more fervent household officers. After that, the word did spread, there was no stopping it. Within a week I found myself making a speech to the Lord Mayor and citizens of London, explaining that nothing would change until Parliament had had its say. I would be guided entirely by Parliament I explained. They took this better than I expected.

I also had to explain to the Council. Or rather, I sat back, mouth closed, and made Stillington lay out all the evidence. There was a great deal of it, and a lot of legal points to discuss. Someone objected that Edward's alleged wife had died before his son was born, and thus that Edward and Elizabeth could have married then, and made all things well. The fact remained that they hadn't, and would have needed a dispensation to repeat the sacrament of marriage. What was more, because of their previous adultery, their relationship had been polluted – that's what Stillington called it, and several of the other bishops and clerks nodded sagely – and they could never have legally married. There was also the point that Edward and Elizabeth had married in secret themselves, which removed any defence of the basis of good faith.

It was all very complicated, and I struggled to follow some of the arguments, but no one stood up and said the Chancellor was mistaken or wrong. The Council, rather to my surprise, said that my claim was good.

After that, Parliament was simple enough. I recused myself from it, saying that I wanted to influence no man's conscience, and would submit humbly to their decision. Then I retired to the Erber, and waited. By the end of the day, a crowd of them came, led by Richard and the Chancellor, with the petition of Parliament that I should take the crown.

Naturally, I did not disappoint them.

✯✯✯

I released Hastings and Rivers and actually allowed them to attend my Coronation. I even allowed Hastings to keep his offices, which – given that one of them was Lord Chamberlain, which kept him close to me – was either naive or shrewd. I'm still not quite sure which. Unfortunately, within six months they were up in arms against me, in the Midlands, and Lord Stanley with them.

I had all three beheaded and attainted. They had had their chance, and I decided I should never be so generous again. I could not forgive them for making me put on harness once more, something which, after Tewkesbury, I had sworn never to do. I gave William Stanley most of his brother's lands. He had remained loyal, and now became Lord Stanley of Chirk.

Elizabeth Woodville and her children still live quietly in the country. I have given them a generous pension, and now that Rivers is dead, I doubt whether they are any threat to me. I keep them watched though, just in case.

Old Harry VI and Queen Margaret are still in the Tower. Some people wanted me to kill Harry, but I would not. He is a harmless soul – I leave them in peace.

As for my Isabelle and me, we were very happy for a time. She gave me a fine son, Edward, Prince of Wales, and a daughter, the Lady Margaret of York, named after my favourite sister the Duchess of Burgundy. After our next child, Richard, though, she sickened and passed from me. In all honesty, I went quite mad for a time. Perhaps one or two were executed then who should not have been. Most of the court survived, however.

My dear sister Margaret soon arranged for me to marry her stepdaughter, Mary, the heiress of Burgundy. While Mary has been no replacement for Isabelle, she has yet been a good wife, and has borne me a fine son, Edmund, who will one day inherit her vast lands. For the present my sister acts as Regent there, while Mary keeps to my side in England.

King Louis of France and I came to an arrangement. Neither of us wanted war, and he certainly did not want one with a united England and Burgundy, so he pays me enough each year to avoid calling Parliament and asking for taxes. We have a truce, and one day my daughter will marry his son. In the interim, if he wants a quarrel, he can seek one in Italy, and hire archers from me at a very modest rate if he so chooses. I'm a generous sort.

The doctors say I cannot live long. I grow weaker by the day, but I am reconciled with God, have made good confession of my many sins, and hope very much to see Isabelle again. I do not despair. Here my good brother, Richard, Duke of Gloucester, Earl of Warwick and Salisbury, will serve as Protector for my son when I am gone, and I am sure he will do as fine a job of ruling England as he has done of ruling the North as my deputy. All speak of his honesty and just dealings – he has never failed me yet.

Soon the heralds will cry it for the last time: 'George, by the grace of God, King of England, and of France, Lord of Ireland, Duke of Burgundy, Lotharingia, Brabant, Limbourg, Luxembourg and Guelders, Count of Flanders, Artois, Burgundy, Hainault, Holland, Zeeland, Namur and Zutphen, Marquess of the Holy Roman Empire, Lord of Friesland, etc.'

The longest style ever claimed by an English King, even if some of the titles – like France – are more or less nominal. My clerks have to be paid a bonus to write it out in full. Not so bad for the younger son of a duke, one everyone called shiftless, lazy and frivolous. Even my lady mother said I would never amount to much.

About Brian Wainwright

In his teens, Brian Wainwright developed a particular fascination with the era of Richard II, another king he believes history has sadly misjudged. There were few novels about that period and Brian eventually came across **White Boar** by Marian Palmer which started him off on his fascination with the Third Richard. His main focus remains with the House of York throughout its existence.

His first published novel, **The Adventures of Alianore Audley**, set in the Yorkist era, was produced by way of light relief during a lull in the long task of researching and writing **Within the Fetterlock**. He was surprised by the number of people who appear to enjoy what he admits is his fairly eccentric sense of humour.

Within the Fetterlock was an entirely different sort of project, one that has verged on an obsession. Fascinated by Constance of York almost from the first time he found a reference to her existence, the novel was whittled down from many previous attempts.

After a long break from writing Brian is currently working on a prequel to **Within the Fetterlock**, (as yet untitled), and has longer term plans for a follow on to that, a further Alianore Audley book (much of which has been written) and possibly a serious Ricardian novel.

Greyhounds and Fetterlocks Blog: https://tinyurl.com/j4uetn2y
Amazon: https://tinyurl.com/yjd5rm8n

April is the Cruellest Month
by
J P Reedman

Introduction

Edward IV died on April 9, 1483, shortly before his 41st birthday. He had returned from a fishing trip and fallen ill, briefly rallied, but then declined and died. Cause of death was not obvious, so unlikely to have been a stroke or heart attack. As is usual with sudden deaths of notables in the Middle Ages, rumours of poisoning ran rampant, especially in France. Most historians have discredited this theory, but certainly some of the Woodville family, who, it seemed, were beginning to fall from Edward's favour, behaved in a rather unorthodox and even slightly suspicious manner upon the king's death...

***

Elizabeth Woodville stared disconsolately out the window of her solar. In the distance, the King's party was riding through the gate, heading out upon a royal fishing trip. Hastings was present, stuck to the King's side like a barnacle. She did not like the man overmuch but had learnt to keep her mouth closed on that matter to keep harmony in the household. She could see Edward clearly, taller than the rest of his courtiers (and now, nearing forty-one, a good deal fatter too), brightly dressed, gems winking on the brim of his hat. He did not glance back, did not give a cursory wave towards the window where he knew she would be watching. He never did these days... Never...

Anthony Woodville entered the solar just as the King's company vanished into a haze of outbuildings and then the busy streets beyond. He noticed Elizabeth's downcast, sour face and rushed to her side. 'You seemed grieved, my beloved sister,' he said, taking her hands in his. They were smooth and white, the nails long, undamaged by work. But they felt cold. He rubbed them to warm her.

'The King is ignoring me, Anthony,' Elizabeth moaned.

'Did you not once say that is for the better, now that he has grown fat and gross?'

'Yes, yes ... but I did not mean to the point where his lack of attention embarrasses me.'

'How is he embarrassing you?' Anthony frowned.

'That harlot, "Jane" Shore. I know Ned always liked a pretty face, but she is actually at court, the little strumpet, and everyone knows he prefers her bed to mine. What's worse is that Hastings runs after her with his tongue lolling like an eager dog, and my own son Thomas strips her garments off with his eyes, and yet ... people like her. They say she's kind, even though she's but a slut. They don't say I'm kind. It's never 'kind Queen Elizabeth'. No, it's greedy grasping Elizabeth, with her avaricious family. I know what the people think.'

'Not all people.' Anthony tried to soothe his sister.

'Enough to make me grieve,' she said. 'But that's not all that worries me about Ned's seeming indifference. Anthony, oh, how can I say it? He has changed his will. He had his lawyers come in for a private meeting. My name is ... gone.'

'What?' Anthony, the handsome male counterpart of his comely sister, blanched. 'Did you confront him, speak to him? Surely you have made some mistake, sister. It cannot be so! You are his Queen!'

'No, it is true! He has removed me as an executor of his will. He was quite open about it. I complained and he laughed it off, saying he would expect me to be too distraught at the time of his death to do the job properly. He also seemed to imply I was too stupid to understand the fine details.'

'Oh, Elizabeth,' murmured Anthony, 'this is grievous news indeed. I must admit I had noticed of late his gifts to our family have been less lavish. He has seemed cooler in temperament. I assumed it was because he was brooding about King Louis going back on his word and no longer paying the pensions from the Treaty of Picquigny.'

Elizabeth shook her head. 'I fear, Anthony ... I fear. As you have noticed, he is not only less enamoured of me, but all the Woodville family. If he has changed his will – what else might change in the future? If he should die before my son Edward reaches his majority, he could choose a regent or a protector that is not me ... or you.'

'Who would he have but Edward's mother, the Queen?'

'He no longer thinks I am suitable as regent, not having had a princess's upbringing.' Elizabeth's eyes flashed with fury. 'He should have married that fat cow Bona instead if he wanted a wife born into royalty. Even that Earl's daughter, Ele ...' She halted, face reddening.

'Calm yourself!' Anthony looked frightened. 'Do not say it, even in private. Men still wonder; there have been many rumours about your marriage to the King being irregular. We've tried to quash them all, but ...'

Elizabeth still looked furious. 'I will never speak her accursed name. It took all of my might to convince Ned to remove his brother, that feckless dolt George, before he opened his mouth and spilt the bitter truth and damned all my children, all my kin, to shame and anonymity.' She began to pace the room. 'As for fearing who might be made Lord Protector or regent in my stead ...'

'You don't think he favours Lord Hastings, do you?' Anthony cried out. 'That would be unfortunate. There is bad blood between Hastings and me. And worse, the King took my side, much to Hastings's chagrin. The man likes me not.'

'Hastings – pah!' sneered Elizabeth. 'No doubt I could wind the man around my little finger with the merest hint of future bed-sports. He is a renowned lecher, as all know ... and always sniffing after

whatever – whomever – Edward has bedded. No, it's not Hastings I fear
… but Gloucester. That runt of the York litter. He does not like me,
Anthony. I can tell. He doesn't … doesn't even think I am beautiful.'

'Oh, Richard is a sombre sort, Elizabeth, but he has always been
loyal to Edward, has he not?'

'Yes, but do not underestimate him when it comes to causing
trouble. He is a stickler for following rules, unbending as a rod of iron.
Jesu, if he should ever find out about El … that, that woman. Add that
to the hate he bears me over the death of George of Clarence … God
knows why he mourned for the wretch; George treated him with
contempt just like he did everyone else, but who knows why these men
of York behave as they do? Each one – unpredictable.'

'It will be fine, Elizabeth.' Anthony touched her cheek. 'Come,
don't frown. We made plans for a dreadful event, didn't we? Great
plans.'

She shivered a little. 'Yes, plans to protect us, to protect the family
… but *such* plans, Anthony!'

'If you are afraid, nought will be said evermore, and we can forget
the past.'

She shook her head, sighing. 'No, no, we were right. Family
comes first. We cannot end up as we were at Grafton. Not after rising
so high. I am not some wilting flower …'

'I know, dear Bess.' Anthony brought her hand to his lips. 'I will
do what needs to be done.'

Her eyes, languid, hooded, green as a dragon's, suddenly became
fierce and steely. 'For my children and for my family. I will do
whatever it takes!'

'Your hand is shaking, dearest sister.' Anthony cosseted her as if
she were a child. 'Do not fret – it ill becomes such a beauteous and
serene lady. Come, I have some new poetry to read to you. You'll like
that, I'm sure.'

Elizabeth pulled her hand away and folded her arms 'You're right,
Anthony. I must not frown. It will give me unsightly lines. My forehead

must remain white and smooth to please Edward, to please my admirers … it must …'

'And the poetry, sister? One is about your unparalleled beauty.'

She sighed. 'Oh, go on – if you must.'

☆☆☆

Edward, King of England, returned from his fishing trip. Larger than life, his middle wide through copious feasting, his face still bore the ravaged remnants of handsomeness. He stalked through the halls of Westminster, dangling a brace of shining fishes from his hand. His long-time companion, Lord William Hastings, trundled along at his side; an incorrigible womaniser, William's gaze travelled over every female from fifteen to fifty in the King's Household.

'Bess … oh, Bess!' Edward cried out. 'Dearest wife, I have a gift for you!'

Elizabeth appeared as if by magic from a side chamber, her hennin tall as a spire, her eyes smoky with imported kohl. 'A gift … for me?' she simpered. Elizabeth liked gifts; she liked them very much, the more lavish the better.

Edward dangled the fish before her face. 'I caught these myself – I even baited my own hook with the worm, didn't I, Will?' Hastings made an approving grunt. 'They will make a goodly dinner, don't you think?'

Elizabeth's eyes narrowed. 'I am sure they will – when the servants, whose job it is to handle such matters, take them away and prepare them. As it is, get those slimy, smelly things away before I stink of fish! Oh, Ned, everyone around us is staring. They think you are making fun of me.'

Edward abruptly summoned a squire and flung the fish to the youth. 'Take them to the kitchens,' he ordered. 'They are offending the Queen's delicate nose.'

'Ned, you're making things worse,' hissed Elizabeth. 'You're making me seem a … a villain.'

'Then stop acting like one,' said Edward, his good mood clearly quelled. He turned back to Will Hastings. 'Will, I think I shall have to call off our evening plans.'

'Your Grace? Ned?' Hastings' eyebrow quirked.

'All of a sudden, a great tiredness has overtaken me,' muttered Edward. 'It feels like a weight lies heavy on my head and shoulders. I will take to my bed – alone – and I am sure I will feel better in the morning.'

Edward strode out of the chamber, leaving a fuming Elizabeth glaring after him. Will followed his friend to the royal apartments, sitting down on a stool while Edward's squires undressed him and readied him for bed.

'Are you sure you are well, Ned?' Hastings' usual grin faded as he gazed on his friend. 'You look ...'

'I feel hot ...' murmured Edward, and he passed his hand over his brow, sweeping away beads of sweat.

'I am calling your doctor, Dr Hobbys.'

'Oh, Will, by Christ's teeth, it hasn't come to that ... I have had a little ague all week, as you know, my nose like a tap, running eyes, nothing fearsome...'

Suddenly he began to cough. He tried to stop himself, but choked. 'Drink, Will!' he croaked, and he coughed some more. 'Need a drink!'

Will Hastings grabbed a flagon from a nearby stand and filled it from the decanter next to it. Edward grabbed it from his hands. 'God's teeth,' the King murmured, between coughs, 'I felt burning hot, but now it is as if ice had entered my very bones.'

Will stepped towards the door. 'Ned, even if you command me otherwise, I am getting Dr Hobbys.'

'Will he live?' Elizabeth stalked around Hobbys, who stood like a black-clad scarecrow – one approached by a particularly malevolent and fearless female crow.

'He is a strong man, your Grace. I have bled him to restore the humours. I have seen such infections of the lungs before. Sometimes they are lethal, but I do not believe this will be the case with King Edward.'

'Can I see him? He … he won't cast his foul sickness on to me, will he?'

'None of his fishing party has sickened, Highness, but I would be wary, for your own sake. This type of ailment does often spread with frequency.'

Elizabeth turned on her heel, flouncing away from Hobbys and into the King's chamber. Inside, Edward was in bed, leaning propped up against his pillows. 'Bess?'

She made the required niceties, but did not draw close to her husband. 'Ned, Ned, I've been so worried about you,' she said hoping her voice sounded exceedingly sincere. She had loved him once, no doubt about it. Loved him almost to distraction. But time had eroded that love – finding out about Eleanor Talbot, then the constant stream of different strumpets, his increasing diffidence to her and her family, even the King's rapidly increasing girth. She had kept her looks despite birthing so many of his children …

'Nice to know, Bess … Is there something else? There is, isn't there?' Edward's voice held a hint of annoyance. 'I can always tell when you want something.'

'When you were taken ill, I was so afraid.' She wrung her hands theatrically. 'Especially since …' She bowed her head.

'Since what?' asked Edward suspiciously.

'Since you removed me as an executor of your will.'

'I told you …'

'That was no reason!' she snapped, fury suddenly flaring in her green eyes.

Edward sat violently upright, covers twisted and falling around his hips. 'Madame!' he roared. 'You come to wail at me in my sickbed over such a trivial matter?'

'It's not trivial to me! I was … am afraid. If you died, others outside our family might take control.'

'You want to be Regent if aught should happen to me – is that correct?'

'Yes! Who better can guide our son? It is my right!'

'Your right?' The King snorted like a mad bull. 'Any rights you possess, woman, have come solely through me! And what did you do to repay me after I wed your sisters to lords far beyond their stations and gave your kinsmen high positions of their own? You just took more, and spent more, and connived behind my back! Christ, Bess, I even did away with my brother George because of you!'

'Edward!' cried Elizabeth, as angry as the King. 'He betrayed you many times He deserved his fate. He might have revealed … the secret and imperilled the throne for our son!'

'I know that. But do you think there isn't a day I do not think of him? Folly dogged his days, but he was still my brother! In truth, he should have gone to the Tower for life instead …'

'Whatever should or should not have been done, it is in the past. It is the future I worry about. Who you would have for Regent, or Protector, if not your loving wife, your Queen?'

Edward's eyes slitted. 'I think you know. Someone who has always been my right-hand man in war, someone who shares the same royal blood as I.'

'Richard. But he hardly knows our Edward, and I – I …'

'You do not like him. I know, Bess. That was clear all along. Nevertheless, your likes and dislikes are immaterial. The Woodvilles could never control the government. You have not the experience and the old blood of the land would never accept you. Now go from me, you are making my head pound with your prattle!' He began to cough violently, clutching his chest.

'Edward, you must listen ...' Elizabeth reached out to clasp his shoulder.

'Get off me, woman!' he roared, his face turning crimson. 'Go, and see to your embroidery or some such. If you continue to harass me, I'll have your whole damn family removed from court, and you can spend most of your time at the Pleasance or some other place – away from me.'

He started to cough again, raising an arm to block the spittle. As he lowered the arm, a smudge of red showed on the white linen sleeve.

'Ned!' gasped Elizabeth.

'Get out!' shouted Edward.

Elizabeth Woodville grabbed her skirts in her hands and fled.

✩✩✩

The Queen hurried to her private quarters where she called for Anthony. Her brother swiftly arrived, rushing in to comfort her. Elizabeth was weeping hysterically, her headdress thrown off, her silver-gold hair in wild disarray. 'Bess, what has happened?'

She raised a tear-streaked face. 'It is happening as we feared ... it is like a hideous nightmare. Ned is sorely sick, no matter Hobbys' assurances. He coughed blood, Anthony, I saw with mine own eyes! He is going to die, and he is going to appoint Gloucester as Protector. Under Richard, my own son will be stripped away from me, taken from my influence. Ned even threatened me just now. He said I'd be sent from court, and the family too ...'

A strange expression flashed over Anthony's smooth, handsome visage. Fear ... but resolve. 'Bess.' He knelt awkwardly at her side. 'Remember what we spoke of recently. If things become grave for us ...'

'It was terrible talk of the most terrible and unholy of things!' she wept, 'and yet ... yet how can we do otherwise? We must move swiftly, Anthony, before he fades, before Gloucester is made Protector, before he is summoned from his hole in the north.'

Anthony's hands reached up to grasp her shoulders. 'What we have proposed ... Remember, if we are caught ...'

'We die, we both die,' she said dully. 'But what we face if we do not act may be near enough to death. Or we may meet our doom anyway – Gloucester hates us because of George of Clarence. Remember when he left London after the execution? Men say he swore to get revenge.'

'I am afraid,' said Anthony suddenly, 'but I will do it – for my beloved family. For you. Nulle le Vault. Nothing is worth it ... but she.'

Elizabeth burst into grateful tears, burying her face in her hands.

In the King's bedchamber, Edward leaned on one elbow and beckoned to Will Hastings. 'I need you to do me a favour, Will.'

'Ned, you are not feeling worse, I take it?'

'No.' He gave a sharp cough. 'I am not. But nevertheless, I feel ... a sense of danger.'

'Danger?'

'You heard me. Will, I have fought in numerous battles. Ever have I been the victor. When I have been on the field, I have sensed, often before it happens, a presence. Death perhaps, waiting for one to make the wrong move. I feel that presence now.'

Will Hastings looked concerned. 'Are you sure you don't want to see Dr Hobbys?'

'Will,' said Edward, 'no. Don't question. I want you to send a messenger – one of yours so as not to draw undue attention. I want you to summon my brother, Richard of Gloucester. Tell him to come to London at once. And I mean with all the swiftness he can muster. Tell him I will personally pay for the change of horses he will need upon the road. But I want him here...'

✫✫✫

Richard, Duke of Gloucester, rode through the night, his mount sweat-lathered beneath him. Periodically he stopped at various towns along the King's Road, demanding at the gates to be let in after curfew to change his mount for another. No one questioned the King's brother and he was permitted to pass, but vigilant townsfolk, the town watch and men peering from crowded taverns and inns whispered to each other excitedly, wondering what was going on in the world of the great.

Richard himself was oppressed by worry, uncaring of stares and whispering. Hastings's missive had told him but little, only that Edward was ill and desired his presence at Westminster. Immediately. The fact that the message had come from Hastings's courier and was written by Hastings' scribe spoke of needed secrecy.

In all his dealings, Richard had always reacted with speed and he was doing so again now. The cause of Ned's illness had not been revealed in his missive, but it must be more than a trivial ague, of that the Duke was certain.

Setting his spurs to his newly-acquired steed's flanks, he sped through the chill, drizzly April night towards London, his little company of Middleham soldiers thundering at his heels.

☆☆☆

The King was feeling much better. He still had a racking cough that sometimes gave him stabbing pains under his shoulder blades, but the fever had broken and his sputum was no longer blood-stained. Hobbys seemed pleased; he had placed his ear to the King's chest and nodded. 'There are no more railing noises in your lungs, your Grace. I believe you are on the mend, but you must rest.'

Edward leaned back against the bolster and popped a sugared almond into his mouth. 'I take it Richard has not arrived yet,' he said to Lord Hastings, who was seated near the fireplace, his legs stretched out before the merry blaze.

'Not to my knowledge,' said Hastings. 'I pray my messenger arrived safely in Middleham.'

Edward scratched his chin, dark with blue-black stubble – he had not had his barber attend him during his sickness. 'I hope I did not overreact, Will, and brought him out on a fool's errand. Yet ... I still sense something.' He pointed to his back. 'A prickling up my spine. As if someone might leap out and stick a dagger in it. Or some such. But maybe that is foolish nonsense, worries brought on by my illness. In all my life I have seldom been sick, save when I had the meazils ... Do you remember that time, Will?'

'I do! We were all surprised you'd not had meazils as a boy like most do. And there you were covered in great red spots and grumpy as a damned bear.'

'Of course I was foul-tempered! It was December, I looked monstrous, and Warwick was down at Bamburgh Castle knocking holes in the wall with his cannons. I wanted to be there.'

A sudden clattering sounded in the hall outside the royal bedchamber. A voice rang out, intense and slightly annoyed. 'I do not need a formal announcement; he summoned me. Move aside, I bid you ...'

'My brother Gloucester is here!' said Ned, with a little laugh that set his cough off for a moment. And then, swinging himself half out of the bed, he roared, 'Richard! Get you in here! You must be frozen from that long ride!'

The door swung open, and in strode Richard, Duke of Gloucester, damp hair windblown and dishevelled and mud caking his long, black leather boots. His heavy travelling cloak was speckled with rain. He threw his bonnet upon the table, nearly hitting Hastings and strode hastily to Edward's bedside.

'Jesu!' he cried, 'I did not know what I was coming to, Ned. I thought I might be too late, that you might be ...'

'Ah, I'm made of sterner stuff than that.'

Richard looked a little peeved. 'Well, all men are mortal, and Hastings' messenger could tell me little of what ailed you. I am sure you did not have me ride many leagues through wild wind and weather just for a friendly chat around the fire.'

Hastings cleared his throat and stood. 'I shall leave the two of you to converse as brothers should.' He bowed in Edward's direction. 'My Lord King.'

'G'night, Will.' Edward dismissed him with a nod.

'Don't tire him out, Gloucester,' Will called irreverently over his shoulder as he hastened for the door.

Once the door had closed, Richard frowned, poured himself some wine from a decanter that stood on the table, and eased himself onto the stool William had vacated. 'Christ, I am frozen to the bones; if this fire doesn't dry me out soon, Ned, I'll end up as sick as you.'

'Dickon, you can change in there.' Ned gestured towards a side-chamber. 'My squires have laid out garments, for I plan to attempt to rise on the morrow. I do not want my subjects to think I am dead!'

Richard looked startled. 'Ah … I do not think any of your garb would fit!'

'I suppose not. You might find some of Will's shirts lying about, though. He is closer to your size.'

Richard raised an eyebrow. 'His clothes are in there?' Edward smirked.

'You do not want to know, Richard, my pious little brother.'

'No, I am sure I do not.'

'Entertainments. Before I became ill, of course.'

Richard made a small disapproving grunt and downed his wine.

Edward's face suddenly grew serious. 'It was a fraught time here, Dickon, make no mistake. I was truly ill as never before in my life. Every breath hurt, I coughed until I spewed. And it got me thinking. If evil should befall me …'

'God forbid!' interjected Richard sharply, fingers clenched on the stem of his wine goblet.

'If it should, I would need a strong hand to guide my son Edward to the throne and oversee his minority. That hand cannot be Elizabeth's, nor Anthony Woodville's. The lords of this land would never obey them. Anarchy would rule and the country would fall back into factional warfare, I fear. I don't trust men like Buckingham, for example. He'd never agree to a Woodville dominated government – even though he's married to one of the brood.'

'That is probably why he wouldn't,' Richard quipped dryly. 'I know you have no love of Bess, but promise to be kind to her if I should predecease her.'

'You won't, you're younger than she is ... but I give you my word, I will give her due honour, always. If she does the same for me and keeps far away from me and mine!'

'Richard, it is my intention to add a codicil to my will. That is why I summoned you. I want you to become Lord Protector of the Realm should I expire before Edward is of age. Will you accept?'

A cavalcade of emotions ran over Richard's features. 'Ned, this is a great honour, but one that comes with great burdens.'

'I know, I understand that!' The King heaved his large body up and swaying over to his brother, clasped Richard's hand in his own. 'Will you do it? For our House. For our father who was lost at Wakefield?'

The Duke hesitated, then gave a brief nod. 'Yes ...Yes I will do it. For all we ever believed in, ever fought for.'

'Good!' King Edward beamed with pleasure and retreated to the bed, throwing himself down and drawing up the rich coverlet. 'But, by God, Dickon, your hand is indeed like ice. You need to get out of those wet clothes, or tis true, you will end up in a sick-bed yourself. And no one wants that. Go ... put on Hastings' things for now. I can assure you the laundry women have cleaned them.'

'And did they help Will Hastings out of them?' Richard quipped.

'More than likely. Now go, get changed.'

Richard nodded and moved into the antechamber, where he began the laborious and annoying task of removing his own garb without assistance from his squires. Hopping on one foot, he struggled with his boot and fell against the wall, nearly knocking down a tapestry that depicted a troupe of peasants stomping on grapes.

Suddenly, in the chamber beyond, he heard the door to the King's bedchamber creak open. Is Will Hastings back, maybe wanting his clothes? Richard wondered in annoyance. No ... he heard muffled voices now. Familiar Queen Elizabeth and her brother, Anthony Woodville, Earl Rivers. Dulcet tones, cloyingly sweet, wheedling.

Almost against his own wishes, he found himself listening as he sat down on the floor, still struggling with the boot.

'Your Grace ...' Elizabeth's voice. 'I must beg your forgiveness for my behaviour the other day. I was impertinent and did not behave as a wife – and Queen – should. Anthony and I have brought you a gift.'

'A gift?'

'We have heard from Hobbys that you have recovered some of your appetite, your Grace,' said Anthony. 'We've brought stewed pigeons stuffed with pepper, cloves and garlic.'

'Very kind,' said Ned, 'but I already have eaten.'

'When has that ever stopped you?' asked Elizabeth, her voice changing – sounding, to Richard's ears, slightly strained and shrill.

There was a sound of a platter clanging onto the table. 'I'll put it here,' Elizabeth's tone was wheedling once more. 'Let me just spoon some of the sauce into your mouth if you cannot stomach anything more. It's lovely saffron ...'

What is the woman playing at? Richard forgot his obstructive boot and sidled over to the doorway, peering out from the shadows, unnoticed.

He could see Anthony Woodville's back as he stood by the table near a silver bowl that steamed and sent off pungent fragrance. Elizabeth was fluttering about Ned, who was frowning at her as if she had gone moon-mad. 'I told you, Bess, I am fine.'

'Oh, just a drop ... *please*. I will taste some for you, if it is the fact your taster isn't here that bothers you.' She picked up a silver spoon and ladled some saffron sauce into her mouth in front of the King. Moments later, she stepped back to the table and leaned close to Anthony, while making much show of replacing the spoon. There was a panicked, almost mad glitter in her eyes. 'Do you think he suspects?'

Edward, half-cloaked by the heavy curtains around the bed, could not see or hear her.

But Richard could. He went cold.

Anthony shrugged and pointed towards the bed, a gesture that clearly said, 'Try again.'

'Edward.' Elizabeth was speaking in that false, sing-song voice again. 'Will you please honour me by eating just a little? Cook made this especially. He will be most upset if he thinks you have not eaten a single bite.'

A loud sigh came from the bed. 'I'll get no peace if I do not, that is clear enough. Bring it over then.'

Richard saw Elizabeth glance nervously at Anthony. Both looked pale and strained. Then he noticed Rivers reach to the pouch at his belt. Opening it, he drew out a tiny crystal phial. His fingers shook as he prised off the lid.

And then he turned it over, carefully tapping the base. Droplets fell into the concoction in the silver bowl on the table. Elizabeth hurriedly whisked the spoon about, stirring the potion in. 'Is it enough?' she hissed at her brother. 'If we have gone this far, we cannot risk him liv ...'

'Halt! Stop what you are doing!'

Richard stepped from the concealing shadows and strode towards the two Woodvilles. Anthony and Elizabeth gasped almost in unison and whirled in his direction. Startled, Anthony dropped the phial and it shattered on the tiles.

'You are trying to poison the King!' the Duke of Gloucester shouted and hurled himself at Anthony Woodville, throwing the older man onto the floor. Elizabeth began to shriek, her eyes filled with terror.

'What in Christ's name?' Edward bawled from the bed. He ripped the velvet hangings aside and stumbled barefoot across the room.

On the floor Richard and Anthony were rolling about, grappling with each other. Anthony was slightly taller than Richard but the Duke was wiry and stronger than he appeared. Suddenly Anthony reached within his doublet and pulled out a long, thin dagger secreted there – no man was allowed to go armed in the King's presence.

Richard's eyes flared with rage. 'So, you seek to cheat in combat just as you cheated in the joust!' he cried, referring to Woodville's infamous long-ago battle with the Bastard of Burgundy where he had been accused of possible dishonesty.

Edward staggered towards the chamber door. Elizabeth, weeping and wailing, clawed at his arm like a madwoman. 'Ned, no, no, it's not what you think. Gloucester is wrong; he is trying to drive a wedge between us with lies!'

'Get off me, woman!' bellowed the King, shrugging her off, and he wrenched the door open, nearly tearing it from its hinges. 'Guards, guards!' he bellowed into the corridor.

A few moments later, dozens of armed soldiers arrived, looking thoroughly confused by the sight of Duke Richard and Earl Rivers fighting and the Queen in hysterics.

By now, Richard had disarmed Anthony Woodville, but he still straddled the Earl, holding his wrists in a vice-like grip. The Queen was standing with her hands pressed to her face as she sobbed, while Edward, red-faced and wrathful, stood barefoot in his nightshirt.

'Him!' Edward pointed to Anthony Woodville. 'Arrest him. Take him to the Tower.' He then turned to Elizabeth. 'As for the Queen … she shall join him.'

'No, Ned!' howled Elizabeth. 'I did nothing, I swear it.'

'That will be determined in time, Madame,' said Edward coldly. 'Guards, take these wretched creatures away.'

✰✰✰

The Lord High Constable of England, Richard, Duke of Gloucester, sat on a high dais in the Council Chamber inside the Tower of London. Normally, he would have been accompanied by the Earl Marshal of England, but Elizabeth Woodville's son, Thomas Grey, had been acting Earl Marshal in the minority of the King's younger son,

amazon.co.uk®

A gift note from Mrs Joanne R Larner:

Alex Marchant said you would like a review copy of our new anthology, in aid of Scoliosis Association UK – I hope you enjoy it! Regards, Joanne R Larner From Joanne Larner

Gift note included with **The Road Not Travelled: Alternative Tales of the Wars of the Roses**

Richard of Shrewsbury, and upon hearing of his mother and uncle's arrest, Grey had gone on the run. Last heard he was taking ship for Brittany.

Ankles and wrists chained, Anthony Woodville stood before Richard, a defeated man who suddenly appeared years older than his true age. 'It was verified by Dr Hobbys and others,' Richard of Gloucester was saying, 'that the liquid in the phial brought into the King's chambers and poured into his food was arsenic. Arsenic has a garlic smell and would easily blend with the dish intended for his Grace, King Edward.'

Anthony Woodville hung his head, and then he mumbled hoarsely, 'Nulle le Vault. Nothing matters but she ...'

The Lord High Constable stiffened. His eyes fixed on a spot somewhere on the wall behind Anthony Woodville's head. 'You have been found a traitor, Anthony Woodville. The usual penalty for that crime is to be hanged, drawn and quartered – but because the King held affection for you in the past, he wills it that your sentence be commuted to beheading.'

Anthony swayed as if he might fall, breath railing through his clenched teeth.

'On the morrow,' continued Gloucester, emotionless, 'after you are shriven, you will be taken out upon Tower Hill and there executed. God have mercy upon you.' He gestured to the armoured guards stationed about the room. 'Take him back to his confinement.'

The guards took the unresisting Woodville away. Richard leaned back in his seat, waiting. A few minutes later Elizabeth was brought in, her hands and feet unbound, but escorted by two stone-faced soldiers holding pikes. She was ashen grey, her eyes red from weeping. She glared at Richard with unrestrained hatred. 'Do not waste time with speeches, Gloucester,' she spat. 'Just tell me my fate and have done with it.'

Richard cleared his throat. 'For the love he once bore you, and because you are a woman and mother to his children, his Grace is inclined to lenience. Your life is in no danger. He will seek an annulment of your marriage, owing to your wedding being clandestine,

103

and you will be sent away- to a convent in the north of England where I can keep my eye on you.'

Elizabeth lunged towards the Duke but was faced with two crossed pikes. 'I will go as Ned wishes. At least, I have my head, but ...' A strange smirk curled the corners of her mouth, and Richard suddenly felt apprehensive. Warwick had claimed her mother, Jacquetta was a witch – and Elizabeth certainly looked witchlike and malevolent at that moment. 'When you get a chance, ask my dear, lecherous husband about ... Eleanor. Eleanor Talbot, daughter of the old Earl of Shrewsbury. Or maybe it is not such a good idea – you might end up joining my poor, doomed brother in the Tower.'

Richard gestured to the guards. 'Escort the Queen back to her quarters. Have her sent in a carriage to Arden Priory near Helmsley before dawn on the morrow.'

The soldiers closed in around Elizabeth, a ring of steel. 'There is no need for that,' she sniffed with contempt. 'I will go peaceably enough.' Head held high, she marched from the room with her gaolers surrounding her, an entourage of dishonour.

Richard rose from his chair, glad the events of the past few days were over. But now, Elizabeth had left a tantalising mystery, one which would niggle forever at him.

'Eleanor,' he murmured under his breath, 'Eleanor Talbot. Whatever could the Queen have meant?'

About J P Reedman

J.P. Reedman is the author of a number of novels on Richard III, Edward IV...and even Richard's enemy, the Duke of Buckingham. The main series is *I, Richard Plantagenet*, which is told in person from Richard's first-person point of view. Future novels (hopefully to appear this year) include part 2 of the *I, Richard* prequel detailing Richard's childhood and youth, and a novel on his father, Richard Duke of York.

J.P. is also the author of a highly successful series of short novels on lesser-known medieval queens and noblewomen – the *Medieval Babes* series, plus a trilogy about a mystical Robin Hood, and an epic set at Stonehenge.

Amazon: https://tinyurl.com/bc93d87v

Of Cousins and of Kings

by
Roslyn Ramona Brown

✫✫✫

Introduction

I have always found the Earl of Warwick's history with King Edward IV very interesting, considering how it ended. What drove King Edward IV to mistrust his older kinsman, who had been a loyal liegeman from before he became king? Was it merely the clandestine marriage with Elizabeth Woodville that put a rift between them?

The Earl was a very powerful nobleman in the North, and his family holdings and resulting wealth exceeded that of the young king. Although Richard Neville was a loyal man, he was also a very proud man, and the unexpected marriage to an older, Lancastrian widow put an end to Warwick's negotiations with the King of France for an alliance with that foreign land.

Even so, Warwick continued to work with his king until another slight put the earl's nose out of joint and humiliated him a second time with King Louis XI of France. The English monarch dispatched Warwick to France to arrange trade negotiations at the same time Edward was cosying up to the Burgundians.

The other members of the Neville clan were singled out by the Yorkist King and his queen consort, when Archbishop George Neville was asked to return the Great Seal to King Edward, and Lord Montagu,

John Neville, lost his Northumberland holding in favour of one of their most hated rivals, Henry Percy. These added humiliations and demotions prompted Richard Neville to instigate a series of uprisings in the North in 1469 and again in 1470, with the unfortunate result that the queen's father and brother were unjustly executed at John Neville's orders. Warwick and Montagu were both slain at the Battle of Barnet in 1471.

My alternate history explores the possibilities of what might have happened had Warwick remained true to King Edward and had not rebelled against him at all. How would Warwick's presence change the outcome of the tragic events in 1483?

Thank you for reading.

☆☆☆

Prologue: Westminster, April 1483

'NO.'

That flat denial caught the queen up short, her startled gaze turning to her husband, just to make sure he had spoken. Edward Plantagenet lay amidst a great mound of thick pillows, but he was not in the least bit comfortable. The damnable ague had him coughing up a noxious yellow phlegm that his healers sniffed and poked at, but still could not get rid of.

'Husband,' Elizabeth said in her most soothing tone, 'you are tired. Rest for now, and we will discuss the matter later.'

'No, Elizabeth,' Edward replied firmly, or as firmly as his illness would allow. 'I have given your family more power and prestige than any other. Do not ask more of me!'

She knew when to push and when to let things lie for another time, but she knew that time was running out for the Yorkist king. Thus far, Edward's healers had not been able to find remedy for this affliction, and the king was getting weaker every day. Edward needed to appoint a Regent for their twelve-year-old son, for the boy could not rule on his own. Elizabeth would guide him, offer him advice and keep anyone else from taking advantage of her son. As his mother, that was her expected role and the queen was determined that Edward sign the document to make it so, before he could no longer sign his name. And should Edward, with God's mercy, survive his illness, doubtful as that was, it was only a precaution. A protective measure that any prudent king, or queen, would take when their heirs were but minors.

The queen drew breath to speak, but Edward's hand lifted to forestall her.

'Do not trouble me, woman,' he told her in a hoarse rasp. 'Leave me.'

'Very well, Edward.' She relented, seeing that she would get nowhere with him for the time being. 'I will come back once you have recovered your strength.'

Whether the king wanted her to return or not, he said nothing as she swept from the chamber in elegantly embroidered slippers.

In the corridor outside, Elizabeth almost bumped into Richard Neville. The Earl of Warwick bowed to her with minimal courtesy, his dark eyes glinting as he said, 'Your Highness.'

'The king is not to be disturbed,' she informed him, fully expecting that he would obey his queen, whether Warwick liked it or not.

'I have been summoned by the king, Your Highness, so I do not think it will be a disturbance at all.' And with that, Warwick slipped through the chamber doors that the queen had just exited.

She glared after him, seriously annoyed that Edward would see that vile man while he ordered her to leave his side! But, what could she do? Edward would not thank her for intruding on whatever business he had with the Neville lord. And she needed Edward's cooperation.

For now.

Westminster, April 1483

Good God.

I put all other thoughts out of mind the moment I laid eyes upon the king in his sickbed. I had not thought Edward was that ill until I saw his pale, sweating brow and the faded brightness in his blue eyes.

'Come now, Warwick,' the king said. 'You have surely seen a man with an ague before. Have you, a seasoned warrior, suddenly become squeamish?'

'Forgive me, Edward.' I found my voice and a suitable reply for my younger cousin of York. 'I have not seen you in so many weeks, I had no idea you were ill at all until a few days ago.'

Edward grunted as he shifted his bulk upon the bed, frowning in irritation that so simple an action weakened him. 'Damnable physics have no idea what to do,' he told me, glaring at nothing as we were alone. 'They would be here now, but I grow weary of their poking and prodding to no effect.' He gestured for me to sit close by the bed on a cushioned stool. 'But that is not why I asked you to come here, cousin.'

When he told me why, all I could do was stare at him in disbelief.

'Me?' I squeaked after a moment. 'Lord Protector?'

The king nodded, blue eyes solemn and a little sad. 'You have been my friend and my advisor, Richard, for all of my years as king; aye, even before I was king. When your own brother turned against me, you did not. You kept your oath to me... though I did not treat you as you deserved. I am sorry, cousin, that I humiliated you in front of the French court.'

By the end of that speech, Edward was out of breath.

I could see that it had cost him dearly, and not just physically. His secret marriage to Elizabeth had been a shock, and my own negotiation attempts in France had been cut down by my very own king and kinsman. This was the first time that Edward had acknowledged his role in that unsavoury business.

'And John...' Edward continued slowly. 'I regret Montagu's death, as he was a good man and loyal.' Here Edward paused, then his hoarse voice continued. 'But, surely, Richard, you understand why I did what I did?' I reached out and took his hand in mine, feeling the unhealthy fever coursing through his flesh, hiding my worry for the moment.

'Of course I understand,' I replied honestly. 'Northumberland was always a Percy holding. I could not convince John to let it go, and he made his own choice in the end. I thank you for your apology, Edward, it means a great deal to me.'

And it did. I would always miss my younger brother, but I had never blamed Edward for John's death. I blamed his wife.

The king's eyes closed in relief and he squeezed my hand with a fraction of the legendary strength he used to have, grateful that I did not hold a grudge against him for Montagu's sake. After a moment, he asked: 'What is your answer, Richard, to my solution?'

'Whatever you want me to do, I will gladly do. But it is only a solution while you regain your strength,' I said, meaning it. 'I am honoured by your trust and confidence in me, Edward.'

A nod was his answer. The king had closed his eyes wearily and was clearly on the verge of sleep.

'Thank you, my king.'

He grunted in acknowledgment.

'Sleep well, cousin,' I murmured as I stood up.

My last words bounced around the room unnoticed, for the king had indeed fallen asleep. I departed the room, my thoughts still swimming in amazement that Edward had named me as The Lord Protector and Defender of the Realm while he was too ill to perform his duties as king.

My smile was inward as I thought how Elizabeth would react to that unwelcome news. With Edward incapacitated for the time being, she would, no doubt, think that she was entitled to complete control of everything as his queen consort.

It had been Elizabeth's interfering that had pushed Edward to reinstall the Percy estates to one of that odious blood, offering my loyal brother a meagre holding in a most unequal exchange. I did not think that Edward had thought of that on his own. John had been a good earl to his people and there had not been any reason for putting the Percy brat back in charge of Northumberland, except that Elizabeth wished to hurt John.

And she had. She definitely had.

I shook my thoughts free of such painful memories and set to solving the current situation. If Edward's healers did not yet know how to help him, it was up to me to keep the government running as smoothly and effortlessly as possible. I was entirely confident in my abilities to do so.

It was a beautiful April day, and if not for Edward's mysterious illness, I was sure that not even Elizabeth Woodville could ruin my day.

☆☆☆

London, June 1483

'Do you remember me, my lord?' the bishop asked me, having gained an audience with me on a late afternoon in June. I had not been expecting a visit from the clergy, nor did I think I had made such an appointment and had forgotten it.

'In a vague way, my lord bishop, if you will forgive my bluntness,' I admitted honestly. The man had been at court during Edward's early reign, but I did not recall him all that clearly. We had had a great many battles to fight in those days, so I was not often at court. 'I do not mean to be rude, Bishop Stillington, but I am busy with the details of the king's coronation. How may I help you?'

In slow careful deliberation, the bishop explained himself.

And an anger that had been long buried resurfaced, and reminded me of other things, of my beloved brother John, who had died all those years ago.

And of a humiliation suffered in front of the French court; a marriage agreement that would never go any further because Edward had already married in secret, while I was pleading his case to King Louis regarding his sister-by-marriage, Bona of Savoy.

To find out that Edward had wed another widow, Lady Eleanor Butler, years earlier and had kept that secret as well? I could not believe it, and yet, knowing Edward, I could.

What a fool Edward had been where it concerned pretty women!

Now, the world was completely turned upside down and as Lord Protector, it was my duty to ensure that our realm did not fall into disaster because of it. It was clear that Bishop Stillington was aware of what he had brought before me.

I focused my attention on my afternoon visitor and the older man met my gaze; wary, yet also hopeful. 'Have you spoken to anyone else about this?' I asked him.

'No, Lord Protector. I thought you should be informed first as you have the legal authority to delay the coronation,' the bishop replied. 'I am completely at your disposal, my lord.'

So, he was leaving it in my hands, to do whatever I felt necessary.

'Bishop Stillington, I think it best to meet again in the morning after I have had opportunity to consider what you have told me. You understand that I must investigate your claim, for I dare not do otherwise. Come back at ten o'clock in the morning and bring any evidence you may possess to prove what you say is true.'

I think he might have been disappointed that I did not accept his story immediately but he nodded and assured me that he would return at the appointed hour with the necessary evidence.

First, I needed to think.

My God, I thought, when the door closed behind the bishop, *this could well disinherit Edward!*

And who, then, would be king?

There was Gloucester, of course. But he had not been trained on how to be a king any more than Edward had been.

Then, it came to me. I was the Kingmaker.

No I *am* the Kingmaker.

I needed to speak with Gloucester. The late king's most devoted and loyal brother would be furious with me if he learned of this in a council meeting. I set aside the work I had planned for the afternoon and turned my thoughts to that meeting.

It was not one I looked forward to.

Westminster, June 1483

'Are you insane?' Elizabeth Woodville wanted to know. 'You think to keep my son from his rightful inheritance?'

'It is not his rightful inheritance, Dame Grey, as you well know and have known for years,' I replied, using the name she held before her clandestine union with my foolish cousin. 'You thought to place a bastard on England's throne, which is treason!'

'My son is not a bastard!' she countered, but I could see that she was scared.

'Your marriage to Edward was not a legitimate one, for he had another wife in Lady Eleanor Butler, and you knew all about it!'

I noticed that she did not dispute that.

Elizabeth meant to leave, but the four guards I had placed at the door prevented it. 'You cannot hold me here!'

Her protest was partially correct. I had no intention of keeping her in her own quarters. 'Here? No, I have other accommodations in mind for you, Dame Grey.'

I gestured to the guards, who immediately strode forward and planted themselves at the woman's side. 'Take the lady to her new residence in the tower.'

She stared at the men as if they had the plague. 'You dare not touch me!'

I nodded and they did indeed dare.

Ordinarily, I did not condone violence against women, but in this instance, I was unmoved when two guards took hold of the former queen by her arms and all four promptly marched her from the chamber. She was still protesting that I could not do what I was doing even as I was doing it. I could hear her cursing my name and my family and anyone who carried the slightest touch of Neville blood in their veins. Well, by the time all was settled, she would have even more cause to curse the name of Neville.

Edward's folly had doomed his own son, which meant the next in line was George's boy, my own grandson, Edmund Plantagenet, Earl of Rutland. His uncle, the late king, had bestowed that title upon his nephew a few years ago, of seventeen-year-old Edmund, who had died at Wakefield with their father, the Duke of York, and for George, who had died under less honourable circumstances; despite their constant bickering, Edward had truly loved his younger brother, and was honestly sad and regretful that Clarence had pushed him to order his execution. Edward had confessed such to me on his deathbed, which brought honesty out of every man in the end.

For my part, I thought it made little difference to England whether the next king was a twelve-year-old or a thirteen-year-old, as they were both minors and would need the same guidance either way. It was personally gratifying that my grandson would be that next king, and that Elizabeth Woodville would finally be thwarted in her endless attempt to grasp and hold all the power she could.

In order to prevent her from marshalling her supporters, I would have to turn them against her through her own actions. And the very person I needed was her brother, Edward Woodville. He was currently residing in Calais, but I still had allies there. I thought I could arrange with Gloucester to exchange one Woodville for another.

Yes, I think that might please the young duke very much. I think that Richard blamed Elizabeth for George's death, and possibly, Edward's death too. I could not prove anything regarding the king's illness, and she only had one neck after all. The charge of treason would suffice to see the deed done.

My mind was clearer now on what I needed to do. And I set off to do it with a firm, confident step, having no second thoughts on the fate Elizabeth had earned for herself.

✭✭✭

London, June 1483

Candles had been lit and there were torches outside in the passageway, offering some manner of light within the windowless chamber. Others might call that narrow slit in the stone walls a window of sorts, but Elizabeth Woodville would not.

Seated in a rickety chair at the small wooden desk she had been allowed, the former queen penned a desperate letter to her brother Edward Woodville.

Brother, why do you not write? she demanded in her urgent plea. *Why have you not come to free me from my unjust imprisonment? Edward, your assistance is greatly needed. Not only for my sake, but for that of your beloved nephew. I have not been allowed to see my children! They do not know how I fare, and I do not know what they have been told. I do not know if they think I am dead! I beg you, brother, for your aid most urgently! Your loving sister, E.*

Elizabeth looked at the brief letter, doubting that it would even reach her brother. The Lord Protector would read it first, and though he would not like the content, there was nothing in it that could be called treasonous. It was a woman's letter, a plea for aid from her closest kinsman, such as any other unfortunate widow would write.

But the widow of King Edward the Fourth was no helpless farm wife.

She would not sit here in the tower and consign herself to her fate, as the Duke of Clarence had done. No, she would not! For all his

115

animosity towards her, Richard Neville thought she was nothing more than a vain, wilful, undisciplined girl who had tricked the king into marriage. She would play upon that false notion and set herself free by her accuser's own hand!

Folding the letter in half, Elizabeth set her signature to it, dribbling a dab of hot wax upon the page to seal it. Her official seal as Queen of England had been taken from her by Warwick, curse the man! "For safety, lady," he had said, as if he cared about her safety! "For when the king takes a wife."

As if the thought of the man had called him to her chamber, Elizabeth was unnerved to see Warwick standing in the doorway, watching her. She had not even heard the door open. Now, she waited for him to tell her what he wanted.

'Since you are in a mood for writing, Dame Grey,' Warwick began. 'Would you write something for me?'

'Your epitaph?' Elizabeth coldly suggested. 'Gladly, my lord.'

Warwick's chuckle was a low, humourless sound and his manner outwardly calm, but his eyes glittered angrily. 'I think your confession might make better reading,' he replied. 'It will also make a difference to whether you spend the rest of your days at Bermondsey as an aide to the good sisters, or whether you are taken to the block.'

He meant to frighten her.

Elizabeth took no pains to hide her disgust for the man. 'I have done nothing that would condemn me to death, my lord, so you may save your threats for those who are guilty of such crimes.'

To her further annoyance, Warwick laughed again. 'You do not consider trying to place a bastard on the throne an act of treason? What would suffice then? Murder?'

'It would depend upon the victim, my lord. Some would not warrant so much as a glance at their rotting corpses,' she replied, turning her back on him to pick up the letter and tuck it into her voluminous left sleeve.

'What is that, Dame Grey?' the Lord Protector demanded, having noticed.

'A letter, my lord,' she admitted. 'I have not yet decided whether to send it.'

'If,' he commented drily, 'it is for your brother, Edward, he will not receive it for a very long time.'

Elizabeth's heart froze for a heartbeat. Was her brother dead? But, no. Warwick would not hold that from her, if only to see her reaction. 'Why is that, my lord?' she managed to ask, even though she wanted to throttle him instead. 'Are you afraid of his hearing the truth?'

'No.' He replied calmly, as if he had not seen the hatred in her gaze. 'Your brother has chosen a different path. He confessed his misdeeds and he has decided to travel to the Holy Land on a pilgrimage to purge his soul of sin.'

'He would not do that unless he does not know I am here!' she protested loudly.

'Oh, he knows,' Warwick replied with a hint of cruel satisfaction. 'You can imagine how distraught he was to learn that you had deceived him in the matter of your marriage. I think he is very cross with you, Elizabeth.' He withdrew a packet from his leather satchel. 'His letter is here. The children wished to write as well—'

'Where are my children, you snake?!' she demanded in a fury, intending to strike him.

But Warwick did not just stand there and let her hit him. He caught her wrists up without any real effort and held her at arm's length. 'Do calm yourself, Elizabeth. Your children are unharmed. They are, however, travelling to Burgundy to stay with their aunt.'

'I did not give my permission for that!' Elizabeth reminded him coldly.

'I daresay, lady, that your permission is no longer required for anything,' Warwick told her. 'Your confession, on the other hand, would be welcome.'

'I have nothing to confess!' she snapped.

Now he gave her a pitying look, as if he knew something she did not. 'Elizabeth, there is a witness to the king's marriage to Lady Eleanor Butler,' he finally said. Then he paused, watching her reaction.

A witness... Elizabeth thought furiously, not looking at him now.

Who? Edward had said there were no others present. Except for the priest— Oh, God. The priest!

'He's a bishop now,' Warwick reported, correctly reading her shocked expression. 'Read your letters first, then send word when you have decided what you will do.'

Warwick left a guard outside the door to relay such a message and turned his steps elsewhere. There was still a coronation to finalise.

Elizabeth tore open her brother, Edward's, letter and began to read. She slowly sank down onto the wooden chair, and with trembling fingers laid it down on the table.

Then, she carefully reached for the other letters, all in a neat little stack with a bright blue ribbon tied around it. Her beloved daughter, Elizabeth, would have done that. After she had read each child's letter, her tears threatened to soil the pages, and she set them aside on the small desk to preserve them.

In a short while, the guard came at her summons and carried word to Warwick on what she would do.

Epilogue: Westminster, 6 July 1483

'You let her go.'

I did not need to turn to see the one who spoke in that quiet voice. 'I had little choice, Your Grace,' I told him. 'If Elizabeth was guilty of treason...'

'So was my brother.' Richard of Gloucester completed my thought, even though his gaze was not on me. 'Where did you send her?'

I watched the heavily laden wagon roll through the city's gate, bound for the abbey where the occupant would live for the rest of her life. 'Bermondsey. But I did not send her there.'

Gloucester looked at me then, puzzled. 'I do not understand.'

'Once she read her brother's letter and the letters of her children, she realized there was nothing else to fight for. She wrote her full confession and I, as Lord Protector, determined that a trial would serve no purpose. None would agree to execute a woman,' I explained to the duke. 'And her son, Edward, believe it or not, did not want to be king.'

'Did he not?' Gloucester was surprised at that. 'From what he told us on the road to Northampton, I would have thought the boy wanted it very much.'

'He was trying to please his mother and his uncle,' I explained. 'He's a good lad, and will do well under your sister's guidance, as will the girls. I suspect Margaret will have young Elizabeth married off before the year is out.'

Richard of Gloucester nodded once. 'She is still the daughter of a king. There will be offers for her hand. Will you leave that to Margaret?'

'The Duchess is a shrewd lady. I think she will do quite well on that account.'

Gloucester nodded. 'Well, cousin,' he said, 'We have a boy who is waiting to become king.'

'And a good king he will be,' I agreed and together we left the chamber for Westminster's great cathedral and for the coronation ceremony of our next king.

I watched the boy sit down with careful deliberation, the crown atop his shining curls not shifting, as he balanced his movements precisely. The spectators erupted in loud, joyous cheers of 'God Save the King!' and 'God Save King Edmund!'

I joined in, of course, dignity and decorum be damned.

England had a king, though he was but thirteen, and would need the guidance of his elder kinsmen, such as Gloucester and myself, to be the ruler we all knew he could be.

Edmund, the firstborn son of George Plantagenet, had the look of his father and Uncle Edward, the late king, but that was where the resemblance ended. Unlike his father, Edmund was not rash and given to impulsive actions that wiser men avoided; and he was not inclined to chase the servant girls like his legendary uncle Edward had done.

No, this Plantagenet had all the charm, good looks and wisdom of his other uncle, Richard of Gloucester, who was beaming as broadly as I'd ever seen him do. As my gaze travelled over the coronation assembly, I was utterly delighted to see that great lady herself seated in the front row, the Dowager Duchess of York, Cecily Neville. Her son's doing, no doubt.

She was elegantly and splendidly attired in murrey and blue and white, a not-so-subtle reminder of her late, beloved duke. Seated beside her on her left and right, my two grandchildren had watched their older brother's coronation with absolute joy on their young faces. Margaret grinned at me and young Edward broke protocol to wave. I saw that their paternal grandmother noticed, but Cecily only sent me a bright smile; I smiled back, nodding respectfully to my own father's younger sister. The Rose of Raby still. I glanced back at King Edmund, and in that instant, I could see Cecily's Richard, the Duke of York, in his young grandson, who was now and forever The King of England.

About Roslyn Ramona Brown

Roslyn has always had an interest in history and in the Wars of the Roses, in particular, and jumped at the chance to write a short story for this publication. Her contribution to this Anthology is her first published short story, *'Of Cousins and Of Kings'*, and she is delighted to be included with so many talented authors in this collection of alternate history tales. Roslyn is a retired US Marine, currently residing in New Jersey, who looks forward to creating future adventures in the realm of alternate history during the Wars of the Roses.

God's Anointed

by
Joanne R Larner

Introduction

When his brother, King Edward IV's, clandestine marriage was revealed to Richard, he seems to have been taken by surprise. He had already sworn allegiance to the young successor, Edward V, and made others do the same. He had got Edward to sign official papers as king, had his coronation robes made, drafted a list of the Knights of the Bath to be created for Edward's coronation and even had coins minted in Edward's name. And, after Stillington's revelation, when Richard was requested to take the throne, he took four whole days to decide. I think this shows he was reluctant to be king, and only accepted out of a sense of duty. But what if he found a different solution?

Also, it seems that there is little evidence for any animosity between Queen Elizabeth and Richard. So, what if she and her family had trusted him and not acted treacherously in taking the prince Edward straight to Stony Stratford instead of meeting Richard at Northampton? What if Anthony Woodville had not tried to ambush Richard's party as seems likely, but had remained on good terms with the Protector?

✩✩✩

121

R ichard, Duke of Gloucester, leaned on the table and took a deep breath, stretching his aching back. There came a familiar knock on the door – he always recognised Francis Lovell's distinctive tap.

'Come,' he called, sitting down and pouring two goblets of Rhenish from the ornate jug on the tray.

Lovell entered the chamber, lowering his head in a bob of deference to the duke. Despite Richard insisting that there was no need for his best friend to make any kind of obeisance to his rank in private, Lovell could not seem to help himself. Richard smiled and offered the second goblet to him.

'Thank you, Richard,' he said, raising his dark eyebrows in appreciation at the wine's quality. 'What is so urgent that it cannot wait until the morrow?'

Of course, he *would* come straight to the point. He had always been a straight talker, one of the main reasons Richard was so fond of him. No flattery, no deception, no calculated self-interest.

'Yesterday, I had a rather interesting, if worrying, visit from Robert Stillington, the Bishop of Bath and Wells. He informed me that my illustrious, late brother was not properly married to the Woodville woman. Apparently, he was already secretly, though legally, wed with another, Eleanor Butler, daughter of Old Talbot, when he married the queen – or technically, not the queen.'

'Jesu, are you serious? Is it true?'

'I am indeed, and aye, it seems so. I need to verify a few things but the Bishop was most convincing and very agitated. This really stirs up a hornet's nest of trouble, Francis.'

His friend frowned and pressed his lips together as he digested this astonishing news. 'So that means all Edward's and Elizabeth's children are illegitimate – including our new king...' He glanced up, his green eyes fixed on Richard's blue ones. 'Christ's blood! That means the rightful king is...!'

'Yes, *I* am. The question is do I want it, Francis? I haven't been raised to be king, never expected it. Young Edward has, although he is yet young. I was content to be Lord Protector and protect his realm for him. Yet an illegitimate child cannot rule, according to law. I shall have to tell Edward he is a bastard, no longer to be king, raise the wrath of his mother and her family. And I am not known in the south, not trusted. It will not be easy, not easy at all.'

'But think of the reforms you could bring in, Richard. You could be a great ruler, the best!'

'You speak as one who is partial, my friend. And as for any reforms, I had hoped to guide the new king and perhaps persuade him to embrace those I would like to see enshrined in law. I would be chief of the Council and I am his father's trusted brother, after all.'

'Are you saying you do not wish to be king?'

'My mind has not yet adjusted to this lightning bolt from the blue. I know not what I wish to do. Nor what I should do.' He raked his fingers through his long, wavy hair. 'A bastard cannot inherit... and yet, he is my brother's son, a fine young man. We spent a goodly number of days with him on the way back from Northampton to London, you and I, did we not? And he is intelligent, considers things well before he speaks and has shown me the respect owed to me. I had always been loyal to his father – how can I betray all those years of duty and devotion? Edward has had him well tutored in the burden of kingship. I have sworn allegiance to him! This news is like a stone tossed into a muddy pond – it will bring all kinds of filth and mud to the surface.' He took a large swallow from his goblet.

'And does anyone apart from Stillington know about this?' Lovell asked.

'He says William Hastings knows, but nobody apart from them and we two. Except perhaps the queen – or should I say, Dame Grey?'

'Then it seems it is your decision to make – Hastings and the queen will be for the boy being king anyway and Stillington has done his duty and reported it; it is up to you how you use the information.'

'Aye, I know. Yet I barely slept last night and I have been turning it over and over in my thoughts ever since I heard – I keep changing my mind on the matter. This is not a decision that can be made lightly.'

'I see that, Richard. And I am positive that you, of all people, will make the right choice.'

'Thank you for your confidence, my friend. But I would be grateful to have your opinion on it.'

'Well, I know you. I have seen how your loyalty to Edward was unwavering, even when you disagreed with him. I know how you hate life at Court, much preferring the peace of the north; you would loathe having to spend so much time here, would you not?' He gave a rueful smile. 'I know, too, you would guide young Edward well in every way. And I can imagine that there would be a fair amount of resistance to you accepting the crown. Also, there is a precedent; there has already been a bastard on the English throne – William, now called the Conqueror. If not for him, many of us would not be here and some might argue he made England the great realm it is today.'

Richard held his gaze, chewing his lip, then sighed.

'Conversely,' Francis continued, 'I know you would be a good king and that you would rule for the common weal – not continue with the self-serving, corrupt system that we have had up to now. I know that the country would benefit from having a grown man, a tested warrior and experienced statesman, as king rather than a young boy, however intelligent he may be. The people remember what it was like to have a minority kingship with old, mad Harry. And would your conscience rest, knowing you allowed a base-born boy to rule the realm?' He tilted his head questioningly, then added: 'But I can tell that you already see both sides of the question and it is for you to decide, not I.'

He sat back in his chair and swigged his wine, watching Richard from over the rim of his goblet.

Richard grimaced and then chuckled. 'Well, you may not have shown a preference for either course of action, but you have, at least, detailed the pros and cons and for that I am grateful. I will think on it some more and let you go back to your duties. You have my thanks, Francis.'

The crowds lined the streets to cheer their new king, arrayed in their best clothes and clutching white roses for the House of York, which they threw into the king's path as he walked barefoot from the Tower to Westminster, where the Archbishop Bourchier waited to anoint him. Cries of 'Long live the king!' and 'God bless King Richard' could be heard as the long, slow procession gradually neared the Abbey.

Inside, the ceremonies began with him confessing and being absolved of his sins so that he came to the throne pure and shriven. It was a long and arduous day, each part of the service meticulously rehearsed so that no mistakes could occur – everything needed to go well for the newly-crowned Richard III, to show that his coronation was approved by God. It had been a worry, but the rites and rituals had all gone off with no mishaps, so perhaps all would be well.

Richard glanced at his wife, Anne, who was by his side, and smiled. It was she who had helped him decide on his course of action after Stillington's revelation. He had gone to visit Elizabeth Woodville in the abbey sanctuary and, when Stillington's name was mentioned, she paled. So, she did know. Before she could protest or say anything at all, he had held up his hand to silence her and told her that she need not worry. That her son would be crowned, despite what the Bishop had told him.

After a long and frank conversation, he had persuaded her that he should remain as Protector of the Realm and help guide Edward. The coronation robes were ordered, a list made of those to be knighted by the new king, coins minted in his name with the Protector's boar etched onto them. Elizabeth came out of sanctuary with her girls and everything seemed to be going smoothly. Until…

✯✯✯

'What is it, Robert? I am run off my feet with the business of this coronation.' Richard shuffled the heap of papers and looked up, tapping his beringed fingers on the edge of the desk.

'Your Grace, I would not disturb you unless it were urgent,' the Constable of the Tower replied. 'But Doctor Argentine is concerned about Edward. As you know, he cut his arm on an arrow while playing in the courtyard with his brother and developed an ague. He has been unwell for over a week and his condition has worsened. He thinks he is about to die.'

'I had better see him and find out first-hand what his doctor says. Do you think Argentine is being overly cautious?'

'Who can tell, my lord? These physicks are strange people. But Edward is at turns burning hot and then shivering, and ofttimes raves in his sleep. In truth I cannot see him being well enough to be crowned on the day decided upon.'

Richard took a deep breath and let it out again in a long sigh. Then he stood and motioned to Robert Brackenbury to lead the way.

When he caught sight of the young prince, he almost gasped. He looked smaller and thinner than he had the last time Richard had seen him. His blonde hair, damp with sweat, was plastered to his forehead and his eyes were red-rimmed and bloodshot.

'Edward?' he said. The boy turned his eyes to meet his uncle's and blinked. 'Can I send for anything to help with your suffering?'

'A... priest, Uncle. I would confess before God takes me.'

'God is not going to take you, Edward,' he said, gently stroking his hand, which was limp and clammy. 'You must fight this off – you are to be king.'

But he could see how ill Edward was and a small voice inside him wondered whether this was a sign from God that he should take the throne himself. If Edward died... but no! It was treason to envision the death of the king, albeit he was as yet unanointed.

Edward breathed his last on June 20th and Richard was crowned in his stead on July 6th.

✫✫✫

On his knees, Richard placed his hands together and the king took them in his, while Richard repeated his oath of allegiance. His nephew, the new Richard III, was even younger than Edward had been and the Protector had hesitated over whether to reveal Stillington's message and take the crown himself, but having met the young Richard again, he remembered how sensible he was, how mature for his age, how like himself at nine. And he loved him.

Elizabeth was reconciled with him now, as was Hastings, and he realised he had no wish to disrupt all their lives for something he didn't really want anyway. It was agreed that he would be the main advisor to King Richard, along with the boy's other uncle, Anthony Woodville, who was a well-educated and cultured man. He had met Anthony at Northampton and, together, they had escorted the tragic Edward into London. He had no quarrel with the Woodvilles and, after much negotiation, his role as Protector was confirmed, along with his place on the Council.

He and Anne could continue their contented life at Middleham, spend time with their young son, Ned, and he would still be a benign and guiding influence on his nephew's running of the country. He would continue to control the unruly Scots for his king, too. The best of all worlds.

He smiled at the young monarch, who returned it. Just then a shaft of light entered the Abbey lighting up the young boy's hair, so that it appeared like a halo.

God approves, Richard thought, as he felt a weight lift from his shoulders.

About Joanne R Larner

Joanne came to be a Ricardian quite late, but she hopes that she has made up for lost time. Richard III helped her to achieve her childhood ambition: to write a novel. In fact, she has now written four, the **Richard Liveth Yet** trilogy and **Distant Echoes**, collaborated on three **Dickon's Diaries** books with Susan Lamb and contributed short stories to several anthologies. Born in London, she now lives in Rayleigh, Essex with her husband, John, and two dogs. Her day job is as an osteopath and she also presents talks to various groups (such as WIs, U3As, Rotary Clubs, etc) on an eclectic mix of subjects, ranging from Richard III (of course!) to Chicken-keeping and Genealogy to Norway.

My Writing Blog: https://joannelarner.wordpress.com/

Amazon page: https://tinyurl.com/2y6ae6jn

Facebook: www.facebook.com/JoanneRLarner

Goodreads: https://tinyurl.com/ju25ca8n

Row, Row, Row Your Boat

by
Sandra Heath Wilson

✫✫✫

*This story has been adapted from one previously published online in the **History Rewritten** blog.*

Introduction

This story sticks more or less to the facts, except that (unfortunately) Bishop Morton lived and continued to conspire successfully against Richard III. Buckingham really did rebel against his cousin the king, he really was unable to cross the Severn because of floods, his army really did desert him, and he really was captured and executed. No one knows what his reason was for rebellion against the cousin who'd rewarded him well. Nor is it known if he intended to support Henry Tudor or take the throne for himself. He was, after all, of more royal blood than Henry could dream.

If Morton had jumped into the Severn that day, things might have been very different, because Henry Tudor's supporters would have been without an arch-conspirer who loathed Richard and was prepared to do anything to bring about his death. That Morton was a man of God is debatable. If you were Lancastrian, yes. If you were Yorkist, definitely not!

✭✭✭

It's October 1483. Imagine the western bank of the flooding Severn, endless rain, relentless gale, pitiless river, one faithless bishop, one hapless army of Welshmen under the Stafford knot...and one hopeless, helpless, feckless, momentarily speechless, Harry Stafford, 2nd Duke of Buckingham, cousin of the new Yorkist king, Richard III. (With apologies to P.G. Wodehouse.)

The furious duke, plump and rather red in the face, huddled in his tugging cloak and gazed at the veritable sea of choppy, mud-coloured water that lacked all sign of the promised fleet of barges. At last he found his tongue. 'You moron, Morton! Where are they? We can't walk on water! Yet. What the feck's the matter with you? Can't you get anything right? This is, after all, your idea!'

'Well, Your Grace, I – '

'Where are all the barges, mm?' Then the twenty-eight-year-old royal duke mimicked the elderly Bishop of Ely's smooth, always reasonable tone. *'Oh, we can't use a bridge, Your Grace, it's too hazardous. Richard's men are everywhere. We'll cross secretly, using barges.'*

'Yes, but – '

'And *that* is the best you can do?' A quivering ducal finger indicated a battered, seaweed-strewn rowing boat that had drifted downstream on the flood and was caught up in the young willows fringing the tidal river. Only, no longer a fringe, for they were at present under water, with only their branches visible.

Dismayed, Morton gazed at the little craft, which would hold two at the most.

Buckingham was livid. 'For Pete's sake, Morton, I've decided not to rebel, but to rally to my cousin the king after all! So I need to be over there, not stuck here like three left legs on a donkey!' The beringed digit now jabbed eastward towards the far bank, where there was an inn – the *Happy Boatman* – with numerous Severn trows tugging at their moorings outside. Trows were splendid vessels, developed solely for this dangerously tidal waterway, but they were of no use to him while they remained on the wrong bank!

John Morton, who resembled a desiccated old fox, saw him move even closer to the water's edge. It was tempting to let the fool tumble in, but perhaps it wouldn't be wise in full view of the fellow's army. 'Take care, Your Grace!'

Buckingham stepped hastily away, but his spur caught on the snake of slimy rope that should have been stretched right across to the far bank for the raft ferry that had long since been swept away. He staggered backward, and winded himself against the trunk of a gnarled old cider apple tree, which he struck with such force that a shower of maggoty fruit splattered down into the soggy Severn clay. He also jarred his back on the numerous pointed folly bells adorning his large leather shoulder purse.

'Plague take it all!' he screeched, jumping around in a fury. He started to snatch off the purse, meaning to toss it aside in a right royal show of pettishness. Then he thought better of it, and to Morton's horror, grabbed *his* purse instead! True aim had never been one of Buckingham's strong points, and instead of flinging the bishop's purse inland, he somehow managed to hurl it into the river instead.

Thunderstruck, the Lancastrian bishop stared as his precious purse swirled and bobbed away downstream on the swift, muddy water.

Buckingham was shocked too. And contrite. 'Oh. I say, Morters, bad luck. I didn't mean it, honest. So sorry. Was there anything important in it?'

The bishop could only stand there, confounded. The purse contained the letter he had spent so long composing and then tricking this idiot into signing! Words failed him. It was bad enough being in Buckingham's custody, without having to endure his brainlessness as well. And to think, the fellow had actually believed for a while that he was destined to take the throne from his cousin Richard III! Sweet God above, Richard could run rings around him without even getting out of bed.

Buckingham realised. 'Oh, lordy, Morters, that's the letter gone west, eh?'

'Another can be written, Your Grace.' But behind the gritted teeth and hastily donned mask of blandness, the plot-riddled bishop was all but spitting feathers.

'Indeed, indeed. I must be sure that Cousin Richard knows I've seen the error of my ways.' Buckingham began to feel a little better about everything. He should never have taken such silly umbrage over what was, after all, nothing much, because Richard now thought he was in rebellion, when it was not so. Well, not anymore.

True, a teensy but temporary thought of such treachery had entered the proceedings, but sanity had returned and the army of Welshmen gathered under the Stafford knot was now going to rally to the king's standards against the expected invasion by the Lancastrian upstart, Henry Tudor. As soon as Richard knew of this noble change of heart, Buckingham was confident he'd hear his dear cousin out and forgive him. They'd soon be chums again.

As for Tudor – or Harri Tydder as he liked to call himself in order to woo the Welsh to his banners – he was nothing without the support of the Stafford knot. His mongrel claim to the throne was iffy to say the least, and he had b-gg-r all chance of defeating Richard on his own. No, no, the Tyddler had never amounted to anything but a useful addition to the Buckingham ranks. That was Harry Stafford's honest opinion. Anyway, it was over with, and all that mattered now was resuming his cosiness with Richard.

Morton's vulpine face remained a picture of mixed emotions. If Buckingham believed an offer of reconciliation was contained in the letter, yet again he proved himself to be eleven eggs short of a dozen. What the letter actually contained, and what this knot-brained Stafford had signed his name to, was a vow of servitude to the Tyddler, whom he, Morton, had decided to put in Richard's place. The bishop closed his eyes faintly. No! He mustn't even think that nickname, for it was what this Stafford fool called the future King of England!

On falling out with the king, Buckingham had first said he wanted the throne for himself, then he said he would help put Henry on it instead, but now he was intent upon crawling back to his royal cousin again. Well, enough was enough. The Tyddler had never intended to back Harry Stafford in anything. Use his support, yes, but support him? No! The bishop closed his eyes again. That damned name just wouldn't go away!

He took a deep, steadying breath. Buckingham was to be isolated, with no chance at all of slipping back into Richard's good books. Hence the letter, which would have found its way conveniently into royal hands. Now a second such missive had to be penned, damn it, and Buckingham tricked into signing it all over again. Oh, this was tedious! And time was short. Richard III was not a man to hang around, hands in pockets, whistling the latest tune, but would be on the move right now. And when he moved, he moved!

Morton managed to respond at last. 'Earthly things are of no consequence, Your Grace. The letter can be replaced. It is to the joys of the Kingdom of Heaven that we must look.'

'That's good of you, Morters. I really should learn to curb my temper. My confessor is giving me management lessons, so when I go back to court, I'll be a good boy at all times. I like it at Richard's court. He has such style. Good singing voice too, although one has to ply him with wine first. They have some damnably good bawdy songs up in Yorkshire, you know. You wouldn't think he had it in him. Oh, I hate being in the wilds of Brecknock.'

'Indeed.' Having been imprisoned at Brecknock by this lout, Morton couldn't help but agree. It was the middle of nowhere. As to Richard III's style, John Morton would as soon strangle the usurping fellow. Well, that was not strictly fair, because Richard hadn't *usurped* anything – the Tyddler would be doing that. Richard had been invited to take the throne because the hitherto candidate was discovered to be illegitimate, as were all Richard's elder brother's children. Edward IV had been a bigamist. Hanky-Panky was his middle name. But that wasn't the point, because the present situation, with the Yorkist Duke of Gloucester wearing the crown, was not to be suffered by Lancastrians worth their salt. Oh, indeed not.

The problem was that Richard was not a man to be manipulated, which meant no juicy plums for the undeserving. Of whom there were many, Morton's good self included. So, it was time for the House of

Lancaster to be top dog again, and that meant the Tyddler. The fellow was no oil painting, nor was he the warmest of souls, whereas Richard – plague take him – was a handsome chap and could be very engaging. Morton sighed. In some ways it was a shame the fellow was a damned Yorkist!

But with the Tyddler safely crowned, who was going to look at his face or worry about how charming he wasn't? No one, Morton prayed, because that face was awful and the Tyddler charm was non-existent. A good deal of spin was going to be necessary to promote him as the new hope of England. Especially as he was sort-of Welsh anyway. There was some awkward doubt about what the hell the fellow actually was. Still, it had to be done. Besides, he, Morton, had been promised the Archbishopric of Canterbury. For that particular plum, he'd plot to put a French ferret on the throne.

Buckingham took a deep breath and ventured to the edge of the riverbank again to look at the rowing boat. 'I suppose I can send two captains across to the inn.'

'I...um...'

'If you've a suggestion, out with it, Morters.'

Morton didn't want *anyone* on the other side of the river now, because he needed to get back to that inn they'd passed on this side, to get His Grace the Buffoon of Buckingham sozzled enough to sign another letter without reading it properly. The bishop cleared his throat. 'I, er . . . Well, perhaps the weather is too bad after all. Attempting to cross will be very hazardous indeed. There's a fine inn back a mile or so behind us, the *Olde Welsh Weasyl*, maybe we should go back there, sit by the fire, have a good meal of fried seaweed and then rest?'

Buckingham shook his head. 'No, no, I want to get my lads over the river. Two captains will . . . No, on the other hand, perhaps *I* should go across. The sight of me, in my highborn splendour, will surely galvanise them all into action. They'll be over here in a trice, and my stout fellows will soon be over *there*.' A highborn forefinger jabbed again.

Morton clutched at straws. 'But, Your Grace, the bore may come at any moment!'

'Boar? *Richard?*' Buckingham's face went pale.

'The tidal bore, the great wave that sweeps upriver twice in twenty-four hours.'

Buckingham's jaw dropped. 'More water? Dear God above. Well, I'll be off over there right now. You can come too.'

'Me? *Row?* Oh, but – '

'A duke *and* a bishop? We'll soon have the prawns eating out of our hands.'

'Pawns.'

'Mm? That's what I said. Prawns.'

Morton gave up, but when he looked at the racing river, and the October murk that was beginning to close in over the late Gloucestershire afternoon, he didn't fancy entrusting his hide to a small rowing boat that didn't look fit for a pond, let alone the Severn in flood. As if to illustrate the lunacy of Buckingham's plan, the tempest blustered even more spitefully, flapping the two men's cloaks around like wild things. To anyone local, that sudden strengthening of the wind would have been a warning of the bore's imminent approach, but our "heroes" didn't know this.

Buckingham's bone-headed mind was made up – for the time being at least – and he squelched back to his army to tell his commanders what he meant to do.

His assembled force of bedraggled Welshmen was fed up to the back teeth with the great Harry Stafford and his dodgy plots, counterplots and counter-counterplots. They didn't like Morton either. In fact, they despised both men, and would far rather be at home by their own hearths. Oh, yes, it was that bad in Buckingham's ranks. There'd already been desertions. If these two irksome Englishmen expected the good men of Wales to cross this demon of a river and risk their lives for *them*, they were very much mistaken. The army rather liked King Richard anyway, because he had more Welsh blood than this Tyddler fellow. So, as soon as the two leaders' backs were turned, the disgruntled army would be off on its toes home to Wales, with suitably insulting farewell gestures and a harmonised anthem of 'Sucks to you with knobs on!'

For the moment, however, it remained where it was, watching as Harry Stafford, Duke of Buckingham, and John Morton, Bishop of Ely, embarked in the wobbling rowing boat. There wasn't room for anyone else, so they had to man the oars themselves and row with all their might. To little avail, as was the case with most of Harry Stafford's notions, because they were immediately washed downstream by the fierce current. Then the heralded bore swept inland as well, and they were driven upstream again, gliding helplessly past the echoingly empty spot where the army had been.

Buckingham was past caring. 'Row, man, row!' he cried desperately, as the bishop caught another crab.

'I *am* rowing!'

'You need rhythm. See? Row – row – row...'

But Morton gave up, shipped his oars and huddled sulkily in his sodden cloak and robes. The thought of jumping into the water and swimming for it was almost too much to resist. Unfortunately, he couldn't swim. If it was the last thing he did, he'd be avenged on Richard for saddling him with this weak-chinned, feck-witted liability.

Buckingham continued to row manfully, but to no avail. They were going to be swept inland all the way to Tewkesbury. Maybe further. Oh, to hell with it. If he managed to get out of this demi-bucket on to dry land again, he'd stick to his original plan and rebel against Richard. Yes, that was it. 'Morton, when we get to an inn, remind me I need to write another letter.'

'Letter, Your Grace?' Morton was filled with trepidation. 'To whom?'

'The Tyddler. To tell him he'll have to rally to my standards after all. I'm going to rid England of Cousin Richard.'

At that point the bishop finally lost it. With a choked sob, he leapt to his feet, almost capsizing the boat, and brandished his fist to the northeast, in which direction he believed Richard to be. Then he howled a vile malediction skyward to his Maker and hurled himself into the welcoming arms of the river. He disappeared beneath the surface, leaving only a thread of bubbles.

Buckingham sat there, gobsmacked. 'I say, Morters, was it something I said?' he enquired as the rowing boat swept on upstream.

The wicked bishop's watery demise was immense good fortune for King Richard III and English history. Even better, without Morton's clever self-interested scheming, the Tyddler's invasion came to nothing. Then the inclement weather caused the would-be usurper's fleet to disappear off the coast of Dorset. No trace of it was ever found, and with it vanished the somewhat dodgy hopes of the House of Lancaster.

In the following decades staunch Yorkists always felt a warm glow of satisfaction at the thought of the two despicable traitors floating in the sea, providing meals for rapacious shoals of hungry but loyal English fish.

Harry Stafford ended up in Cousin Richard's unforgiving hands and paid the ultimate price in Salisbury a month later. He was still changing his mind to the very end. Mid-sentence, even.

The rowing boat, you ask? Well, I believe it's still seen, drifting up and down the Severn with the October tides, looming out of the mist and slipping away again into the murk. Some insist it's only seagulls from the estuary, but others hear a lonely voice calling out in puzzlement.

'Morters? Morters? Was it something I said?'

About Sandra Heath Wilson

Sandra was born in South Wales and brought up in various different places – England, Northern Ireland, Holland, Germany – because her father was in the RAF. Always delighting in historical fiction, and then becoming a firm believer in Richard III, when she was married and at home with a small daughter, she began to write a

137

historical novel of her own. Now, eighty books later, widowed, a grandmother and on her own, she's still writing.

She is also published as Sandra Heath, Sandra Wilson, Betty Machin, Joanie Swift and Sarah Stanley.

You can see her Cicely Plantagenet quartet at:

https://tinyurl.com/379dkdff

Many of her Regency works can also be seen at:

https://regencyreads.com/authors/37

Her titles have been translated into Dutch, German, Polish, Italian and Norwegian.

Amazon: https://tinyurl.com/3mavu55c

Most Untrue Creature

by
Bernadette Lyons

Introduction

Henry Stafford, Duke of Buckingham, was the most powerful and influential man who supported Richard, Duke of Gloucester after Edward IV's sudden and unexpected death and continued to do so when Richard took the crown as Richard III.

Historically, Buckingham rebelled shortly after Richard departed to show himself to his kingdom, as was traditional for medieval kings. With help from storms and floods that devastated the West Country where Buckingham had attempted to raise troops, Richard quickly put down the rebellion; Buckingham himself was captured and executed in Salisbury market place, the king refusing to the last to see or speak to him ever again. He himself described his erstwhile supporter in a letter as 'the most untrue creature living'.

This is my take on what might have happened if the king had decided differently...

☆☆☆

Part One: Under the Blade

Terror. All his life it had been something he caused. Now, however, it had suddenly become an intimate friend, in a way he had never experienced before and had never dreamed would ever be visited upon him.

Oh, there had been moments of uncertainty, discomfort even; when you were the heir to a Duchy and had royal blood in your veins (albeit somewhat diluted), the endless bloody dispute between York and Lancaster was never entirely remote. His own father, Humphrey, Earl of Stafford, had supported Lancaster – a support that had proven ill-advised, as he had fought in the Battle of St. Albans and there received wounds that had reduced him to a semi-invalid, ill-tempered and in constant pain, until three years later the plague finally put him out of his suffering.

He himself, a babe of only two years old at the time, had been a political pawn. Both he and his estates were valuable, especially when two years later his grandfather died and he inherited the even grander title of Duke of Buckingham. The Yorkist king Edward had taken everything under his wing (and doubtless made a handsome profit from having the estates administered by his own escheators!), but saw to it nonetheless that the boy was raised as befitted the rank he would one day inherit. By the time a rich bridegroom was required for one of the Woodville Woman's *innumerable* sisters, Henry Stafford, the second Duke of Buckingham and one of the richest noblemen in the kingdom, was a plum ripe for the picking.

Even now, Henry sneered to himself. Catherine, the daughter of that randy old rake Rivers, a nobody who'd snared a title when he'd crept into the bed of the widowed Jacquetta of Bedford. Even at eleven years old he'd been conscious what a comedown it was for the heir of both an Earldom and a Dukedom to be sold off to the cow-eyed daughter of a *parvenu*. Though it was clearly not advisable to express that opinion to the King or the stunningly beautiful bitch who'd somehow inveigled her way from his well-worn bed to the throne beside him.

140

Witchcraft. He crossed himself. The movement startled the rat which had crept out to investigate the platter of food which had been thrust through the grating in the door, and the rodent fled with a startled squeak.

There had been compensations. Blood clearly told, for his not-so-blushing bride had been indecently eager for her bridegroom to finally consummate the marriage. But for the evidence to the contrary, he'd even have wondered if she'd been able to wait.

The witch must somehow have been aware that he regarded his lowly bride as less than satisfactory, for all that he'd spent enough time dutifully between her legs, siring his heirs with Woodville blood polluting their veins. As a nobleman he was entitled to power and influence, a say in the governance of the realm, and yet somehow Edward had never quite seemed able to find a place for him in his administration. He was in no doubt to whom he owed that particular debt. Catherine had been overly fond of dropping the words 'My sister the Queen' into her conversation, and mentioning how close they'd always been. Possibly if he'd been more adept at masking his contempt for the whole Rivers brood, the Woodville Witch would have whispered sweeter things into her royal dupe's ears regarding him, but marrying a bride with no money, no nobility, no lands, no influence and not even a particularly pretty face had been enough to bear without the mummery of grovelling to her wretched family for the status to which his birth should have entitled him.

But, ah! Revenge had been sweet. Edward had been snatched out of life in his fortieth year (Jesú! Had only seven months passed? It felt like a lifetime... *For you, it may be your lifetime,* whispered the terror.) Henry had acted with decision, partly from contempt for his in-laws and partly out of an opportunist's instinct to earn the trust of the powerful nobleman who would, with his help, become the power behind the throne during the Protectorate that Edward had commanded: Richard Plantagenet, Duke of Gloucester.

They'd had so much in common ... at first. Like him, Richard loathed the Woodville Witch, held her family responsible for his brother's early death. Henry had both admired and gloated as the Duke,

141

finally let loose on the Woodvilles and all their affinity, had gone through them like a scythe at harvest. Catherine had finally fallen silent, aware now who was master in his own household; the Witch had fled into sanctuary, and was no longer in any position to tug on the leash and remind him whose sister he had taken to wife.

But Richard had been so *trusting!* Blinded by grief, hamstrung by loyalty to his dead brother, pathetically thankful for support in a land where he was virtually unknown and little trusted. If they'd been in the North things would have been different, the kerns there worshipped the ground he trod on, but this was London, and whispers ran down the kennels and would not be stilled. Whispers of usurpation and rebellion, and the wrath of God...

Hastings. For all these years his royal master's right hand, now misprized and slighted (as he saw it) in favour of the new king's right hand. Men in Stafford Knots lorded it on the streets, and Catesby saw where his advantage lay. Hastings died and his Woodville go-between Jane Shore did penance as a harlot. It was not every day that a king's whore paraded through the streets; even Henry had been curious enough to attend. In the candlelight her breasts had been exquisite, while above them her face had been that of a weeping angel.

Richard, content with his suppression of the danger and his disapproval of fornication, remained in Westminster.

And then, the thunderbolt struck London. *Bastard slips shall not take root.* Stillington, white-faced and obstinate. Young Edward, never to be king, spitting venom: 'My uncle Rivers was right all along!' The younger of the bastards, seated in a window alcove, watched guardedly.

Henry was a master orator. Given a theme so dear to his heart, he had waxed lyrical, while the citizens of London muttered. But the Lords and Commons snatched at a stable government like men starved of bread, for *Woe to the kingdom that is ruled by a child,* and suddenly Henry was bearing the velvet and ermine train of Richard III, by the Grace of God, King of England.

Support so complete, so timely, so vital surely deserved appropriate reward! The Earldom of Chester was mentioned. Likewise, a betrothal between Buckingham's young daughter Elizabeth and Richard's son Edward.

Edward and Elizabeth ... ill-starred, ill-starred... Men said young Salisbury was sickly, and Anne his mother had never been strong. But Richard himself had been a frail child, if the tales were true, and he had lived and grown strong. If young Edward lived only long enough to sire an heir on his Stafford bride...

Richard, sitting as usual like a secretary amid the mounds of royal account-books. John Kendall, ink-stained and long-suffering. The King's glance up, arrow-sharp as it was whenever his heir was mentioned. 'I think this is for the Council to discuss, Harry. There's the matter of France – England needs allies...'

Harry. A compliment. Richard's private hero, the victor of Azincourt. He dreamed of a second victory, with the Blanc Sanglier flaunting beside the Leopards and Lilies.

True, there was a grant of the vast remainder of the Bohun estates, which 'Harry' had long coveted – subject, the king added, to the approval of Parliament when it next sat. But they were not Chester, and there was no more talk of betrothals; and Henry had been given custody of the reptilian John Morton, taken in conspiracy against the then-Lord Protector and lucky that his Episcopal robes kept his head on his shoulders. Engaged in late-night, confidential conversation, Morton gave it as his considered opinion that so loyal a supporter had been but wretchedly rewarded, and hinted that there were others who would show more gratitude. Especially for one small, but vital, service.

Richard and Anne had gone north. *I leave London in your hands, Harry.*

Brackenbury, Constable of the Tower, could not gainsay the King's authority.

Sometimes, in the night, Henry dreamed...

'On your feet, traitor!'

He must have fallen asleep, though he had not known it. The crash of the heavy door jerked him awake, though for a moment he could not understand who was being spoken to.

143

Lovell. Richard's watchdog. His velvet cloak ruined with rain (yet *more* rain!) and his normally calm brown eyes ablaze.

'Francis!' Life seldom offers more than one chance. The terror that had drawn off for a moment while he walked through the corridors of his past was back full-force, strangling, and in its grip there was no room for pride; only, perhaps, for thankfulness, that his visitor was the one man to whom Richard might still listen.

His chains clinked and rattled as he slithered across the floor on his knees, caring nothing for rank or dignity. Life was sweet, and he had heard the hammers of men working on the scaffold. On several occasions he had witnessed beheadings, and now his inner eye was full of the upswing of the axe, the instant of stillness at the top of its arc and then the downswing with all the executioner's strength behind it.

'Francis – I beg you, hear me out!'

Lovell's lip curled. 'I have nothing to say to you, and nor does His Grace. And there is nothing from you he wants to hear.'

'I was cozened!' Tears sprang to his eyes with very little effort. 'It was Morton – I – he said it was the King's will!'

'Which king? The one you betrayed, or the one you sought to make of the pretender in Brittany?'

'It was for Richard!' How easily the lie fell from his tongue. 'They would have been a threat to him as long as they lived! I did it for him!'

'What a noble act, from my lord Duke of Buckingham! Buckingham the Renegade! Buckingham the Traitor!' He spat. 'Well, my lord, I am come to tell you to make your soul ready to meet God, if it can be done. You have been tried and are condemned. Tomorrow is All Souls Day, and if you can spare a thought from your own miserable skin maybe you will remember those two poor little wretches in the Tower as you die. I will send you a priest after supper.'

'No!' Henry wailed, clawing at the hem of Lovell's cloak while its wearer recoiled in disgust. 'Francis, five minutes with the King! I can serve him, I – I can help him against the Tudor! I have information! Francis, for pity's sake!'

The viscount said nothing, but kicked his hand away and spun back to the door. The violence with which this was slammed after him suggested that if there had been fingers around it they would have been crushed without mercy.

Henry staggered to his feet and clutched at the narrow bars, watching as Lovell's straight back receded down the corridor in the guard's wake, their shadows bobbing monstrously on the damp stone walls.

'If you love the King, Francis, persuade him!' he shrieked. 'I have things he will want to know! I can keep him safe!'

A distant door slammed, and keys rattled. Even the echoes of footsteps were lost.

Outside, the clock in the cathedral's bell tower chimed distantly. The wind gusted, spattering flurries of rain against the wall, and from a nearby alehouse voices rose in raucous song. Presently the walls flung back the sound of hoofbeats.

Henry sagged back onto the cold, flagged floor.

Time was when he had eaten from trenchers marvellously carved with the Stafford knot. Wine from all corners of the known world had danced in goblets of gold on the board before him, and the kitchens had been in a frenzy to produce delicacies at which his guests might marvel. Swans in their perfect plumage, a peacock flaunting its glory, pike and tench and porpoise stewed and served in any sauce cunning could contrive; baked coffyns, gleaming golden in the lamplight, and subtleties fashioned from coloured marchpane to honour lord or guest or saint, depending on the occasion. All along the board there had been flowers in season, anything with colour and scent; Catherine loved flowers. He could feel the press of her thigh against his, warm and amorous. And the music – Richard had been a lover of music. He had spoken of the choristers of York, claiming them unequalled by anything Westminster could produce.

The rat had only chewed a little of the bread. An apple had rolled into the straw, but Henry polished it on his ragged sleeve and bit into it regardless. It was soft, but still sweet. In the South Country – not so far from here – the orchards were famous, though the potent drink they brewed there came between the mind and the legs. He had stolen away, once, when he was being shown his estates, and come across some villagers celebrating harvest. Not knowing who he was, they had made him welcome, and a woman with breasts spilling out of her ragged dress had tipped a mazer against his teeth. He had swallowed perforce, to general laughter, and soon the fire and the stars and the dancing figures had swooned across his sight. Afterwards it had been as much as he could do to make his way back to the manor and slip back into the kitchen and thence to his bedroom, where he lay in a haze of apples and dreamed of fire and a woman's breasts.

There was a stone jug against the wall. It contained ale. Having finished the apple and most of the bread, Henry made his slow way back to the heap of straw.

The jug was almost full. If he husbanded it, there should be some left against the morning. It might give him some courage, at least enough to walk out and face the scaffold, with its scattered straw and the axe half-hidden in it.

The clock was his timekeeper. At each chime, he awarded himself a measured sip. In between, he muttered paternosters and the occasional Ave, and two blood-spattered young faces floated, accusing him.

The clank of the key in the lock startled him. Young Edward gave him a last glare of loathing and Prince Richard stuck his tongue out before they vanished.

It was the priest, come to shrive him; but even as he turned, mustering his sins, the lantern light fell on darkest blue velvet and sable under a cloak of sodden wool.

Presumably Richard would have worn a hat or a hood on the journey hither, but he was bareheaded now, and the face illuminated by the upward gleam could have been chiselled from granite. He no longer looked like the young king buoyed up by hopes of the changes he could make in his realm, the cleansing he could carry out of what he had described as the Augean Stables of the processes of justice. His eyes were as cold as the North Sea in January, and his mouth was a hard, bitter line.

146

'Richard – your Grace!' He pitched forward and pressed his lips to the king's muddy boot. His pulse thudded as wild, desperate hope seized him. Surely now his golden tongue could talk his way off the scaffold after all – Richard had always been willing to listen, always willing to forgive...

'You told Viscount Lovell you had information.' Time was when a nineteen-year-old Richard had had to pass sentence on the men dragged out from Tewkesbury Abbey, having claimed sanctuary there after the Lancastrian defeat. This was the voice of the judge, clear and utterly remote. If he remembered that 'Viscount Lovell' had been 'Francis' in happier days, those days were gone past recall.

'I – I betrayed you, Your Grace.' He risked a glance upward, his face as appealing as he could make it. 'I – I was – I was persuaded. I was a fool. A thankless fool. But Morton – '

'– Was more fortunate than you,' said the stony voice. 'He escaped my justice. You did not.'

Henry swallowed, controlling the urge to piss. 'My lord – Richard –'

'You will address me as 'My lord King.''

'My lord King, I told Lord Lovell I could be of use to you. There is a plot – '

'There are always plots. That is the first thing you learn when you become a king,' replied Richard icily. 'Say on.'

'The Tudor is planning to invade. His ships may already be at sea,' he gabbled. 'I – they told him I would give him my support. If you would only be merciful, I could meet him when he lands...'

'And turn your coat again, like the traitor that you are?'

'I would call it 'returning to my true allegiance'. Your Grace, he has been told to trust me. I can take men, I can pretend to welcome him. How will he know it for a falsehood? Then when he is safely ashore, you can take him, and that will be an end of him.'

'I, too, trusted you once. With my life. With my nephews' lives. And see how you repaid me.' Under the ice, he realised, a terrifying rage was fighting against its bonds. The note of it quivered in Richard's

147

voice for a moment and was fought down again. 'I ride through the streets and hear the whispers. Where are the Lords Bastard? What has he done with them? And now, how can I say they were murdered at your command?

'For who raised you to what you were? I, Richard Plantagenet, King of England. I appointed the man who murdered my brother's sons. Have no doubt that Morton the Fox is spreading that tale already. Christ's Blood, if I lay hand on him again I will have his head from his shoulders, and a pox take the Pope!'

Henry shrank as the rage finally burst out. The king was wearing a sword, and in this mood he might use it.

'Your Grace, once Tudor is taken, the prelate's fangs are drawn,' he whimpered. 'Lancaster is finished. If you spare me, I can serve you...'

'"Lancaster"!' Richard glared at him. 'Speak not to me of Lancaster and Tudor in the same breath! The house of Lancaster breathed its last at Tewkesbury, if the Angevin whelp were truly Henry's getting! This Tudor is a bastard, got on a royal widow by a Welsh knave. The Beauforts would crown a potboy if he claimed his ancestor had been sired on a sheep by old John of Gaunt!'

'They would.' Timidly he raised his joined hands. 'Our Saviour said we should forgive seventy times seven... Your Grace, I beg you! If you will pardon me this once, I swear that never again will I be other than your most faithful servant!'

The king stared down at him through slitted eyes, and for a long moment said nothing. Then, at last: 'In a battle a man must use whatever weapons come to his hand. This crown that men covet so much is a battle without end, and so it seems I must use you.'

Henry drew in a breath, hardly daring to touch hope. He certainly did not dare speak.

'You will meet with the Tudor, and you will convince him you are his good and faithful servant.' The note of terrible irony would have lacerated him if he had had enough pride left to resent it. 'And then, when you have delivered him over to the justice of England I will consider what your fate is to be.'

'Your Grace, I swear to the Lord God you will not regret it!' Instinctively he reached for one of the gloved hands, meaning to cover it with kisses for his reprieve. Instantly the king snatched it back, as though the mere touch of his fingers would soil him.

'Do not mistake my mercy for folly,' Richard snarled, turning to leave the cell. 'And from this day, I am done with mercy. If you play me false, the day will come when you wish you had felt the axe!'

☆☆☆

Part Two: The Blade Strikes

Terror.

Henry Stafford, Duke of Buckingham, sat on his patient courser at the edge of the shingle beach and watched the boat pull slowly closer. The anonymous ship from which it had come sat just offshore, and it was like a bird poised with wings half-lifted, ready to pull away and drive for freedom the instant anyone on board suspected a trap.

Which was precisely what was waiting. And he was the bait, laid out in its jaws, his confident smile and jaunty mien intended to reassure that all had gone exactly to plan.

The Beaufort bastard. It was through his mother that Tudor claimed a right to the throne of England, but all knew that the Beauforts were bastards, descended from John of Gaunt's liaison with his mistress Katharine Swynford. Gaunt's children had been legitimised by their royal cousin (also named Richard), but they had been barred from ever laying claim to the throne. A device that the current claimant had never allowed to deter him for one moment, spurred on by his ambitious bitch of a mother Margaret Beaufort, who cloaked her limitless ambition and far-from-saintly ruthlessness beneath a veil of supposed piety that would overawe an Abbess.

The oars that had pulled the boat slowly in towards the breakers were suddenly stopped and held. A weather-beaten man in his middle years, not known to Henry on sight, balanced one knee cautiously in the prow. 'You are, sir?'

'My name is Henry Stafford, Duke of Buckingham,' he replied, with a proud confidence he was far from feeling. His escort at his back were dressed in his livery, mounted on the matching bay horses it was his vanity they should ride; the bright early morning sunshine glittered on the Stafford Knot on their jerkins and on the pennon fluttering overhead. 'I am here to welcome His Grace King Henry to these shores.'

The other man studied him in silence, not giving his own name. 'And Richard of Gloucester?' he asked at last.

'Dead. Taken in an ambush just outside Salisbury a week ago. He fought bravely enough, but – ' a shrug – 'God's justice was done.' He crossed himself and added piously, for the benefit of the oarsmen, 'His poor nephews' deaths are avenged.'

'He was reported to be moving fast and in strength, when last we had tidings.'

'He was, to begin with. Then God sent the rain. Jesú! How it rained!' Henry's shiver was genuine enough, as he remembered seeing his own army dissolve around him in the downpour. 'Half his army must have been washed away. What was left had lost faith in him. When we attacked, they ran like sheep. My own men cut him down.' He reached into the breast of his jacket and drew out something heavy that glittered. 'If our master requires proof, give him this.'

At a word, one of the oarsmen slipped over the side. The boat was close enough for him to be hardly more than chest-deep, and he waded ashore, eyeing the waiting men warily.

When the breaking wavelets were washing around his knees, he stopped. Henry pushed his horse easily forward a couple of paces, and threw. The livery collar with the white York *rose-en-soleil* on every jewelled link gleamed in the sunshine as it sailed through the air, and the pendant white boar at its base shone.

The oarsman caught it, nodded, and turned to wade with it back to the boat. The man in the prow took it from him before he was hoisted back in, but even before it was in his hands he must have known what it was. An item of such fabulous workmanship would only have been found in the belongings of a Plantagenet prince – or, as he must henceforth be described, a Plantagenet usurper.

'Wait there, my lord Duke. I will show this token to my royal nephew.'

'His kingdom awaits.'

The boat was turned around and began the trip back towards the waiting ship. It was no more than half way there before Jasper Tudor – it could be no other, for the pretender had but one uncle – lifted the livery collar, letting it sparkle, and there was a stir among the faces watching over the side.

Silently, Henry allowed himself to breathe. Inside the elegant embroidered gloves, his palms were wet with sweat.

All around him the beach was peaceful. The sea was calm enough, the sky blue, laced with mare's tail clouds. At the water's edge a few gulls picked at a stranded jellyfish, and a couple of redshank hurried to and fro. Behind him, at the edge of the dunes, there were a few fisherman's huts. Creatures he would hardly have acknowledged as human beings toiled patiently at strung nets, mending the rents; he had ridden past them, glimpsing fearful, sullen eyes in faces burned by the wind to the colour and texture of leather.

They stank.

His horse mouthed at the bit and shifted to stand slack-hipped.

The scarlet velvet between his shoulder blades ached with the anticipation of steel. The frill of marram grass atop the dunes hid archers.

'If you betray me...'

Holy Mary, Mother of God, they were coming. Figures were climbing down the ship's side. The oarsmen who had waited patiently removed the caps from their heads: *Uncover for your king!*

151

The boat pushed off, and backs braced to drive in the oars. There were two new men in the stern of the boat. One was partly shielded by the sturdy figure of his Uncle Jasper (how keenly the treacherous guard against treachery!) but red hair blew from beneath his cap, on which a jewelled clasp gleamed.

Unthinkable, to stand in the presence of his Sovereign Lord, Henry Tudor, rightwise king of England by right of his tainted blood and bastard lineage. Henry knew a single moment of rending temptation to set spurs in his horse's flanks and ride for the surf, screaming out that it was a trap and they should take him on board and set sail for France and safety. But the archers behind him could split a willow-wand at this distance, and doubtless their bows were already bent, the arrows nocked...

Steadying himself as best he could, he dismounted, signing to his followers to do the same. The trembling of his knees was such that it was a relief to kneel, forcing his neck to bend before a man whose claim was infinitely inferior to his own.

The boat rode the waves, and there was the grinding sound of it beaching. Every man in it was now within the range of a child with a bow of crack willow; Jesú, why did they not fire?

The oarsmen splashed over the side and pulled the vessel into shallower water. Unthinkable, for the new king to get his feet wetter than needs be.

Henry heard the sounds of men leaving the boat. The sloshing of legs wading through the surf.

He kept his head bowed subserviently.

Three pairs of boots entered his limited vision. One, even now, a little way behind the others. The sun glinted on drawn steel.

'It seems we have to thank you, my Lord Duke.'

'Aim and LOOSE!' The bawl echoed along the shoreline, scaring the gulls into shrieking flight. Figures rose behind the grass, shaking off sand, arms braced, eyes deadly. The air hissed, and oarsmen keeled over. Some fell into the sea, where they floundered briefly before only the water lent them movement, their bodies bristling with feathered shafts.

The second noble – unknown – was struck in the belly. He folded, clutching the ash, his eyes bulging horror.

The older Tudor was hit in the shoulder. He flung around, pushing at his nephew: *'Run, boy!'*

From beyond the headland, white sails were emerging. The *Trinity*, the *George*, the *Grace Dieu*. At the leading prow Howard's white hair blew in the wind. His breastplate gleamed, though not as brightly as the sword in his hand.

'You *bastard!*' As his nephew churned the sand, seeking vainly for escape, Jasper turned on the turncoat.

Henry had fumbled out his own sword by this time and blocked the downward sweep, his insides somersaulting with glee and triumph and the clutch of honest fear. Red that was not from *Y Ddraig Goch* was staining Jasper's figured velvet, and even as he struggled to recover from the recoil of steel on steel, another shaft thudded home. Blood fountained with a scatter of broken teeth as his lower jaw was smashed, and he fell backwards, writhing briefly on the sand before stilling with a spasm, one arm still pointing vaguely seaward.

His nephew stepped backwards, staring at the body. His face was the colour of a corpse, and Henry looked at him, thinking scornfully what a scarecrow he would have made beneath the crown of England. A scavenger's face, lean and calculating; a miser who would grudge a penny!

'Draw your steel and face me.' From one of the stinking huts a slender figure stepped out. Others followed him, but the November sunlight fastened on the gold about his brow.

'Your life is forfeit, bastard, but I am not minded to sully my courts with your presence. We will have this out here and now, and God will be the judge of who shall wear the crown from this day forward.'

Tudor was unarmed. He bent and pulled the hilt from his uncle's lax hand. 'And if I win?' he asked, forcing a smile.

'Then you take the fruits of your victory.' Richard prowled closer. The boar on his chest savaged the blue velvet. 'At least you will have won it like a man, rather than skulking in the shadows like the coward and knave you have always been.'

Desperate, Tudor lunged. His point was beaten up, the hilt slipping in his hand. Supple as a man two-thirds his age, Richard whirled and struck him across the back with the flat of his blade as he plunged past. The watching nobles applauded as they would have done a skilled blow in the tourney.

Watching, Henry laughed aloud, feeling pardon and freedom slipping into his grasp. After this, what could he not hope to achieve? A brief exile from court might be necessary – a little grovelling, a little penance. Then, stepping back into his place as the foremost noble of the Plantagenet court!

Tudor had been well trained in swordplay, that much was clear. But he had never fought as Richard had fought, never felt the blade searching for his life. He felt it now, as he stumbled and lurched and gasped, parrying wicked strikes and assaying strokes of his own that were beaten away.

The end was never in doubt. Richard toyed with him for a while, studying his chances with narrowed eyes, and then finally chose his moment. He feinted for Tudor's right hip and then at the last moment changed the angle of the blade, slashing upwards with the savagery of Barnet, of Tewkesbury, of a king ending a pretender.

Scarlet sprang across the riven Beaufort portcullis. Tudor's eyes opened in horror. He gasped as the blow opened him from belly to chest, his sword flying wide as he grasped vainly at the bloody things that began spilling out of his body.

He might have tried to say *A priest*, but words would not form. His legs buckled and then he toppled onto the sand.

Richard stepped back. One by one his nobles dropped to their knees in front of him, acknowledging the victory. *Richard of England, King by right of conquest...*

'My lord of Buckingham, you have earned a pardon,' he said calmly, turning his head. 'I revoke the sentence of beheading that was passed upon you.'

'Your Grace – !' Sheathing his sword, he scrambled closer, dropping to his knee and reaching for the hand to kiss.

'Instead, I commute it to life imprisonment in the Tower of London.'

– What?

As the king turned away, Henry was seized from behind and forced to his knees. His arms were grasped and bent behind his back while his sword belt was ripped from him.

'Your Grace!' he screamed. 'Richard, have mercy!'

At that, Richard looked around at him. The expression on the lean face was that of an executioner, the eyes in it harder than blades.

'All my life I have tried to be merciful,' he said coldly. 'I have trusted and been betrayed. Well, the lesson has been learned: a king cannot spare his enemies. And that, my lord of Buckingham, is what you have proved yourself.

Be content with what you have achieved, my lord Duke. You have finally made the king you deserve.'

Without another word he turned back and began walking up towards the path through the dunes.

And overhead the seagulls tumbled against the pale blue sky and cried *'Over! Over!'*

About Bernadette Lyons

Bernadette is a retired civil servant, currently working on a series of fantasy novels. The first of these is available on Amazon, entitled ***The Last Loyalty.***

The Last Loyalty E-book: https://tinyurl.com/ft6kry82

King Henry VII

by
Joanne R Larner

Introduction

Sometimes it is not the actions of man but of chance that decide the fate of men and countries. In this story, the fate of a nation rests on the weather...

I could not help a small, self-satisfied smile as Thomas Bourchier, the Archbishop of Canterbury, placed King Edward's crown upon my head. I could still sense the Holy Chrism with which he had anointed my back, chest, head and hands: I was King Henry VII at last! Finally! After all the years of plotting, of being exiled from my rightful place by King Edward IV, the base-born son of a French archer – at least according to my propaganda machine. I had finally attained my goal and I intend to ensure my reign becomes famed forever and my reputation as a great king endures through the ages.

I rose, being careful not to allow the heavy crown to fall from my head – that would not be a good omen! – and turned to my queen, giving her a smile that I didn't really mean, but I had to keep up the pretence, at least for now. She smiled back at me with equal disdain. We tolerated each other, but neither of us had chosen to be wed to the other; it had been a political match – out of our hands.

'My queen,' I said, offering her my hand. She took it and we, the royal couple, emerged from the Abbey to a great roar from the crowd, although I was unable to discern whether it was a roar of acclaim or disapproval. No matter – I will soon grind the contemptible populace under my heel. I will be a strong king, better than the four or five who have preceded me. But it could so easily have been different...

☆☆☆

I thought back to those terrible times out in the wilderness, exiled, ignored, derided and looked down upon as a man of no influence. It had been by my own wit and cunning that I had risen to my rightful place.

Richard had helped to begin with, my cousin, the Duke of Gloucester and lately King Richard III. I had whispered 'advice' in his ear and he had given me power, influence – he was a good, fair man, but too conscience-driven to be a great king. Not strong enough, not ruthless enough. Although, to be fair, he had shown more than a little ruthlessness towards me, when I made the mistake of attempting to dispose of his nephews, Ned and Dickon, the 'illegitimate' sons of his brother Edward IV. Such a pity the younger whelp, Dickon, had escaped. I heard Richard had called me 'most untrue creature living'. Pah! Loyalty is overrated. Too easily bought. No, fear is the way to rule, as my people will soon see. And his anger forced my decision to rebel, for the sake of the country. England needed strength, not mercy.

Anyway, I heeded the advice of Morton, that perfidious Bishop of Ely, Margaret Beaufort's chief supporter, feigning that I would support Margaret's son, Henry Tudor, to depose Richard. Tudor! He and his mother were deluded if they thought I would support such a weak claim to the throne, when mine was far superior. But I allowed them to think I did, biding my time.

I remember the day that changed my life, the pivotal moment that the dice fell in my favour...

✮ ✮ ✮

'There is going to be rain, my lord,' Morton said. 'Should the Severn burst its banks, your army could become discouraged and desert you and all will be lost. There will be no route through to join up with Tudor.'

'Nonsense!' I replied. 'Don't be so pessimistic. I will beat my cousin, just as we planned, in order to place Tudor on the throne in his place.' I added the last to allay any suspicion that I was seeking my own advancement rather than Tudor's.

And, although there was a mild drizzle, the expected downpour held off and, having crossed the Severn, I met with Tudor on the south-west coast. I bowed to him, gritting my teeth, but patience is a virtue I have long become acquainted with.

We marched on together and met Richard's army at Shaftesbury. Richard fought bravely; I could not help but admire his valour, but I have always found that prudence makes for greater longevity. Tudor and I led from the back and it was our liegemen who died at Richard's hand, before, finally, the weight of our numbers overwhelmed him and he fell, surrounded, but fighting to the bitter end.

As Tudor turned to me in triumph, a relieved grin on his face (he had almost pissed his braies at the sight of Richard charging our bodyguard of soldiers), I smiled my best smile and approached him with respectfully-downcast gaze. The stupid fool thought I was going to offer him obeisance. I, who had more royal blood in my pizzle that he had in his entire body!

Instead, I drew my dagger and thrust it into his throat, before he could even cry out in surprise. He collapsed silently, a look of shock on his gullible face. Blood spurted between his fingers as he grasped vainly at his neck. His uncle Jasper tried to avenge his nephew's death by drawing his newly-sheathed sword again and running at me with a roar. A pity he had spent so much energy defeating Richard's army – he was truly spent and my bodyguard had no trouble dispatching him too. With the head struck off, both metaphorically and literally, the Tudor faction capitulated to me – they had no other choice.

We marched on to London, where I made my claim. Richard, ironically, had paved the way for me. By declaring our nephews illegitimate, there was no one left who was more senior than I was, no-one with such noble blood, apart from Clarence's son, the Earl of Warwick. But he was barred by his father's attainder, thanks to Edward IV. 'Tis always easier when others do your dirty work for you. And he won't last long now I am king. I, Henry Stafford, lately Duke of Buckingham, now King Henry VII.

1496 – The Thirteenth Year of Henry VII's Reign

Why are my subjects so unruly? I have had not one day of complete respite from the constant rebellions, treachery and dissent. I have punished them severely – executions galore, devised by my many torturers – yet still they will not submit. Still the assassination attempts, the plots, the TREASON! Ungrateful curs! I have brought peace to this land, after years of war between my house, Lancaster and York: now York is no more. I have seen to that. Every Yorkist sympathiser sought out and eliminated. For the good of the realm, of course. For peace.

Many were executed after Richard's defeat at the Battle of Shaftesbury: Lovell, Lincoln, Norfolk. But the latter's demise only came after he had 'rescued' Dickon, the younger nephew in the Tower, Richard of York, unfortunately. The only loose end I have never managed to cut off.

My bodyguard perforce surrounds me constantly, for the rabble would tear me apart if they could. They hate me for filling the royal coffers at their expense, but what choice did I have? The king must be seen to be richer than all others.

Even my wife, Katherine, plots against me. She would like to have our son on the throne in my place. She has already tried to poison me, though I can't prove it.

And now, the last straw – I hear of a young man from the Low Countries who claims to be that missing nephew, Richard of York. He inveigles his way into the Courts of Europe, enlisting their support to claim MY kingdom! I fear he is truly the younger of the two boys who ought to have died in the Tower. I curse Norfolk for the hundredth time as I try to convince all that this so-called prince, Richard, is but an imposter – a boatman's son from Tournai named Perkin Warbeck. It was his alias when he was taken there as a child, needing anonymity to escape my clutches – well, now I use it against him. King Richard's sister, Margaret, Dowager Duchess of Burgundy, claims he is indeed her nephew, but all know how she hates me, how she would claim anyone as her kin if it would help her defeat me.

'Sire, a message for you from the North.'

'Yes, Hugh, give it here.'

He handed me a scroll with a respectful bow. It was the seal of Northumberland.

'To my lord, King Henry VII, I greet you well. Alas, the pretender, who claims to be Richard of York, has won over the Scottish king, James, and has even married into the royal family of Scotland, having been given the hand of King James's cousin, Catherine Gordon. Rumours say they are planning an invasion of England soon. I beseech you to hasten north forthwith to defeat them, with my aid, of course. Your loyal and most humble servant, Northumberland.'

'Tis now two months since the pretender invaded my realm, helped by that treacherous bastard, James. I should never have trusted him to keep our treaty. I cannot believe everything has changed so quickly. My army has been routed by their rabble. I say 'routed' – in truth, many of my so-called supporters deserted me. Me! Their rightful king. I am beyond furious. They shall be punished when I regain my throne. I shall have them all hanged, drawn and quartered. I shall make them grovel before me – I shall show no mercy. They have dared to crown the imposter as King Richard IV and his wife as Queen Catherine. And I am once again in the wilderness, exiled, ignored, derided and looked down upon as a man of no influence.

Yet, even if I fail to regain my realm, I still have one thing left to me. I can say I was once King Henry VII of England.

☆☆☆

About Joanne Larner

See after the story *God's Anointed* for Joanne's details.

A Conspiracy Unmasked

by
Bernadette Lyons

✫✫✫

Introduction

The conspiracy between Margaret Beaufort, mother of Henry Tudor, and Elizabeth Woodville, mother of the disinherited Prince Edward, who should have become King Edward V, posed one of the most dangerous threats to Richard III – chiefly because although both of them plotted against him, evidence against them was circumstantial and he was unwilling to execute a woman. He committed the unrepentant and ruthlessly ambitious Lady Beaufort to the care of her treacherous husband Sir Thomas Stanley, who later betrayed him at the Battle of Bosworth; Elizabeth, however, later came to terms with him, committing her daughters to his care and encouraging her stepson – a man Richard heartily disliked, and who was at that time with Tudor in France – to return to England, where King Richard would treat him well (a strange promise to be made by a woman who believed that same king had murdered her sons, his nephews). If the conspiracy had been unearthed earlier, it is likely that Richard would have dealt more harshly with the conspirators and thus quite probably saved his own life. As it was, his gallantry and/or naiveté was his downfall.

✫✫✫

162

'I am sorry. You cannot leave immediately, Master Caerleon. There are some questions we need to ask first.'

Barely three strides from the doorway that would have offered him access to the sanctuary of Westminster Abbey, doctor Lewis Caerleon stared around him at the three men that seemed to have materialised out of nowhere, like demons summoned out of the darkness. 'I – I protest! I am here on lawful business! I have authority to visit!'

He had been around the court enough to recognise Sir Robert Brackenbury, the Constable of the Tower, and the recognition was not reassuring. Brackenbury was a tough soldier, and his face in the torchlight was unimpressed. 'Then, Master Caerleon, you will have no objection to accompanying me to the Tower to answer some questions we have to put to you. If your answers are satisfactory, you may go on your way.'

It did not appear that the physician agreed. He cast a frantic look around as if hoping for some way of escape, but the Constable had laid his plans carefully. Several more men-at-arms stepped out of the shadows, and in the flickering torchlight their faces did not look friendly.

'I am in attendance on Dame Woodville!' he protested. 'His Grace the King is aware of it!'

The heavy face opposite him darkened slightly. 'We are all aware of it, Master Caerleon. Nevertheless, this way, if you please.'

For a moment – just a moment – he contemplated flight. But he was not young and had no weapon, and his only safety lay in being able to bluff his way out of this.

The Tower of London was designed and built to be intimidating. He'd never looked at it without a qualm, even when his activities were entirely innocent. When they became considerably less so – when he was instructed by his patroness Lady Beaufort to facilitate a privy correspondence between her and the still fascinating Dame Elizabeth Woodville, sulking in sanctuary in Westminster Abbey even now – he'd barely been able to bear the sight of those scowling walls as he went about his business.

Now, he would dearly have loved to have had an opportunity to quietly discard the piece of parchment carefully secreted in the hidden pocket of his satchel. It was well hidden beneath the simples and potions of his trade, and a cursory search would not have uncovered it; he was always searched as he entered and left, and so far nothing had ever been found. But as he was pushed onto a borrowed horse and escorted towards the Tower (at one point passing in front of Baynard's Castle, the seat of the House of York's power in London), he couldn't help the terrible feeling that any search that might be carried out in the course of this interview might be very far from cursory. With difficulty he tore his mind from the word interrogation; surely it would never get that far?

But as he rode under the portcullised gateway in those monstrous walls, black against the sky except where the reflected torchlight gleamed on their rain-wet surfaces, his courage shrank. The Tower was a city in itself – not merely a prison, but a royal residence – but despite the fact that much ordinary business went on within it, it had an evil reputation. Even if his conscience had been clear, he would have been afraid; now, his bowels curdled within him and he wished with all his soul that he'd never allowed himself to be inveigled into passing those notes.

He was not reassured by the fact that rather than being taken into any of the houses that lined the inner walls he was conducted directly to the White Tower. The rain that had again started to fall was penetrating even his thick cloak and dripping from the brim of his hat, while his hands were chilled to the bone from clutching the wet reins.

I am innocent. I know nothing. He clung to that even as he mounted the steps.

To a degree, it was the truth. He did not know what was in those letters. But he was quite sure that any correspondence that was written in cipher (he'd once stolen a peep) and so carefully hidden from the eyes of authority was not innocent.

Everything depended on what the authorities suspected. And whether that cunning hiding place was quite cunning enough.

He was escorted to a room, a small bare place containing nothing but a table and a chair. It was cold and damp. Even the single candle burning in a holder on the wall did little to light the room and nothing at all to warm it.

There was a man already seated at the table: John Howard, the newly created Duke of Norfolk and Earl Marshal of England. Caerleon was placed in front of him, a man-at-arms on either side.

'You will now be searched.'

He tried not to follow the satchel with his eyes as it was taken from him and placed on the table. As his clothes were removed one by one, and turned inside out so that even the seams could be checked, he did his best to maintain his air of injured innocence; after all, there was nothing in them to be found. Even his boots were examined, but were blameless of anything save a few splashes of mud.

While the body-search was going on, the duke himself turned out the contents of the satchel. As well as the medicines – Dame Woodville complained mightily of an ague, hearing of which Lady Beaufort had kindly sent her most trusted physician to attend her, or at least that was the tale given out – there were several pages of medical treatises rolled up small, all absolutely innocent even though they looked somewhat suspect. Norfolk unrolled them and studied them carefully, but even he seemed convinced that they were what they seemed to be.

The doctor dared to breathe a little easier...

All of the pouches were opened, the bottles unstoppered. The search was thorough. And it turned up nothing.

For long moments the duke stared at him, unspeaking. Under the thick brows his eyes looked black. The reflection of the candle flame danced in them, twin points of light before the abyss.

Then, as Howard gave a tiny shrug, Brackenbury picked up the documents to restore them to the satchel.

His hand was actually inside it when he paused and drew it out again. And as though in slow motion he laid them down again, took hold of the base of the satchel and pushed it upwards to turn it inside out.

The leather was old and stained, roughened with use. The very bottom of it had an extra layer stitched into the inside for reinforcement. This was almost as old as the bag itself, for medicines sometimes came in heavy bottles and jars and could occasionally leak; but in just one corner the stitching had come adrift.

Nothing showed. His heart kicking in his chest, Caerleon watched the older man peer at it.

Nothing.

Nothing...

The blade of a dagger gleamed. It was as old and weatherworn as its owner, but every bit as sharp too. Its point pried between the frayed stitches that still remained.

The flutter of the candle was louder than the faint rustle of paper. But still, they all heard it.

Only a slight sideways movement was necessary to open the gap wider. Moments later the folded piece of parchment was in Norfolk's hands and being spread to show the neat lines of cipher.

He looked up. His flat black gaze was glittering with triumph.

'It seems we need to talk, Master Caerleon.'

★★★

'The king has not sanctioned this!'

It seemed a long time since he'd shrieked the words. Even then they'd been uttered in sheer desperation, but Norfolk's stare had not changed.

'I will answer to the king. Now, how long has this been going on?'

The dark, smoky ceiling leaned over him. The rough rope sawed against the skin of his wrists and ankles as he struggled, his shoulder joints already starting to ache from the unnatural position. And as yet the pinion had only been turned enough to lift him from the wooden bed and hold him extended. It promised, but it did not deliver.

Yet.

166

He'd seen the whips, the knives, the pincers, the hooks. He could smell the irons heating in the fire. The men employed to use them stared down at him with eyes that measured his resistance and knew how pitifully small it was.

His mouth was parched.

'A – a week only – '

Thud.

One turn of the pinion. Just a few inches. But every joint in his body registered the change.

'A month!' he shrieked. 'The day young Prince Edward should have been crowned – '

Howard leaned closer. 'Hastings was suborned. By whom?'

'The Shore woman.'

'And at whose counsel?'

'I don't know!' This, Caerleon could wail with genuine truth. 'My Lady was remitted to her husband's care after the conspiracy was discovered. But before that, she…'

'Before that, she what?'

There was a creak of wood as someone set a hand to the pinion again.

'She could send messages freely! There were doctors attending Edward, Argentine – he was loyal – '

'Loyal to a Woodville bastard!' Howard straightened up. 'Well, we have people working on this cipher of yours. If they cannot break it, I will have men go into the Abbey and search, and rest assured they will find what they are looking for. 'But in the meantime…' his hard smile gleamed out, 'we have all night to find out what you know.

'Come daylight, I will have a courier go north to His Grace. If you are wise to your own weal, you will still be able to walk out of this place. If not, I still have enough to place your lady under arrest. And depending on what this cipher reveals, I think we will see her head on the block when the king returns to London.'

167

He swooped closer, the Falcon of York with its talons bared. 'And if you would not have yours follow it, Master Physician, I think you had best discover the use of your tongue.'

The Epilogue

It was raining.

It had been raining for weeks.

Buckingham's Water, men were calling it, after the Duke whose plans had been swept away with the flood of the River Severn and who had paid the price of treason on the scaffold in Salisbury market place.

It had swept away Morton's chances of escape too. He was in the Tower. Richard might scruple to execute a priest, but only a fool would wager on the prelate seeing freedom again. However the pope might plead and rage, the king held the keys; and he was no longer the idealistic young knight who had talked of a new era for England.

That man would have scrupled to execute a woman too. But still Margaret Beaufort stood on the scaffold, a plain wooden crucifix in her hands. Her blank gaze stared southward to the grey seas that had swallowed her son's fleet in a storm that men said was yet another sign that the Devil sent foul weather to fight for York. At any rate, Henry Tudor and his hopes were alike ended; and quite suddenly his mother was like a puppet whose strings had been cut, or a child who stares witlessly after a blow to the head.

She had talked too, quite willingly. And the Woodville woman had been sent to a nunnery (rumour said only her eldest daughter's pleas saved her from the same scaffold – Edward had loved her...) and so this was the end. Tomorrow's sun would rise over a weary, war-torn England that could at last draw breath and hope for respite.

At the rear of the crowd, King Richard and his nobles sat their horses, grim-faced and silent. For them, too, this was a turning point. The last Lancastrian traitor, sent to join her son.

There was no wind. The banners hung on their poles, sodden and dark with rain. The sky was overcast.

As she knelt before the block Margaret looked up once, as if hoping to see one more gleam of sunlight. But there was nothing. With a vague smile, she paid and thanked the waiting executioner and submitted to having the blindfold tied about her face; and then, stiffly, bent her head.

The axe flashed up and fell – just once. There was a soft thump of something falling into the waiting basket, and scarlet gushed over the saturated planking, dimpled with rain.

The Duke of Norfolk rose in his stirrups. 'So perish all traitors!' he yelled.

Maybe not all the crowd were convinced. But the spreading blood was the last of Lancaster's, and this was a world where reality was harsh. So first one voice and then another took up the cry, and perhaps most were more grateful than anything else; grateful that the long agony of the Cousins' War had finally come to an end.

And war-weary England could finally look towards the future.

About Bernadette Lyons

See after the story *'Most Untrue Creature'* for Bernadette's details.

Just Desserts

by
Susan Lamb and Joanne R Larner

Introduction

There is a theory that Edward of Middleham, the only son of Richard and Anne, might have been poisoned. His nurse, Ann Idley, had indeed been previously in the household of Margaret Beaufort, Henry Tudor's mother, so Margaret had the means. After their son's death, Richard and Anne were said to have been 'almost mad with grief'. Anne's health had then seemed to decline rapidly, until her own death a year later. Then Henry Tudor, seeing his opportunity, invaded in the August of the same year.

In reality, it was Elizabeth Woodville, Edward IV's queen, who was consigned to Bermondsey Abbey, by Henry Tudor, her own son-in-law.

These were the elements we considered for this story.

Anne gripped Richard's arm like a vice as they stood side by side, gazing out of the window of their chamber in Nottingham Castle. She turned petrified eyes to his, her pale brow furrowing in concern.

'The messenger – it is Piers from Middleham, covered in mud and his horse almost dead beneath him – it must be Edward! You don't think...?'

'Try not to anticipate trouble, Anne, let us wait and see what he has to say.' But Richard's forehead, too, showed deep furrows where his eyebrows drew together in a frown. It must be something serious for Piers to drive his horse so hard in this inclement weather.

He tucked her arm into his and guided her through the chamber door and along the corridor until they reached the audience chamber; the messenger would be brought here.

They had barely had time to seat themselves at the table before an urgent knock came on the door and, with one quick glance at his wife, Richard called: 'Enter.'

The Steward of Nottingham, Geoffrey Haddon, entered, his ever-unruffled expression just the same as usual.

'Sire, Piers Thomson is here with an urgent message,' he said, bowing to the king. He gestured for Piers to come forward and he did so, attempting to wipe off some of the mud from his tunic, before dropping to one knee.

'Your Grace, I have news from Middleham. Your son, Edward...' He hesitated and Anne's already pale face drained completely of colour.

'Well, what is it, man? Spit it out!' Richard rasped.

'There has been an attempt on his life, Sire. Mistress Idley was caught trying to put poison in his bedtime posset.'

Anne swayed and Richard reached out his arm to reassure her.

'Is he well?' he asked, his voice trembling.

'Oh yes, my liege, he is perfectly well, but we thought it only right that the news should be brought to you and your queen immediately. Mistress Idley is in custody in York but it is for you to decide her fate.'

'Has she said anything? She has always been so attentive to Edward. Why would she...?' He shook his head sadly, absently stroking Anne's hand under the table.

'She says Lady Margaret Beaufort is behind the attempt.'

171

Richard's expression hardened. 'It was Margaret who recommended her to us! Now I see she has been plotting against me – against us – for years'

Richard beckoned over his secretary, John Kendall, and dismissed the steward. He told Piers to go to the kitchens for refreshment and began a letter to Robert Brackenbury, the Constable of the Tower in London, with instructions to arrest and question Margaret Beaufort.

☆☆☆

As soon as they could, Richard and Anne made their way to Middleham for an unscheduled visit. Before they had even dismounted, a small figure came flying down the steps leading from the Great Hall and over to them in the courtyard. Normally they might have reprimanded their young son on his unseemly behaviour, but they were both so relieved to see he was alive and well that they let it pass. Edward ran into his mother's arms and she held him close, tears of relief and joy flooding her eyes as she felt his warmth and saw his blue eyes, identical to Richard's, blinking up at her, his lips parted in a happy smile.

'Mama, did you bring me some sweetmeats like you promised?' he said, obviously unconcerned about the near miss he had had.

Richard chuckled, ruffled his son's unruly fair hair and brought out a small parcel from his saddle bag. Edward whooped in delight.

'Thank you, Papa, Mama!' he said. 'May I take it to share with the others?'

'Of course, Edward, I'm sure your cousins will enjoy some,' Richard replied. He looked at his wife and smiled as his lively son ran off to share his loot. 'Well, he seems none the worse. Thank goodness Margaret's plot was foiled. We shall have to reward our loyal staff who spotted Mistress Idley's attempt. By Our Lady, I keep imagining what a state we would be in had she succeeded.'

Anne placed her hand on her stomach. 'Oh Richard, it doesn't bear thinking about. Can you imagine the shock of it – he is such a healthy child, if he had died suddenly…' She faltered and broke off. It was obvious she was also thinking of the child growing inside her. It was well-known that such a shock could result in a miscarriage and this new child was precious too. They had waited so long for another baby, Edward being almost eight years old now.

'I will go on to York tomorrow to oversee the trial of Mistress Idley, but tonight let us enjoy our son and the rest of our extended family.'

Richard referred to his niece and nephew, Margaret and Ned, George's children, and King Edward's two bastard sons, another Edward and Richard, whom Richard had brought secretly from the Tower in London to the north. They had been housed in various places because Richard felt they would be safer if their whereabouts changed regularly. Up until recently, they were at Sheriff Hutton, but Richard had ordered them to be brought here, to Middleham, for his and the queen's return. He wanted all the children to be together for their homecoming. They had not been here for Easter, owing to the requirements of his kingly duties, but they could prepare a feast and entertainments nevertheless. He cherished such times with his family even more now he was king and less able to lead a 'normal' life.

✯✯✯

When Richard arrived at York Castle, which incorporated a prison, he immediately requested to be taken to speak to Mistress Idley. When he entered the cell – as such an important prisoner, she occupied a single cell – he almost didn't recognise the jolly, plump woman whom he had trusted to care for his precious son. She was as pale as milk, her cheeks had grown haggard and her hair, uncovered and long, hung lank and dirty around her shoulders. There were several blood stains on her shift and her eyes were red from weeping.

And well might she weep, Richard thought, as he beckoned her forward. She almost ran to obey him falling down in the dirt at his feet and sobbing.

'Stop your mewling, woman! You know full well what you attempted to do merits far worse than the treatment you have had here. You deserve no mercy, an evil witch like you! God's bones, if Edward had been harmed, I would have torn you limb from limb with my own bare hands.' He found his hands were shaking, almost as if they had a life of their own and were itching to fasten around the woman's scrawny throat. 'I am here to ascertain what part Lady Margaret Beaufort – now Stanley – played in this scandalous deed. And who else might have been involved. Your fate depends on how your answers please me, Mistress.'

He fixed her with his sternest expression and folded his arms as she sank back onto her heels and took a deep breath.

'Sire, as you know, I was in the household of Lady Margaret afore ever I came here, right from when I was a young lass. Both my own son and daughter are still with her. John is a blacksmith on her Woking estate and my daughter, Alys, is a seamstress there. When she sent me here, she warned me that I was still under her command, that if she should call on me to do her a service of some kind, I must do it or my children would suffer.' She paused, taking a shaky breath, her whole body trembling. 'John would be disgraced and turned out and Alys would be married off to a man she hates. The man is violent, Sire. If Alys were to wed him, she would end up dead, like his previous two wives. What could I do, your Grace? I didn't want to harm young Edward, honestly, I didn't and I think I may have deliberately let Matilda see me try to pour the potion Lady Margaret gave me into Edward's bedtime posset. I'm glad I was found out, at least I will go to my death knowing I didn't actually harm him and Margaret thinks I truly made the attempt.'

'Your children will be safe, Mistress. I will see to it that Margaret is arrested forthwith before any possible misfortune befalls them. Who else was involved?'

'I only heard her talking from outside her chamber, but I recognised his voice. I don't like that man; I don't like him at all! It was Bishop Morton, Sire.'

'And you will bear witness to this at your trial?'

'I will, your Grace, and so will one of her maids, Alianora. At the time, I didn't realise what they were talking of, but now it is clear they were discussing how to be rid of you and your line so her son, Henry, could come over and be king.'

Richard's eyebrows shot up at this. He almost laughed, the thought of Henry being king was so ridiculous.

'Mistress Idley, if your story can be corroborated by others – and I *will* ask them – your life will be spared. However, you will no longer have a trusted place in my household, nor will any other nobleman want you.'

Hope lit her eyes for a moment and, just for an instant, she appeared once more to be the kindly woman he had taken on. He didn't wait for any pleasantries – he had to see to it that Margaret Beaufort was justly punished for her part in this plot. And Bishop John Morton, the Bishop of Ely – yes, of course! He called him to mind now and could see him clearly, his eyes always scanning the room as if looking for a lost treasure; he was a shifty and unctuous character. Richard had never trusted him because he knew he fawned his way to positions of power whenever the opportunity arose – he supposed Margaret must have promised him something if he helped her overthrow the Yorkists. What a mess!

☆☆☆

Anne's young son, Edward, looked anxiously through the window of their castle in Middleham as they awaited the return of Richard. His father had told him that a king's lot was not always easy and that one day he would find that out for himself, when he became King Edward V, after Richard's death. He remembered Richard's words: 'Sometimes you will have to make difficult decisions, decisions that will affect not only you, but the whole country.' He hoped his father would not die for a long time; he wasn't ready to be king yet.

Anne sat at the oak table, her tapestry in her hand. Big with child, she shifted uncomfortably in the wooden chair and Elizabeth, her niece, begged her to lie down for a while. She declined.

'I am just a little tired, Elizabeth.' In truth, she was mulling over the last conversation she had had with Richard, before he had left for London...

She had begged him to execute Margaret Beaufort and Morton, when he had discovered their guilt. Apparently, Margaret had done it because she believed she was chosen by God to carry out this heinous crime, so that her own son, Henry, could become king.

Richard had been at a loss as to how to deal with them.

'Richard, you must make her pay the ultimate price,' she had said. 'Do you think she will become a reformed character in a nunnery? Of course not, it will make her even more fanatical and zealous. She will end up bossing the nuns around and acting like a queen. Richard, you must steel yourself to do what is right, and only you can decide what that is.'

'Anne, I know she is as evil as Satan himself, but she is a woman. I am reluctant to kill a woman. And Morton, he is as cunning and sly as a fox, but he is still a cleric.'

He had paced up and down the room, twisting his ring on his little finger, a habit he had when he was struggling to make a decision. Finally, he had stopped pacing and sat down beside her, taking her hand.

'I have made my decision,' he said.

✫✫✫

He called Stanley to him as soon as he reached London, a week or so later. He had received a message that both Margaret and Morton were in custody and Stanley was making a fuss, just as he had the first time Richard had arrested Margaret. Since Stanley was one of the most powerful nobles in the land, having a huge army at his command, Richard had had little choice but to allow Margaret to remain largely unpunished. Not this time though! This crime was unforgiveable.

He informed Stanley of his wife's guilt in the attempted poisoning, calling the maid, Alianora, to bear witness to Margaret's secret whisperings with Morton. Not only that, she had found a half-burnt letter to Morton from Margaret in which she said she would *'get rid of that little brat, Edward. Ann will do it – she knows what will happen to her children if she doesn't.'* Stanley began to open his mouth to protest, but Richard silenced him with a gesture.

'No more chances, Thomas. Her guilt is clear. I have the right to execute her. And Morton. And I can't help but wonder whether you were complicit in this.'

'Your Grace! How could you even think that? I am loyal only to you, my Liege.' Stanley's face had drained of blood at Richard's words. The man was obviously terrified, but was that because he knew he, too was guilty of treason? Or because he thought he might not have a fair trial?

Richard narrowed his eyes, studying Stanley sidelong, his gaze thoughtful. Could he trust him? Well, he hadn't been named among the guilty, but he knew Richard was a just man and so his terror must be from guilt, surely. But having no proof, he could not, in all conscience, punish him for his wife's treason. However, he would watch him closely from now on.

'Very well, Thomas. I have no evidence of your guilt. You will not be punished. You can leave now, but don't expect to see your wife again.'

Stanley's colour rushed back into his cheeks and he mumbled a hurried 'Thank you, your Grace.' He bowed and left the chamber.

✫✫✫

Margaret Beaufort walked into the Abbey at Bermondsey with some trepidation. It was a Benedictine monastery and she felt intimidated by its austere, male atmosphere. There would be no more luxury for her. No comfortable bed, no jewels, no rich food, no good wine... A small tear came to her eye and she blinked it away. At least she had escaped with her life. She could still hear Richard's judgment on her crime of treason. She had trembled as he had stated her sentence.

'I have the right to order you taken from this place and beheaded as a traitor.'

She had almost fainted, but then he had continued.

'However, I am a merciful Lord and I know how pious you profess yourself to be. Therefore, you will be taken to Bermondsey Abbey, where you will have ample opportunity to pray and ask God's forgiveness of your sins. You will never come out from there. There will be no more life of luxury. You will be allowed no visitors nor access to parchment, paper or ink. There will be no more plotting for you.'

Her co-conspirator, John Morton, the Bishop of Ely, was not so lucky. Richard had also declined to execute him but he had a cold, dark cell in the Tower for the rest of his life. He had even pardoned that stupid nurse, Ann Idley. She pursed her lips – Richard was weak. If she had been in his shoes, all of them would have lost their heads.

Now her only hope was that her son, Henry, would still invade, as they had planned. He wouldn't let her down.

✫✫✫

Tudor sat on a chair in his uncle's room and took a sip of the superb red wine provided by the young French king's sister and regent, Anne de Beaujeu. He re-read the letter that had arrived that morning. His mother's plotting had been discovered and she was imprisoned in the Abbey at Bermondsey. Morton languished in the Tower. He let out a deep sigh.

'So, when are you planning to invade, boy, and avenge your mother?'

Tudor sucked his lower lip but remained silent for a long moment, staring at the wall. Then he turned and his gaze met his uncle Jasper's.

'She is stuck in that monastery, Uncle. She will count on me to gather an army, enlist the help of the French king and regent, cross the narrow sea, march against Richard, whose reputation as a formidable warrior is beyond fearsome, defeat him and his band of loyal warriors and rescue her. Then what? I would become king, but who do you think would be the power behind the throne? Mother!' He smiled slowly. 'No, let her stay there in Bermondsey, praying to God and cursing everyone who contradicts her. I think we are well out of it, here in France, free from her constant nagging at last! More wine, Uncle?'

About Susan Lamb

Susan lives in West Bromwich, UK with her husband, Ray, her mom Chris and a black greyhound called Beauty. She has been a loyal Ricardian ever since she read *The Sunne in Splendour* by the late Sharon Penman – in fact she was reading that when Richard III was discovered buried in a Leicester car park!

She is co-author of *Dickon's Diaries*, with Joanne Larner. It is a series of books set in the village of Muddleham, as opposed to Middleham, Richard III's actual home. It's a little bit like the set-up of the film *Brigadoon*. Most people know the tragic but brave ending of Richard III's life, so Susan and Joanne decided to give him an exciting and fun afterlife in Muddleham, with Anne, Lovell and many other fun characters. Book three is coming very soon! But remember you can only cross over when the mist is on Muddleham bridge and don't forget his Jaffa cakes!!

Dickon for his Dames Facebook Group:
www.facebook.com/groups/759076944238959
Dickon's Diaries: https://tinyurl.com/4em9vs7u
Dickon's Diaries 2: https://tinyurl.com/3f83m2s5

About Joanne R Larner

See after the story *'God's Anointed'* for Joanne's details.

The Unwritten Story (Part 2)

by
Maria Grazia Leotta

✫✫✫

B rian was very happy and reading the stories was a pleasure for him. It was time for another break. Maria was determined to speak to the man in black. She was terribly curious now. He was the first one to enter the buffet room and Maria, the second. But, when she went inside, there was nobody there.

'*He probably went to the toilet. He will be back in a minute,*' she thought. '*This time he can't escape.*'

But the man didn't appear and very soon Brian called the participants back for the reading of the remaining stories.

'We are going to read the other stories. I had a terrific idea! I decided to create an anthology of them and publish it. What do you think? Do you want to become Ricardian writers?'

Everyone agreed except the man in black, who was not there.

'Our friend had to go away, but he gave me his envelope and asked me to read his story as the last one.'

Maria was very disappointed but she thought that at least she might discover his name, so she waited for his story to be read, in the meantime enjoying the other stories...

Love Match

by
Terri Beckett

Introduction

His son and heir dead, his wife dying, the king must marry again and get heirs of his body to safeguard the realm. His choices are limited – should he opt for a European princess? Or choose someone closer to home and his heart? History tells us that he had already made overtures to both Joanna of Portugal and Isabella of Spain. He was also to publicly deny the rumours that he intended to marry Elizabeth of York.

The Queen was dying. We all knew that. Even before Christmas, when the first terrible haemorrhage had dyed the breast of her lovely gold-sewn holly-green velvet gown with blood, we knew that for all our wishing, for all the most learned physicians could do, King Richard's beloved Anne was dying.

I remember his face when they told him. He aged ten years in that moment. His face took on a sallow hue, and the lines were graven deeper. It was like looking on a death-mask. And my heart wept for him. Cecily and I, as the eldest Daughters of York, had attended her since we came to Court, and she was a gentle mistress, undemanding. She was almost like another sister to me, so kind and courteous. She

181

liked to have me read to her as she lay in the great bed, saying my voice soothed her. And sometimes, he was with us, and I read from 'Tristan', one of his favourites.

Dr. Hobbes had forbidden him her bed – though in all truth she had been so frail for so long he had not been able to do more than sit by her and hold her thin hand in both of his and talk to her of small matters and try to make her smile. She tried so hard to pretend that she was getting better. But we who attended her, we knew.

'Come spring, lovely, we'll go north,' he promised. 'Leave this pestilential city for the clean air of Wensleydale.'

'I always feel better in the north,' she agreed. 'And spring is so lovely at Middleham.' And he'd make encouraging noises about riding out to see the new lambs frisking with their stolid mothers, and how they'd search for the first violets and the windflowers and bluebells that were her favourite flowers. They both knew that she was never going to leave Westminster.

Dr. Hobbes said it was phthisis, this disease that ravaged a body already weakened by grief at the death of her son. Well, we all mourned the loss of that child, Richard's only heir, but it seemed that his death had broken something inside her.

Perhaps it was her heart. I know mine bled, but it was for him I ached. What did it do to him, to watch her slow decline, watch the woman he loved in this last agony of fleshly decay? I could see it in his face, in his whole being, and when they were together I withdrew as far as I could, because I could not bear it either. It seemed to me that the queen would never die, that we would have to watch her suffering as she fought the inexorable approach of death.

She sent me from the room one time, when she was too weak to even hold a hand of cards. 'Go, Elizabeth. Get some fresh air to put the roses back in your cheeks.' And I was glad to go, to escape the sights and smells and run into the gardens to feel the cold wind on my face, drying the tears I dared not let anyone else see.

'My lady Elizabeth?'

Startled, I swung around. Sir Francis Lovell, the king's boon companion, bowed to me. I curtseyed quickly.

'My lord, I did not see –'

'I did not mean to disturb you, lady, but the wind is chill. The king sent me with your cloak.'

He'd noticed I wasn't there? He'd cared enough to send Sir Francis out to me?

'I thank you, sir.' And the wind was chill, indeed, and I was glad of the cloak's thickness, of the rich marten-fur lining. It wasn't my cloak, I realised, but his, Richard's. It smelled of him, of herbs and faintly of horses. I pulled it close around my shoulders. 'You are kind, Sir Francis.'

'Come inside, lady. The king wishes to speak to you.'

He was waiting for me in the chapel. The air was close with the scent of incense and the faint honey of the beeswax candles. I curtseyed. 'Your Grace wished to see me?'

'Yes, Bessie. I wanted you to know that your care of the queen has not gone unnoticed. I am grateful.'

'It is an honour to serve the Queen's Grace.' I cast my eyes down because I didn't want him to see my expression. 'And to serve you, your Grace. Truly.'

'So formal, Bessie?' he said softly. I felt my colour rise to flush my cheeks, and I was glad of the dimness of the chapel. 'I know how hard it is for you. In the full flowering of your youth and beauty, to be tied to the bedside of a sick woman. It will not be forever. It is time and past time that we thought of marriage for you.'

I thought I might faint. He tugged a ring from his finger, a garnet dully gleaming in the candlelight. He took my hand and slid it onto the third finger of my right hand. 'This, in earnest of my promise to you, Bess. I swore to treat you as my kin. Is there anything you desire?'

I wanted to tell him, then, that I desired only his love. I couldn't find the words. 'I know Bridget would like a kitten, Sire. She had one in Westminster Sanctuary…'

He smiled. I loved to see him smile, it was so rare. 'A request easily met.' He regarded me. 'I could wish to see you more brightly clad, Bess. The gown you wore at our Christmas Court – '

'That was the Queen's gift to me, your Grace.' And it became me well, I knew that. Better than it became the Queen, for it drained her of colour. I had confessed that sin of vanity and done penance for it. Green is the colour of hope.

'She is ever generous, my Anne. Tell Bridget she shall have her kitten.' He smiled again, and kissed my cheek, and was gone before I could stammer out a thanks.

I did not have leisure to speak privily with him again. The Queen was sinking fast, in a delirium of pain, and it was so hard to see. I would catch a glimpse of him in chapel, at Mass, as we prayed for her to be spared more agony. The end came at last on a day when it seemed the sun itself gave up its light and, in the sudden dark, she gave a kind of rattling gasp and coughed and the blood spilled out of her like a tide...

It was horrible beyond description. The doctors came, and her ladies, and I was sent out of the room while they made all seemly. The sun shone again, but she did not see it. I went to the chapel and prayed for her departing soul.

The Court grieved. I hardly saw the king. In desperation I wrote to my uncle Howard, Duke of Norfolk, and poured out my heart to him, thanking him for all his courtesies and friendly offices – he had always been kind to us – and then I begged him to mediate for me with the king, regarding marriage. *'My lord, he is my only joy and maker in this world, and I am his in heart, and in thoughts, in body and in all.'*

Then I begged him to destroy the letter. I did not want my mother to see it. It was too late. She sent for me one evening, and kept me standing in front of her, as if she was Queen still. 'Have you heard the rumour going around, girl? That the king is desirous of a match with you?'

I kept my countenance somehow. 'I place no credence in tittle-tattle, madam.'

'Tch.' She shrugged off my denial. 'He needs a queen, girl, and you are young and from a fertile line, able to bear sons. He could do worse.'

'Except we are uncle and niece, madam.' My throat was so dry I could barely speak. 'There would need to be a dispensation from the Holy Father…'

'It has been sent for, I am told. He has gone to consult with his Council of the North. There would be dissension here, among the old families who were strong in support of the Neville line. He has not spoken to you?'

'No, madam. There has been nothing untoward between us.'

'Well, if you mislike that match, there is another option. You are heiress to the throne. You are the Princess of York, the marital prize of Christendom. There have been offers for your hand. Foremost, Lady Stanley's son. In Brittany. He has sworn a solemn oath, it seems, to take you to wife.'

This I had not heard. And I thought of Lady Stanley's tight little mouth and the gimlet eyes and way she looked at us, and I thought I might vomit on the spot. I controlled myself, however. And carefully, consideringly, I faced my mother. 'I will not thus be married, madam, but unhappy creature that I am, will rather suffer all the torments which St. Catherine is said to have endured for the love of Christ than be united with a man who is the enemy of my family. Nor would the king allow it.'

I turned on my heel, not waiting to be dismissed, and blindly pushed my way from the room. And ran headfirst into Sir Francis. He caught me, steadied me, and seeing my face, led me into the king's privy chamber, dispatching the attendant page for wine. There was a good fire in the hearth. He sat me down and knelt at my feet, plainly concerned. I was shaking, I realised. He poured me wine and made me drink it. After a while I was calm enough to broach the question that was upmost in my mind.

'Is it true, Sir Francis, that the king has announced his intention to marry me?' I was blunt. I knew he would tell me the truth, though. Of all men at Court, I could trust him.

He took the cup from my hand.

'Well, my lady, he must needs have a queen. You know that.' The brown eyes searched mine. I nodded. 'And yes, he has made his wishes plain. Rather an English Rose, he told me, than some foreign chit shipped from God-knows-where for him to wed, will-he-nil-he. The ones he's been offered, like Joanna of Portugal, or a Spanish Infanta – he told me straight he'd liefer have a bride he already knows. And one he loves already.'

'He loves me?' I whispered. My heart beat fast. He smiled at me.

'I've said too much, lady. Forgive me. I will call a page to escort you to your rooms.'

Cecily and I shared a room. She was not there when I entered, and I had my maid help me undress, dismissed her, and got into the big bed. I could not sleep. My mind ranged over the events of the past years.

When my father died, my mother fled the court, not trusting the Lord Protector my uncle. But he was in all things punctilious to do what was right, and met my brother Edward at Northampton to escort him to London for his coronation. Edward did not get that far. We did not know that he had brought plague with him from Ludlow, that his guardian Lord Rivers was deathly sick as well. We were soon to discover it. Stony Stratford was a plague-pit, sorely affected. The young King my brother died there, with only a frightened priest for the Last Rites, gabbling the words through a vinegar-soaked mask, my uncle Richard holding him at sword-point so that he could not flee. He gave all the necessary orders to contain the infection, but it was already in London before he got there. For all anyone could do, my sister Mary died, and Catherine, and my little brother Richard... I wept myself dry in the next weeks. The king was dead, his heirs were dead. Plague is no respecter of rank. England was in turmoil. Parliament turned to the one man of the Plantagenet Royal line who could take up the reins of power.

He had been Lord of the North. Now he was King, and his Anne beside him. But grief had not finished with us yet, when Edward of Middleham died, and again there were no heirs of the Blood Royal, nor would there be from the barren queen.

Richard needed to marry.

He wanted to marry me.

Or so I had been led to believe. But he had not declared himself to me. Nor did he as the weeks past and the land was alive with rumours. Would he be compelled to wed the Portuguese Princess? Or the Infanta? He was King. But he must consider what would be best for England.

I near fretted myself into a decline. I could not eat. I could not sleep. I took the ring he had given me and tied it to a ribbon so that I could wear it about my neck. If he could not marry me, would I have to wed the Tudor?

I resolved that I would go into a nunnery first.

It was Sir Francis who was my saviour. He insisted that I take exercise and walk with him in the gardens or ride out to enjoy the burgeoning summer. There would be a small group of us, and I did not need to pretend a merriment I did not feel, nor did anyone pressure me to be gay. Slowly the summer worked its magic on me, and I began to enjoy myself again.

Then, one afternoon, as the troop of us clattered into the courtyard, we were brought up short by the sight of the king. Suddenly, my companions were gone, and all I could see was him. Sir Francis said something, and the King smiled and replied, and he raised his arms to help me down. I tried to order my grey velvet skirts in order to perform a curtsey, but his strong hands were still on my waist, supporting me. I should have pulled away. I couldn't. I wanted to stay like that for ever, his eyes on mine and the little smile curling his mouth. Sir Francis said something, and the king glanced across at him and said: 'You have our leave, Francis,' and we were alone in the sunny courtyard, the doves croodling to themselves as they sunned themselves on the warm tiles of the stable roof.

'I have been wanting to talk to you, Bess,' he said, 'but I have been much engaged with matters of state. I have today received word that the Holy Father has granted the dispensation I requested. The way is clear, now, for me to ask you if you will consent to wed with me.'

'Your Grace…' I managed to stammer, 'Your Grace does me too much honour…'

'Oh, Bess.' His hand cupped my cheek. 'If you need to think about it… Don't be afraid. We have always been friends, you and I, have we not? Take all the time you need.'

'I don't – I don't need to think about it,' I said quickly. 'Yes, your Grace!'

'Richard,' he corrected.

'Yes, Richard! Yes, I will marry you!' I felt I could burst with happiness. He raised my hand to his lips and kissed it, then kissed my mouth.

'Then we will be wed at Lammastide. I will announce it officially tomorrow. Now I suppose you must needs go inform your mother. I cannot think she will be other than delighted, to be mother of the Queen Consort!'

Privately I thought she would be sick with envy! He released me, and I remembered my curtsey this time, and made for the doorway. And turned. 'Your Grace – Richard… Tell me something? Do you – do you love me?'

He was still smiling. 'We are to be wed, Bess. So, yes. Of course. Whatever love means.'

About Terri Beckett

Married with one son, one grandson and three cats, Terri now lives in North Wales. She has been writing for many years, resulting in two published novels and several short stories in anthologies.

After retiring from twenty years of library work, Terri began to explore the fifteenth century, Richard III in particular. This has led to her current work-in-progress, ***Shadows on the Sun***, an alternative history.

Website: http://kymrukatz.co.uk/
Facebook: https://www.facebook.com/terri

The Butterfly of Bosworth
by
Kit Mareska

Introduction

Many Ricardians dream of having a time machine so they could save Richard from his fate. What if someone actually had one – but all didn't go quite according to plan . . .

✭✭✭

People ask me to predict the Future,
when all I want to do is prevent it.
– Ray Bradbury

Fate and Hope only rarely speak the same language.
– Frank Herbert

The device in Scymon's hand seemed to have a heat of its own – he'd been squeezing, without realising, the casing of the old iPhone 4. Or the Dinofour, as he called it. But that was just its shell. Inside was something far more recent, and more potentially shattering, than anything dreamed up by Apple.

Would he actually be able to bring himself to take a life? That had always been one of the major questions. Even now, standing at the edge of Bosworth battlefield, Scymon didn't know. Which was a big problem. What was the point of all the years he spent researching Henry Tudor's and King Richard's exact locations, recreating the fifteenth-century armour – oh, and the little matter of creating the Time Bender – if he wasn't truly prepared to kill Henry Tudor?

So . . . yes. Of course, he could. That was the only answer. The only reason for all of this.

To right history. And give a good man a chance to rule.

There were solutions other than wading into the thick of battle. He could transport himself to Pembroke Castle and smother baby Tudor in his cradle. Or attack him as he made his way from Mill Bay across Wales. But seeing Richard in his glorious last charge – that was Scymon's personal reward for doing this. Not that seeing the king asleep, or reading his book of hours, or even on a latrine wouldn't have been a thrill. But that moment, when Richard staked his life, his very dynasty, on one slim chance – a moment even his enemies had to admit was fiercely courageous – that was the moment Scymon most wanted to see. That was the moment worth suffering the god-awful burning for.

Heart pounding already, he looked down Fenn Lane towards the used auto sales place where he'd parked his Nissan, not wanting to signal his presence by leaving it on the road. The car looked too new to be there, and he'd left it unlocked, with its key fob under the floor mat rather than risk losing it in the battle. But thieves were the least of his worries.

Keep moving.

The place looked so different in the dark. It didn't help that he purposely chose a moonless night in order to avoid the moon glinting off his armour. But he couldn't come dressed like this during the day, have people think him a re-enactor, have the visitor centre question his presence. It would be daylight once he Bent, anyway.

Dry, firm dirt road beneath his feet, which were clanking and already starting to chafe within the steel, despite his leather shoes. He was no armourer, hadn't enough money to pay a real armourer for a

190

bespoke suit. He'd just cobbled it together from re-enactor sites. It was enough to pass among heavily distracted men but not truly protective. His in-line captive bolt gun, though – that was fully functional. No pitting his hand-to-hand skills, or lack thereof, against an opponent who'd trained his whole life. No bullets to – ugh – retrieve, or more significantly, to be discovered, and no chance of hitting someone by accident. He meant to kill only one man, and not to monkey with history any more than necessary. The drawback – and it was not minor – was that he'd have to get point-blank close to Tudor.

On either side of the road was plain grass now, but back then, much of it had been marsh. Richard had charged down Ambion Hill and his horse became stuck in that marsh, forcing the king to fight his way on foot to the usurper. Scymon left the road, heading north towards Ambion Hill.

He couldn't know, really, the best spot to appear. Where exactly Tudor had stood, watching others die for him. No matter how much research, in the end it was still a guess. Nor did he have any idea what would happen if he chose a spot now that someone else was occupying in the past. Would he land on top of the man? In*side* him?

Nope, nope, nope. Thinking like that won't help. Think about what you do know.

It'll be day.

August-hot.

It'll be loud.

Cannon still firing, maybe.

Men everywhere, yelling, screaming. But, other than the odd word or two, I won't be able to tell what they're shouting. Their English is not my English. Some of it will even be Welsh. Or French.

They'll be real. Not pictures. Not imagination. Some of what I studied will undoubtedly be wrong. Don't be thrown. Just focus on finding Tudor, the standard of the red dragon against the white and green background. He'll stand out . . . somehow. Once he's dead, I can look for Richard.

Air gun in right hand, Time Bender in the left. Can't mix them up. Can't drop either.

He took a deep, shuddering breath.

'I must not fear. Fear is the mind-killer.'

And held down the power button on the Dinofour.

☆☆☆

The first time he Bent, it was just to see if it worked. In his flat, going back only a day. He'd expected to hear a roar, or maybe a rushing, or even a rapid rewind sound. But no: silence. Which left plenty of time to focus on the burning. It started bad, like holding a hand over a candle at the instant the body says, *Too close. Back off.* Except, of course, there was no backing off. And then it got worse. Until his whole body shook with agony. And worse, until he thought he was about to explode, leaving a mess the coroner would never understand. Just when he knew he couldn't take another instant – but not what to do about that – it stopped. His skin wasn't even sunburnt, much less blackened and falling off in hunks.

Like in Dune, *with Paul Atreides and the box of nerve pain induction,* he'd thought. *Except that he, technically, could have pulled his hand out.*

Then he puked, before going to his computer to check the date.

This time the pain was immediately intolerable, as though he'd jumped into a bonfire.

'Fear is the little-death . . . that brings total . . . obliteration!'

He could think no more, other than to become dimly aware that he was screaming at the top of his frying lungs. It went on longer, so long, too long. He was still screaming when he hit daylight.

He didn't land on any people, although he landed less than ten feet from one. The man staggered back, pointing at him, shouting. Scymon understood not a word, and when he made no response, the man crossed himself and fled.

Scymon watched him go, catching his breath. *Real armour – look how well he runs in it! Makes this feel like a Halloween costume.* What am I doing *here?*

Right, right: come to slay a dragon.

More than half a millennium had made a difference to the landscape. Trees he relied upon were no longer there. Others had sprung up. No visitor's centre, of course. And the footing: wetter. Thicker. The marsh extended further than he'd known.

The whole scene, so much louder than expected. Not just human screams but equine. The clang of iron. And steel.

The smell! These men had no deodorant. No daily showers. Only sharp, cutting fear.

Or was that just him?

He retreated several feet to hide behind one of the few trees. After some moments, he spied Tudor's standard bearer, William Brandon, still atop his horse, banner still held high. Which meant that Henry Tudor was close indeed. A surge of excitement made Scymon want to whoop, but then he realised: he was looking at a man who, for certain, had only minutes left to live. This was real. Whatever happened from here on out, he, Scymon, had lived and breathed on 22 August 1485.

He tried to swallow but couldn't. Heard his breath coming far too fast within his sallet.

'I will face my fear. I will . . .'

What was the rest? Usually his recall was excellent. He had known the Litany Against Fear since he was twelve, yet suddenly, when he most needed it, it was gone. He'd read nothing but books about Bosworth and Richard for too long, hadn't reread *Dune* in years. He couldn't just stand and wait for it to come to him, though. Time was liquid. And flowing.

He stepped out from behind the tree, heading towards the dragon standard, only to be nearly run over by a horse and stumble back, cursing the lack of peripheral vision inside his helm. He moved further from the fray, eyes sweeping. Few paid him any attention, perhaps because they saw he held nothing they recognised as a weapon. Or because his armour wasn't fine enough to make him an attractive hostage.

Was he even going in the right direction?

He paused to reconsider and look back. Other pounding riders approached, one carrying a different standard: a white boar, against a blue and red background. Scymon lifted his visor – a terrible idea, but he couldn't help himself. The king was near.

There! *OMyGod, there!*

Thundering not on a white horse but a brown, yet there could be no doubt – the fineness of the armour with its gold trim, but even more . . .

The gold crown atop his sallet.

'Vivat Rex!' Scymon shouted with all his might before he could think better of it. 'Long live the king!'

Whether it was because of the Latin he understood or the English he didn't, the king turned his head in Scymon's direction. Although Scymon couldn't see the eyes within the crowned helm, and although it was only for an instant, he felt their touch, a curious mix of gentleness and power. It felt . . .

Like faith. Like confirmation that everything Scymon had done, and was about to do, was right.

Then the king returned his eyes to his target: William Brandon.

He rose in the saddle, leaning forward.

Another mounted knight in dragon livery, sword drawn, charged the king from behind.

'NO!' Scymon screamed. *'Behind you, Your Grace!'*

This time, he went unheard.

The blow of the dragon soldier caught Richard in one of his only points of vulnerability: the right buttock that was exposed while he stood in the saddle. The Tudor knight's blade pierced Richard's mail skirt – or went beneath it, Scymon couldn't tell.

The king's head flew back, his concentration broken. Yet a half-second later, when his lance shattered against Brandon's throat, the remaining force was enough to bring down both Brandon and his horse.

Having galloped past his opponent, King Richard pitched himself sideways, off his horse.

Of course! He didn't get his horse caught in a marsh. That wound wasn't post-mortem, for humiliation – it was the first! That's why he didn't just use someone else's horse!

And I couldn't save him from it because I never knew.

Scymon sprinted towards the king, then stopped. An unknown man, even unarmed, would never be allowed to approach.

None of the men who knelt around him were recognisable by their faces, but the livery on one – a black engrailed line beneath a black crescent over a silvery-white background – pronounced him Richard Ratcliffe. The Rat.

Scymon, about twenty feet away, stood on the balls of his feet and peered over their shoulders. Then gasped.

The sword was still in Richard.

Was *through* him. Poking out his front. Reddening the grass beneath him.

Richard himself pulled off his sallet. Sweaty-haired, grim-faced, and pale, oh so pale, he spoke an instruction that Scymon couldn't understand. The Rat and another man held the king while a third pulled out the sword.

The king shuddered. Took a moment to collect himself. Then he spoke again, blood seeping from the lip he'd bitten.

Whatever he said, this time, the men shook their heads. Refusing.

Richard's chin thrust, his brow lowered, the iron core of the Plantagenets in full evidence. He spoke far more harshly. Then, unexpectedly, his face softened again, as did his voice. With a gauntleted hand, he touched Ratcliffe's cheek. Managed to smile, and say something that raised a laugh from the men.

That did it. They helped him stand. Blood continued to flow down his leg.

The king took a step, and his mouth formed a puckered O. But it was his eyes that changed the most.

Going into the battle, Richard had said that he would end the day either as a corpse or a king. By the sorrow and the fear – for, yes, that was there, too – in the deep blue gaze, he now knew which it would be.

Scymon knew it, too.

Richard took another hitching step, and though his nose crinkled in pain, he nodded. And drew his sword.

Those around him hefted their weapons as well. Surrounding him, they surged forward. Almost at once, Tudor's men were on them.

And Scymon was running. *Towards* them.

To hell with Henry! I'll grab Richard and bring him into the future. Get him to hospital. Return him to this spot whole and healed.

Not that he knew if he *could* take anyone with him. He had never tried. Never told a soul about the Time Bender.

He dodged men, outright ran from one. Leapt over a body, closing in on the king who had become his sole purpose.

WHAM!

Scymon hit the ground so hard that the Dinofour and the bolt gun flew from his hands. He rolled, saw a small man in an open-faced sallet, his beard so bushy with curls that no visor could have covered it. And something about that, about a little guy with a big beard who fought for Tudor, flickered in Scymon's memory. But he had no time to examine it, for the pale eyes above the dark beard promised that the man meant to kill Scymon.

The gun was closer. Scymon grabbed it, lurched to his feet. The bearded man swung his axe and again made contact, but Scymon barely felt it through his breast plate. He grabbed the beard and wound it around his fist, holding the man tight. The man swung a fist at his jaw, but Scymon shied away, forgetting that his sallet would bear the brunt.

He jerked the bearded head low, brought the bolt gun to the middle of the man's brow and fired.

The little man dropped.

Scymon released the beard, then stood, stunned, for several seconds, watching the oozing red hole he'd made, the pale eyes fixed and staring, before scrambling for the Dinofour. He pulled it from the mud, only to nearly drop it again when the tip of a sword menaced his unshielded eyes.

Without thinking, he slammed the home button.

☆☆☆

He was too stunned even to scream during the return. Just lay on the dry ground, he didn't know how long.

Sobbing.

Who was that? Who was that man I slaughtered?

It made strangely little difference that he'd had no choice.

It made a huge difference that he knew King Richard now.

Not just on paper, or on screen.

For real.

Not just the fierce courage but the determination. The chiding humour. How much younger he looked than his portraits.

I know him. And I failed him.

Scymon cried a while more, then limped towards his car. He didn't know why he was limping – his ribs and back hurt where the axe had struck, but not enough to cause a limp. He just . . . *felt* like limping. So he did. Down Fenn Lane. Still sniffing.

He opened the Nissan's door, sat behind the wheel, tossed the Dinofour and the gun and his sallet into the passenger seat. Reached into the glove compartment for a wad of Burger King napkins, blew his nose and wiped his face.

Blubbering like a baby, for a man I saw – what, three, four minutes? How long was I there?

Doesn't matter. If I didn't love him before, I do now. And he's still dead. Or dead again. Whichever.

I'll go back. I'll get some better armour, maybe a real gun, I'll learn to speak Middle English, and I'll try again.

I'll burn again.

Yes, that too. For him. And for the little man with the big beard.

He gave a final blow and tossed the napkins aside. Then he pressed the ignition button.

Nothing happened.

He pressed again. More nothing.

The button wasn't a button. In its place was a keyhole.

Scymon reached beneath the floor mat for his key fob.

No plastic fob with multiple buttons. Just two keys. The brass one to his flat and a steel key with a black plastic covering on the top that read Nissan.

The entertainment system, too, was different. No more message complaining that it had been unable to establish a Bluetooth connection. There was a thin opening above the radio station buttons for CDs and another, wider opening below it for . . . cassettes?

He had never owned a cassette tape.

Scymon clutched the steering wheel, bowed his head and began to pray. Some time later, he inserted the key and drove home.

He parked in the garage and sat in the darkness, too afraid to get out of the car and trudge up the stairs to his flat. But finally, he did. He had to know what he had done, so he could know what he had to undo.

Slowly, with hands that shook, Scymon undid the buckles and straps that held on the pieces of his armour. When it was scattered all over the floor, he felt lighter. And far less safe.

'I will face my fear. I will . . .' Will what, for pity's sake? Argh!

Of all things to fixate on, given what he'd been through. But if he didn't deal with it, his brain wouldn't let him move on to things that actually mattered.

He went to his bookcase; because he spent so much time staring at computer screens, he preferred to read paper books for pleasure. He pulled out his weathered copy of *Dune*, found the Litany at once.

'*. . . I will permit it to pass over me and through me . . .*'

With that nudge, the rest came gliding back to him so that he spoke it with his eyes closed.

Better. Much better. He closed the novel and returned it to the shelf.

The shelf – something was off. *Dune* didn't usually sit against the edge, it sat in the middle. The Stephen Kings were still there, except for . . . *Pet Sematary*? Why that one?

Scymon started at the beginning. *Fahrenheit 451*, gone, though the rest of Bradbury still there. *Ender's Game*, missing. More fantasy than he had before, including a couple authors he'd never heard of.

Frankenstein, gone. Making sense of *Pet Sematary*, which was really just a retelling of Mary Shelley's story.

Dracula, likewise vanished.

Wait – *Dracula and Frankenstein* – weren't their origins somehow connected?

Come on, Scymon, think, dammit!

A ghost story contest, one rainy summer in Switzerland, that gave rise to both *Frankenstein* and a vampire story that inspired Bram Stoker to write *Dracula* years later. The contest had been proposed by Lord Byron.

Scymon didn't bother re-examining the Bs. There would be no Byron; poetry had never been his thing.

There would be no Byron . . .

That memory flickered again, too strongly to ignore. Byron. Little man with a big beard. Hadn't Henry Tudor knighted some Byron at Bosworth?

199

Scymon's memory was good but not eidetic. That's what computers were for.

He spun towards the opposite wall, where his desk was. And dropped to his knees when he saw it.

His sleek, silver, flat-screen monitor had become a box. A clunky, manilla-coloured box with a corded mouse, a much smaller screen and a . . . floppy disk slot?

He crawled to the keyboard. Woke the computer, which blinked sleepily and greenly at him.

'Come on, come on, give me Google!'

No rainbow-coloured logo. Something called Lycos instead. White against black with a moonlike halo around the O. Seemed a search engine, though. He typed, then retyped to correct the typos, *George Gordon Lord Byron*.

Wait . . . Wait . . .

'Hurry *up* already!'

NO RESULTS MATCH THOSE CRITERIA. PLEASE ADJUST CRITERIA AND TRY AGAIN.

What had been Byron's most famous work? *Childe Harold's Pilgrimage* was the only one that came to him. It produced the same result. No one would ever walk in beauty like the night. Because the Byron of Bosworth was apparently related to the nineteenth-century poet. Who, himself, had fathered . . .

One of the world's first computer programmers.

Scymon didn't know exactly what Byron's daughter had been responsible for – he'd never heard of her until a pub quiz last year – but apparently it was enough to set back the development of computers a good few years. Which meant . . .

'Oh, God! Oh, no! No, no, no!' He repeated it all the way down the stairs and into the garage. The people who would die from lack of better technology! The buildings that wouldn't be built. So many other ramifications that he couldn't begin to wrap his mind around as he ran.

He flung open the passenger-side door, where his sallet, bolt gun and phone still lay on the seat. But it was no longer the Dinofour. It was a flip phone. It worked in 1485 because it was out of its own time then. Must have switched as soon as he landed. And he hadn't noticed because he'd just killed someone. And failed to save a valiant king.

The screen lit when he flipped it open. He dialled 999, the only number he could remember, but didn't press send. It was enough that the option was there. The Time Bender had prevented the Dinofour from functioning as a phone. Which meant that the Time Bender... was no more.

He'd have to start all over. Recreate it. With the new – old – technology.

Sure, and in my spare time, I'll rewrite Dracula *and* Frankenstein, *become bigger than even Stephen King. Do the talk show circuit! Sign autographs!*

Scymon pressed send.

'Emergency – which service?' asked the operator.

All she heard in response was the sound of laughter.

Author's Note:

I had such fun writing this story, in part because, while I'm always writing about the Wars of the Roses, during the pandemic I took a vacation from the 15th century to do a novel about Lord Byron and his tumultuous summer of 1816. This alternative history anthology gave me an unexpected opportunity to combine the two, as well as dabble a bit in science fiction.

In reality, John Byron survived the battle of Bosworth to be knighted by Henry VII and given such lucrative positions as the Constable of Nottingham Castle and Warden of Sherwood Forest. The poet was not a direct descendant of the knight – a great-great (etc.)

nephew rather than a great-great (etc.) grandson – but still such a rise in the family fortunes could have affected Sir John's extended family, not just his own children.

The other alteration in *'Butterfly'* is one I suspect is actually true – that the grievous wound in Richard's backside happened early in the battle, becoming a factor in his death rather than just a cheap shot afterward. I saw this theory presented at the 2020 anniversary of Bosworth celebration, in a video made by reenactor Zac Evans, available on his YouTube channel. Zac came up with this theory independently, only to find that it was a shared suspicion of one of his fellow reenactors. Furthermore, one of the comments agreeing with the video's supposition is from Tim Sutherland, an archaeologist whose paper, *'Killing Time: Challenging the Common Perceptions of Three Medieval Conflicts – Ferrybridge, Dintingdale and Towton'*, convinced me that those three battles took place on one long, single day. So I was really pleased to get the chance to portray that wound happening in this way.

Finally, although they aren't alternate history-related, this story gives a big nod to two others: Ray Bradbury's short story *'A Distant Sound of Thunder'* and Frank Herbert's novel *Dune*. I first read them more than thirty years ago, and they still inspire me.

About Kit Mareska

Kit Mareska is writing a series of novels that centres on the friendship between King Edward IV and William Lord Hastings. She lives outside of Pittsburgh with her husband, daughters and cats. While Pennsylvania is a good place to be, Kit dearly misses exploring castles, eating authentic pub grub and spending time with people passionate about the Wars of the Roses.

Her short stories *'The Play's The Thing'* and *'Let Him Fly That Will'* can be found in the Richard III-themed anthology *Right Trusty and Well Beloved*, and '*With Hasty Speech and Trembling Hand*' appears in *Yorkist Stories: A Collection of Short Stories About the Wars of the Roses*.

Website: https://www.kitmareska.com/

Facebook: https://www.facebook.com/KitMareska

Twitter: https://twitter.com/KitMareska

The Birth of the Renaissance

by
Joanne R Larner

Introduction

Probably the most wished-for change in history for Ricardians is 'What if Richard III had won the Battle of Bosworth?' and that was my motivation in writing my first novel, **Richard Liveth Yet** *– it was the book I wanted to read. Two sequels followed in which I explored in more detail how England and the future might have changed if Richard had won instead of Henry. Just think! No Tudors, no dissolution of the monasteries, no Pilgrimage of Grace, etc, etc. This is the story of that alternative battle, adapted from the battle scene in* **Richard Liveth Yet** *with an additional section added. Please note this novel is not related to the story after this one, which has the same name!*

✭✭✭

22nd August 1485, Bosworth Field

When Richard saw that Lord Howard had fallen, he groaned in frustration – hadn't he warned him not to raise his visor? Idiot! However, there was no time to worry about him now – Howard's men were on the verge of fleeing in panic. He took a deep breath and forced his racing mind to remain calm. He sent two urgent messages to his commanders. One was to Northumberland to reinforce the demoralised men. However, he was doubtful whether Percy would obey, despite Richard having threatened him with dire consequences for disloyalty and promising him great rewards if he stayed true; William Stanley's army was watching from his left flank and Percy wasn't about to commit suicide by crossing in front of it. Richard had found out that Stanley had met with Tudor and was likely to support him if there was any doubt at all of Richard winning the field. If Richard won, Stanley would probably rely on his brother, Thomas's, powers of persuasion to gain forgiveness for his treachery. Richard had to be the winner or all would be lost! His honour, his crown and his very life were at stake.

In any case, he refused to flee like a snivelling, craven coward, perhaps only to end his days under the executioner's axe, or forced to live once again in exile away from his beloved country. No, he would be courageous and execute his defiant charge, attempting to take his enemy by surprise. He would either fail but as the king he was, with honour and courage, or triumph over the upstart Tydder, finally ridding himself of the last Lancastrian pretender.

He still had a few cards left to play. He called his squire over and bade him find out from the scouts exactly where Tydder was positioned. The squire hurried off to do his bidding and Richard turned to his household knights: his loyal followers, his faithful friends and most true lords.

'You can see that the battle is not going as expected – Northumberland is keeping back and Stanley will not commit. We must act decisively if we are to prevail – I will not flee, but will live or die as the rightful King of England. I intend to attack the Tydder directly, a bold, but dangerous strategy. I do not ask you to accompany me; you have served me well and faithfully and I hereby absolve you of further obligation. But I would be pleased to have those of you who will, to support me in this endeavour – who is with me?' he roared, the golden crown shining on his helm and his sword raised in the air.

His huge white destrier, White Surrey, snorted and stamped his hoof, for all the world as if he knew what his master had said. He waited, wondering if he would be forced to do this reckless deed alone. But he needn't have worried – there came an immediate, deafening response from the three hundred or so closest to their Lord.

'À Richard! À Richard! We are with you, Your Grace!'

His heart swelled with pride and he had to fight to contain the emotion threatening to overwhelm him – these men were effectively putting their lives into his hands. They trusted him – yes, they loved him. If he did die today, at least it would be knowing he was loved. At that moment the squire returned and spoke to Richard, pointing over to the east, where it could clearly be seen that a group of mounted men were making their way towards William Stanley's army. The banner of Cadwallader, the Red Dragon, was flying but there were but a handful of men around it. He could see a mounted figure in the centre of the group – it was Tydder. There was no time for delay.

'For England! For St George and for honour!' he bellowed and spurred White Surrey into a canter and then a gallop, not waiting to see whether the men had followed him; for once he had to trust.

White Surrey responded magnificently – he was truly a fearsome beast and the fastest destrier Richard had ever known and he soon outdistanced the men, who had indeed all followed their beloved King. Richard had commanded his blacksmith to double and triple check Surrey's shoes, and he was confident that him losing one was all but impossible. As soon as the enemy group realised what was happening, they seemed to hesitate, as if unsure whether to continue or return to the safety of their army. In that moment of hesitation, Richard galloped madly through the intervening ground, his horse sure-footed and swift. He had sent his scouts on ahead to ascertain where the swampy terrain was and had ensured his route was well away from it. He had his battle axe in his hand, and his helm with the golden circlet atop it shone in the sunlight.

He reached the group way ahead of his entourage and immediately began to hack his way mercilessly towards the Tydder. His way was barred by the huge figure of Sir John Cheney, the giant of a man whom Tydder was using as a bodyguard – what a coward the man was! He didn't allow White Surrey to even break stride, but urged him on even faster and aimed his axe at Cheney's head. The blow missed, but not by much, crashing into his shoulder and chest, injuring his arm and knocking him clean off his horse. Richard galloped on and easily felled Tydder's Standard Bearer, William Brandon, swinging his axe with deadly accuracy, not even stopping to see the colours fluttering down into the mud. He galloped on, slicing limbs and smashing skulls and then he saw that the man he had marked as Tydder could not be him – he was older, much older. With dismay he realised that this was a trap! God's bones! He had not considered that possibility. Tydder was no fool and his general, Oxford, was a wily tactician. They must have counted on him going for a heroic charge, just like his father Richard of York at the battle of Wakefield, who had charged into the enemy in an attempt to rescue his beleaguered household.

He reined Surrey in savagely, the horse whinnying as he slid in the dirt, but he kept upright. Richard's eyes swept the field, searching for the real Tydder. Suddenly the battle seemed to stand still around him and he felt his gaze drawn to a lowly herald, standing in the midst of a group of young soldiers, dressed in a dirty brown tunic and old leather armour. As the man glanced at him fearfully, he saw an uncanny resemblance to Margaret Beaufort, Tydder's mother. It was him! He turned Surrey, with his knees, yelling at the top of his voice:

'Tydder is here! Follow me! À York!'

He swung his axe, felling the enemy guard which had hastened to defend Henry as soon as they realised that their plot was revealed. Tydder was now just a few yards away. He was petrified, Richard could see. And so he should be. He had no armour on appropriate for a nobleman and he was skulking among his servants, trying to hide while his Uncle Jasper, for that was who the decoy must be, was the true warrior. Richard spat on the ground in disgust. His men had, by this time, caught up and he turned proudly, yelling his encouragement to them and then he was face to face with Tydder. He saw the terror in the eyes of the man as he tried to find a horse in order to flee Richard's righteous anger. Richard heard him yell desperately at a passing knight:

'A horse! A horse! My riches for your horse!'

The man rode on, not even recognising the pretender.

'Halt! I command it!' Tydder cried, sounding like a petulant child.

Richard was almost upon him now and he was defenceless. At that moment, he heard a thunder of hooves and wheeled around to see Stanley's forces galloping down the hill to join in the fray. To his horror, he heard the cry 'À Tydder!' begin to sweep across the oncoming men. There was no more time left – it had to be now! He spurred White Surrey forwards in one more swift charge, yelling at the top of his voice, while drawing his sword – his battle axe had become embedded in an enemy's breastplate. Tydder was now fleeing at a run and Richard urged his horse even faster, intent on his prey. White Surrey almost stumbled, but recovered and carried Richard right up to Tydder. But he couldn't bring himself to kill a fleeing man. He was a chivalrous knight, not a murderer. He brought Surrey round Tydder, blocking his escape and Tydder halted his flight – he was gasping for breath. Richard's knights had surrounded Tydder and Stanley's men were still approaching.

Richard ordered his friend, Francis Lovell, to arrest Tydder and he immediately approached him, holding a length of rope. But as Lovell made to take hold of Tydder's arm, the sneaky knave pulled his other hand out of his tunic, holding a dagger, and lunged at Francis, a look of hatred on his twisted features.

Richard acted instinctively to defend his friend. He didn't hesitate, but swept his finely balanced sword around with venomous force in a sweeping arc, taking Tydder's head clean off! The earth became red with the fountain of blood flowing from the headless corpse, which had fallen to the ground with a thud. He leaned down from the saddle and grabbed the Tydder's head, the eyes still frozen in fear.

'The Tydder bastard is dead!' he yelled, his voice hoarse with emotion.

The cries around him suddenly became 'À Richard! À York!', Stanley's men changing their coats even as they arrived at the scene.

'Sire, thank God you have prevailed – we saw your courageous charge and rushed to help – but I see you didn't need it!' said Stanley, kneeling before the bloody but triumphant King.

'Hmm!' muttered the King, fixing Stanley with his cold stare, head slightly tilted.

He turned and saw Tydder's army completely in rout now – he was victorious, as he always knew he would be.

✫✫✫

In his tent after the last remnants of Tydder's rag-tag army had been rounded up, Richard finally felt he could relax. His kingship was vindicated, proven by his victory; God was obviously on his side.

Lovell entered the tent and smiled at his friend and king. 'I would like to thank you, your Grace, for saving my life. And congratulate you on an illustrious victory.'

He made as if to kneel before Richard but the king waved his hand to indicate he should remain standing.

'I know you would have done the same for me, Francis, my friend. I thank the Lord I was in time – if Tydder had…' He lowered his head, his habitual frown creating two lines between his brows.

'Aye, well, he failed in his attempt both at ending my life and your reign. The Stanleys and Northumberland are held under guard – what do you wish done with them, Sire?'

'They will be taken into Leicester and tried for treason. If found guilty, they will face the executioner's axe. As will any commanders left alive from Tydder's men. I have learned the bitter lesson of being too lenient – it is seen as weakness rather than mercy.'

'And Tydder's mother, the Beaufort bitch?'

'I will have her under lock and key for the rest of her days. Likewise, that treacherous toad, Morton. There will be no more second chances. I will have a realm of justice, for the common weal as well as for the rich nobles. I will have a land of culture; I will continue the building works I have begun and commission yet more. England will become renowned for great architecture, wondrous art and heavenly music. And I will have a realm of enlightenment; literacy and education will be encouraged and promoted – for all, not only the privileged.'

'Huzzah! Huzzah! Long live Good King Richard!'

The triumphant king smiled at his loyal friends and hoped his homeland was now safe.

Present Day

'Miss Lambert, could you repeat the essay question we have to do, please?'

'Yes, Daisy, it was 'What date is considered as the birth of the Renaissance in England and why?''

'Thank you.'

Daisy Miller pulled up her laptop and tapped in 'Renaissance, England'. Ah! There was plenty of information to use.

She began her essay: 'The English Renaissance is usually considered to date from the Battle of Bosworth, August 22nd 1485, when Richard III defeated the usurper, Henry Tudor. Once the realm was free of outside threats, he secured the throne by marrying Joana of Portugal, thus uniting the houses of York and Lancaster, ending the Wars of the Roses and bringing peace and prosperity to England. His niece, Elizabeth, married Manuel of Portugal on the same day, and later became Queen of Portugal when Manuel (the Lucky) succeeded his cousin, Juan, known as the Perfect Prince. Joana gave him five children; his son, Richard IV, continued his father's policies and had seven children, ensuring the Plantagenet dynasty was secure, surviving to the present day in the person of Queen Elizabeth II of the House of Plantagenet.

He was renowned for his many building projects, a great proportion of which were religious institutions. He wanted to let more light into the castles and churches and so he commissioned many stained-glass windows in chapels and large oriel windows in secular properties. For example, he completed a beautiful chapel, begun by his brother Edward IV, on the battlefield of Towton, the site of England's bloodiest battle, and paid for priests to pray for the souls of the fallen on both sides.

He also promoted music and dancing, establishing the Royal Choir, comprised of the finest singers he could find from all over the country. It was considered the greatest honour to sing for the king. He was, himself, an accomplished musician and is credited with composing the famous mediaeval song, Greensleeves.

He supported other types of art and design as well, ushering in Renaissance thought and innovation. He became patron to Leonardo da Vinci, whose famous portrait of Richard's wife, Joana, commonly known as *Mona Joana*, hangs in the National Portrait Gallery. Richard commissioned Da Vinci's famous *Last Supper* painting and owned an extensive art collection himself. The most famous portrait of Richard is by the great portrait painter, Hans Holbein, of whom he was also a patron.

He encouraged map-making and exploration, financing Columbus' exploration of the west and the discovery of the New World, Ricardia.

His reign was a turning point in enlightenment, as he promoted trade in printing and books and was the first monarch to encourage everyone, even the poor, to read and write. He had his laws printed in English so his people could understand them and stamped out corruption in the courts.

Richard III is known today as Richard the Just, or Richard the Wise, and his reign is considered the point in history when the Middle Ages ended and the Renaissance began. He ushered in modern thought and is recognised by most historians as England's greatest and most enlightened King.'

About Joanne Larner

See after the story *'God's Anointed'* for Joanne's details.

Richard Liveth Yet
by
Kathy H. D. Kingsbury

✰ ✰ ✰

Introduction

I wrote **'Richard Liveth Yet'** because like so many who are drawn to the historical Richard III's story, I've often found myself wondering what might have happened if he hadn't been killed at the Battle of Bosworth. So I toyed around with various scenarios, and decided on this one in which Richard loses the battle but still survives, leaving open the prospect of further adventures down the road.

I softened Henry Tudor's character a bit, because I simply cannot imagine the real Henry Tudor saying and doing the things I have him doing in this story. St Wynthryth's Priory is a totally fictional place, as are the monks who live there. Sir Owain is likewise fictional, but not Sir Rhys, who I included because he is said to be one of my nineteen-times great-grandfathers. According to family tradition, it was Sir Rhys or one of his soldiers who delivered the death blow to Richard.

22 August 1485 - Redemore Plain near Market Bosworth, Leicestershire

Richard Plantagenet knew that the end was near, but he wasn't afraid. He intended to meet Death head on, fighting until his last ounce of strength gave out. The anger that had overwhelmed him when he realised he'd been betrayed had burned itself out. All that remained was an inner calm and acceptance.

This must be how it was meant to end. First my family taken from me one by one, then my good name, and any moment now, my life.

He only ever wanted to do what was right, but that had never been enough. He recognised the mistakes he had made, but it was too late to correct them now.

Unhorsed, beaten down, his helm gone, he continued absorbing the vicious blows that were raining down upon him. He tried once more to raise his arm, to make one last swipe with his sword, but something struck his wrist and the weapon fell from his hand as he felt the pain of fractured bone. Forced onto his knees, he tried once more to stand but at last his strength failed him. *Not much longer now*, he thought. *So close...so close...*

Someone shoved him to the ground, and he knew the death blow was about to be delivered, but amid the din of battle, someone shouted, 'Cease!' He never knew who it was who shouted, or what he was shouting about, because at that same moment the back of his head exploded with a violent pain that was followed immediately by blackness...and then nothing.

☆☆☆

23 August 1485 - St Wynthryth's Priory, Leicestershire

The sun was low in the sky when Henry Tudor arrived at the Priory of Saint Wynthryth, a small, humble community named for an

Anglo-Saxon saint as obscure as this place that was dedicated to him. Accompanying Tudor was a small retinue, as the fewer people who were even aware of this visit, the better. Among his group of attendants, only two truly knew what was going on – Sir Rhys ap Thomas and Sir Owain ap Gruffydd, Welshmen both who had been knighted on the battlefield yesterday.

Tudor made a point of wearing the crown that had been recovered from the field. He wanted everyone who saw him, whether friend or former foe, to see the proof that the usurper and tyrant, Richard Plantagenet, was dead and he, Henry Tudor, was now king.

But Tudor knew that his opponent wasn't dead. At least not yet.

In the immediate aftermath of yesterday's conflict, Tudor had tasked Sir Owain and Sir Rhys to find a casualty of the battle who bore enough of a physical resemblance to the erstwhile king to pass for him if not looked upon too closely. The knowledge of what they were doing was to be kept to themselves. If they needed assistance, they were to say nothing more than that they were performing a service for King Henry. And so they'd found some poor soul whose name only God knew, who would serve their purpose. That the badge he wore showed he'd served the usurper only made what was to be done that much more appropriate – a foot soldier performing in death one last service for his late master. With the face disfigured just enough to keep the deception from being obvious, arrangements had been quickly made and the corpse taken to Leicester, where even now it was being displayed as that of the man who had called himself King Richard III. Meanwhile, the real Richard Plantagenet, who hung between life and death, was taken elsewhere.

Once inside the monastic precincts, they found it a hive of activity. The complex, hidden away from the outside world and usually a place of quiet contemplation, was today filled with movement as monks bustled about, providing care to the wounded who had been brought to them. Most of the brothers paid little heed to the new arrivals, instead concentrating on performing their assigned tasks, quietly praying as they worked.

An elderly member of the community approached them. This was the Prior, Father Anselm, and he came forward to greet these men about whom the air of battle still clung. Accompanying him was another monk, younger than Anselm but not young, probably in his forties. This was Brother Andrew, the infirmarian.

These men had met with Tudor briefly late yesterday evening, making introductions today unnecessary. What the new king had demanded at that meeting, in the form of a polite request, was more than a little unusual but Father Anselm had complied without question. After all, a man who had an army at his command and who had just defeated God's anointed king wouldn't have any qualms about punishing a small priory that didn't acquiesce. Besides, there had been the promise of a gift of money in return for services rendered, and St Wynthryth's was a poor community.

'You've followed my instructions?' Tudor asked, foregoing any pleasantries.

'Of course.' The prior hesitated briefly, saw the scowl on Henry's face, and added, 'Your Grace.'

'Where is he?'

'Per your instructions, we've housed the patient in a private room, away from the rest of those in the infirmary. As I mentioned yesterday, I assigned Brother Andrew here,' he nodded in the direction of the other monk, 'who is skilled in herbs and healing to care for our...guest.'

'And my other instructions?'

'I have passed along your directives that no one is to speak to the man except Brother Andrew or myself, and only as necessary to treat his wounds.'

Tudor nodded approvingly. 'Very well, then. I will speak to him. Now.'

Father Anselm took a deep breath, concerned at how his next words might be taken. 'I'm afraid that's not possible.'

'Why? Is he dead?'

215

This time it was Brother Andrew who spoke. 'No, Your Grace, not dead, but neither has he regained consciousness. In fact, I am concerned that he may never do so.'

Henry was not to be deterred. 'I want to see him all the same.'

Father Anselm gestured. 'If you will follow me, then.'

When they reached the door to the room, Tudor turned to his knights. 'You two, stay here. I will speak to our *guest* alone. The same for you as well,' he said to the monks, who accepted such behaviour with good grace. Sir Owain, on the other hand, made ready to open his mouth to object, his curiosity as to what the new king had in mind momentarily overcoming his common sense, but Sir Rhys gave him a sharp look, then turned to Tudor.

'Yes, Your Grace.'

Tudor looked around the small, dim room, its lone window shuttered to keep out the light that might otherwise disturb the patient. His nose twitched at the sick-room smell that permeated everything – the pungent aroma of herbs and salves combined with other less fragrant odours. He shut the door tight behind him. The words he had to say were for Plantagenet's ears only, whether or not the other man could hear them.

He scanned the simply furnished room, looking for something to sit on. Spotting a chair by the small table, he pulled it to the bedside and sat down. For several minutes he simply stared at the form on the bed, blankets covering him in spite of the August heat.

Richard was lying on his left side with pillows propped alongside to keep him from rolling onto his back and putting pressure on his injured head, which was swathed in bandages. A dark smudge where blood had seeped through contrasted sharply with the white cloth. Someone had dressed him in a simple robe (Henry wondered which monk had generously given his to their patient) but evidence of bruising was still visible and he lay so still that if it weren't for the faint rise and fall of his chest, Tudor might have thought him dead.

216

It was obvious that the right side of the king's body…no, the *tyrant's* body, he corrected himself…had taken the brunt of the attack. His face bore numerous cuts and bruises, and his right eye was so swollen that even if he were to wake up, Tudor doubted he would be able to open it. His right arm, his sword arm, rested on a pillow, the broken wrist now set and wrapped, immobilised with splints and a cast made using flour and egg whites. Tudor suspected that if he could see the rest of Richard's body, he would find it equally bruised and battered. Armour only protects so much, he mused, and his opponent had been subjected to a savage attack once he'd been unhorsed.

Brother Andrew had told him that most of the injuries were serious but not necessarily fatal – but the head wound? Even if his patient recovered, the infirmarian had expressed doubt as to whether the man would regain all his faculties. He'd seen too many head wounds in his time that, even when the patient recovered, had left the recipient of such an injury little better than an imbecile.

Could this be the same man who had fought with a fierceness Tudor had never seen? The same man who felled his standard-bearer and unhorsed his personal bodyguard with a broken lance before being brought down himself? Even now, having had a day to think upon it, Henry Tudor could not understand what had made him stop his men from delivering the coup de grâce to his Plantagenet foe. It wasn't as if he felt merciful, because he didn't. The last thing he needed was a deposed king hanging around, even if the man were his prisoner.

So he sat, pondering the mess he'd got himself into.

He took a deep breath, then exhaled slowly. Leaning closer, his words were barely above a whisper. Even with the door shut, he didn't want to risk being overheard.

'So, we meet at last. You don't look like a monster. No withered arm that I can see. No hunched back.'

He snorted a small, weak laugh, knowing that those were all lies agents of the French king had helped to spread, but he wasn't going to contradict them publicly. He understood that it was better for soldiers to think of their opponents as something less than human. It made dispatching them so much easier. The last thing he wanted was for one of his troops taking pause to think of his enemy as a living, breathing human being. Doing so made bringing one's sword down to cleave an opponent's head more difficult.

Too bad Tudor hadn't taken his own advice yesterday!

'I was hoping we could actually talk, you and I. I have a number of questions for you.'

Richard made no response (not that Tudor had actually expected one) but remained oblivious to his surroundings, his mind trapped in darkness.

'When you were anointed with the Holy Oil at your coronation, did that serve as some kind of absolution for past and future sins? Were the sins you committed to gain the throne forgiven in that one act? Is it true that you killed old King Henry and his son? Did you poison your wife? Were you really hoping to marry the Princess Elizabeth to keep her from me? Or are these all just pesky unfounded rumours?' He paused, before continuing with what he really wanted to know. 'Most of all, I need to know where your nephews are. You didn't really murder your brother's sons, did you, Plantagenet? If you did, that would save me the trouble of dealing with them. But murdering children is such a cowardly act, and if there's one thing I've learned about you it's that you are not a coward.'

Henry slowly shook his head. 'No, you're not a coward,' he repeated. 'If anyone was a coward yesterday, it was me. When I saw you charging towards me, you looked like some terrible avenging angel. No,' he said, reconsidering, 'not an angel. More like St George determined to slay the dragon. Is that it? Was I your dragon?' He shuddered as once again he recalled his standard-bearer going down, sending his own red dragon standard falling to the ground.

'I will admit this to you and to you alone. I was…alarmed. No, dammit, more than alarmed. For those few minutes, I was terrified for my very life. If your horse hadn't become mired, it's very likely our positions today would be reversed. But you wouldn't have hesitated. You'd have struck me down.'

Tudor said nothing more but remained seated for several more minutes, contemplating the situation. All would have been so much

218

simpler if he'd let his men finish off his opponent. Even now, it would be so easy to snuff out his life. Unconscious, unable to defend himself, even Tudor could do it. A pillow held firmly over the face for a few minutes, then put back in place when the deed was done, and no one would ever know the difference. Richard Plantagenet would simply have succumbed to his injuries. But no, that wasn't something Henry Tudor could do. Killing in the heat of battle was one thing, but killing in cold blood? It wasn't that he objected to eliminating his opponents in such a way, only that he didn't want to be the person doing it.

Finally, he got up from the chair and absent-mindedly moved it back to where he'd found it. He headed towards the door, pondering his next move. His hand on the latch, he turned his head to take one final look at Richard Plantagenet. Maybe, if he were lucky, his foe would give in to his wounds, but he doubted that would be the case.

So he stepped out of the room and motioned to his men that he was ready to leave. But before he left, he stunned Brother Andrew when he approached the infirmarian and said, 'Take good care of your patient, if only because he is a courageous man.'

And Henry Tudor knew that no matter how much he hated Richard Plantagenet and every member of the House of York, he couldn't deny the niggling admiration he felt for the man's bravery.

✯✯✯

Early September 1485 - St Wynthryth's Priory, Leicestershire

It was a beautiful September day, and Father Anselm and Brother Andrew were enjoying what little free time they had by walking the cloister.

'I have a confession to make,' said Andrew.

Father Anselm cocked an eyebrow in surprise. 'So soon? I just heard your confession a couple of days ago.'

'It's…it's important,' said Brother Andrew in a low voice, his eyes travelling across the garth to where Sir Owain stood, slouching against the wall on the opposite side. It was obvious the man disliked being instructed by King Henry to stay here as much as the monks disliked his presence.

The priest acknowledged with a slight nod, already suspecting where this conversation might be heading.

'Shall we go to the confessional?' he said, keeping his voice low. 'That way, no matter what you say, it will be my absolute duty not to disclose anything you tell me. Not to a king's man, not even to the king.'

Brother Andrew gave a slight smile and the two men made their way to the church.

✫✫✫

'Bless me, Father, for I have sinned. It has been two days since my last confession.'

'May the Lord help you to confess your sins, my son,' replied Father Anselm, following the traditional formula. But he knew this wasn't going to be a typical confession, and the Prior admitted to himself that he was more than a little curious as to what the other man was going to say.

'I don't care which side the man fought on, I dislike being put in this position. I don't feel like I'm helping a poor soul, but doing the new king's dirty work for him. It's bad enough having Sir Owain forced upon us. This was a religious house…and I am having uncharitable thoughts about him, and about the king.'

'Continue,' urged Father Anselm.

'If all they wanted was to get information out of him, couldn't they have questioned him on the battlefield?' Brother Andrew asked, frustration in his voice. 'Instead, they bring him to us, wanting us to heal him, no doubt so they can take him to London or wherever and torture him. I was once a soldier before I turned to God and the life of a religious. I understand what goes on during a battle.'

'That was when you and your older brother went off to fight?' asked Anselm, remembering Andrew mentioning something about this in the past.

'Yes, as a young lad, I sought the glory of battle, and my brother and I were foot soldiers in Lord Dacre's army at Towton. So I am no innocent when it comes to what men can do to each other.'

'That was more than twenty years ago.'

'The horrors I saw on that battlefield haunt me to this day, and are why I am troubled by what will happen to that poor man I'm caring for.'

Father Anselm nodded sagely. 'Your concern for the welfare of your patient is admirable. Did not our Lord say, "Whatever you did for one of the least of these brothers and sisters of mine, you did for me"? And in the Parable of the Good Samaritan, does He not bid us to have mercy? Are we not instructed to love our neighbours as ourselves? I'm sure He would have us include both Yorkists and Lancastrians.'

Brother Andrew agreed. 'And there's something else that troubles me. Whoever he is, our patient is no common soldier, nor even a lowly knight. He didn't fight for the new king, else there would not be all this secrecy surrounding him. I don't know if he was a member of the late king's household or one of his advisers, as I've heard they were all either slain in battle or executed shortly thereafter. But he is somebody important. Also, I found this caught on his clothes when they brought him in.'

He showed Father Anselm the silver boar badge he had found and kept hidden to this point. 'This is King Richard's device, and would have been worn by his closest companions, maybe one of his household knights. In short, I suspect that he is a man of very high standing.' He stressed the word 'very'.

Anselm could find no fault in the other's reasoning. 'This may all be true, but none of it is something you need to confess. Well, perhaps your feelings towards Sir Owain, but I suspect many share those feelings.'

'There's more. You see, I haven't been completely truthful when I've reported that our mysterious patient's condition has not improved.'

Ah, thought Anselm, *now we get to the heart of the matter.*

'Although his condition is still dangerous, he has had brief periods of consciousness and these are becoming more regular. He still spends much of the time sleeping, but that is good, as sleep allows his body to heal.'

'And what does he have to say?'

'Nothing. So far, he hasn't spoken. The first few times he opened his eyes, he would stare at nothing as if unaware of his surroundings, but he continues to show improvement. Now when he wakes up he is more alert, and while he still doesn't speak we have been working out simple gestures for things he needs like food and drink. While he hasn't responded verbally to me yet, I feel sure that given time the power of speech will return to him. Whenever I am with him, I make a point of speaking to him as though he knows what I'm saying. I have also learned something else about him. One day I suggested we pray. As I began the Pater Noster, he clasped his hands together and bowed his head without my ever having suggested it. This man, whoever he is, does not deserve to be healed only to face torture and death. And for that reason, I have not reported his progress to you, or to Sir Owain.'

The priest's brow furrowed as he considered everything he'd been told. At last he said, 'What do you propose we do?'

'Simply this. We fake his death and give the man a chance to live.'

Anselm wasn't sure what he expected, but it wasn't this. 'Have you thought this through?'

'I have. Shall I tell you what I would do?' asked the infirmarian. 'It would not be without danger…'

Anselm didn't hesitate. 'I have devoted my life to the Church and to our Lord. If I have to choose between the Temporal and the Spiritual, I will choose the Spiritual every time. I am sure that this is what He would want me to do.'

Andrew nodded, and for the next hour the two men discussed his plan in detail.

When they finished, Father Anselm informed Andrew what penance he was to perform, made the sign of the cross, and pronounced the words of Absolution: *'Diende, ego te absolvo a peccatis tuis in nomine Patris et Filii et Spiritus Sancti.'*

As they rejoined the rest of the community, Father Anselm spoke quietly. 'I think that when this is over, both of us are going to be in need of Absolution.' But there was no recrimination in his voice, only a gentle smile on his face.

Late September 1485 – London

King Henry looked again at the piece of parchment in his hand. The writing was the small, cramped script that he immediately recognised from the many reports he'd received from Father Anselm over these past few weeks.

𝕴t is with deep regret that 𝕴 write to inform you of the passing of the man whose care you charged us with. As Sir Owain will attest, the patient never fully regained consciousness but remained in a mostly comatose state while he was with us. For weeks we attempted to get him to take drink and nourishment, often to no avail. Soon it was easy to see that the end was near. After receiving Extreme Unction, he peacefully slipped away and is now with our Heavenly Father. We buried him in our cemetery. Not knowing his name, his grave is marked with a simple wooden cross...

There was more, but that was the gist of the missive.

Tudor had already confirmed its contents with Sir Owain. Satisfied that all had happened as described, the small hint of a smile played at the corners of the king's mouth. This letter was an answer to his prayers. At last, Henry Tudor would know some peace of mind, at least where the last Plantagenet king was concerned. No need for further clandestine visits to that God-forsaken monastery. No need to explain to anyone what he had done or why. Crumbling the letter into a ball, he consigned it to the flames in the fireplace. At last, he was able to write *fini* to a foolish chapter that should never have been written.

The idea that monks might lie or that Richard Plantagenet still lived never occurred to him.

☆☆☆

About Kathy H D Kingsbury

Kathy is, in real life, a retired telephone company employee who now divides her time between two of her greatest passions – history and reading. She is fascinated with ancient and medieval history, and has been a Ricardian for some 40 years and is a member of the American Branch of the Richard III Society. Her reading tastes include works on the Wars of the Roses (both fiction and non-fiction), Victorian literature, historical mysteries, and modern-day paranormal romances. Previous writing efforts include several **Phantom of the Opera** romances and a couple early attempts at Ricardian inspired stories in which, like too many others, she got the Stanley brothers mixed up.

A Castle Summer

by
Joanna Kingswood Iddison

✫✫✫

Introduction

In April 1483, King Edward IV died, and named his younger brother, Richard of Gloucester, as Lord Protector. Edward IV's son, also named Edward, nominally styled Edward V, was taken to the royal apartments in the Tower of London and joined by his younger brother, Richard of Shrewsbury. The coronation was set for June 1483.

However, the coronation was changed to July and the person crowned was not Edward but his uncle Richard, as Richard III. The young boys were never seen again...

In April 1484 Richard and his wife Anne went on progress. They stopped for a while at Nottingham castle where they received the devastating news that their only son Edward, Prince of Wales had died, leaving the king without an heir.

Anne never recovered from the death of her son; she fell mortally ill (possibly from consumption) and slipped away during an eclipse of the sun in March of 1485. Meanwhile, across the water in France, Henry Tudor saw an opportunity to plan an invasion. In August he and his rag-tag army landed at Milford Haven. Eventually, his forces met with Richard's just outside Leicester, on Redemore Plain. The last English King rode to his destiny.

Henry Tudor, now styled as Henry VII sends Sir Robert Willoughby to collect the royal children from the nursery at Sheriff Hutton. If only things had been different...

✮✮✮

The city bells rang out in entreaty, as the people gazed up in horror. Slowly, the moon passed over the sun, turning the day to night. The people of London fell to their knees and prayed that this was not the day of Gods judgement. In the darkened room, now lit by candles. The little boy sat beside the bed.

'Mama?' There was no reply from the young woman laying still under the covers. 'Mama, please. I haven't finished my story.' Edward was just about to reach over and touch his mother's cheek.

A gentle voice whispered. 'Edward, my son.'

Richard had been standing at the foot of the bed. Listening to his son relate the story of King Arthur, the tale had been faltering, full of gaps and inaccuracies, but Edward was trying to tell it from memory, bedtime tales told by his father in more gentle times. Richard knelt and held out his arms. The little boy climbed off his chair and ran to his father, putting his arms tightly round his neck. Richard tried to hold his tears in check, but failed and they came softly down his cheeks.

'I'm sorry, she's gone to be with the angels now.'

Edward shook his head vehemently. 'But Papa, if we take her back to Middleham, the air is clean there, she will be well again.'

Richard tried to untangle his son's arms from round his neck. 'I'm sorry Edward, but we can't. Mama was so very tired; God has called her to rest.'

Edward looked at his father, then nodded slowly. Richard glanced to the women standing back in the shadows, he motioned to his niece.

'Cecily, please take Edward to the nursery.'

'Papa, please I don't…. I don't want to leave you.'

'Of course, I won't make you leave, I tell you what – come with me and we'll go down to the chapel, light a candle for mama.'

Edward looked to his father and nodded. Just as he did so, the moon began to slowly move away from the sun and daylight returned to the land.

'Look Edward, your mother has arrived in heaven, see how she is smiling.'

Edward looked up at the window, the sunlight beginning to shine through. He slowly smiled and lifted a small hand to his lips and blew a kiss heavenward.

☆☆☆

After Anne's funeral in Westminster Abbey, Richard decided to travel north. The place he and Anne had called home for the last nine years, the land that he knew would bring peace to his soul. The people in the villages and hamlets would help to restore his faith after the sadness of the last few months. Instead of travelling to Middleham Castle, their home in Wensleydale, he decided to take his small party to Sheriff Hutton.

The stronghold had once belonged to his cousin Richard Neville, Earl of Warwick. It was a peaceful place, tucked away in the beautiful Yorkshire countryside. It was now the home for the royal children. Richard hoped that seeing his cousins would bring a smile once more to young Edward's face. His son had been so very sad since the death of his mother and Richard had kept him close, involving him were possible in the day-to-day duties that Richard himself had had to perform. Richard hoped that keeping Edward occupied might help his son; they'd visited the royal menagerie at the Tower, taken trips on the river, but nothing had worked. Edward had been as a ghost, moving around the palace is if in a dream. Only now as they were nearing the familiarity of Yorkshire, did Edward begin to look more animated and took an interest in his surroundings. Each time they'd stayed overnight at an Abbey lodging or one of Richards friend's manors, Edward asked:

'How much further now Papa?'

Richard smiled at the memory, the number of miles slowly decreasing, and his son's smiles slowly increasing with each passing day.

As they rode across through the fields towards the castle gates, he could see his nephew, Jack, standing waiting for them. Richard smiled as he saw his sister's eldest son.

'It's good to see you, Jack. How is everyone?'

As soon as he dismounted, Jack accosted his uncle. 'Uncle!' he cried, not caring about protocol, grabbing Richard in a big bear hug. 'Everyone is upstairs, looking forward to seeing you.'

He looked at Edward, waiting somewhat nervously at his father's side, as if he needed permission to enter the castle, Jack glanced at Richard.

'Well, lad, what are you waiting for?'

Edward didn't need telling twice. With a quick backward glance at his father, he ran through the door and up the stairs. His cousins were waiting for him. As soon as he threw open the door, his cousin Elizabeth scooped him up into her arms.

'Edward!' she exclaimed, 'Oh! We are so happy to see you, come meet the others, it must be a long time since you've seen everyone.'

Edward nodded. Indeed, it was, he hadn't seen his cousins for several months, since he had left for London, and he had missed his playmates. Over in the corner of the room, two boys were playing chess. The older one ran his fingers through his hair in exasperation, as once again he tried to explain the rules of the game to the younger boy.

'For goodness' sake, Dickon, the castle goes that way, not sideways, that's the bishops move.'

Dickon grinned at his brother, 'Ha-Ha, just like old Bishop Morton. That's what Uncle Richard says.' He turned, looked up, saw they now had company, his uncle was standing in the doorway, 'You've returned, at last.'

Richard grinned at his two nephews, he remembered long ago trying to teach Anne chess. He'd been surprised how quickly she had learned the game; the complex moves the small figures made. The game had ended with him feigning sulking as Anne had won, but she had seen through his ruse and they had both ended up laughing together, to the surprise of her sister Isabelle. Isabelle had folded her arms, 'It's a silly game for babies.' She had stomped off in search of the more grown-up company of the Duchess. This had made Richard and Anne laugh even more..

'It's good to see you,' he opened his arms to greet the boys. 'Now, this is all of you. But wait, where's Teddy and Meggie?' he looked round to search for his brothers two children. His castle of the north had indeed become a safe haven for the royal children. The only ones not here, were the youngest of his brother Edward's girls and they had stayed with their mother. Dickon turned to his uncle, his face deadly serious.

'Teddy ran away, Uncle, when he heard the horses. He thought it was the Tudor coming to get us. Meggie went to try and find him.'

Richard frowned, chewed his bottom lip; Teddy had been a nervous child when he had first come to live with them in the north. After his mother and father had died, his Uncle Edward had given Teddy's wardship to Thomas Grey, son of his queen Elizabeth. Whilst Thomas had not been overly fond of having a royal ward, he was very happy with the revenue he had earned in Teddy's stead. Although not directly abusive to the boy, he had not been particularly affectionate either, so that when Teddy had come to Middleham he had been nervous of the strange aunt and uncle he had never met. But over the months, under Anne's kindness and Richard's gentle persuasion he had blossomed and now played rough and tumble with the other boys of the household, he also had a mischievous sense of humour.

'I must go seek them out.' Richard said, 'If Teddy is indeed afraid of the horses, he might misstep and fall, hurt himself on the stairs.'

At this last there was a giggle from behind the door curtain, that led to the garderobe. Richard heard a whispered 'Shhh.' Followed by more giggles... He crept up to the curtain and swept it back, to gaze at the surprised face of his niece and the little boy trying so very hard to suppress the giggles.

'Now you two. Trying to hide from your uncle, are you?'

With that, he went to grab Teddy, but the youngster was too quick.

'Ha, Uncle, you're too slow.'

Teddy set off to escape round the room, only just missing colliding with the table set up with the chess pieces.

'Hey Teddy! Watch where you are going!' Edward exclaimed, and went to grab his cousin; Teddy made a sidestep to avoid Edward's reach.

'Oh no you don't.' Pretty soon all the children were running round the nursery with Richard in hot pursuit. Jumping over stools and climbing on the settles to escape Richard's grasp. The children's laughter rang out around the room. Occasionally Richard would manage to grasp hold of one of them, but would allow them to wriggle free so they could continue their game. After a while Richard slowed, went to sit in the chair by the window. It took a while for the children to realise the game had changed and that their pursuer was no longer in pursuit. One by one they slowly began to come to a halt. The younger children looked to Elizabeth. Elizabeth glanced to where her uncle had retired to the window.

She had always been close to Richard; he had been more of an older brother to her than her mother's sons by John Grey. Before he had married and moved away to the north, it had been Richard that had taught her to ride, showed her and her sisters Mary and Cecily the places he and their father had known in childhood. As a child, her father had been too busy with establishing his claim to the throne and ruling the country, her mother had never seemed to take an interest in her or her younger sisters, so when she tired of the company of the nursery, she had sought out her Uncle Richard. He had made time for her, and together they had kept each other company. He had missed the father he had never really known, she the father she had, but rarely saw.

She tentatively approached her uncle.

'Uncle? Are you alright?'

'What? Sorry, I'm fine, just a little tired that's all.' He looked guilty for having spoiled the children's game. 'You carry on children.

I'm going to wash up and change out of these traveling clothes.' He smiled and left the room.

The children looked at each other.

'Do you think anyone will mind if we go and show Ned the new puppies?' Edward asked.

One of the castle dogs had whelped a few weeks before, and now had a litter of five healthy puppies. Four expectant young faces looked at Elizabeth and Margaret as if daring them to refuse. Both girls smiled, it would be good for them to go outside, especially now that young Ned was back with them again. After the last few months of being away in London following his mother's death, they had been worried that he would be reserved when he returned. But the familiarity of his surroundings and cousins warm welcome would help the boy with his grief.

Now it was up to them to see that all four boys kept cheerful. Elizabeth, Cecily and Margaret shared a room in the castle and frequently discussed their futures whilst the fire burned low in the grate and the candles neared the end of the wick. Many nights had drawn to an end and the suns raise shone through the window, whilst the girls had chatted about what lay ahead, laughing as they played at guessing which noble they would marry. Cecily already knew she would marry Ralph Scrope, but she happily played along with her sister and cousin.

Lately, though, their chats had taken a darker turn. They had heard the gossip in the kitchens and from other servants, that the Tudor was aiming to launch an invasion force against their uncle. Margaret had said that she wasn't worried, their uncle was a great warrior who had been leading armies since he was eighteen. She didn't remember that it had been against her own grandfather that Richard had fought, she only knew of the great battle between her grandfather and Uncle Edward. She had no idea that her father had abandoned her grandfather at the earliest opportunity, even though he had pledged his support. That as soon as Edward had offered a pardon, her father, George had changed sides. This had left the great Richard Neville, Earl of Warwick lacking a sizable retinue. His plans in shatters, his body lying dead on the field.

She knew her uncle had beaten the Scots many times and this upstart Tudor would join the list of his defeated enemies.

☆☆☆

'Look Ned, I like her the best.' Edward pointed to one of the pups, a pure black in colour but with one white ear. All four boys had reached the stables where the puppies were being looked after by their mother in one of the empty pens.

'And what name would you give to such a beauty.' Richard had entered the stable while the boys were engrossed in the new pups.

'Bessie, because she's the only girl and she's very bossy,' Edward said with a smile.

All the boys laughed, as they knew he was having a playful dig at his big sister. Richard looked thoughtful. He turned to gaze into the pen where the pups were playing, biting each other's ears and tumbling around. The parents had been a gift from his sister Margaret. In her letter she'd said they used them in the Bohemian borderlands as sheep dogs. She'd bought them from a traveller who had been passing through her land. Margaret had been so enamoured of the beautiful animals, she paid the traveller a hefty sum. She'd decided that the dogs needed to be busy outside, so had sent them to her dear brother across the sea, so they could work the wild Yorkshire countryside. Richard had been delighted with such a generous gift, and even more so when they had discovered the pair were breeding, so now as much as he was pleased to gift the pups, he was keen to keep at least one of the them to train as a herding dog.

'What about you three, which ones could you give a name too?'

In turn, each boy gave a name to three pups, 'Brunor, Cador and Ector.'

'Well,' said Richard. 'A fine bunch of companions for a fine trio of knights.' He turned to Edward. 'It seems your fellows have chosen names for Arthur's knights, are you sure you still want to call her Bessie?'

'Hmm, but if I change it, I'll have to call her Gwenhwyfar.' He looked a little crestfallen, until Ned passed him the pup.

'Maybe you could shorten it to Gweny.' He looked at Edward and smiled.

Edward smiled back. 'That's a great idea Ned.'

All of a sudden, all four boys seemed to halt, as if struck by the same thought. It was young Teddy that broke the spell.

'Sorry, Uncle, did you say companions?'

Richard laughed, 'Well it took you long enough.'

Four surprised faces looked at him. 'You mean, they're ours?'

'If you promise to take care of them, and train them properly, Rukes here has agreed to help you.'

A man stepped out from behind Richard, the man Ned recognised as Rukes Metcalfe who had been at Middleham as one of his father's retainers.

'Ey, ye Grace, we'll be making fine dogs out of 'em. But for now, they'll have to stay with their mother till they're weaned, but you can come and visit whenever you like.'

The boys nodded and with one last look at their new pups, they left the stables and returned to the main hall.

A couple of days later Richard returned to the nursery, all the children were there, Edward having yet another attempt to teach his brother chess, Teddy and Ned were playing a game of Nine Men's Morris and the girls had set up some needlecraft work near the window. Richard gazed at his family, he loved all the children there, even though they were his nieces and nephews. They were his family and he would do everything in his power to keep them safe. His two natural children Katherine and Johnny had temporarily been sent home to their mother, he'd hated to do it, but felt they were safer far away, only Ned was here, and now when he turned to greet his father, Richard's heart missed a beat at the small face that looked so like the face of his mother.

'I have news for you.' Richard sat on the settle as the children finished their games and came to gather round. 'I have received news from my good friend Francis, that Henry Tudor is launching an invasion soon. I'm afraid I have to go away for a while, I will be staying in Nottingham, until I can be certain where the Tudor will land.'

Four young voices all cried at once, 'We'll come with you, let us help you defeat the Tudor.'

Richard regarded his son and his nephews, he knew they were serious and deserved a solemn response, he replied. 'Sorry, but this I must do alone. I need you here to help Sir Thomas, protect the girls, and hold the castle secure. I will return soon. Tudor is an upstart with no battle experience and I have been fighting the Scots since before you were born.'

He winked at Ned. Ned giggled, but then looked serious.

'Papa, please, can't you send someone else? What about Uncle Jack or Uncle John?'

Richard pulled his son close. 'I'm sorry, but I can't ask someone else to fight my battles son. You will learn as you get older that when you have the command of several hundred men, they will respect you more if you lead them yourself.' He turned to Margaret. 'Your Grandfather taught me that.'

The children still looked crestfallen.

'Besides, I still have business to attend to when I return. I have plans to turn Scarborough into one of England's finest ports.'

He waited for the expected excited response. When none was forthcoming, he added. 'Which means I will need to travel there, and I will need an escort.' This time he nodded pointedly at Edward.

'Hurray, a trip to the sea. We can visit the faire and eat those strange fish they have there.'

'Oh yes, I remember' said Dickon, 'We had to pick them out of their shells, it was disgusting fun.'

The weeks of summer passed. The boys spent each glorious day with their dogs, and each day Rukes spent with them, teaching them the commands to use to train the dogs to hunt and fetch game, he also showed them how to nock a bow and fire at a target the other side of the yard, until they were all very capable archers; the boys had great fun and took to their lessons with gusto. It was great to be out of doors in the clean Yorkshire air, after the stuffiness of the school room. For even though Richard was absent he had left clear instructions that they were not to miss out on their lessons, much to the boys' chagrin.

At the beginning of August, a rider arrived with letters from Richard, sent from his hunting lodge in Sherwood Forest. A letter had been sent to each of them, and they spent the afternoon reading them and passing them round – no-one noticed that Elizabeth had put hers in her sleeve after reading it.

Late that night, as the girls were getting ready for bed, instead of the usual giggles and teasing, Elizabeth was quiet and subdued.

'What is it, Bess?' Cecily moved to her sister's side, concerned that something was amiss.

'It's my letter from Uncle Richard.' She sat on the bed and motioned for Margaret and Cecily to join her. 'He says that if the battle doesn't go his way, we have to get the boys away from here and to our aunt in Burgundy.'

'What all four of them?' Cecily gasped. 'But that's a tremendous undertaking. Has he explained how he thinks you are going to do it?'

Elizabeth shook her head. 'Not me, Cecily, we, and yes he has. Will and I are going to take Edward and Dickon, and you and Margaret are to take Teddy and Ned with Rukes. We are to head for the coast, where we will meet with allies, people we can trust to get us to Aunt Margaret, but we have to go separately to try and avoid suspicion.'

All the while Margaret had sat quietly, staring at Elizabeth. She knew her uncle was just being cautious, that he was only thinking of their safety, but Uncle Richard would win the battle. Her grandfather had taught him all about tactics and manoeuvres.

'We are to prepare clothes and supplies, get them to hand so that we can go at a moment's notice.'

The girls agreed that they would make preparations the next day when they knew the boys would be out with their dogs. They retired to bed, subdued, but determined to complete their task. The next days where fraught with anxiety, none could settle as they waited for news. The three girls tried to keep things as normal as they could. Watched as the boys returned each day to their tasks of training the new pups, each night they would return weary but happy to their room. Until one night, when, as was custom, Elizabeth, Cecily & Margaret peeked into the boys' room to say their goodnights. As they quietly approached the door, fearing the boys would be sleeping, they heard giggles and soft barking. They slowly opened the door to gaze at the sight of three small dogs and three boys, jumping on the beds and running around the room. The fourth, young Dickon was failing to hold a wriggling pup on his bed.

'Cador, no wait, you can't get down, you're all tangled up.'

All three girls started to laugh. Dickon looked up, realised the game was up, and just shrugged his shoulders.

'They can stay for tonight, but they must go back in the morning.' Cecily tried to make her voice stern, but smiled at her little brother. Unknowingly the little dog had managed to break the tension of the last few days.

The next day Teddy and Ned were quietly playing, when Teddy got up to stretch his legs and peered out through the window of the nursery at Sheriff Hutton.

'Look Ned!' he shouted. 'Horses.'

Ned ran to the window, far off they could see the tell-tale signs off horses approaching.

'Who are they? Can you see?'

'Let's go to the high tower, we'll be able to see better.'

The two boys set off from the nursery rooms towards the highest tower, servants jumped out of their way. With the occasional 'Watch out lads!'. 'Eeh slow down there.'

As they reached the upper rooms, they bumped into Elizabeth.

'Woah there you two, where do you think you're off to, at such a speed? Where's Mistress Idley?'

The two youngsters were breathless with excitement.

'But Bessie, there are horses coming.'

Elizabeth's face paled, *'Oh my goodness, which way has the battle gone?'* she thought, *'Has Uncle Richard indeed won?'* Gathering herself, she told the boys to run down and get Sir Thomas. 'Tell him to prepare...' she stopped, realised what she had been about to say, that it could be Tudor at the door. She didn't want to frighten the children, not yet.

The boys scurried off as quick as they could, they still wanted to see if they had time to get to the tower. Elizabeth knew this is what her uncle had prepared her for, the moment had arrived. Her brothers and cousins needed her to be strong now and carry out her task.

When her father's pre-contract with Lady Talbot had been made public, she, her sisters and brothers had been declared bastards. Elizabeth had been the one to look after her younger sisters, kept them amused with stories and games, while her mother had plotted and schemed. It had all come to naught when her uncle had discovered that Elizabeth Woodville had been sending secret messages to Margaret Beaufort. Had even had the cheek to promise marriage with her eldest daughter to Margaret's son Henry.

Her mother had railed against Richard at the time, calling him usurper and betrayer. When her rage was spent, she admitted that the person she was angry at most was their father. She had even accepted Richard's help and come out of sanctuary to live with her younger daughters at Grafton Manor. While she and Cecily had been welcomed into their uncle and aunt's court. She smiled when she remembered their time there, the feasting and the dancing, there had even been some courtly romance with one of Richards young retainers. Elizabeth quickly pulled herself out of her reverie, she had to get to Cecily and her brothers, most importantly she had to make sure her brothers were not here when Tudor forces reached the castle.

Sir Thomas appeared breathless at the door, 'My Lady?'

'Quick get the horses ready, it's now.' Elizabeth told him, already trying to get past him, so she could reach her brothers, get them ready to flee.

The constable gasped, looked at Elizabeth in disbelief. 'No, I don't believe it!'

Sir Thomas Gower had been the constable of Sheriff Hutton for a number of years, another of Richards trusted men, he had been disappointed to not leave with his king, but instead the job he had been intrusted with, to protect the royal children was paramount.

'Thomas, I don't have time to argue, Please....' Panicked now Elizabeth looked at him, tears in her eyes, her whole body trembling with the urgent need to complete her task.

'Oh, Mighty God.' Thomas turned to get the horses saddled and ready. Elizabeth turned to run down the corridor, as she did, she bumped into Margaret, the younger girl took one look at her stricken face, held her hands up in a gesture of denial. Elizabeth grasped them.

'Margaret, we have to get the boys away now. Can you find Ned and Teddy?' Margaret was dumb struck; all she could do was nod her head. Both girls set off to accomplish their task. Elizabeth arrived at the room her brothers shared with the other boys. Thankfully they were both there.

'Quick, Edward, Dickon. Get your things, warm coats on, boots and hats.'

Both boys looked at her, not moving. Two pairs of eyes, staring at her, not wanting to admit what was happening. Then suddenly Edward sprang into action.

'Dickon, come on, move.'

At this they quickly got their things out of the coffer by the window, everything had been made at hand, ready, just in case. Elizabeth was edgy, how much closer were the riders? How much time did she have? The boys ready, she bustled them down the back stairs. Not knowing if the riders were near, they began to creep towards the stables. As much as possible they tried to keep to the shadows.

Jumping at every noise. They reached the door that would lead them to the stables and safety. Elizabeth opened the door and gasped...

Meanwhile Margaret had been tearing round trying to find her brother and cousin. She was getting desperate; she too knew the riders would not be far away now.

'Where are they?' she thought. She knew they wouldn't be in the nursery, then she knew, of course the stables. But Lizzie was heading to the stables with Edward and Dickon, could she really risk them all being caught together. No, she had to stick to Uncle Richard's plan. *'Be strong Meg, you have to find them, get them safe,'* she chastised herself.

As luck would have it, she ran into one of the stable boys, who had decided that the ensuing chaos was just the right moment to sneak to the kitchens to try and steal a sweetmeat or two. No time for pleasantries.

'Sam, have you seen my brother and cousin?'

'No Lady.' Sam shook his head. 'Have you tried the kitchens or the stables?'

Margaret wondered if she could pass round and go by the main door. *'Yes,'* she decided, that's what she would do, she had no choice, she had to find them. She headed towards the main entrance. The heavy bolts had been slid across, Margaret was frantic now, she could hear the horses outside, then shouting.

'Please God, give me the strength,' she silently prayed. Margaret, with everything she had, pulled the bolt across. She gave the handle on the door an almighty heave and pulled the door open. She stepped into the courtyard. The scene that greeted her, made her cry out in shock, she closed her eyes, put her hands to her face in a gesture of denial, not wanting to dare believe what she saw. She opened her eyes; the courtyard was full of men and horses. She couldn't work out what was happening, in her panicked state she didn't recognise anyone there.

All of a sudden, she heard her name; she turned and ran straight into the welcoming arms of her Uncle Richard.

About Joanna Kingswood Iddison

Joanna is a Yorkshire lass through and through. A member of the Richard III Society, she has been interested in history from an early age, watching the classics such as *The Six Wives of Henry VIII*, *The Prince & The Pauper* and *Robin and Marion* as a child, with her father. The constant childish questions of 'who?', 'why?' and 'when?' followed her to adulthood when she read *Sunne in Splendour* by Sharon Penman. This led her to a voyage of discovery about the legendary, vilified uncle figure of Richard III. Through this childhood mantra, she has now begun, with her new partner in crime, her amazing (and patient) husband, a remarkable journey discovering the wider story of the people and places of the fifteenth century.

Revenge

by
Michèle Schindler

Introduction

On 22 August 1485, King Richard III was killed in battle. A lot of his supporters and friends died with him. Others, such as Thomas Howard, Earl of Surrey, were captured by the forces of the victorious usurper and new king, Henry VII. Richard's best friend, Francis, Viscount Lovell, managed to escape capture. What would have happened had he not escaped, but been taken prisoner as well?

★★★

Richard was dead. Robert Percy was dead. Robert Brackenbury was dead. John Kendall was dead. John Howard was dead.

Richard was dead.

They were all dead. Dead, defeated, lost.

Dead like Joan.

Murdered. Murdered as Francis had had to listen, had fought, had not been able to do anything, murdered by the army of a man who had watched as his guards had cut Richard down as he was fighting. Murdered because Richard had been betrayed.

241

Murdered by men who were now trying to take him and Thomas Howard captive, doubtlessly to murder them too. Murdered by the men who were now laughing as they surrounded them.

They had killed Richard. Richard had died, died surrounded by traitors, and when the men came closer, still laughing, throwing taunts at them, when one of them took Francis roughly by the collar, he began screaming. Trying to reach for his sword, for his dagger, for any weapon at all, he lashed out around himself, screaming, cursing.

They had killed Richard. They had killed Richard, they were laughing about it, and they dared touching him with their filthy hands, that had killed Richard –

'Murderers!' Francis screamed, desperate, outraged, beyond all reason, beyond all thought but this. 'Murderers!' His fist connected with the face of one of them, and detachedly, he heard a crunch, heard a yell. 'Traitors, murderers, cowards!' He elbowed one of them, who roughly took him by the arm, away, and then his left hand fell on the hilt of his sword, even as more and more men crowded around him, now no longer laughing.

'Whoreson!' one of them spat, spitting at his feet, but Francis barely registered it, trying to draw his sword.

'Get your – filthy – traitorous – hands off – me!' he screamed, still kicking, boxing, attempting to free some space so he could get to his weapon. Blood was pounding in his ears, mixing with the noise, and the terrible memory of Richard's screams, making him barely responsive to anything but the immediate threat, to the cowards, the murderers standing in front of him, so much so that he did not even think. He fought by sheerest instinct, the instinct that had once baffled the Earl of Warwick so, fought with all means he had. He boxed, he kicked, he spat, he bit, fighting every step they dragged him when they finally could get a hold of him. Fighting, hardly noticing the blows he received himself, the sharp kicks, the slaps. Hardly hearing the curses.

He was still yelling and fighting when they arrived in front of a cart that was doubtlessly meant as his transport as prisoner. As prisoner to whatever place Richard's murderer wanted him brought to kill him too, and the thought – the thought of the whoreson who had watched as his men killed Richard – gave Francis a new burst of strength, making him fight with even more vigour. His whole body hurt, but Richard was dead. They had killed him and were still alive. They –

'Traitors!' he yelled again, voice hoarse and cracking, when they finally managed to force him to the ground, when they twisted his hands behind him and tied it with ropes, when they did the same to his feet. 'Traitors! Cowardly traitors! You'll burn – in hell – burn –'

His last yell was muffled when one of the men took a muddy, bloody piece of cloth, balled it up and shoved it in his mouth, then fixing it in place with another cloth.

'Shut up!' he roared, as Francis twitched, struggling against his bonds. 'Shut up, whoreson! Gloucester's arsewipe!'

A kick hit him in the stomach, and Francis gasped, nearly choked, causing a lot of raucous laughter. The next blow hit his head, and he could feel blood trickle down his brow. Then one of the men lifted him up bodily, spat in his face, before almost throwing him into the cart. Francis gave a muffled groan as he hit the wooden floor, which was received by yet more hoots, and the man who had thrown him cackled, climbing in after him, while behind him Thomas Howard – looking entirely composed – did so as well. He was flanked by two other of the murderers, but they did not seem to manhandle him, as he made no move to resist them.

Coward. Did he accept Richard's murder, then? Did he not care? Did he not care that his father, too, had been killed? John had always said his son had a cool head under fire, but he had not known he would not care if he got killed –

Francis again started struggling, earning himself another kick in the stomach, before his captor spat again.

'Your usurper friend is dead, Lovell,' he jeered. 'No one here to help you now.'

Francis tore at the ropes, but they were strong, and the man's sneer only grew worse.

'He's dead, the deformed pig. What a surprise to see when we stripped him.' He cackled yet again as Francis froze, stared at him. No

– no it couldn't – 'Bled like a pig too. But you know that, do you not? You can taste it. We kept a bit of his bloody clothing, you see. Used it as your gag.'

And with that, he sneered once more as Francis sat in sheerest horror, then slammed the wooden doors of the cart and locked them. Francis stared after where he had left, shaking with pain and horror. There was a metallic taste in his mouth. Richard – Richard's blood –

Bile rose in his throat and he choked, tried to force it down. Richard – Richard – He could not – Richard's clothing – they had – his back now for the entire world to see – the blood in his mouth – he choked again, no – no – trying to gasp for breath –

'Francis,' a soft voice suddenly sounded over his head, and then Thomas Howard knelt next to him, fingers behind his head, working on the knot of the cloth holding the gag in place. 'Only a moment,' he said, and indeed, almost immediately afterwards, the cloth came loose and Francis retched, spat out the gag, retched again, bile running from his mouth. Acidic taste filled his mouth, but it was better than metallic – Richard – Richard's blood –

Thomas simply watched him, said nothing, until his breathing finally evened, then he gave him a tentative smile.

'Better now?'

'Better!' Francis exploded. 'Better?! They killed Richard – killed Richard – they killed your father too, and you ask me if I feel better?! What I –'

'Francis!' Thomas thundered, interrupting him. 'Francis, if they hear you, they will want to know why you are no longer gagged.'

'So?' Francis spat. 'If you did not want to anger them, you should have let me –'

'Let me finish!' Thomas interrupted him again. 'Listen to me and let me finish!'

'Give me Richard's cloth,' Francis answered, and when the earl – duke now? – gave him an odd look, he repeated, roughly: 'Richard's cloth!'

Thomas raised his eyebrows at him, but did as asked, putting the former gag into Francis's tied hands. 'Now will you listen?'

'Doesn't seem like I have a choice,' Francis answered, closing a fist around the cloth. Richard had worn it – he had seen him put it on this morning – he had even smiled slightly –

'They will bring us before Tudor,' Thomas said suddenly, interrupting his thoughts. 'He will make us a speech and tell us we are to be executed, won't he?'

'Coward,' Francis murmured, and Thomas nodded.

'He is, but listen. They will probably search us before they bring us before him. Well, me. They've stripped you of all your weapons, haven't they? You will not be searched thoroughly again. A dagger in your boot will not be noticed.'

This got Francis's attention, and he looked up to meet Thomas's eyes.

'How?' he asked, and the older man gave a small shrug.

'You gave three of them a black eye and I am pretty certain one of them has a broken nose. They did not think of me, nor did they have the time to search me thoroughly.' Smiling very slightly, he reached beneath his thin cloak and produced a dagger. 'They overlooked this when I gave them my sword and my father's dagger.'

Francis looked at him, and after a moment, he said: 'I want to kill him. He killed Richard –' His voice broke, but Thomas nodded, lifting the left leg of his breeches a bit and sticking the weapon in his boot. Then he reached behind him, started fumbling with the ties around Francis's hands.

'You can shake them off when you are in Tudor's presence now,' he said as Francis felt the pressure around his wrist relax.

'Thank you,' Francis murmured after a moment. 'I'll kill him. They – they – Richard –'

His head fell forward, suddenly, as the thought hit him once more. They had killed Richard. He was dead. They had killed him and stripped him and –

'Richard,' he murmured, clasping at the wet cloth in his hand. 'Richard. They – they –'

'Don't think of it now,' Thomas said. 'Don't. Focus. I imagine they will bring us before him fairly soon.'

'Every moment he lives is too long!' Francis burst out, and Thomas shook his head.

'So it is, but focus! Do you want to be discovered? He'll live longer in that case.'

'Don't – don't –' Francis's voice broke and he slumped entirely. 'He's a murderer – a murderer –' His head lolled to the side, connected with the wooden wall of the cart. 'Richard's – Richard's gone –'

The taste of blood still in his mouth…

He did not know how long they sat there, helplessly. At some point, he must have started crying, for suddenly he felt the wetness on his cheeks, heard muffled sounds and only after a moment realised he was making them.

Richard was dead – he was dead, like dear Joan was dead, like –

After a while, the cart started moving, but Francis barely noticed. He barely noticed anything. Not the movement, not the fact that Thomas was speaking to him. Not even when they stopped, when suddenly voices became louder again outside the cart.

'Francis!'

Only the sudden hiss, directly next to him, startled him, and he looked into Thomas's face, saw him frown.

'Focus now! Focus!' Then he reached behind him again, took the cloth he was still clutching from him.

'What are you doing?!' Francis shouted, but was interrupted when Thomas slapped him.

'Use your head, lad! Do you want to be discovered?!'

With that, he threw the cloth down, then moved away again, sitting down across from him. Francis opened his mouth to protest again, but before he could do so, the door of the cart opened again, and he found himself faced with one of the men who had captured them.

'We're –' His grin fell away when he looked at Francis, and then he turned to Thomas with a snarl. 'Did you free him?!'

'No,' Thomas said, quite calmly and coldly, when the man stepped towards him, growling, several others now behind him. 'I saved his life. And yours. What do you think your –' He gave a snarl – 'leader would have said if you had let your captive choke on his own vomit? If you had not let him speak to him?'

Francis growled at the thought, and Thomas gave him an exasperated glance before turning again to their captor. 'I am sure you know who he is. Who I am. And I am quite sure that his wanting to speak to us is exactly why you have come to fetch us. Do you really want to –'

'Shut up!' the man roared. 'Come along now!' He made to grab him by the collar, at which Thomas stepped aside.

'I will come along,' he said, his voice even colder now. 'Do not presume to touch me.'

The man growled even more but did as told, and Thomas stepped out of the cart in front of him and behind another one, while two of the others pulled Francis up, one of them cutting through the ropes at his feet so he could walk.

'Whoreson,' Francis hissed, at which he received an elbow in the stomach, before he was led out of the cart as well.

There were guards all around them, as they walked towards a building Francis vaguely recognised as the monastery of Leicester. They were in Leicester. Where they had been but days ago, with Richard –

He bit his lip, drawing blood. Now was not the time to think of it. He could not – could not –

'We're to bring you to King Henry,' one of the men said as they entered the building, and a growl caught in Francis's throat. King –

'Has he been crowned yet?' Thomas asked, voice still cold. 'I imagine he will want that to be soon.'

How could he be so calm?

'Shut up!' The roar made Thomas shrug, while Francis had to fight with himself not to struggle against the men who were holding him. If he did that now, the ropes would come undone too early. Then – It could not happen, and he looked to the ground. Revenge would come – only a little while more…

He barely saw what they passed, only realised again what was happening when he was shoved into a room behind Thomas, who made a distressed sound, and he looked up, to find himself surrounded by people. Men still in bloodied clothing, and, in the background –

The man was wearing Richard's crown. The crown Francis had seen only hours ago on Richard's helmet, and the man – Richard's killer, who had watched as he was murdered – was wearing it as if it was his right. Francis could not help himself. The growl forced itself up his throat, was past his lips before he could control it.

'Murderer! Cowardly murderer!'

Silence fell following this, interrupted only by a groan from Thomas. For a moment, everyone in the room seemed to be frozen, and then the noise suddenly rose again as a shadow fell over Francis's face and a tall, muscular man stepped in front of him, raising his hand and then slapping Francis with such force his head turned to the side.

'What are you calling my nephew, you churl?' the man thundered. 'Your king?'

Ears ringing, Francis turned again to look the man – bastard! murderer! – in the eye.

'You killed my king,' he answered, spitting out some blood – directly at his opponent, who had to be Jasper Tudor. 'And your king, too. Traitor.'

This earned him another slap, as Jasper roared: 'You will mind your words in the presence of the king!'

'The king gave me permission to speak as I wish before he died,' Francis answered, everything else but sheerest fury now forgot. 'And I will speak in front of traitors as I wish.'

'You will do as I say!' Jasper thundered, at which Francis spat at him again.

'Make me.' He expected to be slapped again, when another voice suddenly interrupted them.

'I take it you do not accept me as your king?'

Tudor. Richard's killer. Who had watched as Richard was killed.

'Traitor!' Francis roared. 'Traitor!'

He just had time to see something akin to surprise on the cowardly murderer's face when suddenly Thomas said, behind him, still sounding quite calm.

'Did you truly expect him to accept your nephew as king?'

At that, Jasper turned to him, opened his mouth. Seeing him turn, Francis knew he only had a few seconds. Watching Tudor approach, he remained standing until he was quite close, slowly straining against his ropes. They fell as Tudor stood directly in front of him, a vile grin on his vile face. Quickly, Francis bent forwards, pulling up his breeches and grabbing the dagger and then, with a fluid motion, yanked it up and rammed it into Tudor's stomach.

He heard his gasp, saw the blood drain from the murderer's face, and felt a moment of satisfaction. There were screams around him, but he barely heard them. Pulling the dagger out again, he grabbed Tudor's arms as his knees gave out. Spitting him in the face, he hissed: 'Burn in hell!' and then rammed the dagger into his heart.

Tudor fell to the ground, and Francis looked at him.

'For Richard,' he murmured, then spun around, heard the screams, saw Jasper come towards him, face pale, shocked and furious, sword raised. Thomas, behind him, was nodding at Francis. He would know what to do.

Francis smiled slightly. Richard was gone. Joan was gone. He could die now. Anne would understand.

He had avenged Richard. He could follow him and Joan now.

He continued smiling when Jasper's sword struck.

About Michèle Schindler

Michèle Schindler is a 30-year-old author of a non-fiction history book, ***Lovell Our Dogge: The Life of Viscount Lovell, Closest Friend of Richard III and Failed Regicide***, and she has several upcoming books as well, including one on mental health in the Middle Ages and one on Alice Chaucer. She has also written a small, self-published novella about Francis Lovell's early life, called ***The Autumn Baron***, and an anthology of short stories about the Wars of the Roses, put together with other authors. Its name is ***Yorkist Stories***, and its proceeds go to Doctors Without Borders.

In her day job, She is a language teacher. She studied at Goethe-Universität in Frankfurt am Main, Germany, reading history with a focus on mediaeval studies, and English Studies. In addition to English and German, she speaks French, and reads Latin. She is from Germany and very interested in both English and German history and culture. Her particular interest is mediaeval history, but in the last years, she did a lot of personal genealogy, which gave her a good grounding in modern German history and culture. Through handling a lot of old letters and sources, she also learnt how to read Sütterlin. Apart from history, she enjoys doing Pilates and other sports, taking photos, and she loves working and playing with animals, particularly dogs.

Amazon: https://tinyurl.com/753vdnmz

The Apothecary's Secret

by
Clare Anderson

✫✫✫

Introduction

Beneath 'The Apothecary's Secret': Despite his incessant plotting, Bishop John Morton survived Richard III's reign. Rewarded for his treachery by Henry VII, he was made Archbishop of Canterbury in 1486 and Lord Chancellor the following year. He became a Cardinal in 1493 and died in his bed.

✫✫✫

Greyfriars Friary, Leicester, August 1486

*P*rime

If he could die anywhere, he wouldn't choose Leicester. He would prefer some quiet spot in his native Yorkshire. But then the choice was not up to him.

Brother Thomas Appleby would not now rise from this bed. This would probably be the last sunrise he would ever see. His eyes went instinctively to the window opposite his cot and watched as the first rays filtered through the window panes. The infirmary had glazed windows, which he suddenly regretted, preferring to greet the new day's light in all its brightness. His last day.

Deus in adjutorium meum intende... Oh God come to my aid, make haste to help me.

The steady young voices of the two friars who had come to pray with him intoned the psalm while he joined in, reciting mostly from memory and pausing when he was unsure of the text. His voice was weak and shaky; he could feel his life slipping away slowly, like a creaky old ship pulling out of harbour and setting sail. But where would be its destiny?

As sunlight gradually filled his room, Thomas thought back to his youth. Born the last child in a family of thirteen, in the closing years of the reign of Henry V, he had spent most of his childhood with his grandmother who lived on the edge of a village near York. A sickly youth, it was felt that he was more likely to thrive as an only child in a household away from the town. Thomas came to love rural life and its cycles, from lambing time to the shearing. His grandmother had been the village 'wise woman', and it was she who first taught him about the uses and lore of herbs and plants. Together they would go in the fields and woods, searching for pennyroyal, comfrey and feverfew. Young Thomas learned which mushrooms were fine to eat and which were deadly and how a mild dose of a certain herb could heal when a strong one could kill.

Like all people who live close to nature, his grandmother respected everything in the rhythm of life, including the animals they caught for food. She taught Thomas to tread silently and watchfully when hunting or simply gathering. He learned to catch fish with his bare hands.

To be young again... running through fields and meadows, in the bliss of youth. His child's limbs knew no pain. Thomas smiled ruefully to himself at the memory; his young heart had been so innocent, so clean.

Terce

He was woken by the sound of the door opening and a soft voice, 'He's asleep. Let's not wake him.'

'We should sit with him awhile in case he wakes and wants to pray.'

The sound of shuffling followed by silence. The end of the bed sagged with a new weight. There was only one chair in the room.

'I'll look in on him later with some broth. What a shame he will miss the King. He was talking about the royal progress and hoping to see the new Queen.'

'I love this king; he is so close to the people. What an honour that he should wish to visit us.'

'They say the Queen is very pious and learned. I hope she shares the King's devotion to St Francis.'

The voices, low as they were, became a distant murmuring as Thomas again fell to dreaming of his past.

Growing into manhood, he had felt torn between staying with his grandmother and becoming a shepherd, or working as a herbalist, which would take him away from the fields and into the towns. With his grandmother's savings and the sums earned from seasonal labour and waiting on guests in York's taverns, he was able to train and qualify as an apothecary. Apprenticed in York, he came to love that city. The years went by – so many it seemed. England became a land of strife, with poor King Harry VI unable to control his warring lords. Lancaster and York fought it out on many a bloody battlefield. Village lads he had known were summoned to march under their lord's banner, carrying nothing but a pitchfork, and many did not return. But life went on in York, mercifully so far north that battles were usually only news. There was a young woman, Alice, who used to come into his shop for remedies for her mistress. She would stop awhile and they would talk together. He could still remember her face, after all this time. He had intended to court her, but then the friar came to town, preaching at the street corner. Crowds would gather round him to hear his message of God's kingdom, a place not of this world.

With a heart strangely free and joyous, Thomas had visited his grandmother's grave to tell her what he would do. She had always told him to follow his heart, so he hoped she'd approve.

Sext

Greyfriars Friary had a large church built into a quadrangle, monastic style. The friars here wore grey, to show they lived in community, rather than the more usual brown of the itinerant followers of St Francis of Assisi. The Greyfriars community was large and vibrant, serving the local townspeople.

His Grace King Richard had been especially eager to visit the Friary as it housed a relic of St Francis, one of his favourite saints. He wished to hear Mass and spend time in prayer; for himself, his new Queen, and the people he served. Crowds gathered in the street and Brother Thomas could hear their voices hum with expectation and excitement.

'How I would love to see His Grace one more time,' he said softly.

Brother Anselm thought for a while. 'We could bring you to the window if you would like. How is your canker?'

'It gnaws, but the pain grows less when I think of other things. I should like to try to move to the window.'

Between them, Brother Anselm and Brother Matthew lifted the old man gently, supporting him between them. Thomas was aware of the canker in his gut, ever there, his constant companion for many months. The window was opened and fresh air washed round his face. It felt good.

A sudden cry went up from the crowd and the royal couple came into sight. King Richard, riding his white destrier, was attired in rich red velvet, with a great chain round his neck with enamelled suns and a white boar at the base. His golden crown glittered in the sun. He looked every inch the king, thought Thomas, and not much changed since they had met. This time, however, he was smiling. Even at this distance it was clear that the care lines were not as noticeable. Beside him on a chestnut palfrey rode his Portuguese queen, Joana. She, too, was smiling. Thomas noted her gentle face and hoped that she was a comfort to the king who had suffered so much grief.

They dismounted their horses and entered the church.

Thomas sighed. 'You may lay me down again, but I pray you leave the window open.'

'But the contagion?'

'I am dying, it will not matter. I love to hear the sounds outside and breathe the fresh air. I grew up in the Yorkshire dales you know. Mayhap tonight I shall hear the birds singing their way to bed.'

He winced as they laid him back on his cot.

'Some willow bark, I think,' he croaked.

Brother Matthew came back with the infusion and a bowl of clear broth. The latter tasted good and relieved the bitter taste of the medicine.

'I met him once, you know,' Thomas said softly. His unfocused eyes took on a dreamy quality.

'You did? When was this? What did you speak of?'

Thomas gave a little smile. 'I must take that to my grave, I'm afraid.'

Brother Matthew nodded; a brother could not shrive a penitent but the friars were often witness to people's most private thoughts and wishes. Thomas was a learned man as well as one of the finest infirmarians in their order. Perhaps he had advised the king on Queen Anne's malady.

'Now go, young man. You are not needed here and you should take every chance to meet this king of ours!'

Brother Matthew needed no second telling and left with the empty bowl and cup. Thomas lay back on the soft pillows and gazed up at the window. He suddenly felt rather cold; he would ask them to close it a little. He was literally wasting away as the canker grew. Even so, there was enough of black bile in his body to feed the thing. He had at first tried milkweed and parsley as well as purging to rid himself of the excess bile, but nothing worked. Now he must sleep and not be a bother to anyone. He sent up a silent prayer for the royal couple and dozed.

'Brother Thomas.' A whisper from the doorway woke him from his disturbed dream. 'The King wishes to see you, if you feel able.'

Thomas blinked. Of course he was able.

And suddenly King Richard was there, smiling down at Thomas. Beside him was his bride of two months, her brown eyes warm and concerned.

'One of your brothers told me you were here. I am glad that I can see you again and thank you once more for the service you did for me.'

'' Twas nought, your Grace. Any loyal man would do the same.'

'I think not, Thomas... It grieves me to see you so pale and changed since our last meeting. You have everything for your comfort?'

Thomas nodded and suddenly wheezed, 'The window... I wish it open, but not so wide... pray ask Brother —'

But before he could say more, the king himself was at the window, adjusting it. Queen Joana moved forward and laid her hand on his cheek, 'Pray for us, holy brother.' she said simply.

'I do, always.'

'And remember us before the face of God.'

The face of God! How trusting they were.

'And I pray you keep me in your prayers also,' Thomas Appleby replied.

'You will have a month of Masses, and one each year on your mind day,' the king assured him.

It was all too brief, but as they said their adieus, Thomas gazed into the king's grey-blue eyes and noted the expression of gratitude.

And if he should go to hell for his sins, it would have been worth it to have this man reign over England.

None

He wished his room had a view over the herb garden, he should like to see it one last time. For many years he had tended it, gathering the healing plants and turning them into concoctions. In his office with its many bottles and instruments he would carefully note each treatment, its success – or not – and the patient's condition. Too much black bile caused melancholy and perhaps that was why he was not at peace. Or perhaps it was the memory of that evening... A sin not regretted, and which could therefore not be absolved.

His Grace had left and there was only the sun to keep him company until the brothers arrived to say the mid-afternoon office of None with him. It was a short office, mindful of the day's labours.

Brothers John and Peter came this time. It seemed as if the community each wanted to say farewell. He smiled grimly to himself; he was regarded as a wise and holy man.

The prayers began and with their familiar words Thomas relapsed again into memory. When you enter religion, you forsake everything else. Above all, you learn obedience. It was this which had taken him from the great city of York to this town in the heart of England. But wherever he was, he would always be a Yorkshireman, seeking news from every visiting friar from the north. He had eagerly followed the career of the Duke of Gloucester, the King's representative in the north. A breath of fresh air, he was; a nobleman with a heart for the common people, intent on giving justice to all. Thomas still had the letter from his friend Fr Matthew Wrangwyssh, a cousin to the mayor of York, in which he wrote: *'In truth, I cannot think of any of his kind who pleases me more. This man is a great blessing of God unto this city. I pray he will long be with us.'*

That prayer was not to be granted, for in 1483 King Edward died and the three estates offered the crown to his younger brother the Duke of Gloucester, King Richard III. The people of the North were comforted only by the thought that the whole of England must now benefit from this man's wise and benevolent rule.

Vespers

Thomas had some more broth, but it came back again leaving him weak and struggling to breathe. Perhaps standing at the window had been a mistake, but he was glad of it anyway. He wouldn't live long enough to see the next royal progress through the town. Now the whole community seemed to want to visit him, sensing that this would be goodbye. He had no objection to it, as long as they wanted just a smile and a "God bless". More than that he could not give anyway, not being a priest. One did not need priestly orders to be a good apothecary. St Francis himself had not been a priest, feeling himself unworthy.

'Would you like the priest now?' Prior Robert asked gently. Thomas looked at the ceiling and wondered if it would do any good. Were there levels in hell? Would cleansing his venial sins give him a milder dose of eternal damnation? If he refused, he risked scandalising the community who regarded him as a wonder worker and wise man. He wondered what his grandmother would say.

'Very well. Is there a visiting priest?'

'Of course, he'll come directly. You can say Vespers with him.'

His grandmother would probably have scoffed 'You did what you felt right at the time, was that so very wrong?' But she was a pragmatist, attuned more to nature's rhythms and its own moral code. She refused ever to see any bad in Thomas. Of course, she would have justified anything he'd done! For herself, Thomas knew she had lived a good, pure and selfless life. All the good in him had been due to her.

The sunlight was weaker now, slowly fading, along with his life. To live in the light is to turn from darkness, and now only darkness remained.

'Brother Thomas? I'm Father John Aske.' An unfamiliar voice at the doorway.

'Come in and close the window,' He was feeling cold again. Not enough flesh on his bones.

'In nomine Patris, et Filii et Spiritus Sancti....'

'Bless me Father for I have sinned. It is a year since my last confession... We are now under the seal, father?'

'We are, and you may tell me anything, God is waiting with his great love and forgiveness.'

'What if I have committed a mortal sin and do not repent?'

Compline

A little over a year ago, when the canker had become more troubling but not enough to keep him from his work, he had travelled to the fens. As he sailed up the Great River Ouse, Thomas suddenly made out the distant outline of Ely cathedral rising from the flat landscape like a ghost. What a marvel in a place which had once been only bogland!

The purpose of his journey was to visit the herbalist and scholar John Mayne. They had been corresponding for some months, each aware that they could learn from the other. Dr Mayne taught at Cambridge University but was also the private physician of the Bishop of Ely.

On the last evening, their conversation was disturbed by a messenger from the Bishop's palace. Dr Mayne was required to attend my lord bishop, who had an ague.

'An ague? You don't mean plague by chance?' Mayne looked doubtful. He had heard that there was an outbreak of sickness among the Bishop's servants.

'No sir. You are not required to treat any of his household that have the puking sickness. You will use the back stairway to the bishop's chambers and leave the same way.'

John Mayne was clearly uncomfortable. He dismissed the messenger and fell into a gloomy reverie. He was a healthy man on the brink of middle age with many more years of useful work before him.

Thomas, on the other hand...

'*I* will go,' he said simply.

'You are my guest... I cannot allow it!'

'I am sixty-four years of age and I have a canker in my gut. I will be fortunate to live out the year. God can spare me more than you.'

'His Lordship may refuse...'

'I will say you are unwell. It's probably an ache in his old joints, any jobbing herb-meddler can do as well as you or I.'

'Keep away from the servants. Take a full case of potions, you won't need them but my lord likes to be impressed. Take that humble look off your face, you're a learned man, Thomas.'

☆☆☆

Thomas the apothecary seldom had dealings with great men. Where he came from, respectable people did not kowtow to their social superiors. He stood in the doorway of the Bishop's palace and insisted on examining the servants. It was possible that the Bishop's 'ague' was connected to whatever was afflicting the household.

'You should see the Bishop first, for fear of contagion.' The liveried servant was nervous.

'I'll keep my distance. I know how to do my work,' Thomas snapped.

He could tell almost at once that he was in no danger, unless he ate something. The servants who were unwell had eaten tainted food, and with rest and fresh clean water should recover soon. He ordered the food stores to be thrown out and the pantry thoroughly cleaned. Then he pulled up his cloak as if it would protect him, and headed to the bishop's quarters.

Treading up the back stairwell, he used the silent tread learned in childhood when hunting prey or catching sheep among the windswept stony crags. Thomas wasn't naturally subservient, but this was a place which commanded deference. Raising his hand to knock on the solid oak door, he paused, hearing muffled voices within. Should he disturb them? Without realising it, he quietened his mind and listened attentively as his grandmother had taught him. There were two people within, speaking clearly enough to be heard if one's ears were attuned. Evidently, they did not expect to be overheard.

'You have my word on it. You can tell Lady Margaret that two thousand men are ready and waiting to meet her son in Milford Haven and more will join as they pass through.'

'My lady knows she can rely on you. You have been the greatest friend the House of Lancaster can have.'

Thomas froze. What was this? A plot against the Yorkist king? In recent years the House of Lancaster had brought little but misery to this land. Who was this Lady Margaret? Hardly the Anjou woman – she had been sent back to France and her son had died in battle.

As a friar he heard most of the rumours from visitors to the Friary. Could 'Lady Margaret' be mother to the Tudor lad who, strong rumour had it, was keen to establish his own claim to the English throne?

'I will write to those I know we can trust, telling them to prepare. The invasion will succeed if we can take the King's party by surprise. His ships are patrolling the coast – they expect a landing further south, but Wales will be better. Who better than a Welsh-born prince, wielding the dragon of Wales, to lead his people to victory! The people will flock to him there.'

'Lady Margaret says that some Welsh lords have sworn fealty to Richard.'

'As have we all...'

'Destroy the letter when you have read it... this is treason, after all.' There was a rustling as if someone had stood up and was reaching for a cloak.

Thomas silently walked backwards down the stone staircase until he was at the bottom of it. He heard the messenger leave, taking the other stairs. Noisily, he trudged up the steps again and rapped on the door.

What on earth was he to do? The blood began to roar in his ears... a plot against King Richard, on the heels of Buckingham's failed rebellion. Was the king to have no peace? Thomas thought hard. A desperate idea came into his mind.

Could he do this?

Matins

I must tell the story, the whole tale exactly as I remember it. I know the hour is late and the sun has long sunk.... but, Father, this is my confession and I need to tell someone before I die. Even if it means there is no hope of salvation left for me. Such treachery. You need to know how far proud men will go in their wickedness against a wise and godly king...

Bishop John Morton was sitting by a fire. It was past midsummer but the night air still chill enough for an old man to need extra warmth.

Thomas bowed and pulled back his hood.

'You are not Dr Mayne.'

'No, my lord, he is unwell so he sent me. I am advising him on certain matters of physic.' *Forgive me, dear Doctor, but if I have to impress him, this is how it's done.* Thomas hesitated, and then added 'I am Friar William Talbot, apothecary and surgeon.'

'Well, I suppose you will do. Talbot you say? Any relation to the Earl of Shrewsbury?'

'A very distant cousin I think, but nothing close, my Lord. Now, what ails you, sir?'

'I have the ague. Comes on when the weather changes. It's the damp, fenland mists, they play havoc with my bones, even in summer.'

With a flourish, Thomas placed his medicine box on a chest by the wall and went over to inspect the Bishop. For a man in his sixties, Morton was not in bad health. He lived well of course, but didn't overindulge on rich food and wine. As Thomas made his examination, he was aware of the Bishop's hooded pale blue eyes watching him. This was a man replete with cunning, a man who could judge others swiftly and with skill. Seldom had Thomas met anyone who exuded such thoughtful intelligence, and who inspired such terror. Fear rose in his gullet, causing him to swallow hard. He hoped the bishop would attribute any signs of nervousness to awe in his presence. Talbot had been a name seized at random. Many of that name were supporters of the Lancastrian cause.

Thomas indicated the wine jug and cup on the table beside the bishop. Morton nodded. Thomas poured some wine and took the cup to his box on the dresser.

'I will mix you something to take now and leave you plenty for later.' Apologetically, he turned away and opened the heavy wooden box. It contained saws and probes as well as decoctions. Briefly he thought of knifing the old man where he sat, but batted away the thought as if it were an annoying fly. It would have to be poison.

He would poison the bishop, find the letter, dump some other document in the fire and leave quickly. The fact that some of Morton's household had been laid low with tainted food would be useful.

The garlic and basil with their strong flavours should mask the dose of digitalis that accompanied them. Not a mild dose, which would steady a weak heart, but a stronger one... to stop it altogether.

He was a friar! A son of St Francis! Was he really planning to kill a priest of God and a senior churchman at that? But Thomas could not find the incriminating letter without searching the bishop's apartments, and for that the bishop needed to be asleep. In a very deep sleep. Should he wake and find the letter missing... plans could be changed.

He decanted an innocent tincture of garlic and basil along with chamomile, a sedative, and placed the full bottle on the table next to the wine jug. 'This is for later, my lord. Meanwhile take this, which should soothe your pains.'

It was so easy. Pray God the dosage was enough. Pray God... *Could one pray God that a poison kill a man?*

Thomas turned to replace the bottles slowly in his box, waiting for the potion to enter the old man's veins.

A little while later, his work done, he stepped out of the bishop's chamber and went on his way.

Lauds

How easy it had been to convince people that the bishop had partaken of the tainted food which turned to poison in his blood!

Thomas had hated to mislead the good Dr Mayne, but England now depended on him.

There was little time to lose, as even now, Morton's fellow plotters might suspect murder and betrayal. Thomas could trust no one. Anyone could profess loyalty to the King but be secretly against him. Travelling from friary to friary, he reached London and prayed desperately that he manage to speak with King Richard.

God appeared to be on his side, at least in this. Dusty and travel-stained as he was, he was ushered into the King's presence. Thomas knelt as low as his knees would let him. 'My liege, I should not presume to enter your presence, especially so filthy and unkempt, but I have evidence of most foul treachery that cannot wait.'

King Richard read the letter and questioned Thomas further. His face, Thomas noticed, was still youthful yet there were frown lines on his forehead and around his eyes. His jaw clenched and a pulse in his cheek betrayed his anger. He threw the letter onto a table and began to pace up and down, fingering his rings. 'You have told no one of this?'

'Not a soul apart from you, sire. I know not when Morton's body was discovered, having come in all haste.'

'It is vital that no one be told, no one! Margaret Beaufort! That traitorous wretch! She must not know her plans are discovered lest she warn her son. Oh this realm of care! What must I do to gain the peace it needs? Will it never end?'

Thomas could not tell if the king was going to burst into tears or explode with rage.

Dawn was coming...

So you see, father, that I can never be forgiven: I lied to Morton and countless others, I killed a bishop and concealed the manner of his death, and not for a moment do I regret it. I saw the look on the king's face, of shock, disbelief and intense sorrow. A sorrow almost too deep for this world. I'm a Yorkshireman, how could I betray such a king, the kindest, best and most dutiful ruler in memory?

'Thomas, I'm a North Country man too and I love and honour our king. I thank God for his reign and pray it lasts long. You came upon a well of foul treachery that would have killed an anointed king and put an untried boy of bastard stock on the throne. Tell me, is it wrong to kill in war?'

Of course not, if it is in the heat of battle.

'But what were you in, if not a battle? They were not warriors with sword and shield, but they were, all the same, at war with our king and that is treason. Tell me, had Morton had no plans of betrayal, would you have done what you did?'

Never. I regret that I had to do it at all.

'Then may God grant you pardon, absolution, and remission of your sins and I, by the authority of Jesus, do absolve you from every bond of excommunication....' Fr John placed his hands on Thomas' head and as the words of absolution washed over the dying man, the first rays of dawn shone faintly through the mullioned window panes.

'You can be at peace, good man. Listen, the dawn chorus is starting to greet the new day, the birds themselves rejoice that we have such a king...'

Dimly, Thomas heard the birdsong, like the angels singing him to heaven.

As the dawn came in and the friars assembled for Prime, the news came from the infirmary that the old friar was finally at peace.

☆☆☆

As a result of Thomas' information, Margaret Beaufort was covertly watched and her letters intercepted, revealing her co-conspirators. The welcoming party at Milford Haven was not as the rebels expected, and Henry Tydder, who would be king, was captured and executed along with his uncle Jasper, Thomas Stanley, the Earl of Oxford and numerous others who would betray their king. The head of Henry Tudor appeared briefly on the Tower gates bedecked with a paper crown, though King Richard did not allow this to remain.

Margaret Beaufort was sentenced to perpetual imprisonment in rather comfortable quarters in the tower, although this did not prevent her from occasionally scheming – not that it did her much good.

About Clare Anderson

Clare finally deserted the Lancastrian cause in 2015 and is now a firm adherent of the House of York. She has four grown-up children and lives with her husband and two dogs in rural Berkshire. Although she has published work on numerous non-fiction subjects, this is her first attempt at historical fiction. She enjoys painting, star-gazing and musing about history.

The Real Story of the Battle of Stoke Field

by
Sandra Heath Wilson

✫✫✫

Introduction

After Richard III was killed by treachery in 1485, Henry VII didn't have things all his own way. John, Earl of Lincoln, Richard's nephew and (it is believed) his chosen successor, soon rebelled, fleeing to Richard's sister, the Duchess of Burgundy. There he gathered an army and returned to England with Richard's close friend Francis Lovell and a boy named Lambert Simnel as his figurehead. No one knows who Lambert really was, or if Lincoln believed he was Yorkist royalty, as claimed.

At Stoke Field on the banks of the Trent the Yorkist rebels confronted Henry's army, led by the Earl of Oxford, who was a fine soldier and commander. Battle was joined, and at first it seemed Oxford was winning the day, but then, as the Yorkists fought back, Lincoln was killed. There was panic, the Yorkists fled the field and Henry's force was victorious. Lambert was captured and, famously, spared by being put to work in the royal kitchens.

Henry didn't participate, arriving late. He always preserved his own hide. He had Lincoln and other dead Yorkist commanders buried ignominiously under willow trees with slender branches through their hearts. Until recently the spring on the site of these trees was still visible at the side of a small lane, but now a new double carriageway has been driven through.

The sad truth about the Battle of East Stoke in 1487 is that the White Rose lost, and John de la Pole, Earl of Lincoln was slain. So my story is pure wishful thinking, and written with a large helping of Yorkist relish. If anyone deserved to be shoved in the ground under those willow trees, it was the vile Henry Tudor! So read on, and see what really should have happened that summer day by the Trent . . .

✩✩✩

My dear friends, today is the twentieth anniversary of the Battle of Stoke Field, and I think the time has come for the full story of that pivotal conflict to be written down. The Yorkist victory has never been denied – thanks be to Almighty God – but what isn't widely known is exactly what happened that day.

I know because my dear father, Tom Sturdy, then a mere crossbowman, witnessed everything. He played a brave role, and I, his firstborn, am determined that he should receive the credit he's due. You see, if it weren't for him, we wouldn't have had John de la Pole, our irreplaceable Duke of Suffolk, who as Lord Protector led the land throughout Edward VI's minority.

When I was small, I could never have imagined that the Sturdys would one day sit here in their own fine manor house in the Kent countryside. The family has indeed moved on since we occupied a very lowly cottage near Nottingham. Tom Sturdy always delighted in relating how our beloved king, Edward VI, ascended the Westminster throne, having already been crowned in Dublin. Oh, I know the tale by heart because whenever my father had a few tankards of ale inside him, my siblings and I had to pay attention! We were word perfect, believe me.

A curious fact that isn't generally known is that King Richard III's nephew and chosen heir, the Duke of Suffolk – at that time the Earl of Lincoln – had a double who might have been his twin. The same coincidence had happened a century earlier, when King Richard II was impersonated after death by his clerk, Maudelyn, who fooled another Lancastrian usurper, Henry IV, that his murdered predecessor had somehow survived and escaped.

In 1487 the land was beset by the Tudor tyrant, Henry VII, whom God curse forever. But as the Battle of Stoke Field progressed, Lincoln's double, a certain Paul Wortham, flashed like a comet in front of both armies before being cruelly slain. Standing over the bloody corpse, the tyrant was to make a fatal decision.

Two years earlier at Bosworth Field the Yorkist king Richard III, of blessed memory, was betrayed by his so-called allies, allowing Tudor to seize the throne. Lincoln survived that dreadful day, and with the late king's loyal friends, Sir Francis Lovell and Sir Robert Percy, fled to Richard's fiercely supportive sister, the Duchess of Burgundy in the Low Countries. She despised the Tudor upstart, and conspired with rebel Yorkists to never rest until he was disposed of. Preferably in a casket.

Henry was cruel, cowardly and cunning, but fate had placed the crown on his head and vengeful Yorkists were hampered because King Richard, who'd lost both his wife and son, had never publicly named Lincoln as his heir. He had in person, of course, but there was nothing formal, otherwise we'd have had King John II on the throne these twenty years.

My father was also in Burgundy back then. Where Lincoln went, he went. He said the fear was that England would only rise against Henry if there was an undeniably premier Yorkist prince to follow. At twenty-seven Lincoln was mature, experienced and inspiring, but he wasn't of the all-important male descent, being the son of Richard's other sister, the Duchess of Suffolk.

But then – wonder of wonders – destiny intervened in the form of Edward Plantagenet, Earl of Warwick, 12-year-old son of King Richard's brother, the Duke of Clarence, who'd been an attainted traitor. Henry set about ridding himself of *all* Yorkist problems, and the inconvenient Edward had been kept a prisoner in the Tower since Bosworth. Not even Tudor dared to commit the execrable sin of executing a child, and his intention was to wait until Edward was full grown and *then* execute him on a false charge. The boy had been rescued by enterprising Yorkists and taken to Burgundy under the unlikely name of Lambert Simnel.

Well, my father always said that simnels were cakes, so no one could understand why such a strange name had been picked. No one knows to this day! But it was as Lambert Simnel that Edward arrived among the delighted Yorkist lords who yearned to restore the rightful line to the throne. Here was a true figurehead, a prince of the all-important male line who could rally dispirited Yorkists. He may have been a boy, but he'd have Lincoln to guide him. And he certainly wouldn't be known as Lambert Simnel for long!

So, in the spring of 1487 a fine rebel army departed the Low Countries for Ireland, where the House of York enjoyed popularity and they could be assured of collecting more men and general support. Lincoln – with Lovell and Percy – were in command of course, but young Edward was on full display as the rightful king. They had many English knights and men, and a trained force of 2,000 fearsome rather gaudily clad German mercenaries under their commander, Martin Schwartz.

On 24 May 1487 in Dublin Cathedral Edward of Warwick was crowned King Edward VI of England. Well, as my father said, Tudor wasn't really a king, he was a murdering usurper and didn't count for anything. The true succession was going from King Richard to King Edward, and that was enough for most right-thinking men, although I confess that many thought it should have gone from Richard III to John II. After all, Richard *had* chosen Lincoln.

After the coronation, the boy king was presented with a dapple pony of the finest Irish breeding, which pleased him greatly. It was saddled and barded for an English monarch and was a perfect miniature courser. Oh, he *loved* that beautiful pony, which was to live long enough to be ridden by his own son.

Then the rebels and new king left Ireland for Lancashire, intending to march south through the realm to take on the Tudor. On landing they were joined by many new supporters, soldiers, gentlemen and knights included. Among them was Paul Wortham, who looked so like Lincoln that he caused great stir.

According to my father, Wortham was a great admirer of the earl and always did his utmost to play upon their shared looks. He was the same age and adopted Lincoln's way of speech and mannerisms, even being impudent enough to wear the earl's personal colours on his surcoat. His antics raised much mirth around the campfires. Even Lincoln was amused, and little King Edward was often helpless with laughter. It was a great diversion, and no one imagined for a moment that just when all was to seem lost, Wortham was to single-handedly ensure victory for York. Well, helped a little by none other than Henry VII himself.

The Yorkists marched south toward the barrier of the River Trent, gathering more support all the time, and posing such a threat to Henry that a great battle was inevitable. The usurper assembled his own army at Nottingham in the centre of the realm. From there an advance force was despatched north along the Trent under the command of the formidable Lancastrian, the Earl of Oxford, who intended to reinforce Newark to prevent rebels from crossing the bridge. The Yorkists would have given much to have Oxford on their side. At forty-five he was in his prime and was no wavering heart, but he supported the red rose and wouldn't be easy to defeat.

Henry was displeased about the whole rebellion business. His ambitions were being thwarted. He'd lost the Yorkist queen foisted on him to supposedly end the warring between Lancaster and York, and now he needed to marry again. He was thirty and needed sons to establish his Tudor dynasty. His chosen bride was a prestigious Castilian princess, and he didn't need this tiresome rebellion to make his future in-laws question his security on the throne.

The rebels crossed the river a mile or so south of Newark at a place where scouts had found a good ford only two feet deep in the summer. Thus Oxford's first plan of defence was thwarted. Now the two opposing forces pitched camp within a few miles of each other on the same side of the Trent.

The colourful pavilions of the Yorkist commanders were positioned on Rampire Hill, in front of a strip of woodland atop an escarpment near the village of East Stoke. Their backs were protected by the Trent and the stretch of river meadow where they'd pitched their main camp. They had a tactical advantage over Oxford and the Lancastrians on the lower acres in front of them. My father was well pleased. Archers could do much damage from up there, especially longbowmen.

Henry and his force didn't accompany Oxford out of Nottingham. Never being one to risk his own hide, it was his intention to delay until the following morning, when he knew the main conflict would have to begin. He'd make his appearance when Oxford had gained the upper hand and he, Henry, was in no danger. So at dawn on the appointed day, he still languished in his bed at Nottingham Castle and his great force remained in its camp. He'd break his fast in due course, select his finest clothes – no, he'd have to at least pretend he was a warrior, so it would have to be armour – and after that he'd amble north with his uncle Jasper Tudor and the royal army, as if to support Oxford, in whom Henry had every confidence. Then, finally, he'd get his hands on Lincoln, whom he'd instructed was to be taken alive. The Yorkist maggot was going to pay dearly for presuming to rebel!

Meanwhile, as the previous night approached, the opposing forces near East Stoke could only wait. Come dawn the main Yorkist force would ascend unseen from the Trent meadows through a cleft known as a gutter that pierced the rear flank of Rampire Hill. As night fell the camps were the usual sprawl of men, weapons, pavilions, makeshift tents, horses, armour, mail, banners and coats-of-arms, campfires, and cannon. Of course, there were the many women followers, who plied a far less warlike trade, so there was singing and laughter, but the atmosphere was charged, as if a thunderstorm were in the offing.

At dawn the rebels awakened for mass and to eat, but then Lincoln's scurriers arrived in haste to warn that Oxford's army was stealing a march by already making for the slope near East Stoke. Yorkist drums rang out battle stations, and the rebel army, nimble after being rested, ascended Rampire Hill gutter at the double.

They outpaced Oxford and were soon deployed, six men deep for three-quarters of a mile, with the village and the hill at their backs. There they waited in brave array, men-at-arms, supported by archers and billmen, with horsemen in readiness at the rear, ready to bear down upon the enemy once the initial advance and conflict was well in hand.

The gold-armoured boy king, mounted on his pony, was prominently visible on the hilltop by the pavilions, with royal standards and all the trappings of his rank, while further down the slope Lincoln, Lovell and other commanders rode up and down the lines, exhorting their men to fight for the true king. They instilled heart, courage and the belief that God was on their side. Lincoln's head was uncovered, his chestnut curls flowing loose as he passed to and fro on his spirited cream horse, so there could be no doubt of his identity.

Oxford's force was beginning to assemble on level ground a quarter of a mile to the south, but he had still to properly deploy when Lincoln perceived that attacking before he was ready was their best chance of swift victory. So, with Lincoln in the lead and full armour and closed armet, the signal was given to advance in orderly but relentless manner, in the hope of throwing Oxford's forces into complete confusion, which initially they were.

The German mercenaries moved forward to the shrill and thunderous racket of fifes and drums. It was the first time this frightening sound had been heard in England. Arquebuses were fired and bolts and arrows flew like hail as the two armies clashed. Terrified horses whinnied as they were caught up in the fray, and the countryside rang with shouting, screaming and the awful clang of metal upon metal.

Battlefields are grim places, and the ground was soon soaked with blood. The stench of death filled the air and numerous bodies cluttered the paths of their living comrades, making things even more hazardous for horses. Lincoln was in the thick of it, lunging and slashing, riding men down and stabbing whichever part of them he could reach. He was every inch the courageous son of York.

Robert Percy fought further down the slope, and there was dismay in the Yorkist ranks as he was cut from his horse and set upon by Oxford's men. No one could have survived such a ferocious and concerted onslaught. Martin Schwartz met a similar end, but his mercenaries fought on regardless.

Francis Lovell held his ground, backing Lincoln at every turn. Two and a half hours of slaughter passed, before an enemy sword found its way past the couter of the armour on Lincoln's right elbow, wounding him badly. He couldn't wield his sword, and had to retreat to the hill, hoping to have the flow of blood staunched and be able to rejoin the fray, but he knew it was a vain hope. His right hand was useless now.

Then a group of Oxford's mounted men broke through to the standards behind him. Blood was seeping thickly from his wound, which was deep and painful, but some Yorkists fought his pursuers back so that he reached the relative protection of the hilltop. His physician and attendants rushed forward, but he had to wave them back. There was no time to take off armour and submit to medical attention! He was swordless, his dagger and left hand his only defence, so he remained on his horse, directing his forces from the hilltop, all the while enduring piercing pain.

Henry's force had yet to arrive and Oxford's men were fighting against great odds and gradually, inexorably, the tide turned in the rebels' favour. Then Paul Wortham appeared from nowhere on a cream horse that was caparisoned with Lincoln's badge and colours. Over his armour he wore a surcoat displaying the earl's leopard arms. Some of his chestnut hair was visible because the visor of his armet was open. To all intents and purposes he was Lincoln.

Oxford's men believed the earl himself was among them, within recklessly easy reach. He was immediately surrounded, dragged from his horse, and a rondel thrust mightily into his face. The rondel's long blade stabbed again and again, but Wortham had been killed by the first stab. My father said that he sacrificed himself in the misguided belief he was helping his idol, but instead he'd handed victory to Oxford because most of the Yorkists also thought Lincoln had been killed!

Yet Lincoln himself was still clearly visible on the hill. Realising that a rout of his confused army might be imminent, he removed his armet to show his face and hair, and then bellowed orders to rally them all again by drawing attention to himself, but there was already such mayhem that he couldn't be heard. Nor did anyone, friend or foe, seem to even see him.! He was suddenly invisible! He cast around for his trumpeters, but they were nowhere to be seen. There wasn't even a drummer. He was helpless. And so was the boy king, now dismounted and standing there in bareheaded confusion, his golden suit of armour gleaming.

The feared rout ensued, with even the mercenaries fleeing. Oxford's horsemen pursued the rebels, and Lincoln could only watch incredulously. Out of the very jaws of victory...defeat! The one good thing was seeing Francis Lovell and his men make a clean escape further along the escarpment. They at least could fight another day.

Lincoln gestured to his attendants to run while they still could and shouted at the king's guards to take the boy to safety as well but those fellows, suddenly craven, saved themselves and left the frightened child behind. Lincoln tried to make Edward escape with him. The boy's pony was tethered nearby, and there was even a fallen tree trunk upon which to stand to mount easily in his cumbersome armour, but the little king slumped to the grass beside his discarded armet and clung to the tree trunk.

When Lincoln struggled to haul him up on his own horse with his one good hand, Edward wouldn't release the trunk. Lincoln could see the enemy advancing up the hill. What should he do? Stay with the boy? Or make good his own escape to join Lovell and take Tudor on another time? He chose to stay. Honour demanded it. He was Edward's cousin and protector and would defend him to the end.

Alighting, he *wrenched* the boy to his feet mightily and then grabbed the reins of horse and pony to lead them and the little king swiftly into the strip of woodland. As soon as they were among the trees, he slapped the animals' rumps, sending them galloping off. Bending low to stay out of sight, he pushed Edward one-handedly into a thick clump of gorse bushes on the battle side of the woods and then climbed in as well.

The gorse was dense and thorny, but the two were protected by their armour. The spiky branches folded over them as they crouched low, and Lincoln impressed upon the boy that the slightest sound would cost them their lives. Blood now covered his lower right arm, the pain was agonising and he knew he'd be hard put to fight off any sustained attack. If the flow wasn't staunched soon, he might even become too weak to survive.

What neither of them knew was that my father had seen everything, having followed the wounded Lincoln to the summit of Rampire Hill. Now Tom Sturdy didn't hesitate to help. Oh, he was a stout fellow, even if he was of low birth. One of Oxford's men had also seen the fugitives' hiding place, but Tom's crossbow aim was always sure. As the fellow's lips parted to call his comrades, a bolt went right through his neck and silenced him forever. Then my father joined the hideaways amid the gorse, prepared to defend them to the very death.

Oxford's horsemen reached the scene, and they cast around for any rebels, but all seemed deserted, except for their dead comrade with a crossbow bolt through his neck. They dismounted and began to ransack the pavilions, looting whatever they fancied. One of them took Edward's armet as a trophy. The gorse thicket didn't warrant a second glance.

The fleeing rebel army had meanwhile streamed down the gutter toward the Trent, but at the bottom, barring their way, waited Francis Lovell and his men who halted them in their tracks. Lincoln's horse and the pony had been spotted, but an alert scout's signals from the hilltop informed Lovell that Lincoln and Edward were not dead but hiding, with a lone archer to protect them.

Lovell confronted the retreating Yorkists, calming them with the sheer force of his personality. It was not without reason that King Richard had trusted him so much and now Lincoln did too. Lovell scanned the sea of frightened faces, telling them that all was not lost, the Earl of Lincoln still lived! As did their true king, Edward VI! Victory could yet be theirs! They had to keep their heads and follow his every command.

Hope began to cheer the hitherto dejected men, and they obeyed Lovell to the very letter, reversing their tracks up the gutter to take on the enemy again. Not a single man would break ranks. They hungered to regain their pride and complete the victory that would have been theirs but for Paul Wortham's loyal foolishness.

On the battlefield Oxford's army was still unaware of what was happening. They thought they were the victors and had no idea that not only were the Yorkists advancing again, but Lincoln, very much alive, was observing everything from the bushes on the hill. Oxford's main concern now was how to tell Henry that Lincoln was dead. He didn't relish the moment. Tudor wasn't exactly amenable at the best of times. Truth to tell, Oxford couldn't abide him. Honour meant everything to him and Henry had none.

Oxford's men moved among the hundreds of bodies on the sloping land, collecting abandoned weapons, horses and scattered banners and pennons. Discarded armour lay everywhere, helmets, breastplates, and various other costly items that were gathered eagerly by the conquerors. The Battle of Stoke Field had been a far longer, more savage and utterly ruthless battle than Bosworth.

The king's divisions arrived at last, and Henry rode slightly ahead of Jasper Tudor, who was not in the least pleased to be involved in such a demeaningly late arrival. He was the Earl of Pembroke, a proven warrior, and had for some time now been struggling to stay true to his nephew's cause.

Henry, on the other hand, was content. He intended to give the battlefield a cursory inspection, make suitably pleased noises, and then ride on to Newark for a fine victory feast. So confident was he, that he'd already removed his armour and was very comfortable in his sumptuous royal robes. He even wore the jewelled circlet taken from King Richard's head at Bosworth.

Oxford's fears were justified because Henry was livid to learn that Lincoln was no more. Viewing Wortham's mutilated corpse, which was one of the few untouched by looting, guards having been set around it, Henry almost jumped up and down in a fury. He was like a spoilt child deprived of a toy, and Oxford was disgusted. So was Jasper.

When Henry had calmed down, Wortham's armet was removed. Even though the face had been butchered beyond recognition there seemed no mistaking it was Lincoln. And yet... Henry hesitated. Maybe the build, colouring and age were convincing, but there was something about the mangled features that disturbed the usurper. If only he could feel certain it was Lincoln and not some fiendishly clever Yorkist trick.

Then he remembered something and indicated the removal of the dead man's right gauntlet. Lincoln always wore a particularly fine amethyst ring, but it wasn't there. Heart sinking, Henry gestured at the other gauntlet. There was no sign of the ring. Jasper shrugged. Amethyst or not, it had to be Lincoln's body. Just how much evidence was needed? The body was clearly Lincoln's, so the amethyst must have been taken before the guards were assigned. It was, after all, a highly desirable, widely known stone.

Jasper was right, Henry thought, glancing at Oxford and his men, who all looked as guilty as sin itself, but now wasn't the best moment to antagonise Oxford. After all, victory was victory. Resigned that the body could only be Lincoln's, he instructed that the remains be carried down toward a small, shallow glen he'd observed earlier. There'd been a spring overhung with willows that would provide an excellent resting place for the traitor Earl of Lincoln.

The bodies of Sir Robert Percy and Martin Schwartz were also transported, with Henry and Jasper following to be certain that Lincoln especially was well and truly buried. Oxford and his men remained on the slope. He didn't approve of this. Lincoln was a prince of the blood, whether Henry Tudor liked it or not, and should be accorded an appropriate burial in holy ground. Richard III should have been interred as a king too, not hastily disposed of in the Leicester Greyfriars. Oxford was very close to having had enough of Henry Tudor.

Henry and his uncle stayed on their horses while some of their men as gravediggers prepared three graves in the soft, damp ground between the willows. The three bodies were put into them hastily, and without a priest in attendance, and when the earth had been stamped down, slender branches from the overhanging trees were driven into the buried bodies. The willow staves would take root and the remains obliterated forever.

At that moment the regrouped Yorkist forces streamed down the slope from Rampire Hill, having collected Lincoln and reunited him with his horse. Edward stayed by the pavilions with new guards.

Henry whipped around in the saddle in horror. The battle wasn't over after all! Terrified, he gathered his reins to urge his horse away to safety, but the mud was treacherous and the animal slithered and fell, depositing its rider heavily in the morass. Jasper and all the men rode off at a gallop, not realising Henry wasn't with him. The gravediggers took to their heels, leaving their shovels behind. Only a wounded soldier remained.

The horse scrambled up again and bolted, leaving Henry too winded to move, even though the Yorkist horde was almost upon him. The soldier made no move to help as the tyrant managed to struggle to his feet. There Tudor stood, his magnificent royal robes covered in mud, King Richard's circlet askew. Henry had once maltreated the soldier who now had no intention of giving his life for such a man, and as the Yorkists arrived he rushed to tell Lincoln what had happened. Pointing at the fresh graves and tell-tale willow staves, he made sure to describe Henry's gloating delight as he observed the shoddy interments.

Oxford and his men watched in silence from further up the slope. The Yorkists were at a disadvantage down in the dell, and Oxford knew he only had to attack now for Henry – and the day – to be saved. Instead, he leaned casually on his pommel and gazed down expressionlessly toward the willows.

Henry observed the solitary figure and knew Oxford had just signalled his changed allegiance. Deserted in his hour of need, Henry was suffering the same fate he'd inflicted on Richard at Bosworth. A sense of sick panic engulfed him, but there was nothing he could do, except... His hand slid inside his robe, where he always concealed a secret dagger.

The royal army remained where it was, out of sight of the tiny valley, but its commanders could see the thronged Yorkists forces down there. They could also see Oxford's force on the slope and took their cue from his inaction. Something important was going on, and they'd wait until commanded otherwise. Oxford was their guide.

My father was still present and had concealed himself behind one of the willow trees. From there he could see both Henry and Lincoln clearly. His crossbow was primed, and he waited.

To Lincoln the three graves seemed to scream aloud for vengeance. He remembered Bosworth, and the uncle he'd loved. He thought of all the terrible lies and accusations the tyrant had directed at Richard's memory. The bastard even wore Richard's circlet! Lincoln's good hand clenched into a fist, and his brow darkened with outrage as he thought of everyone else who'd suffered at Tudor's hands. And now, today, Robert Percy, Martin Schwartz and foolish Paul Wortham had been buried without any nod toward honour or faith.

Anger burned through Lincoln as he studied the loathed usurper, who was in his power at last. He'd waited two long years to be avenged for Richard. Dismounting awkwardly, he prepared to confront the tyrant, even though he was growing weak from loss of blood.

My father always said that Henry went white with dread. Lincoln had removed his gauntlets, and the amethyst ring shone in the June sunlight. Suddenly Henry lost control, a madness seeming to flood his face as he drew his hidden dagger, meaning to plunge it into Lincoln. But hardly had he grasped it when a crossbow bolt penetrated his forehead. Life died in his eyes and his knees buckled as he fell back into the mud.

By the willows, my father lowered his crossbow and smiled. Never had his aim been truer.

Lincoln smiled too, and nodded his gratitude before retrieving Richard's circlet, meaning to place it on King Edward's head at the Battle of Stoke Field, just as it had been placed on Henry's at Bosworth. Retribution at last! And all because Tudor made a fatal mistake about Paul Wortham.

Oxford rode down to them slowly, still alone and unprotected. He was a Lancastrian but a principled man who felt that England was free again. Henry's trial and public execution would perhaps have been more appropriate. But was far from essential.

It was as he and Lincoln talked that the latter lost consciousness and couldn't be aroused. Everyone believed he would die of his undressed wound, from which far too much blood had been lost. He was conveyed carefully to nearby Newark, and there tended by monks who nursed him back to health. Thanks be to Almighty God.

Tudor's naked remains were taken to Nottingham over the back of a horse and put on display. It was another echo of the ignominy he'd heaped upon Richard.

Few would have credited that in the years to come the Earl of Oxford would be entirely loyal to the undeniably Yorkist Edward VI, and that his loyalty would be sealed by a blood bond. Edward would fall in love with and marry Oxford's adored illegitimate daughter, Alice. Oh yes, the good Earl of Oxford was to be very content with future events. To the end of his days he was glad he hadn't gone to Henry's aid in the little glen.

There was great rejoicing as Edward VI's second coronation took place in Westminster. The Earl of Oxford was greatly respected, and his support for the new Yorkist king made all the difference. Many Lancastrians were happy to follow his lead.

My father became *Sir* Tom Sturdy that great day and received generous reward for his loyalty, courage – and flawless aim – at Stoke Field. He also became a close friend of the Earl of Lincoln, who saw to it that the Sturdys rose to be a family of substance. And so I write this in the comfort of our fine Kent manor house. We have others in Nottingham and Suffolk. How the meek have risen.

As for Henry, well, he received a hasty burial to match the one he'd bestowed upon Richard, except that it was casket of stones that was lowered into the ground. Henry's actual remains were conveyed back to Stoke Field to be disposed of beneath certain willows, with a stave where his heart would have been. If he'd had one. His was the only resting place in that place because Robert Percy, Martin Schwartz and Paul Wortham had been reinterred with full honours in the places chosen by their families.

Richard III had also been given the royal funeral of an anointed king. He lay in Westminster Abbey, in the fine chapel Henry had been building for himself. Richard's wife and son were lain there with him, and every day there was a great stream of folk to pay their last respects.

He'd been a fine ruler and in spite of Tudor's lies most people remembered the real Richard.

I will *always* raise a glass to Lincoln, Lovell, Percy, Schwartz and all the others who fought for England's liberty that fine summer day in 1487. And I'm prouder than you can ever imagine that my father saved the life of the Earl of Lincoln, for whom he always had the deepest affection, admiration and respect.

But fine as the outcome was, deep in his heart Tom Sturdy always regretted that Lincoln didn't become King John II, as King Richard had wished.

[Signed by Sir Nicholas Sturdy on 16 June 1507]

About Sandra Heath Wilson

See after the story *'Row, Row, Row Your Boat'* for Sandra's details.

By the Grace of God

by
Richard Tearle

✩✩✩

Introduction

The mystery of the disappearance of the 'Princes in the Tower' is one which Ricardians believe can be explained by Richard having them moved to a place, or places of safety. In this story the place is Portugal, where their siter, Elizabeth, would have gone to be wed to Manuel, Prince of Beja. What if, when they were old enough to be considered men, this happened...?

✩✩✩

Beja, Portugal – September 1490

'He is a fine young man,' Duke Manuel observed.

'He is indeed,' Elizabeth replied, turning to her husband with a smile. 'I am proud of the way my little brother has turned out.'

The object of their scrutiny stood, panting from recent exertion and leaning on his sword, in the courtyard below the balcony on which they stood. He was a handsome youth of twenty summers. Blond hair, dark-soaked with sweat, tumbled to his shoulders, the long fringe sticking to his damp skin. A wispy moustache clung to his upper lip, but his chin was clean shaven and beardless.

The young man's upper torso was bare, displaying an almost hairless chest and finely toned abdominal muscles. As a result of his physical efforts, veins stood out like rivers on his biceps and powerful forearms. He was tall, too. Already he topped six feet, towering over both his sister Elizabeth and their younger brother, Richard. Elizabeth was of the opinion that Edward had not yet stopped growing.

Nearly six years of residence in one of Portugal's hottest regions had bronzed Edward's erstwhile pale skin and now it gleamed in the harsh sunlight.

With a cry, Alfonso, Edward's tutor in all things military, launched a sudden attack. Edward grasped his sword with both hands and fended off the intended blow.

'Unfair!' he yelled in Portuguese, but there was laughter in his voice.

'Nothing is fair in a sword fight, boy,' Alfonso retorted with a growl. 'Always be aware. Be forever on your guard. How many times must I tell you this?'

Although he would not say in words, Alfonso was impressed with his young charge. He had taken the shy and nervous young boy and moulded him into a skilled fighter, tutoring him in the knightly arts – resulting in the lad becoming a good shot at archery, a gifted rider, and more than able to hold his own with a sword, dagger, or other weapon. Grizzled old warrior that he was, Alfonso knew that Edward could now best him six or seven times out of ten. And Edward enjoyed the hunt as well, where he was adept at showing stealth and cunning, an eye for what was around him, natural features of landscape, terrain or woodland. Or suspicious defects. Possible ambush? *De fato,* Alfonso was pleased with his pupil.

The couple on the balcony, unseen to the swordsmen, watched with interest as the two thrust and counter thrust, parried and danced with intricate steps and patterns. The balance of their bodies and weapons, impeccable.

'Where is our visitor now?' Manuel asked his wife, encircling his arm around her slender waist.

'He rests,' she informed him, moving in closer to enjoy her husband's embrace. 'A long sea voyage together with two more days overland has tired him, and he tells me he is not a good traveller.' She laughed. 'I did not know him well, but I do recall he did not enjoy traversing the country with my uncle!'

'Tell me what you do know of the man,' Manuel mused, stroking his long, thin beard. Both that and his long, curly hair which this day he wore tied at the nape of his neck, were so dark that the afternoon sunlight gave off a blue sheen, like the feathers of a raven.

Elizabeth gathered her thoughts.

'He was Uncle Richard's best friend,' she began. 'They grew up together at Middleham. Remember: my uncle was an insular man who made few friends and many enemies. But he and Francis – Lord Lovell – were at times almost inseparable. Lovell was his greatest supporter when Richard became King. Ever loyal to him. *Loyaulté Me Lie* could just as well have been his motto had not Richard already taken it.'

She paused for a moment. 'Richard made him his Lord Chamberlain, a position he still holds. Francis was by Richard's side at Redemore Plain where they met Tydder in battle.'

'That was a fine victory, I believe,' Manuel said, but Elizabeth shook her head.

'No. It was not. Men – good men – from both sides perished. Richard himself was almost killed and though his wounds were grievous, he survived. God be praised.' She crossed herself, her husband echoing the gesture, then continued, 'Tydder fled, saving his own miserable skin and abandoning his army and all those who supported him.' Elizabeth shivered as a memory slid like melting ice through her mind. 'Had he prevailed, I was promised to him. Did you know that, my love?'

Manuel nodded. 'I had heard it so,' he confirmed. 'Did you ever meet him, my sweetheart?'

Elizabeth shook her head. 'Thank God, no. An odious, miserly toad, I was told. No claim at all to the throne. Put up to it by Margaret Beaufort, his mother.'

'What became of him?' Manuel asked, absently brushing a strand of hair, fidgeted by the wind, from his eyes.

'Tydder? He fled to France where he hides in shame to this day, licking his wounds.'

'To fight another day?' Manuel observed, pointedly.

Elizabeth shrugged. 'Uncle Richard mauled him badly. I doubt they will see his cowardly face in England again.'

✫✫✫

'Lord Lovell! Welcome! Please, do be seated.'

The man who stood before them was tall and thin. A nervous tic at the corner of one eye betrayed the apparent calm manner. He was well dressed in clothes that suggested modest opulence. Francis, Lord Lovell, Lord Chamberlain of England, carefully regarded each person in turn. Manuel, the man who had addressed him, was unknown to him, but he acknowledged the Portuguese Duke with a short, polite bow. Elizabeth had smiled at him, a sentiment he eagerly returned, and then took his attention to the two young men.

Edward had a curious frown to his face, trying to remember this Englishman whom he had met before, but had little memory of. Richard, the younger of the two, merely stared, his blank expression unreadable.

Francis returned his attention to Manuel. 'I am grateful for your hospitality, Your Grace. My Lady Elizabeth, I am delighted to see you after so many years. I bring greetings from your uncle. And you boys! Well, I see you are both men now. I also see that you remember me not? That is unimportant for you were both young when last we met. I bring greetings to you both from your uncle, Richard. But I also bring news and I am afraid to say that it is not good.'

The Duke indicated chairs, invited everyone to sit, clicked his fingers for servants to pour wine. Lovell sat, nursing a filled goblet, was silent a while, collecting his thoughts. The words of the speech he had rehearsed to himself many times on the journey here, now evaded him. He took the opportunity to gaze at his companions. Duke Manuel passive but inquisitive, blonde haired Elizabeth, anxiously clutching her hands together. Edward, head cocked to one side, puzzled but patiently waiting. And Richard, so different from his brother in physique, his elbow propped on the chair arm, his slender hand cradling chin and cheek.

'What is this news, Lord Lovell?' There was authority in Edward's voice as he eventually asked the inevitable question. An authority which Francis did not fail to notice.

'King Richard desires your return to your homeland of England as a matter of urgency. Not you, of course, my Lady, although your presence would be most welcome.' Lovell paused and took a deep breath, released it slowly. 'Your uncle is dying,' he said suddenly and with more bluntness than he intended. 'I – I am sorry. I did not intend to state the news quite so brutally.'

'Take your time, Francis,' Elizabeth encouraged, her voice barely above a whisper.

Lovell nodded. Collected his thoughts. 'As you know, King Richard suffered greatly from his wounds following Redemore. There were occasions when he could barely continue even minor daily routines, but he did so. Bravely. In truth, he set about the task of running the country with great energy and resolve. Those who opposed him were reduced in status or banished, but he did not resort to the axe. Not once. But just lately it has all become too much for him. He has taken to his bed. The physician's bleed him regularly but he knows he is dying.' Lovell paused and he struggled to prevent a tear escaping from his eye. Visions of his beloved friend in healthier days invaded his thoughts.

'As you know, he did not remarry following the death of his beloved Lady Anne. He has no heir. Nor does he wish for war – squabbling between men who favour the fit of a crown. He asked, no, commanded, me to seek you, Prince Edward, as he desires to name you as his heir.'

Elizabeth gasped. Edward narrowed his eyes.

'I – I did not think he could do that?' Elizabeth broke the silence. 'Was there not a law? One he drew up and Parliament passed?'

'*Titulus Regius,*' Lovell confirmed. Sighed. 'You must understand, he believed the story Stillington told him. Yet, he did have his doubts. He agonised for days over what he should do, but eventually realised that he had no choice: you were too young, Edward, do you see? Tydder was already raising an army and your life,' Francis looked at the two lads, Elizabeth, 'indeed all of your lives, were in danger. He was afraid of assassins, you understand? The country had been embroiled in war for decades and he could not subject you to the pressure that a continuance would bring. There had been peace during your father's reign, but Richard's accession was, shall we say, controversial? That is why he arranged for you, Elizabeth, to be married to Duke Manuel, and you two boys to be smuggled from England as part of the entourage. The alliance with Portugal he considered to be no bad thing, as has subsequently been proven aright. Richard saw no reason to announce your – er – *disappearance* to Parliament as he felt it may endanger you further. When Tydder began spreading rumours that Richard had murdered you boys, he still declined to declare what had become of you. For the best of intentions, but with behindsight it was a mistake, and many of us have told him so. For many a year he stubbornly refused to discuss the matter further.'

'Nevertheless,' young Richard put in, 'the Act stands. So how can my brother be named as heir?'

'Parliament will revoke it,' Lovell stated, with a small, almost indifferent shrug.

'How can this be?' Manuel interrupted, his brow creasing into furrows.

'King Richard has drawn up a document,' Lovell explained. 'It will be presented to Parliament and will be passed. Titulus Regius will no longer exist. And Edward, you will be crowned King Edward, fifth of that name.'

'How long does the king have?' Elizabeth asked in a low, regretful, tone. Lovell turned in his chair to face her.

'These things are never certain, my Lady,' he said in a low voice, as if to speak the words with volume would conjure them true. 'He may already be dead. Or it may be days or weeks, but not, I fear, months.'

A reflective silence spread throughout the room, reaching to the open windows, seemingly darkening the sapphire blue skies and the hot, golden sunshine beyond.

Edward turned to Richard. Smiled. Clapped him on the shoulder. 'It looks like we are going home, brother!'

★★★

He looked older than his thirty and seven years. Pale and weak, dark rings circled his eyes and there were deep furrows of worry creasing his brows. The cheeks were hollow and his jaw line more defined than Elizabeth remembered. The stern countenance was still present, but his smile when the small party entered his chamber, was genuine and friendly.

'My dear nephews! And my beautiful niece,' he managed with effort. The northern accent she remembered had not changed. 'Is thy husband, the Duke, with you my dear?'

The hand she grasped and knelt to kiss was covered in liver spots and was weak in her grip.

'Alas, not,' she replied, rising to her feet from her deep courtesy, 'but he sends his greetings and wishes for your recovery.'

Richard Plantagenet, King of England by the Grace of God, managed a rasping laugh. 'I fear his good wishes are in vain, but I thank him for them. You are happy in your marriage?'

'Very happy, Uncle. Manuel is a good man and I love him dearly.'

Richard nodded. 'I chose well, then?'

'Indeed.'

'And the boys! By Saint Paul, look at you now! Lovell: help me to sit up so I may see better!'

'We do not wish to tire you, Uncle,' Edward sounded concerned as Lovell assisted Richard.

'Mind my back, Francis: it pains me much today.' To Edward: 'Tire me, dear nephew? Ha! I will soon be in the deepest sleep of all. Tiring me is of no consequence now, believe me.' He winced as he tried to make himself comfortable. 'You knew I have this affliction?' he asked to the room in general. 'Since I was a lad, I have suffered with this back. Tydder would have it that I am a monster, with a full hump, but 'tis little more than a twist of the spine. In truth, it does cause me pain on occasion, though.'

He was silent for a moment. Then: 'Edward. Richard – may I call you Dickon? Come closer, let me see you the better.'

Elizabeth made way for the boys to stand by the bedside. There was a frisson of tension in the air, dispelled when Edward bent to kiss his uncle's hand. Hesitantly, young Richard followed his brother's example.

'Oh, how you have both grown!' the king enthused. 'I can barely believe what I am seeing. Two men – handsome men at that!'

'Uncle, I – ' Edward began, but the king waved him to silence.

'Say nothing until I have spoken,' he warned. Paused. 'I feel I wronged you both,' he began tentatively. 'I believed the story I was told. In truth, I still do.' He managed a wan smile. 'Your father was... promiscuous... in his younger days.' A sigh. 'What I did, I felt was for the best. I was appointed Protector, and there were enemies and danger all around. You were both so young and vulnerable. The country was in turmoil. I was in a position unfamiliar to me. One that I did not ask for. One that was unexpected and for which I was ill prepared.' A grimace crossed his face, an expression that suggested both physical and mental pain.

'But that is as may be. The realm is at peace and has been so for five years. Now, I intend to make amends.'

Richard gestured towards the watered wine beside the bed, drank a few mouthfuls as Francis held the goblet to his parched lips. Nodded his thanks, continued. 'The act that I had made has been revoked. My secretary has drawn up my will and you, Edward, are named as my heir. The kingdom you deserve will soon be yours. I have tried to rule well and, and I trust you will find your kingdom in good order when I am gone.'

'I am grateful, uncle,' Edward whispered, moved to his very soul. 'I – we – bear you no ill will in this. The past is past and well forgotten.'

If this short speech had been rehearsed, it was delivered with sincerity.

The king closed his eyes, smiled. 'Leave me now,' he said. 'We will talk further tomorrow when, perhaps, I will feel stronger.'

But tomorrow did not come. Nor the tomorrow after that. On the third day of October, in the year of our Lord 1490, King Richard, third of that name, passed into God's care in peace, taken in his sleep. The bells of church and cathedral throughout the land tolled their dolorous tones, and a nation from noblest born to lowest servant mourned.

Parliament declared their duty, that King Richard's nephew was named as heir.

Accepted as King, but as yet uncrowned, Edward oversaw the organisation of his uncle's funeral at Westminster Abbey, where he was laid to rest beside his beloved wife, Anne.

In that same holy place, where kings had been crowned from the time before the Conquest, when Harold Godwinson had been legitimately anointed as King, Richard of York's nephew, accompanied by his brother, surviving sisters and their mother, the Dowager Queen, who for so long had enjoyed her retirement from public life at Bermondsey Abbey, was crowned Edward V, King of England.

By the Grace of God, who sees all as it should be.

About Richard Tearle

RICHARD TEARLE
7th May 1948 – 13th April 2021

Richard was an avid reader since childhood when he discovered H. Rider Haggard and Edgar Rice Burroughs. Nevertheless, it wasn't until he retired in 2013 that he began writing short stories, contributing regularly to the Discovering Diamonds Historical Novel review blog, and to a Richard III-based anthology, *Right Trusty and Well Beloved.* His first book of short stories, *Melody Mayhem*, was soon followed by a sequel, *Melody Mayhem: The Second Movement.*

His novella, *The North Finchley Writers' Group*, was based on the various publishing experiences of his writer friends – although he stressed that all the characters were very much made-up.

Richard was in and out of hospital since late 2020 with many problems including a diagnosis of cancer, Covid-19, and a minor stroke. On his behalf, fellow writer, Helen Hollick, took over preparing *NFWG* for publication, and the polishing of the story for this anthology. He took great pleasure from knowing that readers enjoyed his stories.

Richard was a life-long Tottenham Hotspur supporter, liked watching most sports, particularly tennis and the New Orleans Saints in the NFL. He was passionate about encouraging new and novice writers, loved music, especially 'rock 'n roll' and was deeply interested in anything to do with Richard III, Edward Ironside, King Arthur, pub signs and steam trains – but equally, enjoyed anything to do with history.

In his own words, he took neither life nor himself seriously, and was grateful for the overwhelming support and best wishes he received while ill in hospital.

He passed peacefully away in April 2021.

FIND OUT MORE ABOUT RICHARD TEARLE
Scraps and Scriblings Blog:
https://scrapsandscribblings.blogspot.com/

ALSO BY RICHARD TEARLE
The North Finchley Writers' Group: https://tinyurl.com/s9u2b57
Melody Mayhem: A collection of short stories:
https://tinyurl.com/ejf65ent
Melody Mayhem: The Second Movement: https://tinyurl.com/47tt6vet

The Thistle and The Rose

by
Jennifer C. Wilson

Introduction

   This piece of flash fiction was inspired by a line in **The Six Wives of Henry VIII**, by Antonia Fraser, one of my favourite books, which I find myself returning to time and time again. In it, when discussing the potential marriage between Mary Tudor (the daughter of Henry VIII and Catherine of Aragon) and James V of Scotland, she adds a footnote saying that this would have brought the Union of the Crowns into being perhaps fifty years earlier than it did happen, but also that history would "have been robbed of two jewels in its crown" – Elizabeth I, and Mary Queen of Scots. Well, if we were going to lose Mary, one of my personal favourites, we might as well lose Henry VIII too, so I thought about moving everything back another couple of generations. As a Ricardian, I quite liked leaving Henry VII in a position of defeat, knowing he was leaving his crown to another anointed king, his dynasty having survived only one reign before the Stuarts took over. All that effort and upheaval, and in the end, nothing…

★★★

21 April 1509, Richmond Palace

Henry Tudor was dying. He knew his time was coming; the pain in his chest was making breathing harder with each hour, and his poor appetite meant the constant coughing was draining what little energy he had left.

As servants drifted in and out of his chamber, his mind began wandering. Elizabeth. Always back to Elizabeth. His beautiful queen, and the wife he had adored. He would be seeing her again soon, that much was clear. Would she greet him warmly, surrounded by their lost children? So much sorrow had shadowed their marriage: babies who never saw their first birthday, or first steps; their beloved first-born, Arthur, who never had the chance to live up to his name-sake; and second-born Henry, struck down in a joust he had sworn he wouldn't ride in.

So that was it. Henry Tudor, Henry VII, had held the throne for almost a quarter of a century, not far off half his life, and there was no male heir to follow him. To his relief, his mother had stayed away, these last few days; her disappointment would have been too much to bear. In another world, where things had gone right for him, the Countess would have been scurrying around the palace, ensuring Arthur and young Henry were ready for their new roles, as King of England, and loyal royal duke, respectively. He managed a weak smile as he thought of what a king young Arthur would have made, with the devout Catherine of Aragon by his side. England would have stood strong, held its own amongst the courts of Europe, led the way as the new century progressed. Such a shame he'd had to send the poor girl back to Spain. If young Henry had lived, instead of trying to prove himself in the tilt-yard, the lad could have married Catherine himself. Could have followed his father, carrying on his name, his dynasty. But it wasn't to be.

So what was he leaving instead? Two daughters, only one married, and that to one of his country's oldest enemies. Would James of Scotland race to London, Margaret in tow, to take what he saw as rightfully his? There was no living child yet, but both were still young.

He was sure his Privy Council were already moving to make it so, if they hadn't already. Nobody would bother telling him, he was certain of that. What would be the purpose, when there was no longer anything he could do to prevent it.

At least, if neither of his sons could be king, his daughter would still be queen.

As he felt his grasp on life becoming ever weaker, Henry knew he had to find peace, focus on the good he had done. He had taken the throne, and was potentially leaving an expanded dominion behind him. Margaret would rule over both England and Scotland.

He had succeeded. That was what he had to think.

He had won.

He hoped.

23 April, 1509, Edinburgh

'Dead?'

Queen Margaret had known the news must come soon. Reports had told of her father's failing health – it shouldn't have been a surprise. And yet, even in the relative seclusion of her privy chamber, nobody but the messenger, her husband James, and a few trusted servants present, she felt too exposed, as though the grief that struck her was a physical blow, threatening to force her off her feet.

As though sensing her discomfort, James moved half a step closer, squeezing her fingers, bringing her back to the moment.

'The Privy Council send their deepest and most sincere condolences for your loss, Your Grace. And to you, Your Grace.' The messenger turned his head to James, as Margaret realised there was no sense of surprise in the king's eyes. Had he known this was so close? But how?

An hour later, in true privacy within the king's bedchamber, servants dismissed, Margaret stared at James, as he read again and again the message delivered from London. The poor man must have raced through the night for it to reach them so soon. For a moment, Margaret found herself worrying about the state of the horses he must surely have run into the ground. She chuckled at the ridiculousness of her mind's progress, causing her husband to finally look up.

'You have realised what this means then?'

'Husband?'

'You didn't read it in full?' James crossed the room in two strides, pushing the paper into Margaret's hands. 'Go on. Properly this time, don't stop at the first lines.'

If she was honest, she had only read that far. That had been the part which mattered, after all. Her father, the King of England, had died just two days earlier. Leaving her and Mary with only their grandmother. What else was there that could be said? The place she had been so homesick for that she had sent letters home so full of sorrow, no longer held the same draw. Granted, there was Mary to think of. Would she move north, to join the Scottish court? Or remain in England?

England.

The English court.

The English throne.

Now empty.

Margaret forced herself to focus. Perching on the edge of their bed, she ignored James as he flitted about the room, silently marking things off on his fingers, clearly listing something of importance.

The words were a blur, seemingly unwilling to form coherent sentences on the page, but fragments began to form before her eyes:

~~~

A Proclamation... declaring the undoubted Right of our Sovereign King James, and Queen Margaret to the Crown of the Realms of England, France and Scotland. Forasmuch as it hath pleased Almighty God to call to his mercy out of this transitory life, to our great grief, the most excellent high and might prince, King Henry VII of most noble and famous memory... Lady Margaret, daughter of Henry, being lawfully begotten of the body of Elizabeth, daughter to King Edward the Fourth... York and Lancaster united... We therefore the Lords Spiritual and Temporal of this Realm, being here assembled... do now hereby with one voice, publish and proclaim the high and might Prince, James the Fourth of Scotland, is now by the death of our late sovereign, James the First, King of England and France... Beseeching God to bless his majesty with long and happy years to reign over us.

✩✩✩

Margaret realised she was doing the same as James now, reading and re-reading the paper, and tore her gaze away, to where her husband was now rifling through one of his chests.

'Did you know about this?'

James paused, and turned. 'That you and I would be named successors?' He shrugged. 'As soon as Henry died, what other course of action could there be? You are the eldest daughter, Mary is unmarried, and I am already an anointed king. Of course the throne would be ours.'

Of course. Of course it was obvious to her husband. James wasn't the one who had been reading with growing sadness of the decline of her father, wasn't the one who had been trying to be strong, when all she wanted to do was rush to the stables, summon the horses, and flee to London. But he was right. With the loss of her brothers, the crown had to come to her, and James.

As though somebody had thrown open a set of shutters, letting light into every corner of her mind, everything became clear.

Margaret's heart had never truly been in her journey north, so soon after the loss of her mother, Queen Elizabeth. The loss of her horses at Dalkeith had felt like an omen, however hard James had tried to convince her otherwise. But now, she saw the purpose of it all. The death of her father summoned her back to England, just as the death of her mother had heralded her departure. A visit book-ended by grief. But whilst she had left to take on the role of Queen of Scotland, she was returning to a far greater prize, a union their marriage treaty could never have envisaged back when Arthur and Henry were still living. She would have been nothing but a helpful sister with good connections at another royal court. Now, like this, she would be a triumphant, returning Queen of England.

She realised she had been silent too long; James was staring at her, clearly waiting for her to say something. What else was there to say?

'We must prepare for London.'

☆☆☆

About Jennifer C Wilson

Jennifer stalks dead people (usually monarchs, mostly Mary Queen of Scots and Richard III). Inspired by childhood visits to as many castles and historical sites as her parents could find, and losing herself in their stories (not to mention quite often the castles themselves!), at least now her daydreams make it onto the page.

Her debut novel, **Kindred Spirits: Tower of London** was published by Crooked Cat Books in 2015. The full series was re-released by Darkstroke in January 2020. Jennifer is a founder and host of the award-winning North Tyneside Writers' Circle, and has been running writing workshops in North Tyneside since 2015. She also publishes historical fiction novels with Ocelot Press. She lives in Whitley Bay, and is very proud of her two-inch view of the North Sea.

Facebook: https://tinyurl.com/3drr4s94
Twitter: https://twitter.com/inkjunkie1984
Blog: https://jennifercwilsonwriter.wordpress.com/
Instagram: https://tinyurl.com/4vyt4ddp
Amazon: https://tinyurl.com/bbufkct8

Baby Brother

by
Kathy H D Kingsbury

✩✩✩

Introduction

'Baby Brother' was inspired by the ideas I had for a story that never was written. In this alternative universe, King Richard III lost the Battle of Bosworth after being seriously wounded, but survived nonetheless. After being nursed back to health and coming to terms with his losses, he starts a new life as Richard Rutland – going on pilgrimage to the Holy Land, joining Hungarian King Mathias Corvinus's Black Army to fight against the Ottoman – before eventually returning to England. Who knows? Perhaps someday I will write about this Richard's adventures.

✩✩✩

AD 1524 - A village near York

The end was near. Richard knew this and welcomed it. Death did not frighten him. The disease that had been slowly eating away at his body would finally claim him, and the pain that had been his constant companion these past months would at last cease.

He lay quietly in his bed, eyes closed, breathing slowly, willing himself to remain as still as possible, as even the slightest movement was agony. Sitting to his left, holding his hand in hers, was Katherine, his wife of 34 years. Steadfast as ever, he knew she was putting on a brave face for all to see while inside her heart was breaking. He wanted to tell her how much he loved her, how blessed he was to have had her in his life, but even such a simple speech was more than he could manage at this point.

If he opened his eyes, though, he knew what he would see. In the room with him would be Sarah Rose, his daughter, his little princess, now a woman grown and with a family of her own. Holding her in his arms, providing comfort, would be his son-in-law, John. A better man for his daughter he couldn't have wished for. Then there were his three grandchildren. The oldest was six-year-old Richard, named for his grandfather, a bright lad who was always quick and eager to please. Next was four-year-old Stephen, quiet and studious. The youngest was Margaret, a lively and usually rambunctious two years of age. Although not fully comprehending what was happening, the children were silent and solemn nonetheless. Also in the room would be Simon Boetler, his long-time friend and physician. *I'll miss our chess games,* Richard thought, then wondered if anyone played chess on the other side. *Or are such thoughts considered blasphemous?* And of course, there would be Father Petrus, the parish priest, whose youthful appearance belied his wisdom, praying for his soul.

Ah, to have lived a long life and die peacefully in one's own bed, surrounded by those he loved…what more could a man wish for, then a grimace as another wave of pain wracked his emaciated body. If only it would all just end…

'Don't worry, baby brother, the worst is almost over,' a voice reassured him.

What? Who was that calling him 'baby brother'? The voice sounded familiar, but it was one he hadn't heard since…well, hadn't heard in a very long time, from back when he'd been Richard Plantagenet and not Richard Rutland. The end must be close indeed, if his mind was playing tricks like this on him.

'Do you think he heard me, Ned?' It was the same voice again.

A different voice answered, deep, strong and masculine. 'I'm not sure, George. He's in a lot of pain.'

Curiosity finally getting the better of him, Richard forced his eyes open and scanned the room. Yes, everything was as he'd expected; everyone where he'd last seen them. Then slowly he shifted his gaze to the right and was surprised to see two men, both appearing to be in the prime of life, standing next to his bed, smiling down at him. They were tall, much taller than he was. The older-looking of the two appeared to be almost a giant – easily over six feet in height – while the younger was of a more average height. Both had hair a dark shade of gold and were dressed in fashions slightly out of date.

'George?' he croaked to the younger looking of the two, not believing what he was seeing, unable to speak above a hoarse whisper. Then to the blond giant, 'Edward?'

'Surprised to see us, baby brother?' asked George, grinning that mischievous smile of his that Richard remembered so well. It usually meant that his brother was up to something, usually something that bode no good.

'But...but...you're dead. You're both...dead.' Richard took a moment to catch his breath. This was all too much. 'I...I must be hallucinating...delusional,' he whispered.

'If we are a hallucination, then isn't it a splendid one?' That was Edward again. 'What could be better than the three sons of York, together again?'

'Actually, we're here to put your mind at ease as to what's to come,' added George, giving his ailing brother a comforting pat on the arm. 'Don't worry,' he said with a conspiratorial wink, 'they can't see or hear us.' He indicated the others in the room.

Richard stared at his brothers. 'I'm confused.' His brow furrowed. 'Am I dead? Is that it?'

Edward shook his head. 'Not yet, brother. But soon.'

Richard repressed a shudder. Maybe it was the medication Simon had given him for the pain that was befuddling his brain.

'You see,' George began explaining, 'things aren't quite the way we're taught by Mother Church. Don't think of death as the end; it's only the beginning of another journey. However, there will be plenty of time to talk about all this once you've officially crossed over. We just wanted to let you know that we are here to help with the transition, baby brother.'

Richard frowned. 'I'm 72 years old. I don't feel much like anyone's baby brother.'

'He's got a point,' said Edward, who didn't look a day past the 40 years of age he'd been when he died, only without the look of dissipation that had come over him in his final months.

'What's it like…on the other side?' asked Richard, giving up trying to make sense of it all. If this was a hallucination, why bother fighting it, and if it was real…? Besides, it was rather nice to see his brothers once again.

'Once you cross over, all the pain and suffering you've been going through will be a thing of the past,' Edward explained.

Richard closed his eyes for a moment and allowed himself a brief smile. 'That would be wonderful.' Then a thought occurred to him. 'What about my back? Will it be straight?'

Edward shook his head. 'I'm afraid that crooked back is a part of you, but the good news is that it won't trouble you like it has in life.'

'Maybe things won't be so bad after all,' Richard mused.

'And just think of all those who crossed over before you and who you'll be able to see again!' his older brother exclaimed.

'Yes,' chimed in George. 'Everyone's here. Even your bastards!'

'Dammit, George,' Edward admonished, giving his younger brother a jab in the ribs, 'did you have to bring them up now? You know what a pious man our little brother is. Pilgrimage to the Holy Land and all that.'

'Yes, but he was rather randy in his youth. Sowing his wild oats.' George grinned at Richard. 'Isn't that right, baby brother?'

His children. The ones he'd fathered so long ago, and who had gone before him. A daughter who had died in childbirth and a son rumoured to have been eliminated by Tudor...and wasn't there a third one? One he hadn't learned about until just before the battle? Yes, another Richard. Why did everyone have to use the same names over and over? He sighed. It only made things more confusing. Then a thought came to him...what about his first wife and their son? 'They're all there, on the other side? Even Anne and little Edward?'

'Of course they are!' said George. 'It's not as if you're the only person who ever married more than once. At least you had the decency to do it honestly and out in the open. Not like someone we know.' He gave a nod toward Edward.

The topic of Edward's liaison with Eleanor Talbot and its causing his marriage to Elizabeth Woodville to be declared bigamous and his children bastards must surely be a sore spot with his brother, thought Richard, even after all these years. 'Edward...' He hesitated. 'I...I thought you might be angry with me. You know, because of your son being set aside and the crown being offered to me...' His voice trailed off. This was getting awkward. Perhaps he should just keep quiet.

But Edward only shrugged. 'To tell the truth, I was a bit irked with you at first, but when I thought things through I knew you were only doing what you believed to be the right thing. And it's not as if you ever hurt my boys.'

'No,' murmured Richard. 'That was someone else.'

✫✫✫

Edward went on as if he hadn't heard his youngest brother's last comment. 'Besides, no one holds on to grudges here. Can you imagine what a mess that would make otherwise?'

'True,' said George, giving his giant of a brother a meaningful look. 'Can you imagine what it would be like if I held a grudge against you, Ned?'

Richard nearly choked as George's none too subtle reference to his execution at Edward's order caught him off guard. But before he had time to think of something to say to help smooth things over and break up what he was sure would turn into an ugly scene, Edward simply threw back his head and laughed heartily, while George spouted, 'Malmsey, anyone?'

'What about Edmund?' Richard asked, wanting to quickly change the subject and thinking of his other brother who'd been Earl of Rutland and died at Wakefield with their father when Richard was only eight. He'd barely had a chance to know Edmund, and had taken the name Rutland to honour him.

'We hardly see him these days,' explained Edward. 'Remember, he was only 17 years old when he died. Now that he's here, he's still only 17 years old. Prefers to hang out with all the pretty girls. Not that that's such a bad thing.'

'Sounds like he takes after his big brother,' said Richard, slightly reprovingly. Edward only grinned.

'You know, baby brother,' piped in George, 'you made us all proud when you led the charge against Tudor at Bosworth.'

Edward nodded his agreement. 'You most certainly did. You were a true son of York that day! We were pulling for you, Dickon.'

'Then that horse of yours stumbled and unseated you and things got ugly,' George added ruefully.

'I don't remember much after that,' said Richard. To this day, most of what happened after he'd been thrown from his horse was still a blank. 'Perhaps it's just as well that I don't.'

His brothers concurred. 'Most definitely,' said George. 'That was one nasty blow you took to your head. Edward and I were sure that we were going to be needed that day, to welcome you then. But miraculously, you survived.'

'And we're glad you did,' added Edward. 'It's been fun keeping an eye on you from time to time, seeing what kind of trouble you were going to get yourself into next.'

Suddenly an idea popped into Richard's head. 'So, everyone's here? Even Tudor?'

'Oh no,' laughed Edward. 'This could get interesting.'

'He most certainly is,' answered George. 'But remember,' he said, wagging a finger, 'no holding grudges here.'

'Of course not!' replied Richard indignantly. 'I just think it would be proper to thank him for sparing my life that day. Let him know how much I appreciate it.'

Edward sniggered. 'And maybe rub his nose in it, that you outlived him by…what, 15 years? Yes, I'm sure he'd love to hear about that!'

'Well then, let's get started!' George motioned for Richard to join them.

'What? Wait! Don't I have to be dead first?'

'See for yourself,' said Edward.

Richard realised he was standing, free of pain. He turned around and saw his frail, aged body lying lifeless on the bed, his family and friends shedding tears while the priest intoned the prayer for the dead.

He was going to miss his family, but if what his brothers were telling him was true, everyone would eventually be reunited. In the meantime, it would be fun to catch up with all those who had crossed over before him and yes, maybe thumb his nose at Tudor… just a little.

But first, he would have to find something more appropriate to wear. It really wouldn't be seemly to spend his afterlife running around in only a nightshirt!

About Kathy H D Kingsbury

For more about Kathy, see after the story *'Richard Liveth Yet'*.

Lady in Waiting

by
Clare Anderson

✫✫✫

Introduction

One of the most intriguing 'what ifs' for me is the idea of King Richard III having living descendants. The historical record gives him two known illegitimate children, Katharine and John, whom he acknowledged and provided for. Katharine married but died without children. John of Gloucester was probably killed by Henry VII and no children by him are known. A third, Richard of Eastwell, seems never to have married and some doubt exists that he was a child of the King. But what if there were another, unbroken line of descent to the present day?

✫✫✫

R ichard Pettifer looked out from his hotel balcony over the bay of Naples; the view was spectacular but his mind was still back in England. Damn TudorCorp! There was no way out of their shoddy deal if he couldn't stall them. Instinctively he reached for his pocket and remembered he'd given up smoking five years ago. It had been a nervous reaction instilled over the years. Just then his phone vibrated. His secretary's cat avatar appeared on the screen.

'Yes?'

307

'Frank has found a clause in their bid which he thinks can be queried. It will at least give a bit more time. He threw an all-nighter to do it, so he says you owe him a drink...'

'I'll owe him a lot more than that. Let's hope the meeting with Giovanni helps. Talk later, I have to go over the numbers again.' He shut off the call and went back into his room. There were papers scattered everywhere. He sat at the large desk, and with Mount Vesuvius looming peacefully in the background, started to make notes.

Back in London, Annabel White sighed as Richard hung up. It was difficult enough worrying whether she'd still be in a job in a month's time, but being secretly in love with one's boss made it agony.

✯✯✯

Alyse's mother had lied; a life of ease was a tiresome thing. Alyse would rather have her old work back where all she had to do was make and mend clothes. Life in a great house with its bustle and noise at least kept her busy and interested. As Lady Lovell's newest lady in waiting her chief responsibilities now were getting her ladyship up in the morning and readying her for bed at night, while the time in between was spent adjusting the cushions for her ladyship's back, picking up dropped tapestry needles and stopping the kitten weeing on the furnishings.

'You will have your own maid now.' Her mother had remarked proudly. It was indeed a step up in the world for a farmer's pretty daughter.

Alyse would rather be galloping over fields on a fat pony and laughing with the ploughmen.

Life at the great house picked up sharply when it was known that the King would be visiting.

''Tis a solemn time for his Grace,' the Lady Anne noted sadly. 'The Queen ails and there are traitors in every ditch, alas.'

At least at Minster Lovell King Richard could be assured of a genuinely warm welcome. He had known Francis, Lord Lovell, from childhood and they were close friends. Servants' gossip was full of the Queen's ill health, so soon after the tragic death of Prince Edward. Alyse was sure her mother would want to know all the details, but to Alyse the King sounded rather a sad wretch, full of cares. She hoped that there would be some cheerful young knights travelling with him.

This was to be a less formal occasion than a usual royal visit so the king's retinue was not large. Alyse found herself caught up in the excitement all the same as the activity in the house increased. The kitchens were filled with steam and enticing smells.

'Begone!' John Wroxall, the head cook, chased a rather shaggy deerhound from its begging spot beneath the oak kitchen table. A badly-aimed kick failed to connect as the dog scampered out of doors. Alyse, having ordered the honeyed almonds for Lady Anne, followed the hapless dog into the herb garden outside. It was still early spring and not that warm, but there was a scent in the air, and Alyse was glad to be away from the commotion. She laid a hand on the dog's neck and stroked it. Her own dog had looked very like this one and she thought of the comfortable farmhouse where she had grown up. She unlatched the gate and wandered out into the gardens.

She stopped suddenly at the sight of a dark-haired man gazing at a clump of bright yellow primroses. From his dress he was noble – Alyse wished she'd been more attentive to the gossip about the king's circle. Before she could turn away, he looked directly at her and gave a shy smile. She dropped a brief curtsey and, not wanting to be rude, said 'Welcome to Minster Lovell – you are with his Grace's party?'

He bowed in response. Alyse couldn't place him at all – perhaps he was the husband of one of the king's sisters? Nervously she introduced herself, so he would have the excuse to dismiss her. It would not be seemly for her to be speaking to a strange man so obviously above her station. He was still young with no grey in his hair, yet there was a steely look to his blue-grey eyes and a firm chin which denoted no opposition. Perhaps he was one of the king's military advisors?

There was an air of obstinacy and determination about him. The dog had gone straight to him and he bent to pet it.

'There, Rufus, old friend, you should get a good bone from the cooks tonight!'

'He was chased out and I followed him.' Alyse explained. The stranger regarded her thoughtfully, but said nothing. 'I expect you are tired from your journey. The rooms have been made ready, if you wish to rest.'

He shook his head. 'I should like nothing more than to walk in these gardens. I am only weary of company.'

'Oh, I know how that feels! They treat me very kindly here, but sometimes, well...' Alyse made to leave.

'There's no need for you to go, unless you are needed. I would not disturb your peace.'

Alyse, trained to be wary of friendly noblemen, hesitated. The stranger had an expression of strain and weariness and did not look as if he was planning to molest her. Perhaps there were not enough weapons for the army?

'I love this time of year,' she said, admiring the drifts of primroses. 'The new flowers promise the warm weather to come.'

The stranger bent down and picked a small yellow bloom. 'For you, in promise,' he said, handing it to her. Alyse studied it for a moment, hiding her reddening cheeks. The man, whoever he was, had a compelling presence. As a young girl she had played a game with her friends, imagining their perfect knight, who would, of course, become a perfect husband. This man might well have been her own ideal. His bearing was noble but not stuffy, he seemed both confident and shy, and he did not disdain the company of a yeoman's daughter. He moved closer and his hand brushed the flower in her hand.

'Maiden in the moor lay, in the moor lay...' he quoted softly. 'And what was her meat?... The primrose and the violet.'

They had walked some way along the paths around the garden when Alyse realised from the chill in the air that she had been outside for some time. 'Oh, I had forgotten the time! There is so much to do. His Grace will already be here.'

'You had better go then.' He gave a curt nod. 'I expect there will be a packed hall for dinner, so forgive me if I do not greet you tonight.'

'At least there will be more to eat than primroses!' Alyse laughed. 'Oh – I do not know your name, Sir...'

'Richard,' he said briefly and turned away. This time she clearly was dismissed.

Vesuvius was almost hidden by mist. Richard Pettifer stood on the hotel balcony for the last time and thought how ironic that he should not get a good view on his final morning when he was not besieged by worry. The Italians had signed so Regis Energy had a lease of life for at least three months. He began to pack his suitcase, carefully wadding socks and underwear around the bottle of wine which had been left in the room by the manager. He smiled to himself at the thought of sharing it with Annabel; Natasha would have turned her nose up at it. They'd broken up just before he'd flown to Italy; should he get her a bottle of suitably expensive perfume at the airport as a peace offering? He'd get a good bottle of malt whisky for Frank.

He zipped his case and did a final check of his room.

They had fought off the beast that was TudorCorp, at least for a while. It would not have been a good fit – Tudor was all about cheap energy, what they called 'efficient' but which in essence meant anything as long as it was profitable. Regis, a green and renewable energy consultancy, was committed to helping industry find clean, non-polluting solutions to their needs. Richard wasn't an idealist; he had founded this company in response to the rising global demand for new solutions, but at the same time he believed that what Regis offered was not only the future, but the right way ahead. TudorCorp would have used them cynically to keep the environmentalists happy, saying one thing but doing another.

In the limousine from the airport, all he wanted to do was to relax and zone out, but his temperament wasn't suited to this and after calling Annabel he found himself scanning the news on his phone.

'Been away long?' Asked the driver. Richard hoped the man wasn't going to be the chatty kind.

'Only a couple of days; business trip.' He added to forestall the question, 'Sorrento and it was indeed warmer than here.'

'Very nice. You won't have seen the latest on those bones that got dug up under the car park in Leicester. Whole nation has been gripped. They had the big reveal last night on a special documentary.'

'Really?' Richard remembered something about the remains of the so-called lost king. Privately he thought it a lot of hype, some archaeologists claiming they'd found Richard III to enhance their careers.

'Turns out it really is him. The DNA was checked against surviving relatives and it is all kosher. Whatever the poor bugger did in his life, it seems a bit sad him being under a car park all that time.'

'I suppose it does...' Richard scrolled up the news and indeed there it was: 'King's remains identified in TV documentary'. He fell silent for a while.

'They could even work out what he would have looked like. Funny thing, you look a bit like him, if I may say so.'

'Must be my regal air.'

Annabel peered at the label on the wine bottle. *"Lacrima Christi"*, tears of Christ... well at least it's not your tears, Richard. How was the hotel?'

Richard poured the wine into three glasses. 'Fine – come on, drink up, this wine is good but won't keep beyond today.'

'Did you dine on the terrazza where Caruso sang to the guests?'

Richard looked puzzled. 'I ate out with Giovanni's people. I did use the spa though, to help calm my nerves! I gather news of national importance has happened while I was away.'

Annabel went to her desk and returned with a newspaper. 'It has. Here, there's a likeness of King Richard made like those "meet the ancestors" programmes. I always thought those reconstructions look the same, but this guy...'

'Hey Richard,' Frank cut in. 'He looks like you. I mean change the hair and give him some shades and a suit, and you could be related.'

'Have you ever traced your family tree? Maybe you have a royal connection?' Annabel looked thoughtfully at Richard's face and then down at the photograph of the reconstructed face of the medieval king.

'My father was keen on that kind of thing. All I know is that my family is supposed to have come from the Cotswolds, around Oxfordshire.'

Alyse excused herself from dinner saying she wasn't hungry. Well, that wasn't strictly true, Alyse was always ready for a good meal, but after meeting the stranger in the gardens, she felt listless and dissatisfied with her lot. The nobleman called himself "Richard" as if they were on first-name terms, but he had warned her that they wouldn't speak at dinner. In any case, as a junior member of the household she would be sitting on the edge, stuck with a pimply page or most likely Annie Cox, the new housekeeper, a plump woman with a loud voice and bad breath. Alyse would not be missed; there would be more room on the bench for Mistress Cox's ample bottom.

With the entire household fussing around the king and his entourage, the solar was empty. In the candlelight, Alyse found a good book and curled up in a chair with a plate of cold meats and cheeses foraged from the kitchen. Solitude was rare and she cherished it although her mind turned uncomfortably to the man in the garden. She had enjoyed his company, he had been easy to talk to and despite their different stations, she felt there was an unseen link between their souls. But she mustn't get any ideas; even if he were not noble, he was a powerful man of around thirty years, so almost certainly married with a family. She could hope at best for the occasional nod or smile, snatched in odd moments when he was not busy with the King's matters. She must forget all about the Perfect Knight.

Voices from below indicated that the feast was over and the house would again be flooded with noise. Frustration at how life had taunted her girlhood dreams by sending a man she could never have made her yearn to be alone again. She would take the night air alone and in the chill breeze pull herself together. Tomorrow would be another day of tedium. She had better get used to her lot.

Pulling a cloak around her, Alyse managed to avoid the press of people preparing for bed. The servants were mostly clearing up the hall where many of them would be sleeping.

The night air was quiet and still. Swiftly, Alyse hurried along the path through the kitchen garden and went through the gate. She turned left, avoiding the place where she had first spoken to 'Richard'. Beneath some tall trees she could make out the remains of snowdrops and crocus. Soon there would be drifts of bluebells. Meanwhile, while her womanhood wilted, people everywhere fell in love, married and had children. She could see herself waiting on Lady Lovell for the rest of her days. It would send her mad unless she escaped, and even then she would probably end up like the wild maiden in the song. Which brought her back to the mysterious Richard again. Softly, she took up the familiar tune:

The maiden in the moor lay,

In the moor lay,

Seven nights full, seven nights full.

The maiden in the moor lay,

Seven nights full and a day.

Good was her meat.

And what did she eat?

The primrose and the... the primrose and the...

Disturbing the silence, a soft low voice from nearby joined her

 And what did she eat?
The primrose and the violet.

She looked up and saw it was Richard, his eyes dark and shining in the moonlight. Embarrassed, she fell silent while his musical baritone continued

'Good was her drink,
And what did she drink?
The cold water of...
The cold water of...
And what did she drink?
The cold water of the well-spring.'

He paused. 'You weren't at supper.'

Alyse took a deep breath and turned to walk further away from the house. He kept pace beside her, there was no escaping him. 'I wasn't very hungry. Did I miss a good feast?'

'Francis always puts on a good feast, and the minstrels and tumblers were excellent as well. You are unwell, perhaps?'

Alyse shook her head. 'Tired, perhaps, but nothing more. I didn't think I'd be missed.'

'I missed you. You know, this afternoon as we spoke in the garden, I quite forgot all my cares. It takes a great deal to do that.'

She paused and looked up at him. 'Yet you have added to mine. Meeting you reminded me of how dull my life must always be. You can have little idea of it. Your life is full of colour, life and activity, you go where you wish and when...'

'If only that were true. I would gladly exchange your life for mine!' The vehemence of his tone startled her.

315

'Surely not? Have you fallen from the king's favour?' Her face paled slightly at the thought of what that might mean.

To her surprise he turned his head away and gave a low laugh. 'I think more truly the King has fallen from favour, so that he scarcely knows who his friends are.'

Alyse stared at him, this "Richard"... surely not...

'Oh.' Realisation dawned on her. In the moonlight his eyes were dark blue, like deep pools. 'Your Grace, I...'

'Call me Richard, it is my name.' With a stride he had closed the gap between them and enclosed her in his arms. His kiss was light, gentle. Alyse closed her eyes and nestled closer to him.

'Richard,' she whispered.

☆☆☆

The phone came to life on his desk. 'Richard! Welcome back! I hope you bought me something suitably expensive to make up for your beastly behaviour.'

'Natasha, you broke up with me, remember?' He sighed. It was hopeless. He had, in fact, bought her a bottle of "Opium" in the duty free. Just a goodwill memento, no hard feelings.

'Is it true you managed to save your company? I hope you got lots of money.'

He chuckled at her blatant venality. 'Some.'

'Enough to treat me to a deliciously decadent dinner somewhere dark and exclusive?'

He didn't understand how she did it. A week ago, mired in troubles, he had told her curtly that he would no longer have the kind of money to pay for her lifestyle of holidays and shopping. Her extravagance usually amused him, now it grated. He was surprised at the speed at which she dumped him. She reminded him of a Persian cat, beautiful and graceful, but not very bright. When she was purring, she was the best company imaginable, but although she enjoyed money, she had absolutely no interest in where it came from. Nor was it any concern to her that Richard cared about the company he had started with his father's legacy and that he felt responsible for the people who worked for him.

In the restaurant she chattered away in her usual manner. Richard knew she was selfish, hedonistic and immature, but she had a way of making him laugh. She never minded that he found her funny.

'You know...' She bit her lip, studying the menu. It was the kind which didn't show the prices.

'What don't I know?' He smiled indulgently at her, waiting for a hint about some new Manolos.

'I was thinking... you know I don't interfere in what you do, but... well... If you sold the company now, you'd have a lot more money, right?'

'Maybe,' he replied, beginning to worry as to where this would lead. 'But it's not for sale. I can't let it go to an outfit which would asset strip it down to the last paperclip and put my staff out onto the street.'

'Surely it's not so bad. I mean Anna is a capable secretary, she could find another job if TudorCorp won't take her on.'

Richard was surprised that although she got Annabel's name wrong, she had remembered the name of TudorCorp. Perhaps she had been a little bit concerned after all? He changed the subject, realising that as far as Natasha was concerned, their relationship was still on.

✫✫✫

'Shall I see you again?' Alyse gazed solemnly at Richard as they sat together on the turf seat. The chamomile and thyme, bruised from their sitting, gave off a sweet scent.

Richard gave a deep sigh. 'In the past three days I have come to realise that I have need of you. The truth is there is no one else I can turn to. My Queen is dying and I cannot burden her with my cares.'

Ah, the Queen.

'I will not come between any man and his wife.'

Their meetings had been in the grounds of Lovell Minster. They had walked and talked and in the peace among the tall trees, Richard had opened his heart to Alyse, telling her of the many burdens he carried, of the state and of his private sorrows. He told her of his only child who had died and how his Queen grieved and was now wasting away.

She laid her head on his shoulder and ran a gentle finger along the velvet of his tunic. Richard would be true to his Queen as long as she lived; it is what Alyse loved about him.

'If I should ever send for you, would you come? I could command it but would rather not.'

Alyse understood his meaning. He needed her, would need her more and more.

'If things were different,' Alyse spoke softly and sighed. 'I would be yours. My only sorrow is that you are my king, and we must part.'

'If all the world should turn away, would you still stand by me, Alyse?'

'All the world would not keep me away from you, Richard.'

The future was uncertain but Alyse knew if the King should ever need her, she would give herself to him, body and soul.

The royal party left and Alyse took to walking the gardens whenever she wasn't needed.

✩✩✩

'Honestly, it's as if he's under her spell.' Annabel sighed.

Frank nodded in agreement. 'One day he's broken with her, now she's talking about rings. What's got into the man? It's like he is bewitched. Let's get a drink!'

They settled into a quiet bench seat with a high back, away from the bar, where they could be private.

'He used to be my best mate, too.' Frank gazed mournfully into his beer. 'But he's changed. I'm worried for the company too. I think he's toying with the idea of selling. It has to be her.' He laid a hand over Annabel's. He knew how her feelings went.

There wasn't much else to say so they sat in gloomy silence.

The pub was filling up. It was new and currently fashionable. Annabel was aware that the seat on the other side of theirs was taken; the high wooden back prevented her seeing but it sounded like a couple rather than a group. She was about to suggest leaving for somewhere quieter when she heard a familiar voice.

'I think he'll go for it.'

'Great! Just keep on doing what you do. We'll pay the rest when it's settled,' a man's voice with a faint Welsh accent responded. Was there just a hint of smugness?

Frank nudged Annabel and put his finger to his lips.

'Oh, he'll sign in the end. He may be a sentimentalist, but he'll go for the money like everyone else. You coming to the wedding? I'll expect a very handsome gift!' Her husky laugh made Annabel's stomach sink like a stone.

'Really?' He sounded genuinely puzzled.

She gave an explosive laugh. 'Of course not really! But he has to believe I'm in love, it makes it more credible. In any case a "not wedding gift" will do just fine, as long as it has enough zeros. I want my teeny little flat in Knightsbridge.'

'Hand us Richard Pettifer, and it's yours.'

Frank and Annabel stared at each other. 'He won't believe us.' Annabel said in the faintest of whispers. Frank smiled and tapped his phone. It was recording.

✫✫✫

She couldn't bear to see him like this. He had spoken of his cares in the garden, now they seemed to have multiplied. His face bore lines of strain and he nervously played with the rings on his fingers. It had been less than three months since they parted and two since the Queen died. Richard had waited a decent interval before sending for Alyse.

The ride from Oxfordshire to Yorkshire was long, but Alyse was relieved to be out of doors and on a horse again. News of the Queen's death had reached her and in the weeks that followed she had waited until Lord Lovell himself told her privately that she would be coming with his party to visit the King.

She knew nothing of politics and feuding lords, only that the best of men was trapped in a web of treachery spun by people who owed him their utmost loyalty. Francis had told her as much on their journey and she had promised to do what she could to support his Grace. But how would he be, a king in his own court? She had wondered if he would tire of her once he realised she was only a farmer's daughter with no appetite for courtly life. Could their relationship survive a very different setting?

'It is good to see you again, I have missed you, Alyse.' Beneath the silk and velvet and gold, the eyes bore an uncertainty that matched her own. He, too, was unsure! She curtseyed.

'I have missed you too, Your Grace...'

A finger pressed lightly on her mouth. 'Richard,' he corrected.

Later, much later, she knew that nothing had changed or would change but she wondered what people would think of her, dreading their attitudes. Richard reassured her: 'Don't worry, you won't have to face anyone. You are here for my sake, and there is no need to go beyond the gardens and my private quarters unless you wish it. It would also be safest until I have dealt with the Tydder threat.'

'You mean they would harm me also?'

'I would hope not, but I promise no harm will come to you. Let us not talk of that now. Just having you here eases my soul.' He ran idle fingers through her hair and murmured:

'Well was her bower

What was her bower?

The red rose and the –

The red rose and the –

The red rose and the lily flower.'

'That girl had a lot of flowers, primroses, violets, lilies and roses! Shouldn't that be the white rose though?'

☆☆☆

The uncertainty gnawed at her while her coffee cooled. She couldn't get on with anything while Frank was with Richard, revealing the plot they had uncovered. She imagined Richard's face as he listened to the recorded conversation. As a businessman he could make hard decisions and even be ruthless if he had to be, but treachery like this wasn't something he would be prepared for. Annabel would gladly have seen him happy with a wife like Natasha if she cared for him, but...

Really? Would she? Well, perhaps. She wanted the best for him and if she couldn't be the one to give it to him then...

Her peace was disturbed by the sound of a door opening and voices. Frank came into her office. 'Richard's gone out.'

'How did he take it?'

'He was shocked, of course, and disappointed – '

'Broken hearted, I suppose.' Annabel stared dully at her keyboard.

'I'm not sure about that. He's furious with Tudor and Natasha but unless he was showing me his brave face, I'd say he feels a bit of a fool for having been taken in by her. His mind works fast, he reckons the company has been deliberately undervalued. TudorCorp's got a lot of fingers in a lot of pies.'

'Time for digital extraction, or amputation.'

Richard walked furiously towards the car park. The fresh air was helping to clear his mind. So much began to make sense! How Natasha had got Annabel's name wrong but not Tudor Corp. And the sudden difficulties of Regis to turn a profit, when they had been mentioned in the Financial Times as a rising star. Inexplicable, unless a rival company was poisoning Regis' reputation. Well, two can play at that game. Time to strike back! He got into the Lexus CT and sat inside, thinking. He had been planning to drive round to Natasha and have it out with her, but he realised he wasn't as angry as he ought to be. He pulled out his phone and composed a short message. That was how celebrities did their dumping, wasn't it? Natasha should approve.

He got out of the car and headed back to the office. He felt in better spirit than he had in a while. For some reason he kept thinking about Annabel, her loyalty, how he had looked forward to sharing the Italian wine with her. He would ask her to dinner and discuss his next move.

To his surprise, Annabel had more news for him.

'While you were out the phone rang. A genealogist wants to meet you. It's quite exciting, he says you may be related to Richard III. I've got his number. I think you should call him, give you a break from the problems at work. Maybe you are in line for a legacy?'

'Or,' interrupted Frank, 'maybe you're the rightful king of England! My liege!' He gave a stately bow.

Richard gave a tight smile; it would be good to think about something else. He would meet the genealogist and invite Annabel to join them. She was good at logical thinking and her judgment was always reliable.

'This is fascinating, John. You are saying that King Richard fathered a son just before he was killed at Bosworth?' Richard stared down at the sheets of lineages spread on his dining table.

The genealogist, an eminent historian, nodded, his blue eyes bright as he registered the similarity of the man before him to the slain king. Remarkable – and uncanny! After all these years one wouldn't expect such a resemblance. 'It looks at first like an anomaly, but the records are plain. Alice Peverell was a lady-in-waiting to Lady Lovell, and she had a son, Richard, less than nine months after the battle of Bosworth. Her marriage to John Petyfer happened a short while later. The son was given his surname and one might just assume it was a shotgun thing, except that John Petyfer's will specifically names Richard as adopted.'

'That's uncanny – the surname, I mean. Is there some kind of DNA testing that can be done?' Annabel sipped her hot coffee and furrowed her brow in thought.

'Indeed, there is a Y-DNA test which can show a direct link via the male line. It would be most unusual for an unbroken male-line chain after all this time, but my researches show that if your ancestor Richard Peverell/Petyfer were connected to the King, this could be a way of proving it.

'At first I wasn't at all convinced, but the connection with the Lovell family, and the fact that young Richard had clearly some patronage behind him. He had a property, Mellford, near Witney in Oxfordshire, which seems to have been bought for him. His elder half-brother Ralph inherited the Petyfer house. Some money came into this family, but we don't know exactly how. Not surprisingly, if I'm right, the Pettifers lived quiet lives ever after; quiet, but not entirely uneventful. Many were notable soldiers, there was one who fought with distinction at Waterloo.'

'Chips off the old block then?'

'It would seem so. This might interest you. It was found tucked in a priest hole in Mellford Hall back in the 1970s.'

Richard looked at the photograph. 'It's beautiful... what do you think Annabel?'

'Whoever owned this must have been loved – it's exquisite and so delicate. Four flowers, enamel set with gems and inlaid in gold. A gift fit for a king? Or from one?'

'It's been dated as late fifteenth century and is probably the one mentioned in Alice Petyfer's will. Her grandson's will mentions "a jewel, the Kynge's gifte" which might refer to this. But which king? Richard or one of the Tudors? We have no record of the Petyfer family having any connection with the Tudors, but who knows?'

'Where is the piece now?'

'In the Ashmolean museum. I viewed it yesterday. The photograph doesn't do it justice.'

Later, when they were alone, Richard brewed more coffee and joined Annabel on the sofa. She was idly flipping through one of the books on King Richard and his times which had recently found their way into his flat.

He mused, 'I can't stop wondering about Alice. Was she a tragic figure or a fortunate one?'

Annabel thought hard. 'Mmmn, having her lover killed so violently and then discovering she was pregnant. Must have been very hard. Yet she seems to have got money from somewhere. We know that her husband was a bit of a nobody and suddenly he has this nice house, and another one comes for the adopted son. Lord Lovell wasn't the source, he disappeared after Bosworth and Henry VII confiscated his home. If there is a connection with Richard III then Lovell or someone else was protecting Alice.'

'If Richard had a mistress, he might have wanted to provide for her in case he didn't return from battle. Who better than his best friend to help?'

'If our genealogist friend is right, Richard certainly did provide. I hope Alice found happiness with the other chap. Imagine giving birth to a child and another man being paid to marry you? Awful!' Annabel shuddered.

'Not so awful as being out on your ear. Look, the first Richard Petyfer named his second son John. I would think if his stepfather was nasty, the name wouldn't have been chosen. Then there's Alice's will. She outlived her husband and was rich enough to leave gifts to her relatives. I'd say she was canny enough.'

'Meanwhile, your Grace, we have to prove your own descent. Maybe you'll inherit a fine old house.'

'I don't think so.' Richard thought for a moment. 'They have enough proof to identify the bones. Like my ancestors, I prefer the quiet life. Maybe some time in the future...'

It took the tragic early death of their genealogist friend for Richard and Annabel Pettifer to reconsider a genetic test. They sent the record of the king's DNA, unidentified, to a laboratory for comparison with a sample of Richard's own DNA.

'So now it's official, my liege. You're the grandson of the King in the Car Park, only you beat Tudor and your wife still lives. What you going to do now?'

Richard looked out of the window of their new home into the garden. Weekdays were usually spent at his flat in London, but his heart was here.

'Do? Well, nothing, I suppose. Would you mind very much if we just got on with our lives?'

'Well, there is something we definitely should do.'

'And what is that?'

Annabel came over to Richard's desk and wrapped her arms around his shoulders. 'To continue the line, a son would do nicely, and a daughter would be good too...'

About Clare Anderson

See after the story *'The Apothecary's Secret'* for Clare's details.

Episodes in the Life of King Richard III

by
Lisl Madeleine

✯✯✯

Introduction

It has been contemplated before: what would our world be like today if there was never a William Shakespeare? Our culture, language, thought and even the way we understand history would be remarkably different had not this 'upstart Crow' taken to the theatre. Though he is considered the world's greatest dramatist, very little is known about Shakespeare, including his own perceptions of the plays he himself wrote. In **'Episodes in the Life of King Richard III'**, we explore this line of enquiry. To wit: what did Shakespeare think of his own work? What were his thoughts on the sources he used for plays catalogued into his history folio? Commonly spoken of is that he couldn't write much differently about certain historical figures, such as Richard III. But, given the opportunity, would he have? What did he actually know about the sources he utilised, and what might he say, if able to write freely, about the last Plantagenet king? In the following story, researcher Persephone Muir speaks with by-line editor Siobhán Madden-Greyson about her discovery of a batch of Shakespearean documents, and presents readers with a foray into the secret histories the playwright didn't dare reveal and no one alive today has ever seen until now.

✮✮✮

NEW SHAKESPEARE MANUSCRIPT DISCOVERED

by Siobhán Madden-Greyson, Mercury News Staff Writer

In our Special Feature, Persephone Muir discusses the Bard's 'secret take' on Richard III

'It all began quite by accident,' Persephone Muir responds, when asked about her interest in William Shakespeare as related to the deposed medieval king, Richard III, whose remains in recent years were re-discovered in a Leicester car park. 'I knew as much about him as anybody, and *what* I knew, or was taught, was pretty much the same.' The stay-at-home mum-turned-investigative-journalist slowly began to come to the public's attention after a holiday to England, where she visited the National Archives, 'sort of on a lark.' A long way from America, she ended up getting more than she bargained for.

'I studied Shakespeare at university and was a bit of an admirer. I loved what he did with language and pursued as many informational avenues as any non-scholar could. I loved to read his works and anything about him.' Like so many others, however, Muir's post-graduation study had to take a back seat when she married and her family began to grow. 'My first baby turned out to be twins, so I really had my hands full,' she remarked, running her hand through her hair in what seemed like a nervous habit. A business trip on which she accompanied her husband, however, turned that circumstance on its head, when Muir's family ended up re-locating to London for a ten-year stint. 'My husband and I came ahead of the children, who briefly stayed with my mom, and my husband took me back to the Archives, following a visit there on his previous trip.'

During the plane ride, Muir re-read Shakespeare's *The Tragedy of Richard III*, as did her husband, who was unfamiliar with the play in which a usurper who'd murdered his nephews in order to seize the crown is later killed at the Battle of Bosworth, in 1485. 'He was not that impressed with it, Shakespeare's Richard being so overtly and absurdly villainous.' But what does Muir make of the play?

'I never loved it or hated it – I tended to focus on how these stories were navigated as stage productions, and in an era when stagecraft was really kind of new. Theatricals had long existed, of course, but the places in which actors performed them became subject to licensing, which led to construction of the Globe Theatre. I was fascinated with how scenery changed, stage directions were effected, and the relationships not only between audiences and the stories, but also between playgoers and the environment in which these audiences observed, played out. These are the sorts of things I dreamed of finding more about when I sifted through the Archives' documents.'

So Richard III was not on her mind?

'Not especially. I knew his remains had been found in Leicester, but I had to read up some more on him to get a fuller story. He didn't seem like such a great guy to me, but I also saw that the Tudors had fantastic opportunity to legitimise themselves by making him look bad, and indeed may have utilised their chances with grand enthusiasm. But I had assumed it kind of died down as time went on.' Muir discusses this and more in her upcoming release, *Episodes in the Life of King Richard III: Shakespeare's Sources and Hidden Awareness*, an account of her findings and journey from apathy to greater understanding not only of the circumstances of Richard III, but also of those who, in Tudor times, would write about him or any Plantagenet.

'It could definitely be dangerous. Shakespeare, writing for Elizabeth I, had to watch how he presented Richard's character. The queen was the granddaughter of the man whose victory over Richard created the Tudor dynasty. So she was not so far removed from his time and did not tolerate anything that even remotely threatened her position.'

Muir states that we have brought Richard to life, we discuss him, so we must seek to peel back the layers to the extent we can, to avoid judging his case solely by the merits of our own time, and seriously consider the social context and methods of justice which existed in his own. As the vacillating Lord Stanley's relationship with Henry Tudor in 1485 would have been suspect, so too should others we encounter: More with his compromised source, Shakespeare and his own patrons, for example.

'A lot of people seem to know that Shakespeare sourced texts that link back to Sir Thomas More's *History of King Richard the Thirde*, composed nearly three decades after Richard's death. More himself, born less than ten years before the Battle of Bosworth, relied for *his* details upon Morton, betrayer of Richard and a powerful official under Henry Tudor – a clear conflict of interest, especially when we understand the implications of More's younger years spent in Morton's household. Why do we accept this? The material is so blatantly poisoned it demands further examination, and those who utilise it ought to answer for its conflicts or admit its serious defects.'

Want to know More? Read about Shakespeare's famous source here[*]*.*

---

*https://tinyurl.com/3f5w2zcp

When we were getting acquainted before our interview, I had asked her about Shakespeare's own milieu and what it meant for his characterisation of Richard. I remind her of these comments now. Could she elaborate?

'That's a great angle to highlight because it also touches upon the forces the playwright himself had to contend with, and they were powerful ones. Let me step back for a moment: most people are familiar with the concept of patronage, whereby the artist, Shakespeare in this case, of course, receives financial backing in order to proceed with his craft. Since Shakespeare's time to our own, little regarding the money arrangement has changed, and there typically exists some level of quid pro quo: something for something. Compounded with this is that one of his patrons was Fernando Stanley, direct descendant of the Stanleys we know of in Richard's time – those "fickle" souls whose actions propelled Henry Tudor to the throne. Given that Stanley is also said to have had his own aspirations, Shakespeare had to dance a bit, keeping his patron and the queen satisfied, not to mention audiences. That's a lot to contend with; I can't say that Shakespeare himself was out to demonise Richard.'

Hang on – Shakespeare *liked* Richard III?

The hand goes through the hair again. 'This I cannot yet say with any certainty, but in the documentation my team is working on, there is evidence he at least wanted, or perhaps wished he could, portray the monarch as a character closer to what he really was. A lot of the process is currently on hold, but we also had issues with document restoration, so what we have uncovered thus far has provided limited data. Nevertheless, there are clues to other angles and themes Shakespeare considered, even if he knew he could never publish them.'

The questions seem to beg themselves, and my expression serves its purpose as I gaze at Muir.

She adds that it all raises many enquiries about Shakespeare: what he knew, came to believe and kept secret, what other sources he utilised, how close to the vest he kept all of this. Were these drafts or portions of completed manuscripts? Are there other documents that might give us clues as to his discoveries and evolution of thought or belief?

'Within what we had access to, there may be, but we are working in discovery phase. So we really don't know for sure where this will take us. I can disclose that it appears Shakespeare may have written at least two other versions of *Richard III*. In one, he may have worked his way backwards, and this is evidenced in the Act V I found early on. There may be more to this version or not, or it could be this is all he wrote. Whatever the case, there are certainly implications for how we understand both Shakespeare's play and the real Richard III – from here on out. There's no going back.'

What would this mean to the average reader, cinema attendee or playgoer? What should they be looking for?

'In a book I was recently gifted, published in 1844 mind you, Caroline Halsted writes about the growth of research and cultural mores and imperatives that affected how people received what they were told. For instance, Richard Plantagenet was a monster in human form; he killed anyone who got in his way – and why? He was so bad because he was hideously deformed, with a humped back and withered arm. A person's physical anomalies merely reflected what was on the inside, within his soul. We no longer believe this today; even without full understanding, we know that mere spiritual rot is not what causes various maladies of the body and mind. So *why* do we continue to use this as the basis for promoting the ongoing insistence upon Richard's alleged evil character? This especially in light of the definitive findings that Richard suffered from scoliosis and *not* a hunched back, that the withered arm was an egregious work of fiction. Not everything about the last Plantagenet king is favourable, and that's just reality. Sometimes the necessary truth is bitter, as in the case of Hastings' execution. But loyalty to truth should apply to all angles, and just as whitewashing history is unhelpful, so too is lying about it. Upholding stories with no basis in fact or behaviour, or cherry-picking documentation, robs us of the knowledge of where we as a people have been and where we might be going.'

I remark that Muir's passion seems to be revealing itself.

'I don't know about that, at least not about Richard. Perhaps one day. Or maybe it is there and I just don't know it. You know, we're not big on monarchy, where I come from,' she adds with a mischievous gleam in her eye.

And Shakespeare?

'Oh, sure, he is well loved across the land. After all, he pre-dates our own national existence, and colonists brought him with them to our shores. Perhaps one or more of my own ancestors attended his plays. But to answer your questions more directly, it doesn't really matter whether I admire Richard Plantagenet or not. He deserves a truthful accounting in history and audiences are entitled to know what that is. These modern readers and viewers also are not unintelligent; they will often instinctively recognise the shortcomings of villain creation. Even when aware of medieval and Elizabethan belief in disability as moral deficiency, they also are aware this is *simply not factual*. It isn't now and, despite the Elizabethan subscription to the belief, that is all it was then: a belief. So there has to be something else for Richard's guilt to rest on, and there isn't. It was one of the reasons my husband was so dismissive of the play; he later agreed with Halsted's quote of another writer who stated that Richard's character was "too full of discord and animosity to be true". And I have a difficult time believing that someone as brilliant as Shakespeare would have written a play such as *Richard III* without something else to act as commentary upon it. In that way, it is almost unsurprising to me that we found this.'

Despite that aura of American detachment, Muir's words seem quite invested, and I wonder if she is relieved, as if Shakespeare will be vindicated for writing such 'tripe', as she had characterised it.

'Well,' she starts, then stops. 'We must always remember the conditions Shakespeare had to live and write under.'

'And there was Kit Marlowe.'

'Well, yes, but that's—'

'Another angle,' I interrupt, almost regretfully, 'but I mean, given the circumstances of Marlowe's death.'

'Oh, for sure. You may be glad to know I write about this a bit in the book. Not the Marlowe-as-Shakespeare stuff – well, I address that – but I mean I discuss the anxiety Marlowe's alleged spy status and later "assassination" may have provoked.' She uses air quotes to denote her scepticism of the young playwright's manner of death, and I question her.

'It's not that I'm sceptical – to be honest I don't know enough about it to comment, so I suppose I say it that way to communicate that not everyone buys that story. He was, after all, said to have had a fairly quick, and strong, temper, or so I have read. But, you know, I don't want to do the same to Marlowe that others have done to Richard, so I must strongly state the *I don't know* portion of this. One fabulous outcome of my book is that by the time it is complete, or at least goes to publishing, tentatively set for early 2023, I will have learned along the way as well, a great deal, in fact.'

'Can you tell us a little more of what you discuss in the book?'

'Well, we definitely hope to have more results from our findings and therefore more of what I call "Veiled Acts" from *Richard III* to show. These, of course, are the versions Shakespeare had to hide in order to keep his neck intact. The working title, *Episodes in the Life of King Richard III: Shakespeare's Sources and Hidden Awareness*, is also inspired by pieces of the text, in other portions of the folio, that appear to depict biographical details of the real Richard, dramatised for a stage production, unrelated to the play we know. We also discuss what else Shakespeare may have known, or possible beliefs he harboured, to enable him to pen all this.'

Such as the Veiled Act V?

'Absolutely. The excerpt, Veiled Act V accompanying this feature, is different to the play published in the sixteenth century, in that it eliminates some of the Senecan elements, such as ghost visitations, that Shakespeare wrote at least a little about in these papers we have been studying. He may not have held this dramatic device in such high regard, despite its popularity in Elizabethan times. He strays a bit from his iambic pentameter, which was rather popular with Elizabethans, and that may also have influenced his judgement. But one needn't be a poetry aficionado to appreciate what we have coming. And, of course, the story is not the same.'

'Persephone, it has been such a great pleasure speaking with you today, and we hope to meet up with you again.'

'Thank you so much for having me, and a great thanks to those who have shown interest in the project and look forward to the book's release. We appreciate your support so much and look forward to sharing more with you, hopefully as we go along as well as when *Episodes in the Life of King Richard III: Shakespeare's Sources and Hidden Awareness* hits the shelves.'

CONTINUE FOR 'VEILED ACT V' FROM SHAKESPEARE'S *RICHARD III* AND PORTION FROM PERSEPHONE MUIR'S PROLOGUE

From Persephone Muir's Prologue and Special Excerpt Commentary

Episodes in the Life of King Richard III: Shakespeare's Sources and Hidden Awareness

Coming to the study, research and writing of a medieval king is a completely new experience for me, one I had never previously mapped out as even a remote possibility in my life. Closer to my interests were Shakespeare's plays and the environment in which they were performed. The two merged on to one track in the summer of 2019 when, quite by accident, I stumbled upon documents that turned out to be from a lost folio containing what my mother would call 'bits and bobs' – notes, partial manuscripts, outlines and research – from William Shakespeare.

Now of course the Bard needs no introduction; we all know *of* him, even if we don't have much on his personal life or perceptions. So you can imagine what it might have been like for me to draw in my breath (and emit a few dusty coughs!) and then actually say out loud: 'William Shakespeare wrote these very words, on this very paper.' I'd seen in them lots of different references and what looked like what we today would call brainstorming, and did not at first recognise any specific names, not Richard III, nor Prince Hamlet, the star-crossed lovers – no one. Truth be told, I was rather caught up in the excitement and even a bit of nervousness regarding what it was I was holding in my hands.

At a later time, when I'd managed to calm myself and breathe normally, I saw quite a lot of names, but the papers were out of order and it took some time for me to piece some together into any kind of coherent fashion. When I did, the first complete set of something I found dated to 1591, a play about Richard III, or should I say *the* play? More accurately, it was the last act of a play, one recognisable as some other draft, or form, of what we now know as *The Tragedy of Richard III*.

However, this was no mere copy, as I soon discovered. The first scene of Act V in the play we know opens with Buckingham's execution. Here too the execution occurs, but as I scanned the words, I recall thinking, 'Which editions have I been reading?' It veers away from Buckingham's lamentations regarding a false Richard and sorrow over straying from his loyalty to the family of Edward IV, instead focusing on how he wishes he had not doubted his monarch, Richard III. He lays the blame for sowing the seeds of the Wars of the Roses on Henry Bolingbroke, who usurped the throne of his cousin, the famous child king, Richard II. The dynastic wars occurring in Richard III's time have their roots in the lineage in between the two eras, and the players are many, including the antecedents of both Richard Plantagenet and Henry Tudor.

Apart from new perspectives on history, this also gives us a glimpse into the actual individual Richard was, a man of his time and influenced by certain scenarios within his own setting, rather than disembodied from his culture and held up to our judgement. Why? Because Shakespeare's sources may have been far greater than we know, and he was intelligent enough to treat all players, even Richard's enemies, as complex individuals and not one-dimensional characters doing the bidding of our agenda. In my short time studying this set of events, I have read enough to reasonably believe that some historians accrue their agendas from a desire to 'break a case', and habitually draw a conclusion, then seek evidence to support it, rather than first examining what they have and coming to a conclusion, whatever it may be.

Perhaps it should not surprise us that Richard himself has put a stop to this, or at least forced it to change course. When his remains were, after a years-long search, located in a Leicester parking lot, subsequent examinations put paid to some falsehoods Tudor supporters have been claiming for centuries: he had no withered arm, and the so-called hump on his back was also a fabrication, even if sown from seeds of reality. He did suffer from scoliosis, a sideways curvature of the spine typically developed in adolescence and cause of constant pain. This information, paired with our existing knowledge that even Richard's enemies commented on his courage and battle skills, also speaks to what kind of determination and process-oriented patience must have been part of the king's nature. To what other components of his personality did such deliberation and mettle extend?

'Why do you even care?' is a question I have been asked by my own countrymen and British readers alike.

As an American, it is easy to dismiss medieval kings, to gloss over them with the knowledge that our forefathers fought a terrible war to rid us of monarchy. Richard, however, reminds us that in his era, he *was* a forefather to us, and his deeds do the same.

His progressive policies pertaining to bail and property confiscation upon criminal complaint strike us as very American, acts we too might have demanded had he not already done, furthering in English society the ideal that the state has obligations toward its citizens and not only the other way around. Amongst other changes effected, Richard eased the trade and print restrictions on books and ordered laws and statutes be made accessible to all by printing them in English, clearly the work of a man disposed to the free exchange of information.

All this and more speaks to us of the need to continue this policy, for our path forward is impaired when our previous travels are obscured. 'Past is prologue', Shakespeare so wisely wrote. It was true upon the death of Edward, the Black Prince, father to then-infant Richard II, and remains so.

I believe Richard Plantagenet also understood this, and his capacity to reach others has not diminished with his death, which he charged toward, having fully thought out the reality that he would fight for his realm or die trying. An early Patrick Henry, one might consider, with his 'Give me liberty or give me death.' Americans relate profoundly to this insistent demand, and Richard reaches out to us to signify the very deep ties we once had and continue to.

Like him, we can, along with our beloved British cousins and others, be courageous in seeking truth and to it bind our loyalty.

Persephone Muir, London, March 2021

TURN THE PAGE FOR 'VEILED ACT V' FROM SHAKESPEARE'S *RICHARD III*

Act V

Scene I. [*Salisbury. An open place.*]

Enter Buckingham with [Sheriff and] Halberds,
led to execution.

Buckingham. Will King Richard let not me speak with him?
Sheriff. No, my good lord; you must remain patient.
Buckingham. 'Patient'! Who are you to say such a thing?!
    Here I do stand, captive of such mischance!
    Behold Henry, and his act, yet today   5
    In this present time how I be perceived
    Yet as 'the most untrue creature living'!
    The king believeth me not, not even
    When he saw they forecasted the same, these
    Woodvilles, headed for coronation of   10
    An infant, sans protectorate beyond.
    The manticore and the boar, bring upon,
    By dastardly justice, flawed, corrupted.
    Neither to know the long shadow cast, now
    Complete for one, for willingness to turn,   15
    The other not the sunne in place where he
        foreshadows victory.
    But as his revenge, marks my destruction!
    Indeed, spare of spirit was that Rivers,
    Who could trade my claim for treasure
    And forget who I am when peril presents!   20
    [*Starts*] My good fellow, is this not All Souls' Day?
Sheriff. It is, my lord.

Buckingham. All Souls' Day is my day of reckoning
  This be the day into which I surely must fall
  When I was found false to our Protector,   25
  When I dallied with Margaret's false prophecy,
  Determined to respite how I felt I was wronged.
  Hastings! Morton! Oh how 'innocence beguiled'!
  Daily do I attend the misplaced blame of twin
  Atrocity and forecast of same! By false faith of   30
  Those most I trusted, on this All Souls' Day,
  Now with the twist of their wicked swords,
  My word hath come to like fate, though my fearful
  Soul is in determined respite of my wrongs.
  Then I shall be led on to mine own shame;   35
  To thy block, mine own guilt to so reclaim.
                    Exeunt Buckingham with Officers.

Scene II. [*Camp near Tamworth.*]

Enter Henry Tudor, Oxford, Blunt, Herbert
and others, with Drum and Colours.

Tudor. Right, trusty, honourable friends and allies,

  Have we suffered a setback of fortune,
  Which lay upon existing bruises
  Of servitude to a tyrant, laid on
  Us by that usurping boar, one who would   5
  Disembowel you, swill in your blood like wash
  And make his trough as soon as look at you.

This regicidal swine, beloved in the north,
Set discontinuance and kings to sleep,
With willingness of innocents beguiled. 10
Our uprising against his unjust reign,
Chased across the sea, we now return to
A land which he occupies in centre,
Comfortable! Like the suckling swine he is,
A proven villain, we have only to recall 15
Hastings, one victim of many, quickly
Put to blade after loyally serving.
Return we must, our chance of succour
Rests with each other to avenge shedding
Of innocents' blood, to retake our rights! 20
And you bear no unease, you of honour,
Who know he fails to grasp the extent
Of our rebellion, or that it ends not here,
Just as it ended not when traitorous
Misfits brought down Buckingham or made 25
Across the sea like suckling infant swine.
Oxford. The honour of but one a thousand fold
   Against this traitor and his master of
   Guilty homicide! Show us this traitor!
Herbert. I doubt this sea runner has turned to us! 30
   Show us his face! Show us his vile visage!
Blunt. This man knows no friendship, fellows in arms,
   Fear not, we shall allow him view his 'king'
   Who in his dearest need will fly from him.
Tudor. Indeed, he flies from all, no loyalty 35
   Has this utter swine, though Dorset bears no
   Such knowledge in his empty head. Here we are!

Blunt. Bring him to us!

Tudor. Fellows in arms! Have no fear! We are less

    Yet we are mighty! Dorset is captive   40

    And we shall march to Leicester in our ease!

    In God's name, have but courage to declare

    That by this one bloody trial of pain,

    We reap the victory of perpetual peace!

                          Exeunt omnes.

Scene III [*Near Market Bosworth.*]

Enter King Richard in arms, with Norfolk,
Ratcliffe, and the Earl of Surrey
[*and soldiers*].

King Richard. Here we be near the Market Bosworth, so   5

    Let us pitch here. My good lord of Norfolk!

        [*Soldiers begin to set up the king's tent.*]

Norfolk. My liege?

King Richard. We should survey our field of battle for the

morrow.

Surrey. My lord, we hath nigh three times the army of Tudor.

Norfolk. In the main, traitors and mercenaries   10

    Are for him. Two, mayhap mere three thousand.

Norfolk. My lord, the westward village road beckons.

King Richard. Very well. Let us survey the vantage.

    Let us call for men of discipline, sans

    Delay or distraction, for the morrow   15

    Shall be a busy day indeed. Look sharp!

Exeunt.

Enter Tudor, Sir William Brandon, Oxford, Sir Richard Corbet,
Sir Philibert de Chandée, [Herbert and Blunt].

Tudor. Somnolent sun bestows a gilded set,
   Though my bones do feel the blue, and wind shrill,
   [*Shivers in the open air.*]
   Still, the morrow shall be a good morrow
   Especially with you, Sir Brandon, for   20
   You are mine only choice for my standard.
   Ink and paper in my tent! [*All withdraw into tent.*]
   We shall form
   Our model to battle and limits
   For our power is small and must needs
   Limits on each leader as to numbers   25
   In his charge, with proportion to be told.
   But Stanley, where be his quarters, who knows?
Blunt. I am well assured I have seen him, not far
   South of the king's position and power.
Tudor. If it be possible you to slip in,   30
   Gracious Blunt, pass Stanley this note of need.
   [*All move outside of tent.*]
Blunt. So I shall do, my lord, as heartily
   As shall you have needful sleep on this eve!
Tudor. Very well then. Good night, good Captain Blunt.
   [*Exit Blunt.*] Gentlemen! Let us repair to my tent!   35
   This cold doth make my poor teeth prattle so!
   Come, we shall consult inside upon all.
   Our business is inside, away from

The dew, raw and cold.

[*They withdraw into the tent.*]

*Enter [to his tent, King] Richard, Ratcliffe,
Norfolk and Catesby.*

King Richard. 'Tis what o'clock? 40

Catesby. But suppertime, my lord. 'Tis only nine.

King Richard. And all is well. For I tell you the what.

Catesby and Norfolk. Yes, my liege?

Ratcliffe. You will savour, my lords.

King Richard. I bid you update me on position 45
Of that wily Stanley. I have his kin
Yet, though he may play the rook, I warned him,
George may yet fall into a dark slumber.
Though I warrant not his support built in
Duplicitous is that shifty shadow. 50
Catesby, is my armour at the ready
And laid full into my tent for morrow?

Catesby. Yes, my lord.

King Richard. Good Norfolk, stir when all still doth slumber,
After a sure night of rest. Have you supped? 55

Norfolk. Yes, my lord, I comfort you.

King Richard. And you, Catesby?

Catesby. Yes, my lord.

King Richard. Very well. Then I shall bid you adieu,
But mark me, use careful watch, those you trust. 60

Catesby. Yes, my lord, it shall be.

Norfolk. We depart now, my lord.

[*Exeunt Norfolk and Catesby.*]

King Richard. Ratcliffe, we have come through much together.

Ratcliffe. Wretched Bolingbroke!

King Richard. Soothe you, Ratcliffe, what is done is done.   65

Ratcliffe. Aye, my lord, only the obstinacy—

King Richard. We cannot change it. We never could do.

   Our own day is where to find favour.

   Come, let us to our prayers and then sleep.

   Return about the mid hour of night,   70

   Now let us pray and sleep.

        [Exeunt Ratcliffe. Richard prays and sleeps.]

        Enter Stanley, to Tudor in his tent

        [Lords and Gentlemen attending.]

Stanley. Surely destiny of triumph greet you!

Tudor. And comfort to you on this cold, dark night.

   How fares our lovely mother, do tell?

Stanley. Blessings from thy mother, who prays for you.   75

   But as the stealthy hours sneak through night,

   From us too come advantage and surprise,

   For Richard has our kin and under

   Pain of death of he, the king bids us back.   80

   I aim to keep watch for thy best moment

   And at that same time shall compound his grief.

   That is all I can say, I must adieu.

        [Tudor moves to lords and gentlemen.]

Stanley. *[Aside.]* Gentle folk, I am but so very torn.

   Have I other kin, but monster am I not.   85

   Reality shows Tudor's ambition

   To be unworthy and one sans rightness.

   And there is no right in his descent from

Third son of the man with too many sons
And she in his bed before being wed.   90
Mine survival I seek, correct you are
But it goes not without notice that his,
My liege Richard's loyalty to justice
Is great, he often denies self-glory
And gifting to him he discourages.   95
See for thine own selves, his Hornby response.
Thus born from Wakefield, and yet merciful
To mine own self misrule; If he had done
Opposite? I would be not here for this,
This decision, this war might yet not be,   100
For 'tis I brought this interloper here.
I leap wish to wish, appeal to appeal,
I owe Richard that I yet stand upright
Though how can I ever fight Margaret's own?
            [*Exeunt Stanley, lords and gentlemen.*]
Tudor. My sleep shall be troubled, but sleep will be.   105
            [*Tudor sleeps.*]

Scene IV. [*Near Market Bosworth.*]

*Enter Tudor, Oxford, Blunt, Sir Richard Corbet
and others [with soldiers]*

Tudor. Here we finally stand, Richard Gloucester not far!
Richard, the man we shall today fight,
Infanticide, Regicide, Fratricide,

None shall frighten us from our determined path,
For God and the angels fight with us, here,   5
And those there hide their desire to have
Us for the win than him that they follow.
Truly, gentlemen, he falsely sits on
England's chair, gloatingly God's enemy,
A tyrant that if you put down, you will   10
Sleep in great peace, be rewarded by God,
And if the win today is mine, you
Shall partake in the fat for all your pains.
Boldly sound the drums, with goodly cheer and
For God and Saint George! Richmond and our win!   15
Soldiers. Here here!
Tudor. Corbet, leave me, leave me I say!

                         [Exeunt omnes.]

        Enter King Richard and his soldiers and men,
          Norfolk, Catesby, Sir Percival, et al.

King Richard. Catesby, Norfolk.
Catesby. My liege?
Norfolk. My lord?   20
King Richard. Have you news of Stanley?
Norfolk. My lord, he prattles on, straddling the line.
King Richard. Never mind, then. It is done. I have seen Dorset.
    Let us to the men.
[Turns to army.] Sir Percival.   25
Percival. Yes, my liege.
King Richard. [Scans sea of soldiers.]
    Our rich crown of England marks a spring.

Your step is likewise filled with joy of God.
Sons of England, mercenaries await
And by their very nature, they hold no   30
Loyalty: to God, to England, even
Not each other. Some will be slain and
It is up to us to bring them rites on
Death, for no man deserves to lie fallow.
Even their warm-weather leader shall be   35
Given due course.
With calm deliberation we look to
God, as we throw ourselves to the press,
As the fight takes us, we appeal to God,
As we earlier entreated the Lord   40
For blessed victory over these foes
To receive our humble petition
And with great pity loose us from the chains
of sin, help us have mercy on England's foes.
In victory for to be merciful   45
And that our Lord have mercy on us.
Percival. My lord.

       Enter a messenger.

Messenger. My lord, Stanley doth deny his presence.
King Richard. Thank you, good man. Norfolk, no matter,
    Remember that we have spoken, and we   50
    Have the Swiss here with us in their spirit.
Norfolk. Aye, my lord. And here are the enemy.

    Tudor's forces approach and fighting breaks out.

    Norfolk slays Brandon; Stanley rushes in to slay Norfolk.

    King Richard, close to Tudor, sees as his horse's legs buckle.

King Richard. Treason! Treason!

Scene V. [*Bosworth Field.*]

Alarum. King Richard and Tudor in a press of soldiers et al.
Richard charges Tudor.

Catesby. My lord, a fresh horse! Take her, go safely!
King Richard [*On foot.*] God forbid that I retreat eve' one step.
Catesby. My lord, this chaos! Let you to safety!
King Richard. Sir! I will win this battle as king or
   die as one!
Tudor. The press! [*Dies.*]   5
King Richard. Norfolk! You have slain the Tudor!
Norfolk. [*Bleeding, stunned.*] Come, my lord!
King Richard. What not the eye has seen nor the ear heard
   And which the heart of man understands not
   Sweet lord Jesus Christ saved us from the perils   10
   To body, may we be like continue,
   Protected in our souls, O true God,
   Who lives and reigns through Christ our Lord.
All. [*Simultaneously.*]   Amen.
               [*Exeunt omnes.*]

FINIS

About Lisl Madeleine

At age six, Lisl Madeleine announced she would become a spy and shortly thereafter added poetry to her list of goals. She wrote poetry through high school and beyond; by this time spying had lost a bit of its appeal, though she utilised stealthy methods to observe people and activity around her.

Nowadays she writes on a variety of topics and is currently completing a book of poetry. Her other projects include a collection of ghost stories and another of short stories, a series of essays and several works of historical fiction. **'Episodes in the Life of King Richard III'** is her first foray into alternative history. She loves rain, calligraphy and crafting, and looks forward to the day when time travel becomes possible.

Lisl Madeleine can be found at her blog, ***Before the Second Sleep:*** https://beforethesecondsleep.wordpress.com/

The Unwritten Story (Part 3)
by
Maria Grazia Leotta

☆☆☆

'And now the last of your fantastic stories,' Brian announced. 'From our friend in black.'

'I am dying to know what he wrote!' Maria thought, and noticed that an incredible silence had fallen in the room.

He opened the envelope and his face became serious and pale. He didn't say a word and just stared at the parchment in his hand.

'Brian, what's wrong with you?' asked Clare. 'Come on, read the last story.'

'What the heck? Is that parchment? Where the hell did he get that?' exclaimed Joanne.

But Brian was still staring at it in disbelief.

'I won't read his story; you can see for yourselves.'

And turning the parchment towards the participants, he showed mediaeval handwriting and just two lines:

Thank you all.

Loyaulté me lie.

✩✩✩

About Maria Grazia Leotta

Maria was born in Italy and graduated in Modern Foreign Languages and Literature. Eight years ago, thanks to a bursary from the University of Sheffield, she moved to England with her family and she took an MA in Translation Studies. She fell in love with York and she recently moved there. She is an interpreter and a translator, a member of the Richard III Society (she is an active member of the Scottish branch) and contributes to the research for The Missing Princes Project for Philippa Langley, who successfully led the search to locate King Richard III's grave. One of her poems has been published in a collection associated with Yorkshire:

White Rose Bards: https://tinyurl.com/37jrvmc6

Afterword

✭✭✭

We hope you enjoyed this collection of alternative Wars of the Roses stories and we thank you for your purchase, which will benefit the charity that would surely have been close to Richard III's heart, Scoliosis Association (United Kingdom).

Their aim is to provide advice, support, and information to people affected by scoliosis and their families and raise awareness of scoliosis among health professionals and the general public. They do this by:

Providing a helpline where people can call or email the SAUK team for advice, support or just someone to talk to.

Providing good quality, up-to-date information on scoliosis and related health matters.

Running a membership network that allows people with scoliosis to get in touch with others and offers the support of a SAUK Regional Representative.

Organising campaigns and activities to help increase awareness of scoliosis in the general public and among health professionals.

Holding patient meetings where specialists provide advice on scoliosis and people have the chance to get their questions answered.

You can contact them here: https://www.sauk.org.uk/

If you enjoyed this collection of short stories, please consider leaving a review on Amazon or Goodreads. Reviews are invaluable for indie authors.

Printed in Great Britain
by Amazon